NO. 4 IMPERIAL LANE

NO. 4
IMPERIAL LANE

A Novel

JONATHAN
WEISMAN

TWELVE

New York Boston

Twelve
Hachette Book Group
1290 Avenue of the Americas
New York, NY 10104

HachetteBookGroup.com

Printed in the United States of America

RRD-C

First Edition: August 2015
10 9 8 7 6 5 4 3 2 1

Twelve is an imprint of Grand Central Publishing.
The Twelve name and logo are trademarks of Hachette Book Group, Inc.

The Hachette Speakers Bureau provides a wide range of authors for speaking events. To find out more, go to www.hachettespeakersbureau.com or call (866) 376-6591.

The publisher is not responsible for websites (or their content) that are not owned by the publisher.

Library of Congress Cataloging-in-Publication Data has been applied for.

ISBN 978-1-4555-3045-8

For Hannah and Alissa

For God's sake, let us sit upon the ground
And tell sad stories of the death of kings:
How some have been depos'd, some slain in war,
Some haunted by the ghosts they have depos'd;
Some poison'd by their wives, some sleeping kill'd;
All murder'd—for within the hollow crown
That rounds the mortal temples of a king,
Keeps Death his court, and there the antic sits,
Scoffing his state and grinning at his pomp

Richard II

NO. 4 IMPERIAL LANE

CHAPTER ONE

In 1988 I fell in love with an English girl from Leighton Buzzard. She majored in sociology and cultural studies, a combination with great resonance at the University of Sussex, where all things cultural were studied greatly and sociologically, and she bought henna in little paper packets from the Body Shop to make her hair flame-red. She talked about structuralism after a few drinks, a better topic than most in those days. She could have pontificated on that wicked witch Margaret Thatcher or the Socialist Workers Party or the bloody Labour Students and their maddening fealty to that wanker leader of theirs, Neil Kinnock. But that was not her thing.

There were other weighty matters of the day to ponder: how much soap to apply to make your Mohawk ("Mohican" in British parlance) stand boldly erect even in the sweaty heat of Brighton's seaside clubs; the proper amount of eyeliner to prevent tripping from brooding goth to pure poseur, from Robert Smith to A Flock of Seagulls; whether Ian Curtis had been dead long enough to accept New Order as a respectable-if-inferior successor to Joy Division; if overturning Minis in the car park after the student pub closed for the night was an act of political defiance or simple drunken stupidity.

We went to London one weekend to mass in the streets of Piccadilly, protest the latest round of budget cuts, and sing "All We

Are Saying Is Give Us Our Grants," then were back the next to toss Molotov cocktails and demand the removal of short-range nuclear missiles from the Continent. "Hey hey, ho ho, Ronald Reagan's got to go." In between, there was Moroccan black hash, the cheap intoxication of a snakebite—half lager, half cider—and the occasional weekend lost to magic mushrooms, when again the conversation would drift from structuralism to Thatcher to the bloody Labour Students, this time with uproarious effect.

Maggie didn't go in for all that political theater. I remember one particularly self-indulgent discussion of the broken miners' strike, when other students lingered on the role of the scabs, the heartlessness of Mrs. Thatcher, the death of unionism, the fate of the now-laid-off miners.

"I just think it's sad that there are miners," Maggie mourned. "To think that they want to go down in those holes."

For me, Maggie was a respite from the societal battles that animated Thatcher's Britain, condensed and amplified like the outskirts of a black hole at the unlovely but serviceable University of Sussex. That I was there at all stemmed from a sophomoric brew of restlessness and dilatoriness; I couldn't pass a language test to study in a country that spoke a language other than my own, and I had neither the time nor the inclination to correct that. My Midwestern university had an exchange program with Sussex. It was that easy.

I didn't have much preconception of British life when I applied to study abroad; I knew there was an amusing monarchy, and fog, perhaps. I knew nothing at all about the university on the south coast. As it turned out, I enjoyed the cauldron I unwittingly threw myself into, at least at first—the politics, the music, the semiotics and Marxist professors and their minions, the British women with uncombed hair and hemp ponchos or thick, dark eyeliner, who proved endlessly alluring.

I had a "flatmate," Mick, that first year in England, from Yorkshire. He wore battered motorcycle leather and pencil-thin black jeans over his sparrow legs—and talked tough about his working-class upbringing in Sheffield, especially to Richard from Greenwich, who wore buttoned-down shirts, sweaters over his shoulders—never actually over his torso—and played an expensive synthesizer. At a battle of the bands that winter, Richard and some other son of privilege teamed up with a phalanx of lovely backup singers—two synthesizers and ethereal cooing through heavy reverb. They aimed at Depeche Mode cum Dead Can Dance and ended up being booed off the stage.

"That's alright," Richard confided to me, another suburban son of something akin to affluence. "There was a scout from the Zap Club. He said we could play there anytime. I'll have the last laugh."

Not many weeks later, Mick pushed Richard too far in his class-warfare goading.

"Ya li'tle prat, Richard. Richard the Third, right?" Mick taunted, drunk out of his mind. "We're all here 'cuz we earned our grants and escaped our drunk dads. You're here 'cuz ya couldn't manage to get into Oxbridge."

Richard beat the shit out of him. For all Mick's tough talk, it was Richard who was actually fit—played rugby and squash and Ultimate Frisbee when he was feeling a mite free-spirited. Mick's snooker was no match for a childhood at boarding school, synthesizers or not.

It was one of those episodes when I felt my Americanness, the strangeness of the society I had awoken in. We all spoke the same language. Yet somehow I felt like I was living in a foreign film without subtitles or Cliffs Notes. I was beginning to have enough. I needed an out.

Then came Maggie. A friend had introduced me to her months before, and I suppose I counted Maggie as a friend by then. But one night, sitting in the student pub, pondering my escape with a sixty-pence pint of nameless bitter ale, I looked up to the sound of laughter—not so much uproarious as tinkling, a wind chime in the fall.

I saw a girl whose nose crinkled when she smiled, and suddenly I noticed she smiled a lot. She wore the skimpiest of woolen miniskirts, not really sexy, more practical, and had the slightest plump in her thighs. When she turned her smile to me, I drew to her light.

Falling in love with Maggie was easy because she was supremely loving, something I had yet to experience in my years of pursuit of girls slightly out of my league.

She listened to my stories about growing up in the American South—which had sparked polite disdain from the girls I knew in college—with rapt fascination. I provided a window into a continent she would never see. She gently turned my musical world on its head, dismissing my canon and replacing it with her affectless, post-punk British cool: lush, sweeping synthesizers, unrecognizable guitars, elegiac voices full of ennui. She bought me thrift-shop shirts, supervised my haircuts, and cooed, "Oooh, David, you look so hard."

She said "I-Kie" instead of "OK," and she had this way of leaning in to me spontaneously, as if for a kiss, then pulling back with a squinty smile and laughing out, "You're lovely."

She'd tuck her head against my chest, wrap her arms around me, and squeeze, her feet rising just slightly to press the crown of her head against my chin. I'd breathe deep to take her in. She smelled of citrus shampoo. No one had ever told me that I was lovely before. I guess Leighton Buzzard girls do such things, but I knew only one, Maggie. Early in our relationship, we hitched home. Maggie wanted to show me off, an oddity, I suppose, but one she was smitten with. That was alright. I was good with other people's parents. What my friends found annoying, even excruciating, I always managed to manage my way around with something like charm. Maggie's "mum," matronly and eternally worried, did not say "I-Kie." She was not a girl at all. It was hard to imagine she had ever been one. And I was pretty sure her two brothers, younger but harder, never crinkled.

*   *   *

And so, because I was convinced I didn't want to lose Maggie, I found myself standing outside No. 4 Imperial Lane on a wet October morning. I was meant to be back in Chicago. My year abroad was over, and I was supposed to be finishing a degree that would throw me into the workforce of fin-de-Reagan America: sink or swim. But I just couldn't leave Maggie.

No. 4 was two doors up from the end of Imperial Lane, three blocks above Brighton's ridiculous stone beach and two blocks below the Royal Sussex County Hospital, a Victorian institution if there ever was one. I had been in and around Brighton for a year now, but never to this end of the city, Kemptown, as it was called. It was a far more respectable area than I was used to, and far from the student hangouts, the clubs on the waterfront, and the tourist destinations on the Grand Parade. I stood in the road for a while looking at the street number, a single digit that appeared too short for the space and hung crookedly. A couple of cheap terra-cotta planters held desiccated plants. Yellowed flyers visible out of a mailbox attached tenuously to the brick.

There was a quadriplegic inside—at least that's what I had been told. His name, the agency that sent me said, was Hans, Hans Bromwell, which must have made his parents British and German—and cruel. The deal was, I would live here and help the old man out in exchange for room, board, eighteen pounds a week, and a residency permit that would allow me to stay in England. I had never even known anyone in a wheelchair; my only notion of quadriplegia came from the movies: noble invalids painstakingly painting with their teeth or spelling out impenetrable theories about the origins of the universe one letter at a time with their eyes on an electronic board. That would be Hans— heroic, wise, glad to have a set of American arms and legs to help him. He'd be intrigued by my story, ready for my help, and I would be his trusty valet, a less-than-heroic role, for sure, but indispensable to his quest. I took a deep breath and climbed the four steps to the door.

"Are you going to come in, then?"

The door had opened before I could knock, and a cheerful woman appeared. The quadriplegic's nurse, perhaps, or maybe a housekeeper. She looked like a caregiver, frumpy and apprehensive.

"It's David, right? David Heller? Please, come in."

Without any more small talk, she guided me forward and led me to a corpse. Shriveled almost into a fetal position by the contractures of its withered muscles, it shifted ever so slightly and a head peeked out over a pile of thin, wool blankets. I could see the skeletal contours of a human body underneath. The head was a shock—papery skin stretched over protruding cheekbones. Fine, thin wisps of hair were extruded from a scalp in random thatches, gray or blond, I couldn't really tell. It was so sparse. Two blue eyes, once vibrant maybe, now faded toward gray, peered out from deep within their well-defined sockets.

"Ah, Mr. Heller. An American Jew, no doubt," Hans Bromwell said faintly. The woman who had let me in rolled her eyes as she trudged over to Hans and propped up his skull with two overstuffed pillows. "I suppose I'm glad to see you," he continued. "Do you like Woody Allen? Or Maria Callas?"

He interrupted before I could stammer out an answer. His hand, bent stiffly at the wrist, moved haltingly toward a button propped next to the bed. A stick attached to a wristband, with a rubber tip that looked like an oversized thimble, made contact with the button, and a record dropped on a turntable in the corner. The voice of an opera singer drifted from four speakers, one in each corner, to the center of the room.

Fear came rushing in like a hot blast. It watered my eyes and turned my stomach. Clearly, I had made a terrible mistake. The room smelled like a combination of vapor rub and shit. A bag of urine hung off the bed, the catheter tube snaking up from it and under the blanket. The room must at one time have been a parlor, probably the house's main living room, but for obvious reasons, Hans now occupied the first accessible chamber with a door on it. His enormous hospital bed backed into a bay window that overlooked the street, but the heavy drapes looked like they hadn't been opened in decades, and dust bunnies clung to their hems. An open space, maybe five feet wide, separated the foot of the bed from a row of stainless-steel cabinets and a sink straight out of hospital surplus.

The music might have been impressive, but I had no appreciation for opera. My Led Zeppelin phase had given way to seventies art rock: Genesis, Yes, ELO. From there, I had moved on to what passed for avant-garde back home—R.E.M., U2, some Psychedelic Furs—only to get to Britain and find out what a drip I was. Adapting to New Order, the Cure, and the Cocteau Twins had been leap enough. Maria Callas was beyond my abilities.

"Are you coming for a visit or are you moving in, David?" Hans said. You could call the question impatient, but it was wearier than that somehow, more resigned, and it made me feel sorry for him.

"I, I'm moving in," I replied, trying for resolute.

"My brother can be a bit abrupt," the woman said behind me. She was a little peculiar for sure. At maybe five foot eight, she was about my height, her hair a mousy brown, thick but cut into a bob to tame it, which only made it flare outward like a mane. Her head was narrow, putting her gray-blue eyes on either side of her face, where they watched me intently. Her nose was just slightly too large, rising from soft cheeks. Under those cheeks was a weak chin that receded into her neck. She wore her weight in her hips, just enough to make her look too light on top, too thick on bottom, but if there was a time before the padding, I'm sure she had looked alright, all things considered.

"I'm Elizabeth. I live here too. We're going to be friends, whether Hans likes it or not," she said, looking past me, an eyebrow arched toward the body on the bedstead.

*   *   *

The quiet of the Bromwells was a long, long way from the end-of-days tumult of the times. Four months before, I had pulled myself away from a riot in East London, taken the Tube the long way to avoid a bombing in Brixton, and found myself in a muddy field on Glastonbury plain watching a stranger on an ecstatic acid trip, Echo and the Bunnymen thrumming in my ears from a stage not a hundred yards behind me.

"Just one little dot, one little dot," the guy repeated over and over, squinting at the imaginary acid tab between the thumb and forefinger he held an inch from his face, alternately laughing and weeping, weeping and laughing. I stood over him, watching in my own bemused haze of ganja and shrooms. Big Steve, one of Maggie's housemates, had invited me to the grandest of Britain's summer music festivals that June. We hitched from the downtrodden outskirts of North London to Worthy Farm in a village called Pilton, Steve and his blue Mohawk, his friends from Luton, an assortment of working-class toughs and soccer hooligans, and me, a suburban American kid born into casual, upper-middle-class ease.

"It'll be brilliant, spectacular," Steve had assured me from a pub in Luton, a town known best for its airport and football riots. "The Cure, Echo and the Bunnymen, the Mighty Lemon Drops. Have you heard them, the Mighty Lemon Drops? They're like the Teardrop Explodes. You know them, right? And Marillion, they're from around here."

"Marillion? Fuck 'em," a friend jumped in. "Bunch of poseurs."

"Ah, fuck off, you," Steve threatened.

I stared at them, utterly lost, but the tickets were only twenty quid. Steve had tents to sleep in, and the hitching would be free. If we left early enough, we could make it easily in a day.

And we did. Big Steve had the resourcefulness you'd expect from the son of an airport worker who had somehow made it, full ride, to the University of Sussex to study chemistry in combat boots. We pitched our tents, and he and his mates went foraging for bulky, still-green tree branches, which they stripped of their bark, adorned with rudimentary carvings, and traded to the Rastafarians for huge handfuls of oily marijuana, some to smoke, some to trade for food, drink, or harder drugs when the mood came over us.

"Yah, mon, dis walkin' stick is brilliant. Make anoder. My friend will be by for it with da good ganja."

"We'll be ready," Steve said in feigned seriousness, suppressing his glee.

The highlight of those three addled days should have been the Cure's set, with its laser lights and morbid previews of the band's upcoming and last great gothic album, *Disintegration*, before Robert Smith somehow found happiness and went all crap on us. I don't remember a thing, though—just some odd, incomprehensible conversation I had with Big Steve about home, how to get there, when to get there, whether to get there at all.

"Home, David," he was shouting over the music, his voice coming to my ears through some long, distorted echo chamber formed by the toxins clotting my hammers, anvils, and stirrups. "You have to go home."

I wish I could say I was driven by some ambition or some particular reason to be at Sussex. The fact is, I was hardly an adventurer. I was average, from an affluent suburb in the south, but not the real south—Atlanta. I took honors classes in high school, but not too many, kept my grades in the B-plus to A-minus range, got pretty good test scores, had a handful of friends but wasn't super popular. I tried for nice and did alright with it.

Sussex was the Berkeley of Britain at the time, which was a good thing and gave me a little edge. I wore my hair close-cropped and tried to spike it with stiff gel, but a poorly trimmed beard, curly and uneven, probably ruined the effect. I was going for post-punk New Wave: black jeans and weathered shirts, half-unbuttoned over a white tee. In due time I would come to see that the messages were mixed—the beard was all wrong, more George Michael than Che, and I probably came off looking like a hungover Kenny Loggins on a bad hair day.

My cultural confusion was honest, though. It came with the times: punks, goths, New Wave wankers, old-guard metalheads, deadly serious communists plotting their putsches against Whitehall while the real communists across the English Channel teetered toward extinction. The kids seemed more intent on achieving fashion supremacy at Camden Market than any real societal change. The trade unionists of East London, Manchester, and Liverpool were driving the Labour Party further into socialism while their comrades in *Solidarność* were launching vanguard strikes in Poland that would, in short order, extinguish the Eastern Bloc. And what was a modestly well-adjusted American from a good home supposed to do in the midst of all this? Was your hair supposed to stand up in fluorescent spikes or swoop over your eyes in greasy, jet-black curtains? Were you supposed to be swept up in the protest movements or give in to studied ennui? Did antinuclear peaceniks really wear Iron Crosses and Bundeswehr tank tops over combat fatigues and Doc Martens? What about the vegans in soiled ponchos who firebombed the biology labs at the universities? Didn't the poor, unrescued rabbits and rats just end up flambéed in the name of animal rights?

To those questions came my answer, Maggie. To her, none of it mattered.

When I finally asked her out for a drink, casually, she said yes. We went to the student pub near her place on the back side of campus, Park Village, it was called, an unsightly cluster of brick cubes sticking out of the South Downs that had been farmland in the 1960s, before the British government decided to build the country's "new universities," of which Sussex was one. Maggie and I sat across from each other at a heavy picnic table and proceeded to get into a way-too-animated argument over Jacques Derrida, fueled by lager and cider. It was midweek, and the pub was half-empty. I was enjoying myself watching her. She was cute and had this way of lolling her head and looking at me sideways in mock-hostile appraisal. I hadn't noticed it before.

"C'mon Maggie, what does that even mean, 'There is nothing outside the text'? You don't know. It's just gibberish." I leaned in toward her provocatively. "Deconstructionist gibberish."

"Gibberish, maybe." She laughed, stabbing the air with an index finger and a long red nail. "But the French accent helps."

Four weeks after Maggie and I had eased our way into my narrow bed on East Slope, my brother arrived, ready for all the trips on the Continent we had planned. I surprised myself with my misery on that long European excursion. I lay in physical agony one night in a seedy guesthouse in Amsterdam, missing her. I could think of nothing else.

I carried a vision of Maggie with me, locked in from two weeks before. She was sitting up in bed, propped up by a huge red pillow wedged against the wall, mulling structuration while reading Anthony Giddens's *Capitalism and Modern Social Theory*. I lay beside her, Dickens's *Bleak House* taunting me, only a quarter read, and watched her work from behind the pages. She looked over, took off her glasses, and smiled. I reached for her, and we kissed.

"In a bit, David, I've got to get through this chapter."

It was an odd image to linger over, stoned, in a room full of cheap metal bunk beds above a bar in Amsterdam. House music rumbled beneath me, its bass line crushing my skull with its monomaniacal thudding. My brother was off somewhere exploring the debauched wonders of a city that only a twenty-four-year-old could love so much. My affections were completely elsewhere. It must be love, I moaned.

Maggie didn't seem to wonder. She was sure. As the end of the school year came into view, she grew to dread my return to Chicago. I contacted my school; if I were to want to take, say, a year off, how exactly would I go about requesting that? The letter from Illinois came back quickly.

Dear David,

We are in receipt of your request for a year off from your studies. We are happy to oblige and hope you have a grand adventure.

Besides, the letter didn't say, tuition would be higher the following year.

That summer had been the leanest time of my life. We traveled for a while, Maggie and me, mostly on an ill-fated trip to Africa. Maggie indulged me on that one, even when I drove us far beyond our physical and financial capacity.

"If we can get through Sine Saloum, we can make it to Gambia," I assured her in Senegal.

"Just a little further south is Ziguinchor. There's a beach town, Cap Skirring, I swear, and maybe from there, Guinea-Bissau," I told her in Gambia. "It'll be amazing."

We didn't get that far, and I kept that failure to myself, even when that oddest of Shangri-las, the benighted little country of Guinea-Bissau, entered my consciousness in a big way. We returned flat broke, having accomplished nothing beyond wrecking my gastrointestinal system. Unwilling to ask my parents for money after forsaking them for another year away, I looked for work, illegal without a permit and scarce to begin with in Thatcher's England. We sold junk out of the "boot" of Maggie's mom's car, until finally I signed on with Community Service Volunteers, a wage-slave organization that apparently took all comers, and it was CSV that found Hans. All that was expected of me was to muddle through until June, when his friends would come take him to Tuscany, as they did every summer. Nigel at the volunteer agency was encouraging. He wore a cardigan sweater with holes at the elbows that clung tightly to his bony frame. His teeth were crooked, and he looked at me earnestly.

"I twust, David, that you will find the Bwomwell household to be a warm and wonderful place to spend a few months," he said.

Hans's white, two-story row house was nice by Brighton standards, small and tidy with a pub down the street called the Imperial Arms. Maggie was two bus rides away in a grungier part of town. The furniture in Hans's house was strangely spectacular—grand armoires too large for their cozy spaces, bowed chests of drawers carved exquisitely, gilded bookcases with fine gilt grilles, commodes of the antique British sort—and decorated incongruously with African objets, carvings, masks, delicately inscribed gourds, and musical instruments. I felt like I was in a museum.

Before our adventure in Africa that summer, Maggie and I had hitched to her cousin's farm in north Devon. He had some camping equipment to lend, and he wanted to show me how to use his old army Primus stove. While we were visiting, he took us to a manor nearby. It was something an American was supposed to enjoy. Maggie had mocked the opulence of the place, preserved in state by the National Trust. I didn't think much of it one way or another at the time, but it came back to me as I toured the Bromwells' home. I was no expert, but this furniture seemed to have a pedigree.

Hans asked nothing about me that morning, nothing in the vein of an interview at all. I asked him what he thought of my girlfriend spending the night every once in a while, to which he replied:

"Fuck like bunnies, for all I care, just as long as you come when I call."

The panic that had overcome me that first moment with Hans was overwhelmed by my inability to think up an alternative living arrangement. I could hurry back to Nigel and ask for a different assignment, but I saw little chance of getting a better one in or near Brighton. I could cut the cord, say "That's it. I'm done. I'm going home." But I was no closer to that than I had been when I let myself stay in the first place. My resignation snuffed out my panic like a heavy, damp blanket. So I did what I told the volunteer agency I would do. I moved out of Maggie's overcrowded group house, away from Big Steve the punk and Little Steve the rocker, Astrid the hippie and Suzy the normal one, and in with Hans and Elizabeth Bromwell.

A week later, complaining already of my absences, Maggie came to visit for the first time. I went to meet her at the bus stop on the Grand Parade and saw her tumbling down the steps and out the door, lugging an overstuffed overnight bag. I didn't know she had planned to spend the night.

"How long did you say this was going to last?" Maggie asked, slightly winded and laughing as she pulled down her skirt. Leighton Buzzard girls, even those who read sociology and cultural studies, didn't talk like Hans and Elizabeth Bromwell. They said "dunno" a lot and called people "prats" and "wankers" and "willies." They got their knickers in a twist. They didn't dress like them either. An overstretched sweater—a jumper, in English English—draped over Maggie's torso and obscured most of her tartan skirt. She wore round, steel-framed glasses that might have been called cool-chick glasses in the States had they not come from the National Health Service. Here, they were just cheap, free actually.

I assumed in ignorance that all of Britain would be more or less the same, not some Merchant Ivory fantasy of posh accents and white trousers but without the variations of region, race, and wealth that I grew up with. Maggie taught me about class, the true working class, Brits living north of London, warehoused in row after row of identical houses, with a pub, a cup, and a Sainsbury's to get them by. Her mom, Maryanne, had a harelip, mended badly, and a boyfriend, Alf, who traveled the Midlands selling stuffed animals— "plush toys," he called them—out of a suitcase. When Alf asked for butter at the table, he'd say, "Would you pass the fat, love?" Her father had abandoned them, first for a construction job in Abu Dhabi, then for a younger sheila, who dressed like Maggie but grew fat on chocolate digestive biscuits. In ways I could never, Maggie would have understood Hans's sarcastic greeting for me, the implications of Woody Allen and Maria Callas. The British grasped class stratification at a visceral level. They were born to it.

"You know, David, you can't be fooled by that old blanket on what's-his-face's bed," she said, walking up the steps to the front door.

"Hans," I said.

"Hans isn't like your friends at Sussex. He's not from Luton or Sheffield. He already hates you."

She turned in time to see my face droop, and gave me an encouraging smile.

"Alright then, 'hate' might be a bit much. He just doesn't like you, love. But I do," she added, kissing me on the cheek. "It won't be for too long anyway, right?"

"Until May." I dropped her suitcase on the stoop with a thud and fished out my keys. The summer had long given way to the grayness of an English autumn. The air was dampening but not yet cold. "Then he goes to a villa or something in Italy for the summer. I guess he goes there every year."

"You're joking," she gasped. "May?"

"That's what I promised the agency."

"It's October. You'll never make it."

"It hasn't been a good start," I agreed.

Elizabeth opened the door with a smile. She beamed in fact, not at me but at Maggie. A girl I had not yet seen, only a few years younger than us, sixteen or seventeen, but tall and dark-complexioned for a Brit, came out of the kitchen and smiled. Her black hair streamed down her back, over a tight-fitting T-shirt that clung to her lovely breasts. "I'm Cristina," she said with a wink, then dashed upstairs, leaving Maggie to glare, first at her, then at me as my eyes followed Cristina's breathtaking backside.

"My daughter, David. Remember I said she'd be coming back from her uncle's farm this week?" Elizabeth said to me, catching my gaze and bailing me out. "Got back just now, while you were out fetching your girlfriend. Maggie, right?"

She smiled at me.

"Come into the kitchen, both of you. Hans is listening to *Die Fledermaus*. His beloved Maria," Elizabeth said. "You don't want to disturb him."

She whirled around the little kitchen in great excitement, not doing much but doing it quickly. She offered us tea in stained, delicate cups, not Maggie's usual mugs. They had dainty roses that wound upward from the bottom toward slightly chipped rims. She took out a quart of vodka and poured herself a shot.

"As I've been telling David here," she said excitedly, "I'm going to the poly now, so I need him more than some of the other volunteers who have come through. I'm learning to type and some maths too."

"Really?" Maggie chimed in. "What kind of maths?"

It was the kind of question I would have shied away from. Elizabeth was nearing forty, I suspected. Unless she was studying advanced calculus or linear algebra, there could be no easy explanation for a math class at the community college at her age. But Maggie seemed to understand that Elizabeth didn't care. Elizabeth was different from Hans. She showed no disdain. She absently brushed aside her unruly hair. Her mouth worked itself to one side, the right, as she blew away a hair. She reminded me of the nervous girls I went to middle school with—always wanting so desperately to be liked, never expecting they would be.

"I'm going to get a job," she said, a smile breaking across her face like a beacon. The sentence and the expression seemed completely unrelated, at least to me. She said it as I would have said "I'm going to win the lottery" or "I just saw the most amazing movie." There could not have been a more genuine look of delight.

She poured herself another shot, then downed it as she took her seat on the kitchen stool.

"It'll be my first. ' 'Tis my vocation, Hal; 'tis no sin for a man to labor in his vocation,' " she said with a flourish of her arm.

Hours later, Elizabeth called us down again, to discuss dinner. She'd be making *canard à l'orange*, she announced, one of Hans's favorites, with a duck bought from a butcher on the east end of Brighton, a butcher who hung his venison for six days, prepared his own pheasant, and made sure always to save Hans his very favorite: pig vagina.

"You're joking," I said, venturing familiarity for the first time since I had arrived and using Maggie's British inflection, an affectation I had picked up but insisted I hadn't. The trick was never to end questions with a rising tone. The most inquisitive phrase always sounded like a statement. It's no wonder the British never sought any answers from the world. Their language and tone offered only advice and opinion.

"Amazing what parts of an animal are considered a delicacy, isn't it? I won't eat it, but Hans relishes tastes. When you can't shag, you can't walk, hell, you can't wipe your arse, what do you do? Eat, really. Taste. Taste anything. It's his last adventure."

To watch Elizabeth prepare dinner was a marvel. It focused her mind. I had been so broke for the past two months, I was reduced to buying rice and Brussels sprouts in bulk at the Brighton farmers market, just off the lorry depot. I'd prepare them with curry powder, or chili powder, or cream and cornstarch, or tomato sauce. It didn't much help. It was still Brussels sprouts and rice. But just when I had grown despondent over my poverty diet, I found myself watching this strange, flighty woman patting down the duck she had filleted and trussed, preparing a citrus medley for the sauce, reducing it, baking, broiling. The smell was overwhelming.

When it was ready, Elizabeth carved up a plateful, included some parsnips and broccoli drenched in butter, set it on a tray that had been sitting on the counter, already set with cutlery and a starched white cloth napkin, and pushed the meal into my hands.

"You're on," she smiled, a phrase she had taken to using as my cue each evening.

Hans was lying utterly still, opera music still drifting around him. His eyes opened slowly to meet mine. Maggie walked a step behind, uncharacteristically shy.

"Is this your bunny, then? Prop me up and come round."

I set the tray on the nightstand beside his bed, reached under his head, and lifted his torso as I pushed down the pillows, careful to grab more this time than just his head as I had my first night, when he had jolted to life to admonish me.

"No, David, not just my bloody head. You have to prop up my body. Don't be shy about it. I won't break. Reach under my shoulders and heave."

I was glad I didn't follow his advice. I would have thrown him across the room. His back had been warm and moist. I don't know why I expected otherwise. I could see the vertebrae so prominently, I guess I thought I'd be pressing cold, bare bones. But lifting his upper body was no more difficult than supporting his head. He weighed nothing.

Now propped up, he looked more squarely at Maggie. They locked eyes, neither of them smiling.

"She can go home now," Hans said. "Cut the pieces small, like I told you. And I like a bit of duck, a bit of parsnips, and a sprig of broccoli on each forkful."

Maggie and I exchanged glances as she walked out. I looked at her helplessly, she left without a word, and I heard the front door shut.

My first option at Community Service Volunteers had been working with juvenile delinquents on the Isle of Wight. It wasn't that far from Brighton, but Maggie and I would have seen each other only on the weekends, and with eighteen pounds in my pocket a week, probably not every weekend. Hans came up a few days later, before I had given CSV an answer on the delinquents. Maggie's mum believed it was a sign from God that we were meant to be together forever, but after that first encounter between Hans and Maggie, it was clear this would not be easy on our relationship. A sign from God, maybe, but so were Job's boils.

Hans's bed was massive, an oversized hospital number that could be lifted and lowered, with side rails that seemed to serve no purpose for a man who could not roll over. Hans lay on a rubber sheet of air nodules—penises, he liked to say—which worked to lift his body from the bed top and keep away the bedsores, imperfectly maybe, but this was a technological marvel compared to previous prevention devices: foam pads, cashmere blankets, anything that felt soft to the touch but flattened into what might as well have been sandpaper against an unmoving, deadweight body. One of my main jobs was to shift him from side to side every few hours during the day. Two nurses with tight white costumes that delighted Hans came in the morning to bathe him and clean his catheter, thank God. But I'd have my share of dirty work: emptying the urine bag, wiping his bum, adjusting the catheter when his penis would inexplicably grow hard.

"Damnedest nuisance," he'd say, aware of the hard-on but unmoved by it. "I can't feel the bloody thing anyway, and it just gums up the works."

As I sat down on the bedside stool, knife and fork in hand, Elizabeth peered in.

"Try to be nice, Hans. How's the duck?" she asked.

"I haven't tasted the damned thing," he replied. "The American takes his time."

"The American will leave us high and dry if you can't be civil. Small bits," Elizabeth advised me once again. "The chewing isn't a problem, but the swallowing can be."

Hans sniffed. "You'll see she likes to repeat what I say," he said. "Treats me like a baby. Do I look like a baby to you?"

No, he looked ancient. I moved faster now, cutting, feeding, cutting, feeding. I was twenty years old and had never cared for anything in my life except a few goldfish that needed to be fed in the morning and some hamsters that died. This was surprisingly unnerving.

The meal didn't last long. After a few bites of everything, carefully assembled, forkful by forkful, Hans gave a little gasp, rolled back his head, and said, "That's fine. You eat the rest." A quarter of the plate was gone, if that.

The first night, I had offended him by asking, "Here?"

"Yes, of course here," he had said with exasperation, breathing heavily as if I had taken him for a brisk walk.

I looked at the partly eaten meal with chagrin, but I ate it, with the extra fork that Elizabeth had supplied for this unspoken purpose. I was not experienced in hierarchy, but I knew to be ashamed. Hans got something out of it, though he didn't say what. Humiliation aside, from the first week, I knew I would eat well, though not all of Hans's culinary adventures would sit well with my palate—long-hung venison was like eating rot.

"Put ketchup on it," Cristina would say, shaking the Heinz bottle until the deer meat was drenched. "Trick I learned as a little girl in Africa with antelope meat. I hated it."

I would follow suit, laughing with her, pleased with her attention. It still tasted horrible. But most of Elizabeth's concoctions would be a surprising treat. I learned to love pâté de foie gras. Pheasant, rich and gamey, made any other poultry seem tasteless. Sheep's kidneys in cream sauce were like succulent sautéed mushrooms, but with more substance. Calves' brains in garlic took some getting used to. They offered no resistance as your teeth bit down, but as Hans noted, neither did Camembert or that stuff that we poor students ate, tofu. Skate, purple and firm, was like a steak fish that was more steak than fish. My portions, generous as they were, were almost always his leftovers.

Every evening, after some time in silence, Hans would ask if I was through, which was my cue to return to the kitchen with the tray. Elizabeth would always be there, smoking a cigarette and paging through the *Evening Argus*. She seemed to be pretending to be engrossed in the story she was reading—usually some young girl gone missing from the council flats on the edge of town.

" 'Night, Mum, I'm going out," Cristina's voice would sing in the hall, a delicate hand holding her up in the doorway of the kitchen. She would flash me a smile. I would nod, dry-mouthed.

"I'd tell you to leave my daughter alone, David, but you don't stand a chance," Elizabeth murmured as the front door slammed that first night of Cristina's return home. "She likes basketball players, really big ones. 'Black men are pearls in beauteous ladies' eyes.'"

I had gotten an important lesson in the thin walls of No. 4 Imperial Lane that first night. When I walked into Hans's room for any final instructions, he cackled, the first hint of merriment in his voice, "My niece and the Moor are surely now making the beast with two backs."

He let out a breathy little laugh, then told me to strap the six-inch, rubber-tipped stick back on his wrist. I strained not to wince as my hand encircled his bone of a wrist.

"Cover my head completely, and close the curtains tight," he said. "I'll wake you if I need you. Good night."

"Completely? Can you breathe?"

"Does it look like I suffocated last night? All the Italians sleep this way."

CHAPTER TWO

"Our father was a man of some importance," Elizabeth began in a weary voice. We were in the kitchen again, tea for me, vodka for her. She needed to talk, it seemed. I had no idea what to say.

"What was his name?" I mustered.

"Gordon, Gordon Bromwell. If you are of a certain age in the UK, you'd know of him."

Gordon Bromwell, I came to learn, was a gentleman farmer from Hampshire—not the sort that planted anything but the kind that trod over his land in a tweed suit and Wellington boots regardless of the weather, an uncocked shotgun bent over one arm. His estate, Houndsheath, it was called, on the North Downs south of Basingstoke, wasn't the largest, but it was worthy of his title, viscount. It was outside a little village that proudly included one last thatched roof and a few miles of charming old fences. A meandering, one-lane road from the village center ended in a sweeping, circular driveway of yellowed gravel. The manor itself dispensed with the flat roof favored by a particular type of English aristocracy. It was topped instead by a more Continental steep slate pitch plunging down to stone walls, unpainted and multihued. It was elegant and lovely, but Sir Gordon preferred to call it "a heap," as in, "My father died and left me this heap."

"'Houndsheap.' That's what he called it in Parliament when the inquisitors learned that the taxpayer had paid for the dredging of our pond," Elizabeth said with a rueful little laugh. "Didn't work. The *Sun* called it a moat."

Gordon set aside his title in middle age, along with his seat in the House of Lords, to pursue the less genteel but more effective politics of the House of Commons, where he became a Tory MP. That was in 1968, before Africa and the unpleasantness with his daughter and son that had wrecked all their lives. As young Margaret Thatcher was penning her conservative manifesto and pursuing her grand vision of a dismantled British welfare state, with its broken miners' union and poll taxes, Gordon had more parochial ambitions. He cheered her on, no doubt, but he was driven to politics by two more personally pressing issues. Foremost was the estate tax, which had forced his father to sell half their land to their banker neighbor, whose fortunes were swelling as the Bromwells' waned. Indeed, the tax was threatening to end the Bromwell claim to North Hampshire altogether. His second cause was inspired by the scruffy students of the Animal Liberation Front, who invaded what was left of his land with their infernal pepper and garlic sprays to disrupt his foxhunts. It was the latter crusade—saving the hunt—that made his name. He figured that anyone would be driven to activism if he had the maddening experience of sitting astride a befuddled horse as a pack of dogs scattered in the woods, unable to find the scent.

Toward the end of his life, licked by the forces of ALF progress, various parliamentary inquisitions, and the misfortunes of his own family, Gordon Bromwell retired with his rifle to a sun-filled, sparsely furnished guest room upstairs, where he fired down from the picture window at rabbits, foxes, or any living creature, save the help. He would then tally his kill with chalk hash marks on the wall. Foxhunting may have been out of favor, but the foxes still needed taking care of. The occasional guest would ask who was scrawling graffiti on the walls, wondering if old Sir Gordon had finally taken leave of his senses.

"Goddamned right, I have," he would grumble to himself if he had overheard.

"By that time, I had pretty much taken over the affairs of the manor as best I could," Elizabeth continued. She loaded it with flotsam from Angola and the place she called Portuguese Guiné, and sold off most of its prized contents to a couple of traders with an antique shop in London. Hans was by then a hopeless cripple.

Gordon was in his pajamas, standing at the top of Houndsheath's sweeping front steps, the first time he saw the agents of his estate's demise. A burly bloke with a Mohawk and another with peroxided, spiked hair were carting off the mahogany trestle table from the breakfast nook. He drew the line when his daughter came for the sixteenth-century kingwood bookcases adorned with fronds of ormolu, which had been in the family for centuries. They had shielded his first-edition Thackerays and Coleridges behind their finely carved gilt screens, and they would continue to, thank you very much.

Gordon would resist, but he couldn't deny that the Bromwell empire was being dismantled before his eyes. Though Hans and Elizabeth had moved back home, everything else appeared to be moving out. And it wasn't just the furniture. As the bills began to mount, the neighbor who had already done away with half of the Bromwell estate had offered to take the horses and hounds as well. His skittish daughter—"What a burden I had proven to be"—had been too quick to oblige.

Well, Gordon thought, a lot of good the animals will be, once the fight to preserve the hunt is lost completely. Two benders—Wills and James, they were called—prattled on about first-edition books from the family collection with his cripple of a son, who had requisitioned his study. Yes, first floor and all that, he understood the reason his stricken son was now sleeping there, but that didn't make it any easier, especially since the study lay directly below the guest room he had taken up residence in. The staff appeared to be leaving as well, one by one. When the cook left with her underlings,

Elizabeth began handling the culinary duties, whipping together one overwrought Continental confection after another—venison, duck, sheep's innards—all in indulgent cream sauces or wine reductions, under the orders of his paralytic son.

His son, he thought. It pained him, that thought. He was loath to express it, but just the image of him downstairs made Gordon Bromwell ache. Sure, he had some wild oats to sow, who didn't? But the boy had finally been coming along and would have soon been in position to assume his place in society. Gordon had no doubt he would have taken his peerage, a seat in the House of Lords, or, if he caught the political bug, on the backbenches in the Commons.

That wouldn't be happening, not now. A cripple would be useless on the stump.

How different it had all turned out. Gordon and Charlotte Bromwell had had only two children—Hans, much loved and totally unappreciative, and Elizabeth, not loved much at all. Hans got his German name from his father's softness for Oswald Mosley, the baronet, philanderer, and British fascist. He liked the sound of a single-syllable Teutonic name followed by his unmistakably Anglo surname. "Hans" was Germanic without all those guttural noises that sounded like dragging up phlegm after a dusty summer day. But the politics of the right or left were not to be Hans's "thing," as they say. He was a rogue from the start. He had charm and looks and he knew what to do with them.

At eight, he was sent to boarding school, Ludgrove, and at thirteen Eton, of course, on the shoulders of his lineage. His academic skills weren't much, but that was hardly worth noting. He was a success from the start.

"Elizabeth has the brains. I have the charm," he became fond of saying by the age of thirteen. "I'd take charm any day of the week."

Elizabeth, two years younger, with none of her brother's smooth sophistication, was not sent to school at all. She had a tutor, a kind and well-meaning woman who knew nothing but Shakespeare. So that is what Mrs. Parsons taught—no maths, no science, nothing practical even, like knitting—just Shakespeare. Charlotte Bromwell did not see much use in mathematics or science for her daughter. Penmanship was good, as were reading and writing. And what better to read and write than Shakespeare? The 1960s were bursting out all over. London was swinging. But Elizabeth's mother saw nothing odd or impractical in the education her daughter was getting.

"'He reads much; he is a great observer, and he looks quite through the deeds of men,'" Charlotte would tell her daughter, as she yanked back Elizabeth's nest of hair into a tight, taming bun that would hold maybe half the day, quoting *Julius Caesar* as if she were preparing Elizabeth for the greatest of deeds. And maybe she was. Algebra and calculus could carry you only so far. Shakespeare, well memorized and properly sprinkled in speech, could make you a force.

Charlotte's personal contribution to Elizabeth's education was piano lessons, most often bellowed at top volume. "It's *pianissimo*, Elizabeth. Can't you read?" Or, "No, no, no, *forte, pianoforte*," screamed in her own forte. She would run over and bang at the instrument in brutal demonstration or take her daughter's hands in hers and pound the keys with them. Elizabeth took it stoically and went on tinkling at the keys without expression. She silently plotted the day when she would never have to look at a piano—or her mother—again as she neatly put away her sheet music at the end of each daily practice session.

Before Hans's escape from Houndsheath, to boarding school and beyond, he and Elizabeth had been as close as you'd expect children who live miles from any others would be. There was a creek that meandered through the estate before spreading into the marshy, useless pond that would later become such a scandal. They would catch tadpoles and try to fish, without understanding that a fishing pole needed more than a line on the end of a stick fetched from the woods. Their father hadn't bothered to tell them about such things as hooks and bait, although he would shout out a warning if he was going shooting. Their mother allowed them free and unsupervised rein over the out-of-doors, as long as she did not have to be involved. The governess made sure the children were scrubbed clean of mud and bathed to a ruddy, high polish before meals.

Once Eton began, such adventures were relegated to summer vacations and spring breaks, and then disappeared altogether. Elizabeth grew up without her brother, alone, unkempt, and fanciful. Her eyes could be wide open but see nothing, as she sunk into the depths of her inner life. She would mutter to herself and make little dancing motions, tiny outward manifestations of the elaborate choreography playing out inside her head. Once Charlotte gave Elizabeth a Madame Alexander doll she had picked up on a jaunt with Gordon to New York, a Scarlett O'Hara in a flowing, green Christmas gown—not that her daughter had a clue who that was. For a time, Scarlett was her best friend—until she reverted back to her Paddington Bear, whose face was smeared with marmalade in keeping with her storybooks. By ten, her favorite companion was Suzy, a sad-eyed, droop-eared hound from her father's hunting stable. Suzy's short coat and rubbery countenance contrasted wonderfully with Elizabeth, all hair and arms and legs, sharp elbows and kneecaps going every which way.

"Oh, Suzy," she would say as the two sat beside the pond, its sulfurous smell masking the dog's, "whatever will we do with that big, boxy head of yours?" She would then grab her by the ears and plant a wet kiss on her spongy black nose, thankfully out of sight of her mother and the governess.

As for Hans, given his station, his choices at nineteen boiled down to Oxford or Cambridge. Naturally, he picked Edinburgh. It put the entire country of England between him and his father, which suited him fine.

Hans began his culinary adventures with internal organs in Scotland. He quickly learned to discern between true haggis—sheep's pluck (heart, liver, lungs, suet, and assorted offal) encased in stomach—and the modernized variety squeezed into sausage casing. He pulled off a fine Robbie Burns after a few drams of Glenfiddich.

Ye Pow'rs wha mak mankind your care,
And dish them out their bill o' fare,
Auld Scotland wants nae skinking ware
That jaups in luggies;
But, if ye wish her gratefu' prayer,
Gie her a haggis!

He read politics and dabbled in art history, not with any great passion, but he did fine. He also flirted with Shakespeare to please his benighted sister. With enough Shakespearean knowledge, he could tease her at her own game. Besides, he liked the bawdy bits. It was a revelation that Shakespeare thought of the beast with two backs, better yet that the context was interracial, delicious in a household so steeped in Oswald Mosley.

Hans's only regret about rejecting Oxbridge was the quality of his classmates. He was certain he could have gotten a richer, better sort of friends farther south, which would have come in handy later. But he did alright. Julian, who came from London via an estate outside Norwich, could be unctuous, but his father had a villa in Tuscany where the help fattened geese for foie gras, mixed up something he called corn porridge and the Americans called grits, and bottled their own red wine. The cold, gray weather of southern Scotland suited Julian's pallor. His skin matched the sky on its brighter days. His ill-defined chin and sharp nose foreshadowed the jowls that would one day swallow his face and make his neck disappear altogether.

Simon, Hans's other best mate, was a Francophile with a father who had left his mother and him in Lincolnshire for a spacious flat in Paris and a posting at the Organization for Economic Co-operation and Development, whatever that did. He appeared to do nothing but entertain. He owed Simon for this abandonment, and

Simon intended to take full advantage as soon as he could sweat out his exams.

Vibrant primary colors were in style then, even in Edinburgh: tattered fishermen's jumpers along with bell-bottoms, ripped at the ankles then enlarged with bright-colored weavings. Long hair was meant to signify freedom and androgyny. But somehow, at least a decade early, Simon was something of a goth. Black, pencil-cut trousers clung to his sticklike legs. His jumpers were properly tattered, but they were colorless and hung limply, as did his hair, which did not so much signal freedom as surrender. Gravity and grease relieved his mane of any buoyancy with which to match the Age of Aquarius. Despite all this, Simon Fellowes exuded magnetism. Women were drawn to him as they were to an urchin that needed their care. He lapped it up, though he was careful not to express too much joy in their affections.

"All the girls wanted Simon, God only knows why," Elizabeth said, giving me an appraising glance as she took a deep drag from her Silk Cut. "He's still a bastard about it."

For Hans too, there were women at the University of Edinburgh, drawn to his father's title, even if the politics attached were frowned upon, and impressed by his posh accent. And since ease was Hans's most cherished attribute, he didn't bother much with his female classmates. Edinburgh wasn't London in the late sixties, but that only made the women that much more eager to please.

"When they graduated, Hans and Julian—Lord, I can't stand that one—decided it was time Simon prevailed on his father to 'mind the gap' with his poor, estranged son," Elizabeth said with quotation gestures and thespian inflections exaggerated by vodka. She put a kettle on with a wordless query to me to see if I'd like a cup of tea. I nodded. She continued, "You know, it was all about healing the pain caused by a broken marriage, reestablishing contact between *père et fils* and getting him a bloody flat in Paris."

Gordon Bromwell, settling into his backbench in Parliament, was only too happy to send his wild son to the other side of the Channel, far from the headlines of the *Daily Mail*. After all, Hans didn't hide his fondness for an easy lay and Moroccan black hash, not the sorts of dalliances that fit with the politics of a Tory MP preaching law and order to the fed-up folks of North Hampshire. So yes, the elder Bromwell would supply the francs, but the younger one had to figure out what to do with himself in the City of Light.

"Just don't look in Montmartre," Hans ordered Simon. "I'm not bloody Toulouse-Lautrec, staring up dancers' nostrils. Find something on the Rive Gauche, in one of those little lanes near the Seine—preferably near a brothel. I'll stare up something, just not a nostril."

That opening conversation was exhausting for me, cathartic for Elizabeth. She took up in the morning where she left off late the night before, once she had lured me into the basement laundry room to help her sort clothes.

"Here, love, tug on the end of this," she ordered gently as she tried to smooth a weathered slip over an ironing board. Her voice was groggy and a bit slurred from the drinking, but she appeared functional. I blushed a bit, gingerly took the lace hem, and pulled.

She laughed. "Nothing to be afraid of, dear. No one's hand has slipped up this in years."

As she worked, she talked, racing to fill the airtime before the nurses left Hans's bedside and called me to duty.

"I knew damn well I was missing the fun," she lamented.

On the occasional breaks from university when Hans felt like traveling home, he would swoop down on Houndsheath like a knight-errant. Their mother would make a fuss, prepare a regal feast with the best china, and dust off the formal dining room. When Hans and Elizabeth were young children, they ate in there routinely, waited on by staff, Hans looking like Little Lord Fauntleroy in his suit and knickers, Elizabeth prim in a stiff dress. But with Gordon more often than not at the pied-à-terre near Parliament and Hans with the Scots, the great mahogany table with its heavy, carved legs had fallen into disuse. Mother and daughter ate instead in the breakfast nook, hardly a nook with its huge square English oak table nudged into a great bay window overlooking an overgrown field. But it was certainly more casual.

"We weren't much for conversation in those days, Mum and me," Elizabeth sighed.

Charlotte would mainly glare at her daughter, whose nervous manners and vacant stares unnerved her. "Dear God, Elizabeth, chew with your mouth closed. Do you think you're a horse?" Or, "If you slouch like that at the table, you'll have permanent scoliosis. Imagine trying to find a husband bent over like a doddering great-grandmama." Or, "Move your chair closer to the table, Elizabeth. You already smell like bangers and mash from that dog of yours. You don't want to be wearing your breakfast as well."

When Hans was there, neither that setting nor that conversation would do. Around the dusted and polished Louis XIV dining room table with its parquetry inlay, he would regale his mother with witty but chaste stories of university life. Charlotte would be on her best behavior, ostentatiously displaying kindnesses to son and daughter alike.

Hans would later sneak into Elizabeth's room to tell of his drug- and booze-addled sex life. It was amazing what a shot of Glenfiddich would do to a town girl who had never been able to afford much more than a half pint of cider or a shandy, he'd tell her. He pleased the girls with his wallet, his accent, and his attention. They pleased him with what was at their disposal, which for Hans was quite a lot. Elizabeth would listen, rocking slowly on her legs, tucked underneath her on her bed, and biting her lower lip as her brother sat on the floor against the wall and laughed at his own exploits. She figured he was too immersed in his storytelling to pay much heed to her squirmings, but he was well aware of the education he was imparting. He felt it was a duty, cheerfully rendered.

Hans's stories sent Elizabeth searching for a way out of Hounds-heath. A cousin, "Victoria Tunbridge was her name," soon became her link, however imperfect, to the outside world. Vicki, as she insisted on calling herself, was not nearly as isolated as her Shakespearean cousin. She had gotten through her first set of exams to continue her schooling, but her inbred academic sloth had gotten the best of her before she could complete the exams for university. Which was fine, really. She had graduated to the party circuit, where she had considerably more energy.

Physically, Victoria—slight, elegant, and effortlessly sexy—was Elizabeth's opposite, and she quite enjoyed the contrast. Elizabeth's uncertain presence, her perpetual motion, her 360-degree glances at her surroundings, gave Victoria the confidence of a well-protected politician, and in her more honest moments, she had to admit Elizabeth could be a damned better conversationalist. At a party, she could draw the attention, let Elizabeth do the talking, then let the bloke take her home. By that point, the lads weren't looking for talk. She found it odd that Elizabeth didn't mind the arrangement. Of course she did, "but that's only because she couldn't fathom my isolation," Elizabeth said, folding the last of Hans's briefs, grayed with age.

In a sense, Elizabeth's escape was inevitable, especially once Hans had abandoned her altogether for Paris. In Vicki, she had an escort out. In Hampshire, she had a launch pad. And in the summer social season of 1970, she had any number of practice runs, testing the pull of gravity to see how much force was needed to escape the orbit of the North Downs.

In September, as the party boys headed back to university, Elizabeth plotted her most daring excursion yet. Hans went to France. She would go someplace warmer, Malaga, perhaps, or Majorca.

"Don't be stupid and boring. You can be so conventional," Vicki chided her. "Let's go to the Algarve."

"Where?"

"Portugal, darling."

We were still talking that night, after Hans had retired beneath his blanket.

"Aw, Mum, have you noticed how serious David looks at you when he's listening to your stories? You've got yourself a real audience for once."

Cristina was calling into the kitchen before heading out for the night. She was wearing a diaphanous white chiffon shirt over a tight black miniskirt, bare legs, and sandals, though the fall chill had set in. Behind her was her new boyfriend, who was hulking, six four, I guessed, built, and black, with an almost pretty face. I was doing the dishes.

"Oh, David," she said, "this is Kelvin from some city called Detroit. Kelvin, this is our resident Yankee, David."

Kelvin had played college ball at Michigan State, I would learn over the course of a few visits, but he failed to be picked in the NBA draft. Undaunted, he was playing for the Birmingham team, hoping to impress the scouts. The Midlands were far from Brighton, but he earned enough money for quick weekend trips. They had met at a dance party at the Zap Club, just off the boardwalk in a cave of a structure built into the Brighton seawall.

At that first meeting, with Kelvin standing behind Cristina, a wave of self-pity had passed over me; I understood how out of my league she was. It reminded me of the feeling I had had a year before, on a visit to Florence to see a college friend teaching English there. I had arrived in tattered jeans, an oversized sweater, and high-tops, with my filthy green backpack on. I smelled a little. Watching the northern Italian men dressed in their elegance, their hair and nails trimmed perfectly, courting women of absolute perfection, I hadn't felt so sexually irrelevant since my awkward midteens, when I battled acne and waited for a growth spurt.

"Birmingham's a ways from here."

"She's worth it," he said, and gave Cristina a gentle squeeze around her waist that I tried to ignore.

"How's the season going?"

"Not bad. We're over five hundred."

"What are you averaging?"

"Twenty-four points, about a dozen rebounds," he answered quietly.

"Double double a game? Man, that's fantastic. You'll be in the NBA next season."

He gave me a dazzling smile.

"Keep your fingers crossed for me, man."

Cristina let her body fall back onto the rock of a man behind her. She crossed an arm across her chest to rest her hand on his enormous forearm.

"I have no idea what you blokes are on about. Mum, when are you going to make David and me one of those Portuguese dishes from Africa? I think our guest deserves that, don't you?"

"I thought you didn't like those? 'Reminders of scary times,' you'd say," Elizabeth responded absentmindedly. "Food's like that," she directed at me, "an instant association with the first time you recall eating it."

"I know, but really, I wouldn't want an adorable bloke like David to be denied foo foo in piri piri sauce," she sang out, glancing at me from under her thick eyelashes. "David, don't keep Mum up too late. Mum, you've got a test tomorrow," she said reproachfully. "Have you even cracked a book?"

She turned her head to Kelvin's chest, lingered for a moment in admiration, then looked up at him.

"Let's get out of here."

Kelvin gave Elizabeth a shy little wave. I turned back to the dishes. Elizabeth's glance lingered on the open doorway as Kelvin's back faded from view.

"It's been a long time since I've had a shag," she muttered.

Elizabeth took out a drink and a cigarette. If she still wanted company, I would acquiesce. I didn't relish climbing the steps to my barren little room.

Elizabeth poured me a shot of vodka along with her own.

"It's been thirteen years since the neck snapped. I'm sure you've been wondering. Everybody does." She tapped the ash off her Silk

Cut and took a swallow of vodka. "'Such an injury would vex a very saint.'"

She paused to enjoy my perplexity. "Baptista, in *Taming of the Shrew*." She took another swallow. "But my brother's no saint."

"This might seem very American to you, but do you mind if I ask you about the way you talk? I mean, it's Shakespearean."

"It *is* Shakespeare, my darling. You don't know *Taming of the Shrew?*"

"I'm sorry. I always mix it up with *Turn of the Screw*."

"Ah, James. I'll be reminding myself for the next year that you're a Yank."

"James died a British subject," I showed off.

"Yes, poor dear. Anyway, Shakespeare is just about all I know, and I know it bloody well. 'I could a tale unfold whose lightest word would harrow up thy soul, freeze thy young blood, make thy two eyes, like stars, start from their spheres.'"

It sounded impressive, but I have to admit, I didn't know Shakespeare. This was the fall of 1988, and my education consisted mainly of liberation theology, Gabriel García Márquez, and a little Faulkner to burnish my southern upbringing, but not a lot of Shakespeare. I had intended to take a course on the Bard the year before, but there was a mix-up, and I ended up with Dickens. Elizabeth's words amazed me, though—lyrical, expressive, at once anachronistic and timeless. Even disembodied from their context, her little snippets had the power to move, and to grace her with erudition and eloquence.

"Though I suppose I've already started to unfold it for you, you'll want the whole story," she said. "'The true beginning of our end.' It was all my fault, this."

She lit a cigarette.

"It all started with Vicki, you see, and our little seaside escape."

Portugal. The sun streamed through thin, salt-weathered white curtains that undulated in the ocean breeze. The rough cotton sheets were not what Elizabeth was used to, and she had kicked them in the night down below her waist. She glanced over to the twin bed not four feet away and watched her cousin sleeping soundly in her diaphanous nightgown, one strap over a shoulder, one breast exposed, a slight smile on her lovely lips.

Vicki had entertained the troops well on the journey down, laughing with the businessmen on the ferry crossing from Dover, some students on the train from Calais to Paris, a couple of soldiers from Paris to Madrid, a bemused, dark-eyed Spaniard from Madrid to Lisbon, and a passel of tourists on the final leg from Lisbon to Faro.

The sun had grown warmer and more intense, the sky a deeper blue, as they moved away from Hampshire. Their parents had given them the money without bother. The girls were twenty now, and a little adventure and independence would do them some good. The Algarve was becoming all the rage among the upper-middle class in and around London. Besides, the fascists of the Iberian Peninsula— Spain and Portugal both—kept a lid on the local undesirables. Elizabeth and Vicki would be safer in Praia da Marinha than on Brighton beach, Gordon thought approvingly.

Elizabeth wondered if she should wait for Vicki to wake up before heading out. But Sleeping Beauty was not stirring. She brushed through her hair, instinctively pulling it back into a tight ponytail, and hoisted on her one-piece suit, cut low on the hip and high on the chest, a few small flowers breaking up the field of navy blue. Elizabeth's body wasn't half bad really, she thought, breasts pert, firm, and youthful, waist trim if not hard, sloping out nicely to hips still on the narrow side. She gave herself a last once-over in the mirror and opened the door to the sun.

The resort in Albufeira was nothing special, just one of a jumble of whitewashed blocks above an expanse of beach and palms. But to Elizabeth, it was exotic, or at least not British, even if many of the lads and louts swilling bitter in the bars talked football in unmistakable cockney. Her father had misjudged the exclusivity of the

Portuguese beachfront, understandable considering how long it had been since he had ventured into the sun. But there were palm trees, an old Latin town square, a few narrow lanes, and enough steeply sloping tiled roofs to maintain the feel of Iberia. The prawns were massive, served with the heads on and no adornment. The ham was blood red, finely sliced with pungent cheese on the side. The Spanish tangerines were divine, and the air smelled of sea foam and salt.

After arriving the previous night, they had gone to a seaside bar where Vicki had turned heads. Waifish in an almost sheer cover-up (and shivering), she was chum for the clumsy, circling sharks.

"Vicki, really, how long are we going to stay?" Elizabeth queried, looking piteous after the second hour at the bar. She really was tired. She was beginning to feel sorry for herself.

"Oh, come on, Elizabeth, we've only just gotten here. I like it."

Elizabeth had sat at the bar and pouted, watching the men come and go, chatting up her cousin, who deftly deflected the attention of one by turning to another. Vicki was well practiced at this, and with one room between them, she had no choice but to be discerning. And in the subtropical heat, she had no need for a conversational assist from her cousin. Libidos needed no priming on the Algarve.

With the next day's sun climbing higher, Elizabeth primly stretched out a knotty, threadbare towel she had nicked from the room. It was not long enough, so she sat with her knees awkwardly bent, reading *Portnoy's Complaint*, all sex and American and New York and Jewish and foreign.

"There you are," her cousin's voice broke through.

Elizabeth looked up at the pink bikini Victoria was wearing, the material gathered at her narrow hips in little macramé rings, the halter top tugging gently at her chest. She swallowed her resentment and smiled.

"Well, may I join you?" Vicki asked, her hand on a casually jutting hip, her smile self-satisfied.

The cousins chatted about home, their respective brothers, how jealous they would be if they could see them now, and the boys they—well, Vicki—had met on the way down. The sea was calm. The surf lapped the sand hypnotically. Vicki went silent, pointed her delicate face to the sun, and slipped into sleep. Elizabeth picked up her book and scanned it for the naughty bits. The day passed pleasantly, without the adventure or excitement Elizabeth had expected but as a good holiday should. Her skin browned, then burned, but just a touch, enough to prickle and feel alive. She wandered up and down the beach, sometimes with her cousin, sometimes not, waded into the sea and felt blissfully far, far from home.

That night, Vicki seemed to find a man to her liking, a young Portuguese business type visiting the coast to assess property for the burgeoning tourist trade. But as the night was giving way to morning, she was taking ill.

"Excuse me, just for a moment," she told him with a sweet smile. She casually slid off the barstool and sashayed to Elizabeth, who was nursing a beer and talking to a British student about life at one of the new universities.

"Liz, would you please come with me to the loo?" she asked, her body as casual as ever, her eyes beginning to panic. They walked off together, Vicki clutching her cousin's arm, leaning more and more heavily as they approached the restroom. As the door swung shut, Vicki lunged for a stall and exploded in obnoxious sounds and smells.

"My lord, Vick," Elizabeth chuckled, covering her face with cupped hands and secretly enjoying her cousin's exertions.

"I know, I know," came a moan through the door. "I am so sick. It must've been those prawns we had for dinner, all that cinnamon and pepper."

"Not to your English sensibilities, I s'pose." Elizabeth laughed. Finally, she had something to lord over her cousin, however unexpected—her more rugged stomach.

They left Vicki's expectant beau in the lurch, and Vicki, leaning heavily forward, clutching Elizabeth's arm with both hands, climbed to bed.

It would be a fleeting sanctuary. For the rest of the night, Vicki didn't know which end to stick in the toilet, an unfortunate state of affairs for her and the rest of the hall, which shared the WC. Elizabeth slept soundly, content that this was divine retribution. By dawn, Vicki, already wan, was spent. She crawled into bed and slept for the morning, then begged Elizabeth to help her find a doctor.

There was a clinic not far from the hotel, it turned out. The hotel clerk hailed them a taxi, and once in, her cousin drooped her head on Elizabeth's shoulder, which was enough to prick her conscience. She laid her hand on Vicki's.

João Silva Gonçalves had been making a few halfhearted notations on a clipboard, his stethoscope dangling from his neck. His patient, a barrel-chested old veteran of the Spanish Civil War with arteries hardening beyond a doctor's reach, sat quietly humming to himself. The man was lonely and looking for company, and Gonçalves had nothing much to do anyway. He listened to the soft whoosh of blood through the man's carotid artery, as his enlarged heart tried to push the fluid through the thickening plaque. It was a pleasing sound, João thought, not a death rattle but signaling death was coming nonetheless. He wondered if it would be a stroke or heart attack.

"You know, young fella, I have to confess I fought on the wrong side," the old man confided. "I didn't think so at the time. I hated the Republicans. That's what I was taught. But just think if they had won, if they had beaten Franco and his fascists..."

He shook his round head, his wattles a beat behind. "How different things would be. You know, Salazar couldn't have stuck around. Franco gave our own fascists the air to breathe. And look where it got us."

The old man laughed quietly to himself. João nodded, unwilling to commit such overt subversion but by no means eager to defend the regime either.

Keeping regretful old men company wasn't what he had gone to medical school for. He had been one of the top students in his class. He had been a particularly distinguished diagnostician among the international student body at King's College in London. He was too young to be this weary, he thought, to sigh, as it were, at his fate.

The clinic's one and only nurse stuck her head into the exam room.

"Doctor Gonçalves, two young Englishwomen are here. Vomiting, diarrhea. Acute dehydration, it looks like."

"Both of them?"

"No, just one. The prettier one," she said with a sly little wink.

"Senhor Sousa, I'm sorry, but I must see another patient."

The old man flashed João a lascivious smile as he pulled on his trousers.

The lab room, one of two, was surprisingly cheery, a light peach color suffused with the sunlight that poured into a small window. Vicki miserably pushed herself up to the examining table and sat in exhausted silence. She tried to remain as still as possible. The crinkling of the paper stretched over the cracked vinyl upholstery hurt her head. Elizabeth was glad of the quiet. She perused faded anatomical drawings tacked to the wall, their genital areas prudishly omitted. There was something charming about a repressive Catholicism that reached even into this rural health clinic.

"Hello, ladies, I'm Doctor Gonçalves," a voice said in mellifluous but hushed English. João extended his hand first to Vicki, who barely glanced up and did not meet it with her own. He pivoted to Elizabeth without a thought, a gesture she appreciated immediately.

If she had had to guess what the doctor in this clinic looked like, Elizabeth would have conjured an old man in the twilight of his medical practice, semi-retired but in need of some spare change to supplement his pension. He'd be portly from a lifetime of good eating, or leathery and thin, browned by decades of sun reflecting off white sand, his excess skin hanging off bony arms. She hadn't guessed she'd be looking at a man not much older than herself, with brown eyes so dark they were almost black. His cheekbones were prominent, hollowing out an olive-skinned face and making his lips delicate as their corners stretched to fill the hollows. Black hair, a lot of it, with waves that defied a comb, sat atop his small, nice head. Elizabeth smiled.

He lifted Vicki's shirt to press on her abdomen, then reached around her back, probing with his stethoscope. Elizabeth watched his movements across her cousin's creamy, hairless expanse of skin, watched as the tips of his fingers sunk gently into her belly, above, then below, then to the left, then the right of her naval. If it had been her, she thought, she would have let out a little sigh of encouragement, a purring, low "hmmm."

"I studied medicine in London. King's College. Hated the place," the doctor said quietly as he took Vicki's pulse with bare fingers. He was a little awkward; his white lab coat hung off his shoulders like a shroud. He was not as tall as he looked, but six feet seemed willowy on a man so thin—and young, twenty-seven at most. *He must still be a student*, Elizabeth thought, a resident, interning for the summer by the sea.

"You would be surprised how many patients we see like this," he said, addressing Elizabeth. "Salazar's revenge. We don't exactly have the same meat storage standards as you do. It's justified as free-market principle, but really there's no money for inspectors. Two bags of IV fluid, and she'll feel good as new."

Vicki had not uttered a word.

"Ah well, 'sweets to the sweet.'" He smiled at her, patting her hand as he turned to fetch the nurse.

Elizabeth unconsciously reached to check that her ponytail was in place, that her unruly hair was not escaping around her forehead, before venturing forward. "Oh, come now, doctor, *Hamlet* is a bit overwrought for the occasion. Vicki here is not Ophelia."

João looked at Elizabeth with a sideways glance. He was not expecting to hear from the escort at all. The patient was indeed the pretty one, although her pallor—a very light green—and her sour expression took some of the charm out of her delicate features. There was something about this other one, though. Her eyes were some searching shade of blue-gray. She had soft cheeks, doughy but not flabby, and a kissable mouth. And she gazed into his face straight on. *British women*, he thought. Having a reputation for frigidity, born of century-old Victorian novels and etiquette manuals, they could always be counted on to bridle at the stereotype and be quick to buck it. He could imagine, moreover, how frustrated this one might feel in her prettier companion's shadow, how needy that might make her.

"Yes," João said, his mouth turned upward. "Yes, and how would you have known that?"

"Does a Portuguese doctor quoting the Dane mean to ask an Englishwoman on the Algarve how *she* knows Shakespeare? And *Hamlet*, no less," she asked, straining her tone of incredulity. "If you're testing me, try something slightly more obscure. 'Take note, take note, O world! To be direct and honest is not safe.'"

"*Othello*, hardly more obscure in this Moorish part of the world," João responded. "And technically, I was quoting the queen of Denmark, not the prince." He smiled shyly again and ducked from the room.

The IV bags took hours to drain. Vicki slowly perked up, sipped water the nurse brought, and took an antiemetic when she felt well enough. The doctor came in to look over her vitals one last time, deliver the discharge papers, and urge her to take a rest—and stick to soup, "not gazpacho either, a clear broth." They packed up and prepared to leave, when Elizabeth did something she had never done before.

"Doctor Gonçalves," she chimed sweetly. "Would you care to meet us for a drink tonight? You can make sure Vicki here is drinking her tea."

He wrinkled his eyebrows in misgiving. He was no novice with British women and their forward flirtations, and he wasn't a bronzed cabana boy, there for the *touristas* to throw off their inhibitions and grab a taste of guilt-free Latin.

Undeterred, Elizabeth put on her quotation voice. "'I have seen a medicine that's able to breathe life into a stone.'"

Alright, this is an odd woman, he thought to himself. He knew the type—upper crust, no doubt. She didn't have a trace of cockney or even middle class in her voice. But she was different somehow, not as put together, not as sure of herself as the well-to-do Brits he had known. Her boldness was a little forced, meant to overcome a truer nature, perhaps a shyness not usually associated with her class. He admired the effort and wondered at the inadequacy. He was intrigued.

"Where are you staying?" he asked.

"*No Hotel O Peixe No Mar*," she answered a little too quickly.

João laughed. "I know the place, 'the fish in the sea,' a little joke on the tourists, as in, 'There are other fish in the sea.' Not my usual hangout. 'Hither they come, to see; hither they come, to be seen. This is a place for the chase, not the chaste.'"

Elizabeth gave him a querying look.

"Ovid," he said slyly.

She cocked her head gently and gave him a look of appreciation. "Ovid," she repeated slowly. "So, nine o'clock?"

Elizabeth looked at Vicki, who sighed. She had this coming.

"I suppose I could make that."

"Wonderful," Elizabeth replied.

João Gonçalves approached the bar, where Elizabeth sat alone. His white shirt ballooned around his chest, a well-worn linen that waved under his arms in the ocean breeze. His jeans were fashionably tight around the waist and edged outward from his knobby knees. His eyes darted, looking at the other men at the bar, a small sign of discomfort with these surroundings. He spotted Elizabeth and walked cautiously, though he had rehearsed his opening line for more than an hour.

"*All's Well That Ends Well*," he said, half meeting her eyes. "Act two, scene one."

"Doing your homework, I see."

"I must admit you stumped me back in the clinic. And a medical quote from Shakespeare should be something I have in my bag of tricks. Where's your friend?"

"Cousin, actually. She's sleeping off her illness. Didn't get much rest last night."

Elizabeth expected the doctor's face to darken at this news. They always did. Not this time, though. He seemed to have no reaction at all. In truth, João Gonçalves figured the pretty cousin was out of his league. He never could see himself as attractive to women. He knew intellectually that a young doctor would be desirable to a certain sort, craving stability and stature if her own position in society was tenuous or low. But Elizabeth's and Vicki's were clearly neither. As a boy, he had been gangly and uncoordinated. The park near his home in Lisbon was crowded with his schoolmates playing soccer or playing tough. He stayed away. He feared them, or more accurately, feared their response to him. He was not athletic. He was not funny or silly. Honestly, he was a bit of a mama's boy, being all that his mama had to live for. He was Maria Gonçalves's little man, the insubstantial rock she leaned on while his father was out with his latest mistress. She would wake early, at five in the morning during the school year, to cook his eggs and sausage and order his books and fuss over his outfits. Such tasks had given her so much pleasure in an otherwise pleasureless existence that he took it upon himself to enhance her happiness in any way he could, mainly by eating her breakfasts with relish, wearing her foppish little outfits without protest, and studying diligently. All of which helped isolate him from the other boys. Medical school was his sole concession to his father—a thing, it should be noted, he did not do without protest.

João stared at the girl for some time, trying to divine her appeal. It was not immediately obvious. Her face was oddly featureless, a plain collection of sleepy eyes, weak chin, unremarkable cheekbones, a nose that was slightly too large for its frame. The countenance was slightly sallow, her hair seemed unattended to. But there was a subtle curve of her waist into her hips, and an athletic firmness to her ass; he could imagine running his hand from the base of her spine and resting it there.

He began to understand that the appeal of this Elizabeth was less the girl than the girl looking at him. Her eyes searched his face as he spoke, waiting for the next word, and her mouth turned up in approbation at his turns of phrase. He felt handsome under her gaze, and it flattered him.

Elizabeth fixated on his throwaway line, "something I should have in my bag of tricks," and was equally surprised by her own stirrings. She had focused on his shy manner, the way he averted his eyes before the end of each sentence. But the promise of some sort of expertise attached to the self-effacement sparked some excitement. Funny, she thought to herself, how men are so attracted to the virginal, while women craved some sense of experience. To be taught.

"What are you drinking?" Elizabeth asked.

"A Sagres is fine," he said, "but..."

He realized he should be the one ordering for them, but Elizabeth had already caught the bartender's attention before he could recover.

"Doctor Gonçalves," Elizabeth went on, "it's a bit embarrassing to ask, but I don't know your first name."

"I'm so sorry," he said, genuinely ashamed. "João, João Silva Gonçalves."

She offered him her hand, which seemed appropriate to her but which of course was entirely inappropriate. He recognized the gesture from film more than anything else, took her hand, and kissed it so as not to embarrass her.

"Tell me about your grasp of the Bard," she continued.

"Well, I wasn't only studying medicine in London. I wanted to act. That was to be my life, but my father had other thoughts, and I was dutiful. 'In time, the savage bull doth bear the yoke.'"

"*Much Ado*"—Elizabeth smiled—"and 'savage bull' does not exactly fit the man."

His love of Shakespeare hadn't started as a cheap come-on. He read it in Portuguese at first, and it was what inspired him to learn English, so he could read it in the original language. He would never have bothered studying medicine in London if he had not fallen for Shakespeare. The Globe Theatre was gone, but he figured he could still find some of that Elizabethan inspiration. This strange woman was reminding him of that.

"What brings you to Albufeira?"

"Isn't that what I'm supposed to ask you?"

"Well, you could, but the answer would be obvious," Elizabeth replied. "But a young doctor, from Lisbon, I'd imagine, educated in London..."

He nodded.

"In a little tourist village for the summer, ministering to the likes of my nauseated cousin, it hardly seems like a challenge, much less a career."

"It's something of a summer off, a gesture from my government before it puts my skills to its chosen task."

He stopped there, took a long draw from his beer bottle, and looked out over the bar to the sea. The two listened as the waves gently lapped the shore. "Ever heard of Angola? Guiné? The British call it Portuguese Guinea. I'm heading to Africa soon to ply my trade. The Americans haven't won the hearts and minds over in Vietnam, but they've given our own fascists an idea on how to calm down the colonies. 'How can tyrants safely govern home unless abroad they purchase great alliance?' With a little medicine, first aid more like it, they seem to feel we can make some allies yet."

"*Henry the Sixth*...Part three," Elizabeth chimed in.

João couldn't decide at first whether this game was captivating or annoying. He really was heading off to war, and it was no laughing matter. Then again, he was entitled to some fun, especially because he wasn't particularly adept at having it. As he drank more, he found himself giving in to Elizabeth's Shakespearean advances. He genuinely enjoyed the conversation. They talked of tutors and Tudors, London and Lisbon. They had a lot in common—overbearing, aristocratic fathers, aimless childhoods, a love of literature that threatened to blot out too many other pursuits. Of course, João's parents ultimately forced him on a path to useful adulthood. Elizabeth's practically precluded it. Then again, where did it get the two of them? The taxpaying citizen was about to go off to war. The isolated, barely educated one felt like she had torn off her blinders and could do as she pleased.

"'Doomsday is near; die all, die merrily,'" João, now drunk, said of his draft notice.

"Oh dear, João, how horrifying," Elizabeth said with a slight slur. "War? How dangerous will it be for you?"

He shrugged, his gaze drifting above her head.

"I'll be a doctor, maybe very far from the fighting, but if all goes poorly, the fighting will be coming to me, won't it?"

"Do you see a role for an assistant? Me, for instance?" Elizabeth chimed in coyly.

He looked her in the eye and smiled.

"Florence Nightingale in Bissau. That would be something."

As he expected, Elizabeth knew nothing about Portugal's wars in Africa. And though he evoked doom lightly now, if such a thing is possible, in quieter moments he feared what Africa would bring. The draft board had assured him there was no real danger involved in battlefield medicine. He would not literally be on the battlefield, far from it. But there was a vagueness to those reassurances that let his mind fill in the blanks. This was war, after all, and a war that most of his contemporaries were trying mightily to avoid. They were not fools. Such thoughts were surely far away from the privileged head of this vacationing Englishwoman, next to whom he now sat very closely. In more animated moments, he allowed his hand to touch her thigh, which gave softly under the thin cotton of her dress. And she allowed her fingers to graze his, he noticed. Their eyes would meet, and she would smile, her eyes crinkling at the corners, her shoulders rising. A strap would slip off and down her arm, and linger there long enough for his eyes to drink in her nakedness. Then she'd brush it back up and smile at him again. He had to admit it, he was enjoying himself.

They parted around one in the morning, as the last call went up. He kissed her cheek and a rosy blush forced her gaze downward. He could see she was smiling tenderly.

"Would you come back tomorrow night?" she said to the floor. "I'll make sure Vicki shows up for a check-up."

He reached two fingers under her soft chin and guided her face up to his.

"See you tomorrow," he said.

Elizabeth had no intention of bringing Vicki along. On the contrary, she bought her cousin another room, which Vicki happily accepted with a giggle and a playful push.

"Elizabeth, what has gotten into you?" she said, happy for her.

"Don't jinx it, Vick. There are no guarantees in life, certainly not my love life."

"My one piece of advice, Lizzie: Be careful. First-timers fall hard."

João had not been sure he would come back. He had obviously had too much to drink last night—they both had. And what was the point? He'd be in Africa before he knew it, and she could sleep with any number of brown-skinned men to fill her vacation fantasies. This was 1970; sex was supposed to be everywhere, even in Portugal. To that point, his summer on the beach had been sadly chaste. His father wouldn't have approved of Elizabeth Bromwell, that was sure, but he wouldn't have approved of his son's failure to get laid either.

He had to admit he liked her. She was vivacious, bright, an effortless conversationalist once she got going, a little needy, yes, but so was he. So he went. That evening, he put on a pair of loose-fitting linen pants, untucked his shirt, and walked to the beach by his place—so he could approach Elizabeth from the shore, trousers rolled, with the sun low and at his back. She was at the bar as promised. Vicki, of course, was not. They began to talk and drink and, without struggle, the night marched on. Soon after midnight, Elizabeth held out her hand and led him to her room. "'In thy face, I see the map of honor, truth, and loyalty,'" she whispered, actually believing it.

"'She's beautiful and therefore to be woo'd. She is a woman, therefore to be won,'" he murmured in response, and to his surprise, he meant it.

I too had left my home country to escape something—maybe not an aristocratic upbringing in a gilded cage but something pretty potent. I listened to Elizabeth's story and tried to avoid my own. My parents had dwelled now for ten long years on my sister, their eldest child. We never faulted them for it, my brother and I. We felt their pain, not as acutely maybe, but in our own way. We understood their inattention, the days, sometimes weeks, when our parents didn't seem to notice us. We had been young—I was ten, my brother twelve—when our sister, Rebecca, was stricken, but that was old enough to learn to care for ourselves, even to appreciate a little the benign neglect that let us get into trouble without ever really getting into trouble. By the time our parents could tune back in to their sons' lives, we didn't feel like we much needed them. So they didn't.

The truth was that I did need them, but without my mother's attention, in the shadow of my dead sister's frozen room, I expressed my need—really my longing—in other ways. I was perpetually falling madly, painfully in love with some girl or other, usually with one who could never love me back enough, certainly not the way I loved her. It was riveting in its painful, animating way, the constant string of one-sided pinings for fourteen-year-old girls who preferred the company of their girlfriends and Bonne Bell Lip Smackers and trips to the mall to the mess of poetic and slightly pathetic me. This was followed by engrossing, unrequited love affairs of slightly more maturity and imagined sexual content that at least involved talking to the object of my desire. That phase was finally capped by something that felt equal, but was fueled more by my need to be noticed than to offer love. Once I got my first girlfriend, I was never long without one. Even leaving for England meant leaving behind the latest love of my life—Lisa, a scattered college beauty with icy gray eyes, self-consciously staggering musical taste (King Crimson, Mike Oldfield at Montreux), and the same propensity for love with distant, invisible partners. That affair, again, was ultimately unrequited.

Now I was with Maggie. I had managed to escape the tug of Rebecca, the detritus of her unlived life: proms never attended, kisses never received, the Faulkner she never got to, exotic tropical fruits never tasted, European trains never missed. The black hole of loss marred my parents' faces, so I put an entire ocean between me and them. But I was no more whole for the journey.

"Can I make you some tea before bed, Elizabeth?"

She looked at me with a rueful smile and picked up her shot glass, tinkling it a little in shaky hands.

"No, David, you go ahead. I'll be alright." She poured herself another drink, and, I imagined, thought too about love, about being loved, about a man's touch. As she had said that night with Kelvin, ogling her daughter's latest, it had been some time.

Elizabeth was giddy with joy. The sun hadn't risen yet, but the room and the world outside were beginning to glow. She released her hair from its constricting ponytail and looked into this man's lustrous, black eyes, her left hand slinking behind his head, her fingers parting his curls. He moved toward her, lips softly parting. *My God*, she thought, *my mother's bizarre educational curse has yielded this gift to me, this most wonderful gift, the most wonderful gift I have ever imagined. I will never again muster an ungrateful thought toward Charlotte Bromwell in my life*. That happy pledge swirled into the excitement overtaking her as she realized that she had done it, she had rid herself of her virginity, finally.

She had tried to whisper to João that it was her first time, but she wasn't sure it had come out through her quickening breath. He had sunk into her hurriedly, with one of his hands on the small of her back, the other on the curve of her waist. His grip had been fierce. He didn't squeeze or pull, just held her in place, and as the first shock of pain shot to her head, she remembered she gasped but didn't flinch. With a deft, single thrust, he had staked a claim, and Elizabeth wanted nothing more than to honor it, to belong to someone, someone who wanted her this badly. He had obliterated her, and it was far, far better than she could have ever prayed for. She was gone from Hampshire, gone from Vicki, gone from tutors and aimless non-expectations. She was in someone's grip now. Better yet, he was in hers, cradled in her thighs, held in her arms. She had arrived.

CHAPTER THREE

It's possible that Elizabeth's stories had been embellished over time. How often she had told them I could only guess by the number of volunteers who had preceded me, a number I had not worked up the courage to inquire about. Of course, I may be embellishing myself, filling in some gaps, some carnal detail Elizabeth didn't actually share. But the detritus of the Bromwell past was certainly everywhere at No. 4. It all fit together. This man she described, João, had sounded like a reluctant but effective Don Juan, and if, as I suspected, Cristina was his, he may well have been Jupiter incarnate.

It was Cristina I was hoping to see when I peeked into the kitchen the morning after Elizabeth's most recent long night of storytelling. Instead I found Elizabeth standing by the counter in a dressing gown, intent on a textbook, her hair wild and unbrushed. It was early still, before she had prepared herself for class, and the glance we gave each other was almost intimate, a lover's view before the morning ablutions. She smiled shyly, beneath sleepy eyes, as I hurried past, toward the sound of Hans's buzzer.

"David, come take a letter."

The two nurses were grabbing the last of their things as they headed out of the room, cheery in their tight little dresses. I still hadn't learned their names, which was shameful considering how much I already owed them. Years of paralysis had left Hans's ass pretty much gone. The flat, flabby surface that was left behind was smeared with whatever dribbled out. It festered into small infections that would grow into larger ones without constant minding. The attention to such medical issues, particularly the irrigation of the anus, was, lucky for me, mainly the responsibility of the professional help, the ones paid more than eighteen pounds a week. On occasion, I did clip Hans's nails and nostril hairs. He was remarkably fastidious about such things.

The nurses smiled at me as they swished out. "Morning, love," they cooed. They didn't remember my name either.

Come take a letter. *What am I, a secretary?* I thought, stepping in and rummaging through the polished and bowed chest of drawers next to his bed for a pen and paper. *I realize this guy's my employer, but has the guy ever heard of asking? Or saying please? He hadn't said that word to me once since my arrival.*

The chest of drawers had a twin, less used so the inlay stood out more clearly, a delicate filigreed pattern. It had been carted away on my third day by two broad-shouldered men under the watchful gaze of a little, balding antique dealer. They had wrapped it carefully in quilted blankets, secured the blankets with duct tape, and loaded it into a beat-up green van with "Haversham Fine English Antiques" painted on the side.

Elizabeth had watched impassively, leaning against the open doorway and smoking a cigarette. The little man produced a wad of one-hundred-quid notes and began counting. I couldn't make it out, but there were quite a few of them. Elizabeth hadn't seemed impressed, slipping the folded bills without so much as a glance into the side pocket of her denim dress. "Haversham indeed. Rubenstein more like," she muttered as he sped away. "Who does that little Jew think he is?" Her eyes met mine briefly as she turned around to reenter the front hall before a flicker of shame averted them.

"Second drawer," Hans said wearily. "There's a lovely Montblanc, unless Elizabeth's nicked it and sold it off."

Hans was always weary to one degree or another. His condition meant he could never expend enough energy for real, sleep-inducing fatigue, but in the absence of deep sleep, he was always in need of it. From my end of the bargain, I was convinced he never slept. The stick strapped to his wrist with the rubber, studded thimble at the end could do a remarkable amount of work. It could put on Maria Callas at all hours of the night, for one. For another, it could hit the buzzer.

I hadn't noticed the wires when I moved into the room upstairs. They were connected to an electronic buzzer, the kind you'd see on a game show, high on the wall, in a corner. Whoever put it there must have been in on the joke. No one would ever notice it until it fired—which was for me, as I'm guessing for most, on the first night of occupancy. It made a particularly heinous noise, a wrong-answer kind of noise, perfect for wrenching your eyes open out of a deep sleep.

"Oh, David," Hans would say as I stumbled down the stairs at four a.m. "What on earth are you wearing? I'll have to get Elizabeth to find you some decent pajamas if you're going to insist on stumbling around in your knickers. Anyway, a little light is streaming through the drapes. Can't get any sleep. Close them up better, that's a lad."

"Oh, David, nice to see you. Still in your underthings? My throat is positively parched. The pitcher of water is next to the bed."

"Oh, David, the bedclothes have slipped off my head and I can't seem to get them into place."

I began to imagine all this was intentional, a way to make me miserable. He seemed to be particularly needy when Maggie was spending the night. "Fuck like bunnies for all I care," he had said, neglecting to say how difficult he could make that.

Clearly I had to toughen up. This was what I signed up for. "You will be his awms and legs," Nigel from Community Service Volunteers had told me. I guess it hadn't occurred to me that this would be a twenty-four-hour-a-day task.

"I will need you to type this up later, neatly, no mistakes. But jot it down for now," Hans said crisply. "Elizabeth can show you where the typewriter is when I'm napping."

"'Dear Voluntary Euthanasia Society,'" he began. "'I have been a dues-paying member of your little association for a dozen years now, and I'm still bloody alive.'"

He stopped to consider his words. His pause was so pregnant I thought maybe he'd given up on the whole venture. I stood there dumbly waiting.

"Strike the 'bloody.' Sorry," he continued again. "I'll try to keep this a bit more formal. Make it, 'and I still appear to be alive.' Yes, 'I have been a dues-paying member of your little association for a dozen years now, and I still appear to be alive.'"

I rushed to catch up. As the meaning of his words had begun to register, my handwriting had slowed.

"'Across the Channel, in Holland, doctors are snuffing out quadriplegics like me by the dozen. Nobody seems to be complaining. Yet I cannot seem to get so much as a decent dose of painkillers from the National Health Service. I would like an update on your efforts with Parliament. Surely you can find a cranky Tory with fascist roots, keen to rid Britannia of the likes of me. Pity my father, Gordon Bromwell, has passed on, but he must have progeny in Whitehall.'"

He paused again. "I wonder if assuming knowledge of my ancestry is unreasonable. Does anyone remember Gordon Bromwell?"

"Umm," I let slip, unsure whether he was talking to me, continuing with his dictation, or muttering to himself.

"No, no, that's fine. Let's carry on, David."

"'I am at my wit's end,'" he said more forcefully. "'I have also exhausted my patience with the society. Please inform me why I should maintain a membership that has gotten me nothing beyond a newsletter devoted to assisted suicide in lands I cannot hope to reach, given that I have broken my neck, and unhelpful hints at making life somewhat bearable as you dither on your assignment. Sincerely, Hans Bromwell.'"

He paused for effect, then ordered, "You'll find the address of the society in my black binder, top drawer."

"Hans, you don't really want me to send this."

"Well, why the hell not?" he said, turning his head away in disgust. I shuffled silently back to the newly twinless chest of drawers to find the binder and an envelope. I could tell this wasn't the first letter of its kind.

After breaking his neck, Elizabeth told me, Hans was brought to the spinal center at Stoke Mandeville Hospital, just northwest of London, "the best in the UK." It cost a fortune, but those debts would become clear only after their father died. Houndsheath was sold to the National Trust to pay off the private practitioners—the doctors, nurses, and physical therapists brought in to supplement the National Health Service—and the estate taxes that Sir Gordon's hopeless legislative efforts never succeeded in killing. Stoke Mandeville may as well have been a hospice on the beach, and those high-priced specialists might as well have been buxom, twenty-one-year-old candy stripers, for all of Hans's efforts. He implored the staff to let him drink himself to death, but they did not consent. And since he couldn't lift so much as a dram to his lips, he was shit out of luck.

For a high spinal injury, physical therapy is not supposed to be optional. It is not just for would-be Paralympians. With even a modicum of effort, someone like Hans could have at least maintained bladder control and spared himself life with a piss catheter.

"'With the help of a surgeon, he might yet recover, and prove an ass,'" Elizabeth muttered in exasperation.

But Hans had had none of it.

He loved to share the disdain he felt for the physiologist who had broached the future of his sex life. He would get spontaneous erections, he was told by the well-meaning imbecile, but they were not the product of sexual response, just some mysterious nerve firings that could not be counted on with a lady friend. Of course, the physiologist chimed in cheerfully, Hans's tongue, mouth, and facial muscles would be fully functioning. "You might be surprised at the wonders you can provide with a flick and a twitch."

The withering contempt with which Hans told this story, to lady and men friends alike, surely could not match the look he must have flashed the physiologist, who slithered away without so much as dropping off the booklet on sex and quadriplegia. That was the end of Hans Bromwell's post-accident sex education, the end of sex, period, or as he would say, full stop. The movement he could muster with his right arm, well conditioned and exercised, could have been put to good use. He certainly could have operated an electric wheelchair. But when the National Health Service sent him one—an expensive one at that, at least a thousand pounds—he ordered his nurse at the time to toss it into the street.

"If I'm going to be a quadriplegic, someone can bloody well push me. I've earned that at least," he growled.

No one would be earning an Oscar playing Hans Bromwell as he struggled nobly back to honest citizenship.

Maggie and I were lying on her futon, pondering over the impenetrable sounds of the Cocteau Twins' "Head over Heels." She was insisting that yes, those were lyrics. I had my mind elsewhere.

"I have to tell you something, Maggie," I said, turning on my side and propping my head up with the palm of my hand. "I don't know how much more of this I can take. He doesn't even like me. I don't sleep. I don't have anything to talk to him about. Maybe I should just leave now." It was late November; the wet, cold grayness was already getting oppressive outside, and I was thinking about Thanksgiving at home, which had always seemed modest when I lived there but the memories of which now filled me with awe. It would still be warm there, the leaves colorful and unfallen. I had been with Hans and Elizabeth nearly two months and was feeling bereft. I nestled beside Maggie's soft, pale body, as she listened, or pretended to anyway.

"Leave for the States?" she asked mildly.

"Hmm," I answered without much commitment.

Maggie didn't have much more to say. She had told me from the beginning Hans would not like me. But she didn't think that would be of much consequence to me personally. She figured she would be enough to keep me glad I stayed in dreary old Brighton. I was not so sure. Her second year of studies was considerably more difficult and intense than her first. Comprehensive exams were still more than a year away, but she was now able to size up the competition, to know what it would take to graduate with a "First," top of the class, to make something of her degree. And she had all the ambition of a working-class girl whose dreams had been mocked by the schoolmates she had left behind. I was now sharing her with Derrida and Giddens and mountains of books and Socratic professors I would never meet. And since I didn't have any such pursuits, I felt half-abandoned.

"David, you're not thinking of leaving me, are you?"

"Well, not leaving you. Just, leaving."

Maggie fixed her gaze on me, fully engaged now. I looked sheepishly at her. She had that look of exasperation I sometimes got from girls, the look that told me I was whining. I wasn't particularly mindful of the way I sounded before I made my sounds, but I was self-aware enough to see it in retrospect, to catch an immature neediness in my demands after they had slipped from my lips.

"David, I love you, but I can't help you through everything. You need to do something. I don't know, write or take up jogging or something. Find a hobby. Americans jog, don't they?"

"Maggie, my problem isn't my hobbies. My problem is my job."

"Job? Is that how you think of Hans?"

"I shouldn't?"

"I dunno. I s'pose."

She thought for a moment. Her look of annoyance faded. I could see her mind working, then coming on something.

"David, if Hans is a job, you don't bloody do it very well, do you?"

"Whadya mean?"

"You don't do much of anything. I mean, I know you do what he asks you to do, but you don't take any initiative. Surprise him."

"Surprise a quadriplegic?"

"Have you thought about taking him somewhere?" she asked.

"Taking him somewhere? Like where?"

"Anywhere, you great idjut. The two of you just need to get out of the bloody house."

It made perfect sense. If I was stir-crazy, Hans must be too. An excursion—damn, I loved Maggie. So two days later, I took the first step (which was no mean feat). I learned to use the winch. It was a contraption next to Hans's bed, a hammock of sorts hanging from a stainless-steel boom. You lowered it until the black canvas fabric lay flat by Hans's side, then you carefully rolled him onto it, straightened him up, and lifted. I had to laugh at Hans's expression as he rose, a mix of genuine fear (he had no defense if he fell), bemusement at his condition, and some excitement at a change in routine. As the harness closed in around him, his arms involuntarily hugged himself. His knobby knees drew up toward his chest. His eyes darted around him, willing his dead body back to earth. I lowered him into his wheelchair and gingerly tugged the canvas from under him.

Hans had a way of attracting interesting friends. It may have started with pity, but he roped them in and kept them around. And they rewarded him. One of the more handsome rewards was the coyote-fur coat he would wear when he went out in his wheelchair, made for him by James and Wills. His friends could be divided into pre-accident and post-accident. James and Wills were post-accident friends, which is why I liked them. The pre-accident friends, mates from school or Europe or Hampshire, were insufferable.

"You know, Hans, I went riding the other day. Wonderful exercise," one of the pre-accident friends droned on once, a porcine man named Cecil, a classmate from Eton. "Really, the up-and-down motion, the squeezing of the thighs, all that running about. Really wonderful for the constitution."

"Sounds like all the exercise belonged to the horse," Hans replied.

"Oh yes, quite right," the man allowed. "Very droll, Hans. Say, Hans, how is Elizabeth these days? I take it she never re-married, no?"

"No, no, Cecil."

"Yes, well, it was something of a miracle she landed a husband the first time," he said with an insolent chuckle. "But I suppose all young flowers can catch a bee when their blossoms are most tender. A little more difficult when the petals start to wilt and droop."

I don't know if it was out of malice or some notion of politeness that Hans would laugh softly at such comments.

James and Wills were nothing like that. Gay, flaming actually, they gushed over Hans's newest Callas recording and regaled him with stories about the latest gorgeous boy who wandered into their London fine used books store.

"You should have seen him, his smile. Really, Hans, I had to bite my palm, like this," Wills said, demonstrating with relish as he shoved the heel of his palm into his mouth and clamped down.

"I had to run into the back of the shop. My heart ached," James chimed in.

"What were you doing back there, you old queen?" Wills slapped his friend with mock ferocity.

They also joked about Hans's past live-in helpers.

"Remember that first, fat one a few years back, when you were getting ready for Tuscany?" Wills launched in. "We were talking about this boy's ass or that boy's ass. 'Who will ever want my ass?' he squealed. I swear, I didn't think he had it in him."

"I don't think he ever did have *it* in him," James responded on cue.

The two of them dissolved into squeals of laughter.

"I wish the image had never been allowed into my aching brain," Hans replied.

The one sensation Hans could not escape was cold. He felt it in his depths. He dreaded going outside for that one reason more than the many others on his list. And putting a jacket on Hans was practically impossible. You had to lean him forward in his wheelchair to slip it behind him, then pull back his arms and somehow feed them through without breaking his increasingly brittle bones or tearing his papery skin. He wouldn't feel it if you did, but that was all the worse; infections set in quickly and mercilessly.

James and Wills had the answer, a shop they knew of in London that specialized in fetish wear, bondage and domination, straitjackets and the like. A straitjacket could be slipped on from the front, no need to twist arms or wrench shoulders. But the ties or zippers in the back would dig into the bony spine, producing a bedsore without even a bed. So James and Wills's friend designed for Hans a fur straitjacket, the sleeves protruding from the front, with one side so long it wrapped neatly behind Hans's back. The two sides of the jacket met at Hans's side and zipped up diagonally over his left shoulder. To top it off, he was given a coyote-fur mat to cover his legs.

"But why coyote?" I asked. "It's like a mangy wild dog."

"David, must you always destroy my images of your country? Occasionally I can muster some romanticism about the call of the wild and all that," Hans replied.

"Those were wolves, Hans. Actually, if you really must know, they were huskies."

"Well there you are. Mangy dogs."

We were heading to the pub. Not the Imperial Arms down the street but a much brighter place in a hotel overlooking the sea a block down toward the beach.

"You sure you don't want me to come along?" Elizabeth called out in a singsong voice from upstairs. She hurried down, still buttoning a flouncy white blouse that she had just thrown on over a prim skirt that fell below her knees. She looked at me with a harried smile. "I could be good company for a handsome young man on his own." She gave me a playful nudge.

"He won't be on his own," Hans sighed wearily.

There was no use in me trying to mediate. I was paid, however woefully, to take the cripple's side. I gave Elizabeth an apologetic look.

"I'm sorry, Elizabeth. I'll join you for a drink tonight."

For a skeletal wraith, Hans was, it turned out, surprisingly difficult to wheel around. Even strapped in, his body fell with gravity, exaggerating the slopes and turns and forcing me to stop every few feet to hoist him back up. He was used to it and good-natured about the whole thing.

Inside the pub, I ordered us both a bitter, a pint for me, a half pint for him. His money. I held the glass to his mouth and turned it up nervously, watching for the little gasps from his chest to signal when to pull away. And then I noticed them. The stares. Not everyone, but quite a few, just staring, without an ounce of shame. If Hans met their gaze, they didn't flinch. Do you look away when the gorilla looks back at the zoo? It was like that, like Hans was a different species. Like they had total license. I flashed them a glare and tried to swat their gazes away, but their eyes wandered back, if they moved at all.

"How can you take this, Hans? Do you want me to say something to these people?"

It dawned on me that Hans had agreed to this little expedition for my benefit.

"That's kind of you, David, no. One gets used to it. You should have seen your own expression when you walked in that first day."

Hans, clearly exhausted, ate only a few bites of sheep kidneys for dinner. I set him up with his reading easel and rubber pointer, then cleared the dishes away.

"I'll be fine, thank you," he whispered, almost inaudibly, so quietly that I almost didn't notice that he actually thanked me.

"How did you get on then?" Elizabeth asked as I walked into the kitchen with a plate of food even I couldn't pick clean.

"With dinner?" I asked, setting the tray down by the sink.

"No, David, this afternoon."

She stood instinctively to relieve me of the dishwashing. It was one of those infrequent nights when Elizabeth and Cristina had eaten together, and mother and daughter were sharing a cup of tea. It was childish of me, I know, but I always got flustered and self-conscious around Cristina, like I was around Kelly Hill in fifth grade. I cleared my throat and tried to sort through a response.

"I think it went OK, I guess."

"David," Cristina chimed in, "I think you can do better than that."

I could feel my face flush, but I appreciated the challenge. It woke me out of my torpor.

"Well, I was taken aback, I guess, by all the staring."

Elizabeth considered that, her face slightly knit.

"You'll get used to that soon enough," she said. "This was your first time out with my brother."

"I was a little more concerned about him."

"Don't be, David. Hans is a big boy. He won't let you do anything he doesn't want to do, believe you me."

"How are things at home, David? I saw you had some letters from your parents," Cristina said by way of rescue.

"Fine. I mean, nothing ever really changes at home."

"It occurs to me I don't know anything about you, David," Cristina probed. "Do you have any brothers or sisters? You're so far away from family."

"I have a brother, Noah. I know, very Jewish, right? 'Parently he's going to law school."

"'The first thing we do, let's kill all the lawyers,'" Elizabeth jumped in theatrically.

"I had a sister, but she died."

I hadn't meant to say it. I talk about Rebecca almost never. But it slipped out, like a shroud over the little party.

"I suppose I shouldn't have killed off your brother just then too," Elizabeth muttered to break the silence.

"Mum!" Cristina snapped.

"No, no, it's OK; it was a long, long time ago." I waved my hand and smiled wanly.

Elizabeth looked at me with a sad, sweet smile. "'Everyone can master a grief but he that has it.'"

"My parents have never mastered it," I said softly. "My sister gets a mention at least once in every letter. Her room has never been touched."

"They must miss you terribly, David," Cristina said. Elizabeth shot her a silencing look.

"I don't know. They never seemed to need me much when I was around, but they are writing more, I've noticed, a lot more."

"Well, David, don't bugger off too fast. We need you as well," Elizabeth rang out.

That night, after I had emptied the urine bag one last time, adjusted the blankets, and wrenched the drapes shut, I fumbled in the gloom for Hans's hand stick. The top left drawer was a cluttered mess, the convenient repository of volunteers' shortcuts, Elizabeth's hasty tidying, and flotsam deposited by Hans's friends over the years. My hand brushed across a pile of old onionskin correspondences.

"What are these?" I asked, raising a few letters aloft and into Hans's view.

"You Americans are as impertinent as your reputations."

I turned to shove them back into the wreckage that had moved to fill their spot.

"You are curious about our story, are you not? Me, Elizabeth, Cristina?"

I hesitated. I wasn't sure whether a yes would be proper or prying.

"Oh, come now, David. You are. I dare say Elizabeth has told you something. I can hear through the walls well enough."

I didn't know what to reveal about our nightly story-time ritual.

"Those are letters, evidence."

"Evidence...?"

"Yes, of all that happened," he snapped, then sighed. "Hand me that top letter."

"Now?"

"Yes, David, now."

I set the reading table that propped up on finely carved pegs across his chest and smoothed out the letter in front of him.

He cleared his throat.

"Oh, this one." He laughed. Then he began.

Dearest Biggest Brother Hansy,

Oh, I've been a naughty girl. You'd be so proud. I hitched up with Victoria and fled Houndsheath, to Portugal! We are on a beach in the Algarve, dear brother, eating blood oranges, dark ham and gigantic prawns—yes, there is such a thing. The sun is hot, the wine is cheap, and Hans, I think I'm in love—not that you would know of such a thing. Perhaps a turn on a tropical shore would soften even your cynical heart. Come unto these yellow sands, and then take hands: Curtsied when you have, and kiss'd—The Wild waves whist.

I wanted to jot off a note to say, alright to boast, that I too have found lift. I'm not too bashful to admit, Hansy, that your own flight across the Channel gave me some inspiration and more than a little courage—not that I could have done it without Vicki. But now I am feeling so free, to live, to love. The isle is full of noises, Sounds and sweet airs, that give delight, and hurt not.

Well, in truth the delight did hurt a touch, but we women suffer even in pleasure. I hope I'm not shocking you, brother, but I have lost my virginity here. Oh what joy!

Mum is just fit to be tied, not that she knows the gory details. She has an inkling that I'm up to no good. I must admit I think Dad is quietly glad to be rid of me.

But enough about me, you should be well ensconced in Paris. I want to hear all about the City of Light and your latest, spine-

tingling adventure. I'm sure it involves a lady of exceptionally ill repute. I'm all ears. Of course, I don't have a fixed address at the moment. Please send your sporadic correspondences to Houndsheath, care of dear mama and papa. They'll have a better idea of where to find me.

Oh and Hans, although your stories from university were wonderfully graphic, they could not hold a candle to this "heaven that leads men to hell." If it works out, I'll tell you all about my Joao Goncalves. Just the name will titillate you, no doubt. If not, there are otros peixes no mar, no?

Take care, dear brother.
Your loving, beaming sister,
Elizabeth

CHAPTER FOUR

"Just a minute," Cristina yelled from behind the bathroom door.

It was morning at the Bromwells', which meant the usual scramble for the upstairs toilet, and if I didn't have such a weakness for Cristina, I might have been angry, like Greg waiting for Marcia in *The Brady Bunch*. Instead, I thought of Hans's catheter; there are advantages to his condition. I slinked into the study to look at an African carving—a woman on her knees, with pendulous breasts and a curious smile, holding on her head a great bowl, which Elizabeth, or perhaps Cristina, had filled with cowry shells.

"It's from Portuguese Guiné," Elizabeth broke in, startling me. She reached out a hand, and I handed the figure to her. She studied it for a moment.

"What do you know of the Portuguese wars in Africa?"

I shrugged. "Wars of liberation, right? Angola and Mozambique are still fighting. Reagan keeps pumping them with money to fight the communists. 'Our man in Huambo' I remember reading somewhere. I can't remember who the guy is, bad though, I'm sure."

"'Huambo.'" She laughed. "'There is a tide in the affairs of men, which, taken at the flood, leads on to fortune. Omitted, all the voyage of their life is bound in shallows and in miseries.'"

She paused to look at the statuette, but her eyes were elsewhere.

"'On such a full sea are we now afloat.' Are you interested, David?"

*   *   *

Italy had Il Duce, Germany the Führer, Spain El Caudillo—murderous one and all, but flamboyantly evil. Portugal had a mama's boy economist who went by the honorific title of "Doctor." What António de Oliveira Salazar's fascism lacked in flare, it made up for in longevity—forty years of absolute control. Maybe his dullness explained his durability.

After the assassination of King Carlos in 1908 and the hapless two-year reign of his son Manuel II, the Portuguese Republic commenced what would be sixteen years of chaos—enough revolution, government change, corruption, and anarchy to give democracy a bad name and the Weimar a run for its money. It was a relief when the generals put an end to it by launching a bloodless coup on June 17, 1926. Portugal was the laughingstock of Europe when the military government summoned Dr. Salazar in 1928 from the University of Coimbra. And at the tender age of thirty-nine, the quiet, precise economist performed a miracle: He balanced the budget. For that simple act, he became the *Ditador*.

From his poor redoubt on the western edge of Europe, Dr. Salazar commanded a ragtag empire: to the east, half the impoverished East Indian island of Timor, the seedy, corrupt outpost of Macau, and the exotic beaches of Goa; to the south, the desert outcroppings of Cape Verde, the lush isles of São Tomé and Príncipe, and the tiny sliver of West Africa known as Portuguese Guinea—Guiné—not to be mistaken for the only slightly larger French colony of Guinea. Then there were the jewels of the Portuguese empire—the *ultramar*—Angola and Mozambique. That empire was proof of Portugal's once and future greatness, the legacy of da Gama and Magellan, men who had brought a planet to fealty, and Salazar was not going to cede an inch of it, not a fragment of fetid mangrove swamp.

These were not colonies, he declared. They were provinces of Portugal, equal in every way to the lands of Iberia, save the forced labor, the whippings, the poverty, the caste system, and endless war and violence—all in the service of empire, *o ultramar maior.* Strong-willed men were dispatched to do Salazar's dirty work. General António Sebastião Ribeiro de Spínola was such a man, *o toureiro mais destemido*, "the baddest bullfighter of them all," and in 1968, for his long service to empire, Spínola was made the new governor and commander in chief of Guiné.

Spínola flew in by helicopter and found himself in the interior of the province, in a colonial outpost in the town of Bafatá—and in utter disgust. The forces of flamboyant rebel leader Amílcar Cabral, the PAIGC, the African Party for the Independence of Guiné and Cabo Verde, controlled half the country—malarial mangrove swamps to the west, razor-sharp elephant grass hiding guerrillas in the east, with scorching, soaking heat all over its 36,125 square kilometers, not much bigger than the state of Maryland. But Spínola wasn't worried; he'd seen worse. In 1938 he had commanded a Portuguese contingent fighting on the side of Franco in the Spanish Civil War. He spat at the Lincoln Brigade, the Commune de Paris Battalion, the Internationals, the communists, all those idealists who had flooded Spain to fight for the Republicans. They knew nothing of the chaos and corruption that lay in the hearts of Iberian men when they lacked proper supervision and authority. The defeat of those pompous pretenders was one of his life's greatest pleasures. In 1941 he had the good fortune to study German cavalry techniques as the Nazis rolled eastward, unstoppable. He was an observer on the Nazi side as German artillery reduced Leningrad to rubble.

But damn if the Soviets didn't survive that.

If the Russians could walk out of Leningrad, we Portuguese can stand tall in the ultramar, he thought, as Soviet-made rockets thudded down from the east. It did not occur to him that the Russians had been defending the motherland, a different proposition than a bedraggled imperial army subduing Africans in three different parts of their continent. Nor would it. He, like any good Portuguese officer, was convinced Guiné, Mozambique, and Angola were inseparable from the *metrópole*. As far as he was concerned, he *was* defending the motherland.

But by the time Spínola took command in '68, his forces were sulking and demoralized, harried as much by guinea worms and botflies as they were by the guerrillas slinking through the ten-foot-high grasses or plying the rivers and swamps.

With his monocle in place, his white gloves pressed to his skin, his camouflage fatigues neatly pressed, and his cap tilted jauntily on his head, the new governor looked over the sullen men and aimless officers. The villa stunk of sweat and bat guano. It was not so different from his venture in Angola in '64, but it was more manageable. That colony was also teetering under assault, but from three different guerrilla armies. Angola was fourteen times the size of Portugal. Guiné he could cross by helicopter in an hour or so. Sure, Amílcar Cabral was wily and organized, his forces united and well supplied, unlike those buffoons in Angola. But now, Spínola was in charge, not some junior officer. He would win this thing.

"Roust your troops and array them in the courtyard," Spínola told a disheveled little major, Almeida Bruno, who snapped to and followed orders. The men, no more than three dozen, stood at attention in the heat. The air was so saturated with water that sweat flowed without the slightest motion. Thunderheads rolled in from the Atlantic not far to the west, their rumble joining the mortar thuds to the east.

"Gentlemen, sons of Portugal, subjects of Senhor Salazar's *Estado Novo*, know this: We will not be the generation to lose empire," Spínola said, loudly but not angrily or urgently. He projected authority without bullying. Bruno stood by his side. "Our great-grandchildren and great-great-grandchildren will ply the rivers of Guiné, walk the highlands of Angola, and work the majestic seaports of Mozambique. They will fish from these shores, farm in Nova Lisboa, drag diamonds and coffee onto the ships of Beira because of what we do here today.

"This town, this, this intersection of two dirt roads, this pit, this is

Cabral's birthplace. Bafatá. You will hold it. You will not let the criminal communist see where his mother suckled him at her Mandinga teat."

He paused for dramatic effect. Who knew when these men had seen a true commanding officer? Who knew what these men believed they were fighting for, if they had given it a thought? António de Spínola allowed his monocle to drop into his white-gloved, outstretched palm. He looked up, surveyed the line of men before him, and straightened to an imposing height. "We will not fail," he concluded, almost in a hush, then headed to his helicopter. Bruno stood silent, afraid to drop his salute.

In the coming months, General Spínola would traverse the little colony by helicopter, staring down at the mangrove swamps in the northwest, the lush islands of the Bijagós, grasslands in the east, and forests along the Senegalese border, all crawling with the enemy. He studied Cabral's methods. If the PAIGC broke its combat forces into small, roving teams, so would he. If Cabral ran education camps to teach an otherwise indifferent peasantry to loathe the colonial oppressor, he would wage his own campaign for the hearts of Guineans. He would exploit divisions, between the Muslim Fula of the north and the native religions of the rest of the country, between the educated *mestiços* from Cabo Verde who led the PAIGC and the *pretos*, the dark-skinned Africans who took their orders. He needed thirty thousand troops but had only five. The young men of his country were slipping out of the country and into France in ever increasing numbers to avoid conscription. Cowards.

But what he needed above all were doctors. Cabral ran pathetic shanties he called clinics in the "liberated" zones. Spínola would build hospitals, health centers, mobile dispensaries. He would show these *selvagens que vivem nas matas*—these people who are no more than savages living in the forest—what civilization had to offer.

Elizabeth remained in bed and watched João dress in the clothes he wore the night before, her head propped up on a hand buried in her riot of hair. She enjoyed the show, the way he raised his arms high above his head to slip on his loose shirt without unbuttoning it, the way his slender midsection was exposed, the muscles and cavity of his armpit, the way he gave one little hop as he pulled on his trousers, his still-mussed hair, his smell, mingled with hers. She had fantasized about this moment for years in lonely, furtive breathings at Hounds-heath, and like those fantasies, the next act was hazy and beside the point. She might see him again. More than likely, the curtain was fall-ing, but it had been a jolly good show—her first, after all.

"Will I see you tonight?" she asked as casually as she could.

"Of course," João replied blankly. He kissed her forehead, a filial gesture that left her with a vague sense of loss.

He headed off for a quick stop at his summer bedsit for a change of clothes, then on to the clinic. He was surprised to find that he couldn't stop thinking about the Englishwoman. As he was leaving O Peixe, he had halfheartedly resolved not to return, at least not while she was there. There were other fish after all. But his resolve was breaking of its own accord. She was interesting. Other English-women he had known were good conversationalists, charming and intelligent, without all the Shakespeare of course, but certainly Eliz-abeth's equals, yet better looking, more feminine, more sexual. They were always toying with him, though. Their snobbery, their sense of superiority, that they were more experienced, more urbane, more, well, British, than he, was maddening. But Elizabeth, from all she had said, appeared genuinely to want nothing to do with her priv-ilege. She was enriched by it, but not *of* it. And the way she was in bed, she hadn't been snobby, aloof, or "above it" at all. She had wanted it, badly.

"Huh." João grinned. He did like her. Plus, he could really stick it to his father with this one. Times had changed. He wanted a part-ner, an equal, not a series of chippies or one exceptionally tolerant doormat who would bear and care for his children, no questions asked. He certainly was not interested in Portuguese women, with their cloying shallowness. Gustavo Gonçalves would chastise him, would tell him Elizabeth was not beautiful enough, her breasts were all wrong, her jaw too small and ill-defined.

"What the hell are you doing?" he'd say, holding out two hands and shaking them as if he had his son by the throat. The son would ignore the father, leave him with arms outstretched. João smiled at the thought.

A week later, at the hotel bar that had nurtured their quick courtship among the many other fish in the sea, they toasted their daring. On their second night together, Elizabeth had been more nervous than on their first, just twenty-four hours before. She had time to think about approaching lovemaking, to consider what she had done right and the many things she was sure she had done wrong. He had sensed her fear as they ate anchovies drenched in olive oil, nibbled on sweet cherry tomatoes, and drank a bottle of *vinho tinto*. "Do you want to call it a night? You know, we can," she heard him say. She blushed, looked down at her hands folded primly in her lap, and shook her head in short, subtle spasms. He touched her chin and lifted her face to his.

João had gone more slowly that night, held her gently for a long time, allowed her to come to him, and she was grateful. It grew easier from there until finally, she sent her cousin home alone to pursue her future in British society.

"But Elizabeth," Vicki had protested, "what will you be?"

What would she be? She hadn't thought of it that way. She had thought only of what she would do. She would continue on, the further the better. This lovely Portuguese man was offering her the ride, and she was going to take it. For João, Elizabeth offered help as well, a different kind of ticket, more like an upgrade to a better version of the harsh life to come.

A married doctor, João couldn't help but think, would have certain privileges, private quarters—maybe a house of his own, a remove from the barracks of the colonial army—a social standing that would go with the rank that would automatically be conferred on him by way of his medical degree.

There, he had said it: married, marriage. Could he really take it there? Yes, he thought, yes, he could. He had never been one for the company of men, and he was going off to war. Africa, "the kingdom of perpetual night," as Elizabeth had murmured. The thought of it induced panic. He would be lonely and at the same time, with all those men, entirely socially overwhelmed. But a woman in the picture changed his entire vision of the chapter to come. The image of Elizabeth by his side eased his anxiety like an opiate slipping into the bloodstream. Why not get married? He could inject her into his life just as simply.

Elizabeth was only beginning to acquaint herself with men and love and the bewilderment that came with it all. She had not known the painful, quicksilver love of high school. There had been no high school. But she was sure the sympathy that swelled in her chest as João spoke was love. And there was something else: João needed her. All those mornings in the breakfast nook with her mother telling her to sit up straight, to sit still, to chew with her mouth closed, for God's sake, all those nights glued to her brother's words and his side, all that longing for her father's attention—always, always, she was the burden, the hanger-on. *Never again*, she thought. João Silva Gonçalves needed her. She wanted to touch him, to soothe him. She leaned in close over the rough-hewn table.

"Take me with you, please. I want to see."

"'Hasty marriage seldom proveth well,'" João warned with a wry smile, knowing well the words would have the opposite effect of their meaning. "'For what is wedlock forced but a hell, an age of discord and continual strife?'"

Elizabeth smiled. *Marriage*, she thought, *he said it. What heaven this will be, swapping lines as we sweep across Africa.* She pictured herself as Katharine Hepburn in *The African Queen*, or perhaps some lonely figure in a windswept, arid desert, *Lawrence of Arabia* as a love story.

"'In time,'" she quipped, "'the savage bull doth bear the yoke.'"

"Elizabeth"—he dropped to his knees, her hands in his—"my lovely surprise, will you marry me?"

It was as if a cell door had swung open with a clang, and Elizabeth, without pause, ran for freedom. The tears gushed from her eyes. She squeezed his hands, brought them to her face. She cried on his hands, soaked them in tears, then smothered them with kisses as her head nodded over and over and over again.

"I am in love, truly," the Bromwells' daughter wrote to her parents in a letter mailed from the Algarve before she boarded the train for Lisbon. It was more defiant than confessional. "I will bring João to you in due time. He is a doctor, and no doubt, we will settle in London, where he studied medicine. But first, there is adventure to be had. And Mother, remember what you taught me: 'Such duty as the subject owes the prince, even such a woman oweth to her husband.'" She didn't mean that part, of course. Even she had absorbed enough of the times to laugh at the notions of *The Taming of the Shrew*. But her mother would recognize the irony and feel the slight. Elizabeth was turning the anachronism of her education against the parent who had foisted it upon her. And it felt fantastic.

Elizabeth knelt before the priest in the small church in Lisbon, her husband-to-be kneeling beside her. An elopement would have done just fine, but such things were impossible in Salazar's Portugal. Fascism was not the proper word for what afflicted Portuguese society; it was more repressed than repressive. The PIDE, Salazar's secret police, was hated. They lurked, fostered paranoia, and could strike at random, landing you in prison for an unpleasant but usually brief stay. The generals—geriatric, pathologically conservative, but wholly ineffective—ruled the body politic. But the church had frozen society in amber. To Elizabeth, who had never been to a Catholic service before, the ritual was remarkably short, quaint, romantic even. She could not understand a word the little man said, but as she knelt before him, staring into his flowing cassock, she could feel the power of supplication.

João's parents were every bit as furious with their son as Elizabeth's were with their daughter—more so, perhaps. They had seen the bride. Off an alleyway in the Alfama, one of the seven hills across from Bairro Alto, João had brought Elizabeth home to Dr. Gustavo Gonçalves. He had sent his son abroad, to medical school. In a nation ruled for decades by a professor, Gustavo had raised João to join Lisbon society, to meet an olive-skinned beauty who would bear his grandchildren and care for him in old age. João's ticket was punched, and what had he done? Fallen in love with an Englishwoman on vacation, a plain one at that.

"Son, may I have a word with you?" Gustavo had asked, mildly, but João knew what was coming. In his darkened study, the elder physician ripped into his son. "You go off to the beach for the summer. You're supposed to chase girls, fuck a few—many if you want. You don't marry them. And this one, this one..." The anger had stolen away the words. He fumed, stormed around the room, bounced on the balls of his feet as he silently gesticulated, then blurted out, "You could have at least found one with bigger tits."

João wasn't listening. He had grown inured to such drama, to his father's fits of boorishness. As a child, he would hide behind a closed bedroom door as his mother raged about some new girlfriend of his father's, discovered by a friend or relative, which only added to the shame. She was leaving, Maria Gonçalves would scream. This time she was serious. She had been pushed too far. No matter how many times he heard those words, João felt them like a stabbing. His mother was to abandon him; she meant it. And where was he to go? His father certainly wouldn't care for him. At best he would get a governess, some sagging, rotund *dona* from the church to tug at his earlobes. At worst, he would be taken, put in an orphanage or shipped to a distant relative's farm in the country.

"Oh, come on, Maria, we've been through this before," Gustavo would say.

"Yes, yes, yes, we've been through this before, and never again."

She might storm out of the house for a day or two—and send João into a paralyzed panic. She would come back, though. His father would give João a little wink or a playful shrug, nothing to be concerned about. They had played their roles perfectly, he was saying. All's well that ends well. João would return a shy smile, shaken to the core, but he would never show it.

As he knelt beside his bride, he imagined his father's eyes burning into the back of his skull. He was marrying for love, he thought with satisfaction. Elizabeth Gonçalves would never abandon him, ever. Tiny Portugal had brought mighty Britannia to its knees in this little church. The screams of his mother, that little wink of his father's, those were experiences he would never repeat in the long life that stretched before him. He made the decisions now. He commanded the silences.

He and Elizabeth reported the next day to the military Forte de São Bruno at Caxias, in the shadow of the vast prison where the secret police brought their captives. The structure jutted into the sea like a jagged star on the beach, its walls and corners sharp, its rooms without warmth. There would be no real training. By 1970, the Portuguese military understood that the imperative was to get the conscripts to the continent as soon as possible. Better to acclimate them there anyway. The heat, the bugs, the smell of raw sewage, cooking fires, and bat shit were things they could not be prepared for from Portugal. Besides, they couldn't change their minds once they were there.

"I will be taking you to Guiné," Renato Marsola Araujo, the head of the medical corps, told João when he arrived at Caxias. "General António de Spínola pampers his medical corps there. You and your wife will find it, well, more comfortable than most. Guiné is a shit hole. I will not lie to you. It is useless to us beyond a decent port for refueling and some peanuts for export. Why the hell we are there I cannot tell you. But it has its charms. Besides, it will fall soon. Spínola won't tell you that part, but he knows. Deep down, he knows. I don't expect you will be staying long."

CHAPTER FIVE

I knew what Elizabeth meant when she spoke of sewage, shit, and decay, of rotting refuse and spoiled slaughter, the stench of urban Africa. I'd been there myself, rebuffed legless beggars in Dakar, leaped across putrid, green rivulets in Banjul, and now I held a mild facsimile in my hands, inside a bulging paper bag, greasy on the bottom and breaking open as I rushed it into the kitchen. I couldn't look inside. I was afraid to. I heaved it onto the counter and sat on the barstool as Elizabeth cheerily poured me a cup of tea.

After more than a year in Britain riding public transportation, I felt a guilty pleasure driving to the west side of town, past the local Sainsbury's to the exotic butcher that met Hans's peculiar demands. Having suffered through so many aging double-decker buses, slow-motion local trains, and endless chitchat about the miserable weather, I found driving alone to be a joy I had never experienced in the States. The air was crisp and biting now. The autumn mist was giving way to a clearer, thinner sky on most days. And I was driving a blue Vauxhall van emblazoned with the word "Ambulance," heat and radio blasting. The traffic parted for me. I was invulnerable.

This particular run was to pick up pigs' ears for dinner that night with guests, unfortunately from the pre-accident days. I figured pigs' ears would look something like pork rinds, a meat product of indeterminate shape and origin. I was wrong. As Elizabeth rattled on, she casually lifted the enormous things out of the bag, two hairy, floppy, unmistakable animal ears joined by a flap of skin that was once a scalp. They were still pink. You could wear a pair for fun, like Mickey Mouse ears for the porcine, if they didn't stink so much.

"Elizabeth, are you sure you can eat those things?" I winced.

"Never seen one of these?" she queried, picking a pair up casually. "Really, they're quite edible, but I won't lie and say they're delicious—an acquired taste. Maybe not worth acquiring for you, I realize. 'For sufferance is the badge of all our tribe.'" That one made her laugh to herself as she pivoted toward the sink. Not knowing any other Jews, she believed me to be somehow complex and secretive, a Shylock. How was she supposed to know I hated *The Merchant of Venice*?

"They're a bloody lot of work," she called over her shoulder as she reached under the sink to pull out what looked like two Brillo pads. She tossed me one and started scrubbing.

"Give us a hand, then. You don't have to eat them, but we've got to get all the wax and hair out. Terribly bitter otherwise."

Maggie didn't believe me, but I was starting to enjoy life on Imperial Lane. Hans's letters and Elizabeth's stories kept me up late when Maggie wasn't around, which, as the term progressed, was getting to be more usual. And then there was Cristina. She liked to leave black, laced thongs in the hallway outside my door. I hadn't realized women really wore such things. Maggie, with her cotton Hanes French cuts, certainly didn't.

I had by then become adept at hoisting Hans out of bed and into the world and found myself surprised at what good company he was, though he still refused to let Elizabeth tag along. Whether it was hostility or indifference I couldn't be sure, but it was clear I was the communication bridge between them. Turns out his first-day dig at my choice between Woody Allen and Maria Callas wasn't such an insult. He really loved Woody Allen, and I had taken it upon myself to watch the film listings and festivals at the Duke of

York's for showings. *Hannah and Her Sisters* had been playing a few weeks back, and I was proud as we left the theater, feeling like my country had something to offer Hans.

The holidays were approaching, and even Hans was making some effort. He suggested we make a shopping run, and I took him out hunting for a piece of jewelry—I had suggested a necklace—for Elizabeth. The Bromwells were feeling temporarily flush. Haversham, their London antique dealer, had come down to offer more than ten thousand quid for a desk out of the upstairs living room. The wood tones were a deep, rich red, the grain smoothed from hundreds of years of use. The pulls had a delicate, lotus shape. Even an untrained eye—mine, for instance—could appreciate its beauty. I imagined it carved from the forests of Burma and gracing a colonial parlor somewhere in Singapore. As his lads carried it out, the antique seller riding herd on them to avoid even the slightest scratch, I could feel the ebb of empire, I swear.

"That was a beautiful desk," I said, sidling up to Elizabeth, who was leaning casually against the open doorway as the men loaded the truck.

"An escritoire, if you must know. Konbaung Dynasty, before ornamentation was forbidden in Burma," she said, watching the little antique dealer direct the movers into his truck. "British Colonial is quite big these days. I should have asked for more"—she gestured toward him—"but the little Jew—" She pulled up short. "Oh, David," she stammered, "I am so sorry." She looked away from me.

Elizabeth was studying hard now for an eventual career as a secretary or an even less distinct office-girl post. The furniture and its proceeds would last only so long.

"See you in a few months," the dealer called out cheerfully as the engine of the truck idled.

"We'll call you," Elizabeth replied. She wasn't angry or sad or wistful. Losing a desk or armoire was nothing like losing the farm or her father—or her brother, for that matter. The end had been approaching for some time.

Hans and I had decamped to The Lanes, the warren of precious shops just above the Royal Pavilion. There was a jewelry store I knew of there, and a Belgian chocolatier. I wheeled Hans down the ramp of the ambulance and swung him into the street. A hippie was striding purposefully toward us, his woolen poncho and woven, Andean Indian hat dulled to a kind of beige but his eyes intent. His breath blew from his open mouth in little dragon puffs. Hans's eyes moved toward him, alert to the danger I hadn't detected.

"Is this fur real?" the stranger hissed in my face, sneering at the coyote straitjacket cinched around Hans's torso and the fur cover-up warming his legs. "Is it real? Because if it is, you're really gonna need an ambulance, mate."

I stood there, dumbfounded. Hans said nothing, but the belligerent man, somewhere nearing thirty, hadn't asked for a reaction from Hans. He didn't seem to notice him. In public, there were two reactions to Hans, staring and denying he was there. I guess when you're attacking a cripple's fur, it's best to ignore his presence.

"Are you going to say something?" he shouted in a vaguely East London twang, now an inch from my face.

I took a step back, turned, then hit him in the cheek with a gloved right fist. Besides sex, it was the most satisfying thing I had ever done. And sex usually ended in disappointment. This didn't. The hippie bent over, holding the side of his head.

"Bloody hell, bloody hell, bloody hell," he kept muttering. "I'm gonna kill you, I will. I'm gonna kill you."

But he made no move to do so. He just crept away, overmatched by all five nine, one hundred fifty-five pounds of me.

I'll admit it, I had a violent streak in me. I kept it well hidden. It didn't clash with my effete image, but it was there. When I was in fifth grade and Frankie Hellman was in fourth, I had beaten the crap out of him for no reason at all. We were both little, but Frankie was pathetic. It wasn't a fair fight. Later, much later, in high school, when Frankie was still an underdeveloped, snot-nosed tenth grader, I had lunged at John Rich, a junior like me, after John had dumped a bag of dirt on Frankie's head to please the other football play-ers. That time, I was taking on someone a lot bigger than me, but righteousness and surprise won out. John Rich fell back against the lockers, took a harmless punch to the jaw, raised his hands in sur-render, and walked away. He knew he was in the wrong. Frankie scurried away, trailing dirt in the hall, too embarrassed to thank me.

Rebecca had been in the hospital when I gave Frankie that beat-ing. I couldn't stand visiting her. I couldn't stand seeing my big sister like that, pumped full of steroids, her head shaved, puffed up and orange as a pumpkin, a livid scar across her scalp where the sur-geons tried—and failed—to remove every vestige of brain cancer, tubes tumbling from under her sheets, from her wrists, from her elbows, from her nose. I didn't understand what those tubes did, whether they were delivering to or taking from her depleted body. I couldn't ask, and by then she couldn't answer anyway. Toward the end, I begged my mother to leave me at home, and sometimes she did. One of those days, I beat up Frankie Hellman. His mother did nothing to punish me. Mine never found out. Later, I punished John Rich for my transgressions.

The hippie gone, Hans did about the best thing I had ever seen. He laughed. It was a breathy, faint laugh. He couldn't muster any-thing more. But it lasted a good two minutes and nearly stole what little breath he had left. His head had slumped into his woolen muffler, and as I watched him, I realized that he had enjoyed that altercation more than anything I'd done for him so far. Short of pushing him in front of a bus, it was the greatest gift I could have given him.

Elizabeth was still laboring over the pigs' ears in the kitchen when the doorbell rang. "Could you get it, David? That'd be Julian and Simon."

I had heard tell of Hans's old university pals. Elizabeth insisted I would enjoy the evening, though she hadn't been very convincing. Simon Fellowes stepped in first, taller than me by a good six inches and carrying it imperiously. Julian, whose chin was nowhere to be seen, followed.

"Ah, you must be the American volunteer we've heard so much about," Simon said, handing me his coat and rolling his eyes. Julian peered around to look for a coatrack. Seeing none, he tossed his long, tweed cover-up over the banister. In unison, they pivoted to the right and waltzed into Hans's room without a knock.

"Punctual as always." Hans sniffed, glancing at the clock but smiling. I had propped him up well for the occasion, combed his hair, trimmed his nose hairs, and strapped on his pointer tool. Music was at the ready.

"Well, Hans, some of us have things to do, places to go, little walks along the promenade," Julian replied.

"Maybe even a little jog," Simon chimed in, "like the Americans do."

The abuse was what Hans loved from these two. They had taken so much of it from him in university, they were not about to let paralysis and pity get in the way of revenge.

"Hans, I see you have still not bothered to learn bladder control," Simon said, playfully squeezing the catheter bag hanging beside the bed as if he were pinching the poor invalid's scrotum. "Volunteer," he shouted over his shoulder, though I was standing not three feet behind him, "please dump the piss before dinner. It's mildly revolting."

"Mildly?" said Julian, an arching eyebrow cutting through the folds of skin piling on his forehead. "Well, at least it's not streaked with blood.

"Hans, *you* look positively revolting. Whatever happened to that hot little nurse who was supposed to stretch out your fingers and ride your willy? You never did take her up on that, did you? Refused to live up to your end of the bargain, as I recall, letting her straddle your face for a little in-and-out on the cripple's tongue. Well, you get what you deserve, lying there, shriveling. 'I'm meeeelllllltiiiing,'" he said in mock horror, folding toward the floor before thinking better of it.

"You never were one to please the ladies on their terms, were you?

Anyway, enough of all that. I've brought you a little something. Papa's latest," he said, fishing from a deep canvas bag a label-less, dusty bottle of deep red wine, which he put on the chest next to the bed, "some porridge"—he pulled out a sealed tin of something— "and your favorite." Out came maybe ten tins of foie gras, again un-labeled. "To get you ready for the summer."

Hans smiled. "If it'll ever come. David, open that bottle and pour three glasses. I'll sip a bit."

"Here's two more," Julian said, pulling out a couple more dusty bottles, then tossing the sack on the floor.

Elizabeth was pulling a pan of sizzling parsnips from the oven, baked in olive oil and rosemary. The house smelled of sweet, sautéed pork, baked parsnips, garlic and onions in a reduction sauce for the ears. And vodka, which Elizabeth was laying into with gusto. As I poured three glasses, two full, one just a nip, Elizabeth grumbled, "S'pose Julian didn't invite me to partake."

" 'Fraid not, but here, let me pour you a glass."

"No, no. I wasn't expecting any. Special stock. I'll stick with my own," she said, throwing her head back and finishing her shot.

"You mean Elizabeth's learning maths?" Simon was saying incredulously as I walked back in, carefully carrying the wine glasses on a small tray. "Elizabeth, doing something useful? What would your parents say?"

"They bloody well should've thought about that before they spent the inheritance," Hans said wearily as I propped his head up more and leaned the quarter-filled glass to his lips.

"Hans," Julian chimed in, "it was you that spent the inheritance, you bloody fool.

"Well, you know," he continued, "maybe it's best we British start letting the cream rise and the waste fall, like the Americans, a bit of meritocracy. I think Elizabeth will make a jolly good secretary. She's been wiping your arse all these years. Let her kiss someone else's. At least he might have the strength to pinch her bum."

"That'd be a thrill," Simon said with a sneer.

"I think you tried once," Julian said accusatorily.

"I bloody well did not. I was never that desperate."

It went on like that for a long time. They tried to cover their snickers when Elizabeth approached to ask my help serving dinner. They sat in momentary silence as the steaming plates of food came to them. They accepted the service naturally. They were used to it. But on their own turf, they would not take such delight in insulting the servants. That would be no fun at all. Elizabeth, on the other hand, was fair game. They had been insulting her most of their adult lives.

I cut Hans a small corner of ear and fed it to him gently as the conversation veered from the cruel to the dull. "Have you seen the new newspaper, the *Independent?*" Simon was asking. "Not sure what to make of it. It's bloody wide, though, lots of flash."

"I'm still reading the pink," said Julian, stifling a yawn. "Best paper in Britain. Bet young David over here reads the *Yankee*," he said dismissively, no doubt assuming I wouldn't recognize the nickname for the *International Herald Tribune.*

"The *Guardian*," I said defensively.

The three of them looked at one another for a moment, then laughed. They had been talking to hear their own voices and chase away the silences. What a strange kid this was, they must have thought, taking the conversation seriously enough to defend his choice of reading material.

"That's a good boy," Julian said, pretending to reach toward me to pat my head.

As I entered the kitchen with a tray of greasy dishes and half-eaten food, I found Elizabeth on the barstool, her plate of reheated baked beans and white-bread toast barely touched. She was silently weeping. Her face was turned away from me, but I could see the wracking of her shoulders, the fluttering of her thick head of hair. I took the few steps across the galley and laid a hand gently on a shoulder blade, tenderly, I hoped. It was enough to elicit a low moan, a barely audible wail of grief.

"You've been listening to them, I suppose," I said feebly.

"'Why should a man whose blood is warm within sit like his grandsire cut in alabaster?'" she cried softly, but so clearly I was startled. It was a voice that could hardly emanate from this hunched, wracked figure. Deep, resonant, thespian—like something from a lit stage in the West End.

Simon and Julian let themselves out, calling good-byes to Hans as they fetched their coats from the banister. A cold wind blew down the hallway, then stopped with the slam of the front door. The two were still chattering to each other as they got in their car and sped away.

I put a tentative hand on Elizabeth's back again, this time just below the nape of her neck. She reached over her shoulder to clasp it. She didn't let go for a good long time.

"I gather Elizabeth did not take the evening well," Hans whispered as I prepared him for sleep.

"No, how did you know?"

"One knows. You must think me cold, David."

"I don't really like your friends."

"No, you shouldn't."

I rolled him a quarter turn to smooth out the sheets and take a quick look for the beginnings of any welts that could blossom into a bedsore.

"There are things you don't understand about my sister and me. We don't like to speak of it, but it creeps in. We were born with so much, and look at us now. We destroyed each other."

Dearest Hans,

I think of you often in your flat, wherever it is, wondering what you do to fill your days. The thought comes to me often, since I have nothing to fill mine.

Hans, I have done a foolish, foolish thing. I write to you from a military base outside of Lisbon, a married woman. You would like Joao, really. He's a doctor, but don't hold it against him. He quotes Shakespeare like a true scholar of the man from Stratford. He believes in it. We met on a lark Vicki and I took to the Algarve. That's Portugal, darling. I think I wrote of it already. I have not heard from you, but I have not been easy to reach. You would love it, Hans, all palm trees, whitewashed houses, olives and squid. But now he is taking me to Africa, to a little speck on the map called Portuguese Guinea.

I have not told him this, but I will tell you. I am scared. It seemed so wonderful and romantic. I was intoxicated with love, with the newness of it all, with the adventure. But watching Joao put on his uniform this morning and lace up his boots for whatever training he is heading off to, I realize I'm off to war. Cry Havoc! And let slip the dog of Hampshire.

The Portuguese are still fighting for empire, Hans, as father presides over the decline. Joao doesn't believe in it. He was drafted. And I fear he has drafted me. I have to believe there is more to it than that, that he does love me and we will return from Africa, find a place in London where he can practice medicine and I can do whatever, and you and I will be friends again, gallivanting across the English Channel like it is our own private moat. That seems so far away.

I will write as soon as I know where you can reach me. I know we have not been close these last years since you left for university. It may sound pathetic, I know, but I need you, brother. Please write to me. You will be my anchor to sanity.

Your loving little sister,
Elizabeth

CHAPTER SIX

António de Spínola reached for another bottle of Portuguese red as he implored his guests, "Don't believe everything you read in the newspapers. Reporters are gullible creatures, easy marks for rebels and communists and anything emanating from the well of the United Nations." The West African night air was thick as porridge. The general poured for his guests before taking a glass for himself.

Elizabeth sat uncomfortably across from this imperious man, at a rough-hewn table in what passed for an officers' club. She understood almost nothing. His Portuguese flowed beautifully but torrentially, sparsely translated to her by her husband hours later, then filled in by her creative mind until it made sense. She tried to dab the sweat from her forehead inconspicuously, but it was pouring out. Night had long since fallen. The air smelled of bodies, wine, peppers, and fragrant smoke from the mosquito coil on the table, a cheap, glowing centerpiece at a very downscale restaurant. Major Otelo Saraiva de Carvalho, a favorite of Spínola's, sat with them at the table, smiling serenely.

"I hear Cabral will be in New York soon, to claim the seat of an independent Guiné. He came so close to winning, but he has lost. He flooded his so-called liberated zones with schools and hospitals, but what does he have, really? Communist propaganda, some Soviet aspirin, and a Cuban volunteer or two."

Spínola raised his glass and leaned toward João. He let his monocle fall from his eye and bounce from a light, gold chain.

"I"—he paused for effect—"I have you. Major Carvalho here has been pushing for your presence for some time now. 'Just one more doctor,' he'd say." Spínola reached to give the major a friendly punch on the shoulder. Carvalho looked pleased.

"Otelo is our perfect man of the *ultramar*, born in Mozambique, got a touch of Goan in the blood, gives him his dark good looks. His parents were literary sorts. They named him after the Moor of Venice."

"Really?" João spoke up. "You'll have to tell my wife that, sir. She's a Shakespeare scholar of sorts."

Elizabeth had been watching her husband, his lean body, his drawn face almost pretty in the candlelight. She was bathed in sweat, excited by her husband's prowess with power. At times, he looked flustered by what he was hearing. He would very subtly shake his head, glance away as he absently picked up his glass of wine. At times, his eyes would drift to the darkened corners of the room, the patches of mold or peeling paint. Then he would lean in to the two uniforms and slip into the river of rapid-fire Portuguese. If they were back in the Algarve, she could have at least touched his leg lightly with a toe. Here, she would wait until they were alone.

As her mind wandered, João had leaned forward to say something conspiratorial to the general, nodding to the attaché at Spínola's side, then glancing over his shoulder at his wife.

"Ah, Senhora Gonçalves," Spínola said, smiling, in loud, bombastic English, as if volume would help him communicate across the language barrier, "your husband tells me you're a Shakespearean. I was just introducing my companion here, Major Otelo Saraiva de Carvalho, named after the Moor."

His voice was deep and resonant; his accent reminded her of the lyricism that had drawn her so powerfully to João in Albufeira.

"You're joking." Elizabeth couldn't help herself. She had met him earlier that day on their arrival to the country, but he had paid her little mind.

"I'm quite serious. His parents were odd that way. He and I spent most of the sixties fighting together in Angola."

"'You may relish him more in the soldier than in the scholar,'" Elizabeth replied haughtily.

Spínola gave her an appraising look-over, a long, lingering examination, from her eyes down to the hands that rested, crossed, on the table, to her breasts, and back to her eyes. An involuntary twitch of his upper left lip telegraphed his opinion. Then, with an abrupt pivot, he switched back to Portuguese.

"Major Carvalho will run the operation to win the hearts and minds of Guiné," the general said to João. "But you, Doctor Gonçalves, you will actually win them for us.

"And you, my dear, my Florence Nightingale from England," he said to Elizabeth, again in English, "you will be my one hundredth military nurse. A nice, round number for one as soft as yourself."

"Me?" Elizabeth chimed in, incredulous, an open hand on her chest, eyebrows raised. "I've never so much as changed a bedpan. What use am I?"

"Ah, you would be surprised," the general responded. "It is rich, rewarding work, to care for our boys. The communists and the savages too. The wounds infect quickly without care. The flies in Africa are a pestilence. I hate them, carrying shit on their little legs like couriers of doom, pardon my language. You will want to be useful, Senhora Gonçalves, and unless you fancy ironing the botflies out of our men's drawers, I think you will find nursing suits you."

Elizabeth glanced searchingly at her husband. Their eyes met, but all he offered was an affectless nod.

Four weeks had passed since their marriage, three and a half since they reported to Caxias for João's training, such as it was. Elizabeth and João's few days at Caxias had been a bore but a useful one. Forte de São Bruno looked severe but romantic from the outside. Inside, it was all cold, sterile corridors and slits for windows. The Cadeia de Caxias, the prison of the secret police, loomed next door, a threat unnoticed by the Englishwoman. João busied himself learning tropical medicine, sitting in narrow classrooms under the glare of fluorescent lighting in his starched fatigues. As old military physicians yammered on about parasites and maggots, yellow fever, schistosomiasis, and kwashiorkor, he wondered what he was doing there, and whether his new wife would actually be waiting in the room he left her in, or would disappear like a dream disturbed.

Elizabeth had imagined this at first as a honeymoon. "'Come, let's away to prison; we two alone will sing like birds in the cage.'" She soon came to see she was alone in that cage. "How was your day, darling?" she'd say to João in the early evening. "Fine," he'd respond.

So, as her husband brushed up on West African parasites, trauma care, and the treatment of dysentery in rudimentary clinics, Elizabeth had not much to do but think. She still had only the clothes she had packed for a couple of weeks at most on holiday: a few pairs of jeans, a white calf-length pair of trousers, some gauzy thin shirts, a couple of sundresses made of embarrassingly heavy cotton, courtesy of Mother, and a flower-print dress, well below the knee but not to the ankle, that João had bought for her wedding day, proud of his find and satisfied with his gift.

A woman may tire of a husband, Elizabeth had to admit to herself. Even that nightly greeting, "How was your day, darling?" might grow to be too futile a gesture and too much of an effort to muster. Still, she pictured that, with age, a husband would grow into a puppy—cute, in need only of a pat on the head and a decent meal. Even the churlish ones, once housebroken, would be merely grumpy, in an endearing way. If the passion that had thrown man and woman together so violently faded, what of it? Surely it would fade for him as much as for her. *But a girl's wedding dreams are not so easily disabused*, she thought frowning. A wedding ceremony, it's true, is so fleeting it's meaningless. The reception afterward becomes just another party, topped several times over by other, better parties.

But the opportunity to wear a breathtaking gown and veil, to be the inspiring center of attention with that much flamboyance and that little shame, that comes once in a girl's life. For her, it came not even once. A spinster could dream of what might have been had that man come along. Elizabeth was forced to rue what had actually been. She had a store-bought flower-print dress that would follow her through life like a haunting.

In those hours at Caxias, for the first time in weeks, Elizabeth began to doubt herself. In fact, the absurdity of her decisions came crashing in. João was a diminished man beyond the resort on the Algarve. That was to be expected, she told herself. He had defended his choice of bride to his parents, and she had observed that his behavior around them wasn't exactly meek. He talked back to his mother and father in a joking, filial way, and didn't accept judgment that was obviously off. Still, it was all less than manly. He was *politely* rebellious, willing to take the rope he was given but not break it. She would feel those misgivings whether she was twenty or thirty, she told herself. They were commonplace, petty, feminine. Women expected too much of men. They were only human. He still made love to her every night with the same steady intensity. She still hungered for him. She would wake him long after midnight by reaching over and stroking him stiff. He always responded, a sign, she insisted, of his love. They still bantered Shakespearean. He would come home from a training session, forgo the mess, and take her to the PX to scrounge up some rice and vegetables, maybe a little pork or sausage. They would cook dinner in a little kitchenette in the officers' quarters. They were the only couple passing through at the time, and they had the place to themselves, such as it was. They slept on two twin beds pushed together. They tried to sleep on one, but invariably, in the middle of the night, after their second lovemaking, went to their separate mattresses.

"'Unarm, Eros; the long day's task is done,'" she'd say, nuzzling his naked neck. "'And we must sleep.'"

Perhaps the glow of marriage had faded a tiny bit, she reasoned, but Africa's allure remained undimmed. Though it was getting more complicated. Her visions of a young couple exploring the jungle or standing resolutely on an arid patch of land against a desert wind had to be reconciled with her new glimpse of military life, the drab mechanization, the antiromance. Her destination remained exotic, exciting. But she would not be Stanley to some Portuguese Livingstone exactly. She would be an interloper in someone else's army, a witness to, if not a participant in, a war she had no understanding of and that no one cared to explain to her. It seemed now she would have to make her own adventure.

"What have we done, João?" she asked dreamily one afternoon, as he set off to something or other, somewhere on the base, a white lab coat resting on an arm sheathed in camouflage. She sat in a stiff, wooden chair in front of a window unadorned with molding or curtains. A glimpse of sea could be had, and even enjoyed if the tin military barracks and sterile, whitewashed concrete buildings in the foreground were overlooked. This was her purgatory. Beyond it was the unknown.

He stopped and turned to her. A rush of love and pity and resentment washed over him. What he had done was snare a partner for a journey he did not want but had no choice but to make. Whatever was coming in this war he could not avoid, wife or no wife. Seeing her, sitting uncomfortably on that frail chair, he realized what he had done to another human being—conscription. Or what did the English navy and Spanish Armada call it when young men were simply kidnapped from the bars? Impressment. He had impressed her into service. He let his lab coat slide to the floor as he approached his wife, kneeling at her feet and holding her tight and close.

"It will be a great adventure. 'Screw your courage to the sticking-place, and we'll not fail,'" he murmured, stroking her hair, pressing it gently into place.

"I trust you, João," she responded.

They held each other for a long, lonely time in silence. She breathed in the smell of industrial detergent and the faint burn of the military irons on his fatigues. What comfort she took from his embrace was diminished by those smells of war. She longed for that billowing, weathered white shirt that smelled only of him and the sea.

He kissed the top of her head, picked up his white coat, and headed out.

"Were you scared?" I asked.

The transition from her stories, from the fetid heat of Africa and the briny breezes of Portugal to the damp cold of Brighton, was always a little jarring to me. But occasionally I had to chime in, to break it up or just to put on a new pot of tea.

"Hmmm?" Elizabeth murmured, rousted from her reverie. It was very late, and she had been talking uninterrupted for a very long time.

"Scared, you know, war. You had no idea what you were getting into, right?"

She waved a hand dismissively. "I was a child. Fear is a learned response, and I had learned nothing by then. I do remember how short the flight was. The world is very small, David."

Elizabeth knocked back a shot of vodka, and the story resumed.

CHAPTER SEVEN

After flying low over the Atlantic for only a few hours, their plane turned inland. Elizabeth looked down through the windows of the Douglas DC-9 at the brown, foreign landscape of Africa. Her grandfather had been a member of the Royal Geographical Society. Granted, he hadn't gone to Africa, but he had funded the chaps who had, Stanley and the like. They knew how to travel to Africa, by elephant or some such, with long lines of porters and servants carrying all manner of equipment and supplies. They built decent cities like Cape Town and Mombasa, taught cabdrivers to say things like "Madam, I believe you are to alight here," or "It is time to do what? Drink tea!"

Renato, Elizabeth, and João had set off that morning in a jeep for the military terminal at the airport in Lisbon. The morning air had begun to turn slightly crisp in October, a fitting farewell. Elizabeth carried the same cloth suitcase she had hustled onto the train a few weeks back, heading from London to Dover. João and Renato hoisted their bulging, green duffel bags into the back, chatting amiably about emergency medicine, the progression of infections in the tropics, the sterilization of medical equipment over wood fires. João liked to pretend he didn't much care for medicine, but such conversations brought a joy to him she hadn't seen before. Though she barely understood a word, only the slightly Latinized versions of scientific terms, Elizabeth was still seduced by the soft *zh* sounds, and the cool whooshes of the *x*'s of Portuguese.

The battered DC-9 was half-empty, emblazoned with the Portuguese cross, which resembled Germany's iron version but was more delicate, brittle, weaker. The doctors and the doctor's wife sat in the front, with a wide gap separating them from a few soldiers returning to Guiné from leave. To Elizabeth, there was a shocking casualness about the whole thing. Shouldn't there be more ceremony with every deployment into a war zone? Shouldn't a brass band be playing at the foot of the stairs, with officers saluting the heroes of Guiné smartly, young women crying for their sweethearts, children hugging the legs of their daddies for perhaps the last time? There was none of that, just a klatch of young soldiers drinking beer, laughing, and heading off to work, as if they had nine-to-five factory jobs and would be returning for supper.

The thrum of the propellers sent a dull roar through the plane, making conversation impossible. That was something of a relief. Elizabeth sat on a canvas jump seat, two rough straps crisscrossing her chest uncomfortably. This was a setup for broad, muscled male chests, not soft English breasts. For the trip, João had secured an auxiliary nurse's uniform: a polyester-blend green skirt, brownish shirt, and cropped jacket. She was glad for it. She blended in, even looked as if she belonged. She would have to get a lot more of these costumes when she landed.

Bissau being a port, they were on the ground seconds after they banked inland. The aircraft skipped over the compacted-dirt airfield, then taxied past military transports, Portuguese choppers with their vulnerable-looking glass-bubble cockpits, and a few American helicopters like the ones Elizabeth had seen in Vietnam War footage on the telly. Mechanics were working on a couple of old biplanes that looked like they would be used for crop dusting. Coconut and oil palms ringed the airfield, but after weeks in Portugal, that seemed ordinary enough. The whole scene seemed ordinary enough, a decrepit version of southern Portugal—until she stepped onto the landing of the stairs.

The heat and humidity were searing, a physical blow. Sweat

erupted from Elizabeth's hairline. It soaked through her shirt under her arms, over her chest, down her back. As she stepped gingerly down the stairs, she moved to take off her jacket, saw the dark stains forming on her shirt, and thought better of it. By the time the three had crossed the dirt tarmac and entered the perfunctory terminal, the jacket was off anyway.

A couple of Portuguese soldiers manned the security desk but waved the whites through without stopping their conversation. An African man, his tattered shirt unbuttoned, his muscled chest glistening, carried the bags from the plane, three or four at a time, dropping them gingerly on the dirty, curling-linoleum floor. Two much lighter-skinned men, their uniforms neatly pressed, went through the manifest, checking the cargo and recording receipts. The smell was like nothing she had come across before, sweat, body odor, mildew, wood smoke, mosquito coils, and raw sewage, mingled together in a stench that nobody but she seemed to notice.

"*Bem vinda a Bissau*" a Portuguese officer called out, his brushy silver hair contrasting against a deep, rich complexion, a prominent chin incongruous against a thick neck, strong but a bit pudgy as well. "Welcome to Bissau," that Elizabeth could understand. He reached to give João a swift hug, thought better of it when he saw the young doctor recoil, and instead ordered his African driver to grab the bags of the three travelers and toss them into the back of the truck.

He introduced himself to João and Elizabeth as Major Otelo Saraiva de Carvalho. "Civil affairs and army public relations," he said in English, then shrugged. "Propaganda, more or less.

"This is the moment we have been waiting for," Carvalho continued in Portuguese with a chuckle. "The meddling UN can't say we haven't made an effort. Our medical corps is the envy of West Africa. You, my friend, Major Gonçalves, yes? You are the last brick in our little Potemkin village." He laughed heartily at that one. João looked down at his feet.

João was not an antiwar activist. Most of those had long ago fled to France. In 1967 alone, out of eighty thousand men caught in the dragnet of Portuguese conscription, fourteen thousand had failed to show up. More young Portuguese men escaped to France each year than took up their nation's generous subsidies to settle the *ultramar*. He was not a surreptitious believer in the cause of independence either. He was a doctor. He believed he could put his medical training to good use here, for Portuguese and African alike. He relished the chance. But to get it, he now knew the humiliations he would have to endure, the conspiratorial jokes between the white overlords, the clique he was joining.

Bissau was tiny, a small warren of narrow streets and Portuguese houses off the Rio Geba, clustered around the port of Pijiguito. The military hospital was there, just a few blocks from the water. The country was so small that the Portuguese wounded from any battle—from the mangrove swamps of the northwest to the grasslands on the eastern border with Guiné—could be airlifted to Simão Mendes Hospital. Spínola moved into the graceful, whitewashed governor's mansion nearby, but he favored socializing in the military barracks just out of town, with his prized officers—and their wives.

Carvalho insisted that João sit with him in the front seat, next to the driver, who had stashed their bags. Renato climbed into the back with Elizabeth.

"That's where it all started to go wrong." He signaled toward the waterfront, where a dozen or so Guineans loaded hulking sacks of rice and peanuts onto small Portuguese cargo boats. "That's where we white Portuguese opened fire on our supposed black brethren. It was just a labor dispute really, a strike. Now it's a lot more." The Portuguese buildings clung to the edge of the waterfront, whitewashed, with sloping, red-tiled roofs, charming but faded. The shipping clerks inside, marooned by one company or another, tried their best to keep up appearances, but holding at bay the greenish mold that crept up the walls from the puddles on the ground or scrubbing away the gray slime that trickled from the bat-infested rafters was futile. The Portuguese there counted their days, as if their jobs were fixed tours of duty. The guerrillas were still no threat to Bissau, but they were moving inexorably toward the center. The port functionaries would be lucky if their eventual escape brought them home and not to the next doomed port, to Beira in Mozambique, maybe, or Luanda in Angola. At least in Luanda, they were told, a decent meal, a nice hotel, and a white whore could be had with their paychecks. Enough of their countrymen had been lured to Angola by the promise of land and riches to effectively build up a white underclass: failures in Portugal, failures in the fertile highlands outside Nova Lisboa—now cabdrivers, maids, stevedores, and whores in Luanda, wondering if they'd ever see Lisbon again.

João was to work in the military hospital in Bissau at first. Elizabeth and he would live on base, in the officers' quarters. After a time, they could decide whether to stay or move into town, into one of the more graceful flats, with mahogany floors and great, hardwood ceiling beams. They would be colonials, Elizabeth imagined, sitting on a veranda with servants bringing peppery dishes under languid ceiling fans stirring dense, tropical air. Or they might be moved to one of the forward bases, where João would show the natives the miracles of modern medicine, or at least dispense some aspirin and antibiotics. Elizabeth would befriend the native women, play peekaboo with charmed children, and doze in the shade of oil palms.

The jeep drove past the governor's mansion, surrounded by palm trees that were sculpted into giant fans, ready to cool Spínola's troubled head. The city then quickly gave way to tin shanties and roadside shacks where men sat drunk on palm wine. Children squatted around little fires and cheap hammered-metal woks where they braised corncobs and peanuts in salt and garlic. Goats stupidly chewed their cud. It was a fine, sunny day, but the air stunk, a pungent mixture of wood fires, charcoal, and human shit. In her imaginings of Africa, Elizabeth could conjure movie images: *The African Queen, Zulu, Stanley and Livingstone*. She never thought to wonder about the smell, but it was that and the heat—not the tumult of greens and browns, the palms, the children, or the market women in their colorful print wraps—that were overwhelming.

The jeep driver pulled up to an unconvincing guard post in front of a rusted barbed-wire fence. Carvalho lifted an arm casually, and a white soldier waved them into a compound of barracks, narrow, single-storied, long buildings arranged in military order. The grounds were stripped of grass and foliage. It was a scraped landscape of rusty brown hardpan, deeply rutted where jeeps and troop carriers slogged through mud in the rainy season—which was just about on them. Off along the fence line, a dozen or so Guinean women were laundering fatigues and pressing military-issue khaki boxer shorts with heavy irons. They heated the irons to a glowing red over charcoal, dipped them in water to clear off the ash, and then bore down on the shorts tossed casually over a split log that had been flattened and smoothed with use.

"Lord, in this heat?" Elizabeth exclaimed. "Why are those women ironing knickers?"

"You'll be thankful for them. I assume they'll be ironing ours as well," João replied over his shoulder. "Botflies. They lay their eggs in damp clothing left to line dry. The eggs hatch into tiny larvae that burrow into the inviting flesh of your buttocks. At first, you think it's a mosquito bite, then a maddening boil that grows harder and more painful by the day, until one day it bursts open and out of your flesh come a new crop of flies that scatter to find their next victim. Those irons kill the eggs. Worth the price of their service, no doubt, though I imagine their price is not high."

"That's just the beginning," Renato jumped in cheerfully. "Then there are the round worms you pass in your stools, the guinea worms that hatch on your legs. You wrap a stick around the head and slowly tug them out, little by little, day after day, so they don't break and leave part of their body to rot under your skin. Schisto-somiasis, passed on from freshwater snails that pick it up from the human piss in the creeks and rivers. The lesions are unsightly, but then there's the fever, fatigue, diarrhea, abdominal pains. Guiné is a parasite paradise. It's not hard to imagine why we Portuguese pretty much left it alone until the Guineans wanted to formalize the arrangement."

The driver dropped the four off at a low-slung, white building. An exceptionally thin woman, so thin she looked tall though she wasn't, rushed out to greet them, speaking in rapid-fire Portuguese. She met their eyes only in fleeting glances, deferentially looking down at the ground as she excitedly motioned them inside. The Guinean women who worked on the base had been anticipating the arrival of this new Portuguese couple. Husband and wife was something they could understand, and newlyweds, well, that was cause for celebration.

"Ask her her name," Elizabeth told João, who passed the request on to Carvalho. The officer fired off a quick question.

She looked puzzled. He tried again, then again, gesticulating to her, to himself, to Elizabeth, until finally he elicited a simple enough answer: Maria.

"I don't think she speaks Portuguese," Carvalho told João.

Renato shrugged. "Most don't," he said. "Their tribal languages come first, dozens of them. They've converged on the capital, really just in the last few years, with the war, the bombing, and all the soldiers and officers and people like you arriving to pay them. The Tower of Babel that Bissau would be with all these different tribals is bridged by a kind of pidgin—Kriolu. Creole."

Maria motioned to Elizabeth, smiling through crooked yellow teeth and leading her to the end of a long hallway that smelled of disinfectant and mold. The room she showed her was larger than it should be, given local standards, even for the soldiers. But it was as depressing as Elizabeth had imagined—bare white walls, a dirty, tiled floor, a ceiling fan that hadn't worked in years. The Portuguese army—or the Guinean women it relied on for such things—had found an extra-large piece of foam to lay across a square of plywood perched on cinder blocks to make a conjugal bed. A thin cotton sheet and blanket added a measure of domesticity, but yellowing stains from the humidity diminished the appeal. The women of the base had procured a small bamboo chest of drawers, handcrafted, on top of which whirred a marvel, an oscillating, slightly rusted steel fan.

Maria, as the representative of the women who had acquired these treasures, beamed with pride. This was a welcome gift worthy of a queen, they clearly believed. Elizabeth, aware of Maria's obvious satisfaction, thanked her profusely, theatrically, in a language she could not possibly understand.

"João, I need to learn Portuguese," she said, turning to her husband.

"I don't think this woman can help you, but we will find someone who can. Rest up, Elizabeth, we're to have dinner with the governor tonight."

After their dinner with the general and Major Carvalho, Elizabeth and João returned to their room in silence. João understood what was expected of him. He was to help bring respectability to colonial suppression, to help make it clear that Portugal had only the best interest of its subjects in mind.

"What was he saying back there?" Elizabeth asked furtively.

"Not much that would have interested you. A lot about tactics to counter the guerrillas, the size of the medical corps, that sort of thing. He was very big on the notion that I am somehow a decisive part of the campaign to win over the natives."

"You?"

João looked at his wife.

"Well, don't look so surprised."

"I didn't mean anything, João. It's just that, you know, how's one additional doctor going to change a war?"

João looked down at the tiled floor. "I wish I knew."

"João, I loved watching you in there. My doctor and the general." She stepped toward him and laid her hand gently on his cheek, the base of her palm cupping his chin. "You were beautiful."

He smiled and gently kissed her waiting mouth.

In the heat of the Guinean night, she slowly unbuttoned her drab military shirt and unzipped her loose-fitting skirt. Never had she felt more attractive than she did shedding so unattractive a sheath. João feverishly followed suit, and they fell onto their slab of foam drenched in each other's sweat. The thin walls silenced their outcries but not their fervor. Elizabeth wanted to be taken by João, this doctor, this caregiver, this man facing so many horrible expectations. She lay on her side, his chest pressed hard against her back, and held his right hand to her breast, urging him to grab her hard as she lifted one leg up and back, guiding him. His breath quickened in her ear.

The medical chief was busy the morning João arrived at the colonnaded colonial hospital, so he wandered the main ward on his own, dazed by what he saw, bed after bed of wounded men. A few Africans stared vacantly at the ceiling, recruits to the colonial army, maybe even a guerrilla or two making good on Spínola's hearts-and-minds order. Their black skin only highlighted the whiteness of the rest of the patients.

Infections were wasting men away. They lay trembling with fever, vomiting into cheap tin buckets, or virtually comatose. Their eyes darted aimlessly or sunk into their skulls beneath papery lids. Nurses wiped sweat from foreheads, changed bedpans, and held hands as they gently tried to coax the pus out of wounds. João had introduced himself to the more lucid men as a new doctor on the ward. He smiled gamely, wondering what he would do beyond the initial trauma treatment. He also felt strangely exhilarated.

A young man shuffled from bed to bed pushing an IV pole, his hospital gown falling off his rail-thin, otherwise naked body. As he approached their beds, some men would bark and swat him away; others vacantly watched his progress, while still others took no notice. Moans created a low hum in the emptiness. Morphine muffled the ward like a pillow over the face. The squeak of the nurses' rubber soles reverberated across the polished terra-cotta tiles.

João drifted to the side of a moaning soldier, his left arm amputated just below the elbow, his right with a gaping wound. At first, he thought the small white shapes were bone fragments, but then he caught their movement. Maggots. He absently reached his fingers toward them, when Renato Araujo startled him.

"Leave them. They're debriding the wound. Some bugs are useful."

Araujo gently swatted away João's bare hand, snapping him out of his trance.

"Let's make rounds together this morning," he said. "You're not in medical school anymore, Doctor Gonçalves. You're about to embark on an entirely new education."

They floated down the ward, Renato flipping through clipboards at the foot of the beds, João mainly staring.

"We have learned much from the Americans in Vietnam—the golden hour, the rush to treatment. The soldiers that are wounded in ambushes will generally survive if we can get them here quickly, and the helicopters do it well. NATO has blessed us with the Huey Cobra for air ambulance work. Our biggest problem is infection. Bacteria grow here like topsy. Amputation is too often our only recourse. In many cases, it's not enough."

"Where do the wounded go? The amputees?" João asked. The beds were arranged neatly, side by side, spanning the long hallway, but each of its inhabitants seemed to display a unique horror show, a blasted jaw, a lost eye, a suppurating wound on an elevated arm, an infected stump. "We don't see them in Lisbon. I had no idea this was happening."

"You wouldn't. We have convalescent hospitals in Luanda, settlers' communities in Nova Lisboa. If you stay long enough, you'll see it all. German engineers, on Portuguese contract, are building this massive dam in Cabora Bassa. That's Mozambique. Caetano intends to settle a million Portuguese there. A million." He paused for drama's sake. "The first inhabitants will likely be missing a few limbs.

"Look here." Renato paused at a young man's side and lifted his sheet to show off a ghastly abdominal wound, livid purple around the edges. The smell was putrid, like rotting meat over whatever stewed in his bedpan.

"The initial wounds usually aren't horrendous—small-arms fire from ambushes. We're the ones that really wreak the carnage, with bombs and incendiaries, the kind of weaponry that sears flesh and mangles bodies. The guerrillas don't know it, but their most effective weapons are the flies that swarm the bullet wounds and the filthy water the soldiers wash the blood away with.

"And the heat—you've noticed it—grows flora like a hothouse. We've got bacteria you've never heard of. It grows like weeds."

The soldier's eyes—dirty, brownish yellow—looked searchingly at the new doctor. João recognized the jaundice, probably liver failure. Renato frowned as he halfheartedly lifted the urine bag hanging from the bedrail, its tube snaking up to the catheter hidden from sight.

"Not a drop in it," Renato confided quietly as they wandered to the next bed. "His kidneys are shutting down. He's a dead man."

"So young," João muttered.

"We're all so young."

Just before noon, João heard the *thump-thump* of a helicopter approaching the roof, and then a higher pitch as the rotors slowed to a halt. A single soldier was wheeled into the operating room with a bullet lodged in the inner curve of his hipbone, a bleeding hole in his groin showing its path. He had snapped out of his torpor and was screaming with every bump of an errant wheel over the rough tile floor. Blood soaked through the sheet hanging half off the bed.

"Triage," a male nurse shouted, as he inserted an IV.

"He's yours, João," Renato said calmly. He leaned a shoulder against the doorway of the wounded ward, arms crossed casually. He wanted to watch the reaction of his new doctor.

João followed the male nurse, a woman nurse, and a uniformed soldier as they pushed the gurney. He was unsure of what to do, but when the wounded young man was in position and sedated, João acted on instinct, quickly scrubbing down, donning a surgical mask and cap, then reaching in for the bullet without the aid of a scalpel. He could feel the warmth of the body through the surgical gloves, the squish of human tissue softened further by trauma, then the bullet, hard, jagged, and so foreign.

It was remarkably small given the size of the wound. *A higher-caliber weapon must do horrible damage*, he thought. He irrigated the wound with sterile water, scanned it for bleeding arteries, and asked the nurse beside him for forceps to remove a few bone fragments. Then he suctioned it, inserted a clear tube into the wound, then a rubber instrument with a bulbous end so fluid could be drawn out even after the wound had sealed.

As he began suturing, he allowed himself a long look at the boy's face. Fine wisps of facial hair helped bead the sweat on his upper lip. His eyes were closed, as if he were summoning the concentration needed to stay alive. The wound was not life-threatening, but one whose life had been so short and circumscribed to that point could not have known that. His cheeks were almost chubby. Black, wavy hair was plastered to his forehead.

I'll have to write a letter to his parents, João thought, as he reached to touch that forehead, *tell them their son is going to be fine.*

Later, the patients would all blur together. It wouldn't be long before João stopped allowing himself such indulgences—the promises to himself, the searching looks into the wounded soldiers' faces. He never wrote a letter.

His heart raced again a little more than two hours later when the same low thumping broke through the hospital clatter. This time, he ran toward the roof with the other medical staff. Four soldiers lay groaning on litters. One soldier had tripped a mine. His right foot was ripped off, his lower leg mangled to halfway up the calf. Bone fragments mixed with muscle tissue, raw beef in a blender. This was trauma João had never seen before. Another appeared near death. The others were collateral damage: shrapnel wounds from the mine, a bullet from the guerrillas that had lain in wait.

Another doctor, Andréas Pelegrin, took the most grievously wounded, calmed the patient, sedated him quickly, and without hesitation amputated what was left of the leg just below the knee, leaving a flap of skin from what was his shin to tuck over the stump. João peeled off and took the bullet wound.

In the time it took João to deal with that one bullet wound, Pelegrin had amputated a leg, pushed aside a soldier he deemed well enough to wait, and written off a patient with an abdominal wound that had spilled out too much of the contents of his large intestine. The dose of morphine he injected had stopped the screaming; even from a slight distance, João could see the quantity was enough to kill him. The boy would not be waking up.

That's the man I want to be, João thought. *Just give me a few months. I can do this.*

"Nasty work," Pelegrin said as he ripped off his surgical garb and scrubbed his sticky arms. "You get used to amputations, really. The worst part is watching the men wake up. They often have no memory of the explosion. They're disoriented. They're out of the bush, out of their base, in this strange hospital. There are women around, white women. Heaven. Then they find they've lost a leg, or an arm, or both."

"Is there something you say, some kind of formula?" João asked.

Pelegrin looked at him sympathetically, a slight smile crossing his face.

"You do what you can," he replied. "That's the moment you learn what kind of doctor you are, really, what kind of man."

Renato told João he could go back to the base, "check on that wife of yours," when the last helicopter came that day. This time, the response was a little less frantic. The nurses walked up the ramp to the rooftop with a couple of orderlies, drew open the steel storm doors, tilted against the sun and rain, and casually wheeled in two patients, jet black, bathed in sweat. João looked at the African patients and thought back to that first night in Africa, when Spínola had tried to explain his role in the war. "We will take care of them all," the general had said, "hearts and minds and all." But that simple formula yielded one bit of complexity. What of success? Do you return a guerrilla to his people, to his battlefield? João had asked.

"No," Spínola answered. "There are prisoner-of-war camps in Angola. I haven't seen them. I'm sure they're grim. Yellow fever rips through them, but we try to keep that quiet. Work camps in Mozambique, the Cabora Bassa dam. I guess they figure the fight in Guiné is not the fight in Angola or in Mozambique.

"I wouldn't be so sure, though," Spínola had continued, arguing with himself as he poured from what must have been the fifth bottle of the night. "Look at the PAIGC leadership: Cabo-Verdianos, light skinned, they don't even look like Guineans. But they fight hard. Why wouldn't a Guinean fight in Nova Lisboa or Beira? Perhaps we do go too easy on them."

"Perhaps we do go too easy on them." João played the line in his head as the softening light of the late afternoon fell on one of the new arrivals, a boy who couldn't have been more than twelve. He was in shock, glassy-eyed, with a head wound that was deceptively grave. He was bandaged well, but from the pink seepage, João could tell the skull was open. In another hospital, in another country, he might be saved. A large enough piece of the skull would be carefully removed to allow the brain room to swell, then heal, with the patient monitored closely in a medically induced coma. Not here, though, not with this child. The boy's father was conscious. He looked fierce, angry, even on the stretcher, a wounded animal choosing fight over flight but unable to land a paw. A bullet was lodged in his thigh, not serious at all. But he had an intensity to him, a panic in his face, that told João there was something else. His speech was raspy, a light breeze from the shallows of his lungs, and he coughed with the little force he could muster.

João moved to his side, then tore away what was left of his pant leg. As João leaned over to clean the wound, the patient grabbed his shoulder roughly. Surprised, João turned and locked eyes with him.

"Doctor, save my son if you can," he said in accented but clear

Portuguese. "I have seven others, three wives, all soldiers of Guiné. We will keep coming. Doctor, when you are done with him, get out. Get out of Africa. This is not your fight. The Tuga will be driven off this continent soon. The dam will break, and when it does, it will not be water that flows."

There were only a handful of other European women on base, the wives of officers. They weren't that much older than Elizabeth, in their young thirties at most, but Elizabeth felt the deficiency of her twenty years acutely in their presence. They chatted in Portuguese, a language that slides and swirls, unforgiving for outsiders trying to understand but lyrical to listen to. In their shrugs and sighs, they seemed like prisoners, jaded and waiting for release. But they tried to make the best of it. Some joined the auxiliary nursing corps. Most devoted their time to domesticity, a complex task on a military base in West Africa, involving the organization of help from Guinean women happy to have the work but mindful of their collaboration, and the procuring of some decent ingredients, if not from the PX then from care packages ordered from home. In a pinch, the market in Bissau would do. Certainly, it was good for basics: peanuts, garlic, chilies, onions, dried macaroni, bananas—small but sweeter than any in Europe—and mangos by the crateful in season. But staples like manioc did not agree with the Portuguese palate, and the produce was generally bleak. Tomatoes were shriveled and flaccid. Greens, actually leaves of indeterminate provenance, crawled with bacteria.

Her first morning, Elizabeth stood staring at the unmade bed, wondering if she should smooth the still-damp sheets into place or find a laundress. She had already unpacked her suitcase and João's duffel bag. The small dresser was plenty large for the few items she had to put away. The room had a narrow closet and a few wire hangers. A mousetrap inside, long sprung, held the decayed contents of its target. *Well, at least it's a little one*, she thought, mentally noting a task for her husband when he returned.

It felt good to be domestic, and as she folded João's military-issue boxer shorts, she fantasized about feeling his arms wrapped around her from behind, supporting her weight as she leaned against his thin body. She decided to make the bed, when there was a knock on the door. A welcoming crew of base women stood, one of them holding a bouquet of tropical flowers—orchids plucked right out of the notches of trees on the base perimeter, some birds of paradise, others Elizabeth had never seen.

"*Bom dia*," they shouted, practically in unison. "*Bem vinda a Bissau. Meu nome e Paula*," a tall, handsome woman said as she stepped forward, her hair jet black and lustrous, swept back into a ponytail, her white, loose cotton shirt and flowered skirt pressed taut, not for the sake of fashion but the elimination of botflies.

As she went on in machine-gunfire Portuguese, the others all giggled, Raquel blushing as she looked at her feet, shuffling in still-bright white canvas sneakers. Not that Elizabeth had understood, but she had just been informed that the young woman named Raquel was the envy of the lot, the wife of the Portuguese Air Force commander, dashing in his little Fiat G.91, which he buzzed low near the military base, with a dipped right wing, to show off for the women.

Raquel was a honey blonde, a rarity of rarities in Lisbon. A beauty. Her angular nose was more Roman than Iberian, her cheekbones swelled to perky soft mounds in a round face bronzed in the African sun, then flushed in the rising morning heat. She was petite, maybe five foot three, one hundred fifteen pounds if that. Her sundress demurely covered her shoulders but the backline plunged seductively. She was everything Elizabeth wasn't, and quickly, the thought arose that João would see this woman and regret his choice, that this gorgeous woman's presence could cause her endless heartache.

Elizabeth shook hands, smiled broadly, and fumbled for words. Pointing to herself and speaking as if to children, she managed, "I am Elizabeth."

There was a pregnant pause before Paula ventured, "*Você fala Português?*"

This, Elizabeth understood from the first day of her arrival on the Algarve. She smiled sadly. "*Não, eu não falo Português. Sou inglês, da Inglaterra.* My husband is Doctor João Gonçalves." She had picked up the message of husband-as-identification even through a language she could barely decipher.

Raquel stepped forward. "I speak leetle Englis," she said, smiling. It could have been a moment to heighten Elizabeth's jealousy to a new level of dread, but that smile melted her. Raquel's teeth were lustrous white, a little too big, an endearing flaw, Elizabeth thought, and those high cheekbones were now accented with little dimples. "I am Raquel, not Raquel Welch," she continued, the others laughing. "Rachel in Englis, like de Bible, de wife of Jacob."

"I have to learn Portuguese," Elizabeth said earnestly.

"That is no problem," Raquel assured her.

The woman called Ana set down the flowers in a plain glass vase on the dresser, and arranged them to perfection. They would be an explosion of color and smell for João's return.

They set off to show their new charge around: the laundry where Guinean and Cape Verdean women washed clothes, hung them to dry, and ironed them to the edge of burn; the PX stocked with Portuguese dry goods; the officers' mess where Elizabeth and João had dined with the commander and governor of Guiné the night before. There was a room set aside for the base wives, a simple affair with low ceilings and terra-cotta tiled floors, but successive waves of women had adorned it with femininity: rugs of baby blues and pale pinks, tasseled couches and love seats, chairs with embroidered pads, knitted blankets, and doilies on side tables. Spínola had said Elizabeth would be wise to keep herself busy with hospital work, and maybe it was so. But it was obvious most of the women had found hobbies of a more prosaic sort.

As Elizabeth looked around the room appreciatively, Raquel walked in with a willowy Cabo-Verdiana, her hair clipped short, her skin the color of café au lait.

"Thees ees Angélica." Raquel motioned to her. "She ees speaking de Englis better dan me." Raquel turned to the girl, smiling broadly and motioning for her to step forward, her right arm gesturing in a rapid circular spin. Angélica smiled as she looked down but quickly covered her mouth, missing a tooth, with one hand. Angélica, like all the Cabo-Verdianas Elizabeth had seen, was remarkably thin. By now, Elizabeth had decided this was a national trait, not a sign of mistreatment or starvation, some end process of centuries of inter-mingling blood.

The Cape Verde islands had been uninhabited rocks far off the coast of Senegal. One island, Fogo, had the drama of the live vol-cano that had created it and continued to rumble and spew, lifting it farther and farther from the sea. Beyond Fogo, the islands were dead. Rainstorms more often than not could be seen dumping freshwater into the ocean a mile or so offshore. The archipelago's biggest asset was the vast airport that Portugal had built on Praia, just outside the capital. It served as a refueling point for Portuguese planes flying to Mozambique and Angola—and not wanting to brave what passed for an airport in Bissau. More important were the South Africans and Rhodesians. Commercial flights from New York and Europe to southern Africa, unwelcome anywhere else on the continent, stopped in Praia for refueling, sometimes for mechanical repairs as well—and always for the extortionary landing taxes de-manded by the Portuguese authorities.

Cabo-Verdianos came to understand the value of currency more than work as their barren islands attracted commerce in the oddest ways. Portuguese fishermen, eager to harvest the rich waters off Cap Skirring, could not land their catch in Senegal, lest the French colo-nials take their cut. So they skittered to the rocks of Cabo Verde and built fishing communities in coves devoid of rain and vegetation, bringing Africans with them for help. Passing fishing vessels de-posited their own refuse or stowaways over time. Cabo Verde stewed with colors that ultimately blended into a lovely, light brown.

Those fishermen eventually made their way to New England, establishing Cape Verdean communities far larger than any that existed on the mother isles. They invariably called themselves Portuguese, and the New Englanders never thought to quibble. But these were not Iberians. They were toughened on desert islands and trained to haul fish by the ton.

Angélica had learned her English in the rough bars and waterfront restaurants of New Bedford, Massachusetts. Her father had brought her over with him when she was young enough to attract a good husband and old enough to be put to work, washing dishes at first, waiting tables later, where the tips were good even if the weathered hands were far too liberated for a father's taste.

Angélica's few years in those back kitchens had ended badly. The *migre* had launched one of its crackdowns in the spasm of law-and-order anger that swept Richard Nixon to the White House. They may have called themselves Portuguese, but the angry whites in Southie didn't see Ireland or even Italy in that olive skin. An INS raid swept Angélica into a holding pen outside Boston. With her father out to sea and without a lawyer or money or a clue what to do, she found herself back in Praia, penniless. A cousin told her there was work in Bissau for the Portuguese military. The colonialists were increasingly wary of bringing Guineans onto base. Angélica's English would put her in good stead—an educated African, good to show off to the NATO and Red Cross inspectors.

"Good morning, ma'am," she said, extending her hand toward Elizabeth. "My name is Angélica Cardoso. How are you adjusting to Africa?"

The voice rang out forcefully, the accent pure New England. "Cadozo, how ah you adjusting?" Elizabeth was overjoyed. She understood then how isolated and lonely she had been without someone to talk to, the struggle it had been to reach out with so limited a tongue. Beaming, she took Angélica's hand a bit too eagerly.

"Very well, thank you, now that I've met you, Angélica," she said with palpable relief. "We're going to be great friends."

CHAPTER EIGHT

Under the terms of my contract, I was granted one weekend off a month, and I needed to claim it. Little Steve, one of Maggie's housemates, was in the hospital in Haywards Heath. He was a mess. He had been on his motorcycle, not going fast really, but motorcycles are exposed things. A little old lady had swung open the door of her Reliant Robin outside the Sainsbury's in a village north of Brighton. Little Steve crashed into it, really just clipped it. But that was enough. "Oh dear, quite sorry I'm sure," I imagined her saying as the young man writhed on the street.

Little Steve's right leg, after three surgeries, was an inch shorter than his left. He had been short to begin with, too short to look hard in the heavy cowhide biker gear he sported. To make matters worse, he had a head of curly black hair that he wore long, like a seventies rock star.

"Steve, if you're going to be a poseur, why don't you at least stay current with the other poseurs? Depeche Mode or something, not Jimmy Page," Big Steve would say before that unfortunate accident.

"Whadya know of Jimmy Page, you lout?" Little Steve would reply.

Poor short Little Steve would now have a limp to go along with his stature. We figured we needed to pay him a visit.

*   *   *

Maggie's house was a pit. The red brick on the Buxton Road row house, just off the five-way intersection above the railway station, had weathered to brown. The carpeting in the hallway was threadbare and hadn't been cleaned for decades. The living room was a parlor of sorts in the front of the house, strewn with pillows, ashtrays, and wrappers from the chippy down the road. The electricity ran on a meter fed by fifty-pence pieces kept in piles in a basket—no change, no juice. There were two kitchen sinks but one was out of commission. In that one, dirty dishes had been stewing for months, but the greasy water had grown so rancid, the film on top so toxic, that no one would reach in to pull the plug and let it drain out. So it was ignored, never to be spoken of.

The house captured the moment. Britain was a nation exhausted by decline, sullen in its defeat, with a dominatrix in No. 10 Downing Street trying to whip it back on its knees. Margaret Thatcher had broken the miners' strike in the north. Just down the road, in Brighton's Grand Hotel on King's Road, Patrick Magee of the Provisional Irish Republican Army had nearly blown her and her government to smithereens. The near miss of the Brighton bombing left everyone I knew terribly disappointed. Her bathroom was destroyed, but the damned sitting room where she was poring over her speech to the Conservative Party conference was unscathed. She changed her clothes, calmly walked from the hotel, then privatized British Telecom. We shook our heads as we passed around the bong.

The house was big and full. Big Steve, from Luton, always tried to look hard, in his dirty fatigues and torn flannel shirts. He wasn't all that big, maybe just over six feet, but size is relative. His body would build up over the summer on construction jobs, then soften slowly over the course of the school year. The resident philosopher, he led discussions of the present—"It's like God has killed love," he moaned over AIDS—and of the future, which usually revolved around which city offered the best housing subsidies for the unemployed (Edinburgh), where the dole could be stretched the farthest (the Lake District), or where the best squats were opening up (London). No one, it seemed, had any intention of ever working. The amount of effort, the soaps and gels and dyes, that went into Big Steve's Mohawk made him more a misguided fop with a working-class accent than a threatening punk. No one should have to work that hard to look like a thug.

Little Steve's motorcycle was the most prominent signifier of his identity. He was maybe five foot five, shorter than me, with pallid skin made more pallid by the curly rocker locks that framed his face. He studied engineering, something no one would have guessed by looking at him, and was the one member of the house who more or less eschewed dope. Then there was Astrid the hippie, with her tattered poncho from Mexico and her hand-knit beret covering long, unkempt, sandy-blond hair, a joyous literature major, enamored actually with my world: Kerouac, Dylan, Burroughs. She gave me a book of poetry written by Lawrence Ferlinghetti, who waxed credulously about the Sandinista revolution in Nicaragua. The diehards in the States, probably Ferlinghetti too, had grown weary of the whole thing. Reagan was on his way out. The struggle with the Contras was ebbing. But Astrid thought Iran-Contra had something to do with her poncho, and I wasn't going to stomp her buzz.

Suzy was the sanest one of the bunch. Tidy, she had a closely cropped head of dark, curly hair and told mundane stories of a suburban childhood south of London. She was particularly fond of the one when she mistook the bathroom cleanser—the Brits called it Flash, the Americans, Comet—for bubble bath when she was filling her tub. "'Mum,' I screamed, 'I got Flash in my vag!'" She'd laugh uproariously every time. One of the thrilling little things about Britain, I discovered, was the absolute immodesty over all things to do with genitalia: "willy," "fanny," "vag," even "cunt," all words for genitals, all used in the politest of company. There wasn't anything physically attractive about Suzy, nothing exotic or exciting. But her relative affluence and suburban childhood reminded me of home, and I think I craved her company because of it.

Phone calls to the States were out of the question. My parents had been sending updates on thin, crinkly aerograms that would inevitably tear around the edges as I struggled to get them open. Their contents were like messages beamed to me on radio waves from distant galaxies. "We've installed a new, self-cleaning pump in the pool," my mother wrote. "Dad is horrified at the price but thrilled at how well it works. Now all we have to do is fish out the leaves after a storm."

"Your brother is taking his LSATs. He's looking at law schools and is leaning toward the University of North Carolina. Your father has fallen in love with the idea of UNC basketball games. He hates Duke as much as he hates the Yankees. Your brother says law school isn't about basketball."

I couldn't share any of this with Maggie. I could imagine the scorn she would heap. She'd mock the pool cleaner for sure. The worst part was, I couldn't mock back. For all their affectations, the students of Buxton Road had made it through their O levels, their A levels, scored grants from their government and secured a place at a university. Not Oxbridge, but Sussex, which was still pretty damned good. That showed infinitely more ambition and resourcefulness than most of the white, suburban kids I knew, who had gone on as a matter of course to higher education, be it Georgetown or Georgia Southern.

When I was at Maggie's, I'd lay my head in her lap, moderately stoned, and feel her fingers in my hair. She had a double futon on the floor, very innovative for the times. Her housemates had old mattresses. Her turntable was some strange Japanese brand I had never seen. It stood up on its side, so the records spun perpendicularly to the table. They spun invariably one of the four pillars of her spiritual existence: Julian Cope, New Order, the Cure, or the Cocteau Twins.

Maggie had taken it upon herself to educate me on musical taste. She made me cassettes, one after another, genre mixes but also the most important songs of the most important artists in her library. Her innovation was the tape case cover; she would paste a collage or find some paper print that captured a mood of, say, Dead Can Dance or the Teardrop Explodes, and then cover it with a sheet of translucent paper to complete the effect. It was a show of love, and the cassettes with their delicate cases piled up quickly.

"What is that?" she gasped one night, walking in on me listening to Bono croon "Bad" from *The Unforgettable Fire*, my own face contorted with the emotions of the singer. It was as if she had caught me masturbating.

"Isn't he embarrassed," she asked, her face twisted with scorn, "exerting himself like that?"

If the house on Buxton Road felt far from No. 4 Imperial Lane, it felt in some ways farther from the university outside of town where I had spent my first year in the UK. In its apocalyptic state of utter disregard, Buxton Road was a refuge from the overbearing, comical politics of Sussex—politics, I must admit, I fell into almost immediately. It seemed like the thing to do, like backpacking at the University of Washington or skiing in Boulder.

The University of Sussex was built at an unfortunate period in British architectural history, one of the first and best of the new universities, more accessible than Oxford or Cambridge, and more brick—a lot of brick, arranged in variations of the rectangle. The students lured to the south coast of the UK for the university's arcane academic strengths gathered in the smaller brick corridors around Jacqueline Rose to hear her disquisitions on female sexual fantasy and the hauntings of Sylvia Plath. The brooding shoe gazers, attracted to the languor of Sussex's social scene, would linger in their cramped flats to find meaning in the feedback reverberating from the Jesus and Mary Chain. The political groups, though, dominated, and at the student union, one of the larger brick blocks, they would argue endlessly, plotting the next assault on the Barclay's Bank branch on campus for its neocolonial investments in South Africa, on the science labs to release whatever innocent animals were being tortured that day, on the visiting Tory politician, on the weekend foxhunt on the South Downs, or on the administration building for, well, administrating.

The balkanization was enough to make Josip Tito proud. There was the Revolutionary Communist Party, the Spartacus Youth League, the International Committee Against Racism, and the Socialist Workers. The one thing they hated more than each other was the Labour Students, but that was understandable. While the communists plotted revolution, the Labour Students—scions of progressive London—had more important aims for their disruptions. They were venturing into Politics earnestly, not as a passion but as a career, not as a cause but as a job in Parliament, maybe a seat in the House of Commons someday. For the more committed leftists, job Number One was to convince the Labour Students how ridiculous they were and what a wanker the current Labour Party leader, Neil Kinnock, was.

The lovely Labour Students couldn't care less. They laughed and tossed their hair and were all reasonable, once they had crawled out of the beds they shared, and since they were popular and numerous, they'd invariably win. It was galling.

I fell in briefly with a Revolutionary Communist, Mary Brewster. She was a flatmate of mine, and I suppose that's why I got into the revolutionary politics that infested Sussex. As I fraternized with known or professed communists, I became aware of my own Americanness. I would show up to meetings, talk gamely of the manifest injustices of capitalism, just two years before the truly manifest collapse of communism, and crash in some dingy flat for the weekend in the East End of London. I even spent a long four days in Manchester that November for a conference on the Irish Problem.

"You cannot be truly committed to revolution in the UK till you've taken a side on the Ireland question," the main speaker intoned in a church hall, his northern accent thick in his throat. Since he never said exactly which side we were supposed to be on, I was certain the Irish Republican Army had sown doubts even here. The Brighton bombing was one thing—targeting Tories. But the series of bombs in London had gone too far—and gummed up the traffic something dreadful.

My relationship with Mary ended before winter break, and with it my flirtation with communism. I had a quick fling with a Labour Student who brought me back into the mainstream. Though an avid attender of the endless political discourses, Natalia Weston didn't seem to care a lick about the discussion of the day or the politics of the era. She laughed a lot, whispered in the supple ears of her beautiful friends, and smiled this broad, toothy smile that soon became an infatuation of mine. Her buckteeth only added to her appeal. Otherwise she was perfection: long, wavy black hair that flowed down her back; creamy, light, impossibly smooth skin; legs and arms that glided through space like a dancer's. She approached me as a curiosity, the American who kept showing up, and once her curiosity was satisfied, she told me flat out to leave her life.

That was how I came to Maggie, a friend of a friend in a squat brick flat in Park Village, on the other side of campus. I knew her already. She made me laugh, was bright, interesting, had great taste in music and no politics whatsoever. She hated Thatcher, but at the University of Sussex, that went without saying. Otherwise, her opinions were distinctly unorthodox.

Her friends, Big Steve, Little Steve, Astrid, and Suze, were mercifully removed from the Sussex I had known. What passed for conflict came when Little Steve nailed a baggy to the wall above the sink in his flat with a yellowy, waxy remnant and a note, "Who ate my cheese, you fucking bastards?"

They welcomed me with no expectations, just as Maggie had that first night we made love.

"You're lovely," she had said, her nose crinkling with her irrepressible smile. She held my hand in hers and softly kissed my fingers. I sunk into the bed sheets, my relief and gratitude immeasurable, and smiled.

*　　*　　*

Now it was time to repay a few of those favors, to cheer up Little Steve and reconnect on a bit of a house outing. We were convinced Little Steve's weeks in the hospital, marooned somewhere between the university and London, had to have dragged him down. Maggie had the idea of brightening him up with homemade hash truffles. "Big Steve's got the hash. I can handle the truffles."

So that Saturday, freed from the Bromwells and No. 4, I joined in as we meticulously shaved Steve's stash of Lebanese black tar into flakes to mix with Maggie's chocolate confection. Then Maggie, Big Steve, Astrid, Suze, and I climbed aboard the London-bound local train, our candy offering tucked discreetly into a canvas bag.

By Hassocks, we were getting a little nervous.

"We don't know the medications Little Steve is on," Suzy said, her voice squeaking anxiously. "What if there's a reaction?"

"Oh, c'mon," Big Steve said. "There's not much hash in there. He's probably on stronger opiates than this anyway."

"That's the point," Astrid rejoined. "What if he OD's? What if we're piling drugs upon drugs?"

"Blimey, what if he OD's?" Big Steve sniffed.

The train rumbled on with us biting our lips. By Burgess Hill, we were sampling the wares, reasoning that maybe we should hold Little Steve's portion down. By Wivelsfield, we'd figured we'd keep Little Steve to one truffle. By Haywards Heath, the truffles were gone.

"We did the right thing," Astrid said, with a little giggle. "Better to not take any chances. I'm sure Little Steve just wants company."

Maggie let out a huge laugh at that.

Big Steve asked directions to the hospital, an easy walk. I was impressed by his initiative, since I was next to him shouting out, "Con-tsen-trat-sion Camp? Con-tsen-trat-sion Camp?" in a thick, ridiculous German accent. That was a faint echo of a trip I had taken the year before to the Austrian town of Mauthausen, where I arrived at sunset and gamely asked the locals with those two words and the same ludicrous accent which direction I should head to see where they had slaughtered my forefathers. Of course, none of my fellow stoners understood the reference. I barely did. Astrid and Suze were pretending to be zombies bumping into each other and stumbling into the gutter.

"Take me to Pigeon Street," Astrid cried out, which I think was another of her endless references to English cartoons that I had never seen. Suze mused she had read that the show was a vague reference to Pakistani immigrants.

"Here are the people you could meet. Here are the people who would say, 'Hello, good-bye, hello, good-bye, every dayyyyyyyyy,'" the two scream-sang.

"Wha' about Seaman Stains and Master Bates?" Big Steve interjected.

By the time we reached Little Steve's bedside, the world seemed soft and pastel, a cloud of memories and possibilities all at once.

"Company!" Astrid shouted, laughing uproariously.

His leg was in a thick, primitive-looking plaster cast, elevated in a sling. His corona of rock star hair was plastered down against a greasy face drained of color. His reddened eyes looked miserable. Nothing could be funnier.

" 'Ey, ya li'l wanker, you look 'orrible. You gonna die on us?" Big Steve asked earnestly.

"He's not gonna die. He's just gonna limp, poor little man," Maggie scolded. "You poor, little, little man," she cooed, touching his face.

"Why don't you give it a go, Mags, ri' 'ere? We won't look, promise," Big Steve said.

"You cad," she said, laughing.

"What is wrong with you people?" Little Steve demanded, as we ringed his bed, giggling.

He looked at us intently. Then the muscles in his face relaxed with recognition.

"Oh," he sighed.

We burst into uncontrollable laughter.

*   *   *

Hours later, the buzz mellowing but far from gone, Suzy sat cross-legged, drinking a lemon squash in a living room more dingy than usual with the approaching exams. "That was a really rotten thing to do to Little Steve," she said.

"Better than plying him with hash and watching him go to code," Big Steve said.

"You can't argue with that," I offered helpfully.

"Big Steve did," Astrid said, shooting him a look. "Now I see you've come round to justify your appetite."

He got up and wandered toward the kitchen. He came back with two Newcastle Brown Ales in Britain's standard, absurdly tall cans, one of which he tossed to me.

After nearly two years in Britain, I still sipped my ales and bitters. How Brits put so much of the thick, yeasty liquid into their bellies I never figured out.

"So what are you two gonna do when it's time for David to go home?" Astrid asked, looking at Maggie and me. "You're not just breaking it off, are you?"

I gave Maggie a searching look. She shrugged. It dawned on me that she had been a little cool all day. We were too stoned for me to draw any conclusions, but I listened to her answer.

"Dunno, really. Maybe I can earn some money this summer and join David in the States in August," Maggie said without much conviction. "I've got a job lined up at Sainsbury's in Leighton. I'll be thinking of him every time I check through a courgette or cucumber. I'll give them a little squeeze."

"You mean a gherkin," Big Steve chimed in.

"Funny, that," I said.

Big Steve's head lolled to one side, his still-stoned eyes resting on my face. "I dunno, David. I really want you to be my friend, a real friend."

"I am your real friend."

"No, I wanna be close, but there's somefing about you, somefing ya can't break through." He paused, his mind in thought.

"You know, I once had this friend, my best friend from primary school back in Luton. One day we were up in my attic, high on hash, and you know what we did? We touched each other's willies."

"Steve," Maggie tittered. "Are you trying to shag David after all this time?"

"No, no, nuffing like that," he said, shaking his head. "I'm not a hot grod, if that's what you mean." I swore I saw Maggie and Steve exchange quizzically hostile glances. I figured it was just one of those British exchanges that were beyond my comprehension. Big Steve got up, teetered on his black leather boots, then retreated to his room.

I lay that night with Maggie on her bed, both of us on our sides, facing each other, our bedside arms sticking upward toward the wall, fingers entwined. She seemed a thousand miles away.

"That was a fun day," I said softly.

"Hmm." She was looking at some point over my head.

We lay in silence for a long time. Julian Cope crooned quietly on her funny vertical turntable. "The greatest imperfection is love, love, love, but I can't keep the fire away."

"I'm tired, David. Could we just go to sleep?"

"Yeah, that's fine."

I kissed her on the forehead. She smiled, closed her eyes, and fell asleep. I watched her for a few minutes. Then I headed home, to No. 4 Imperial Lane.

Sitting alone in the kitchen the next morning, I realized this was my world now, tiny and drawing in. Haversham had come around the day before to cart off a weathered, five-drawered dresser on finely bowed legs. The base above the legs flared outward with three smaller, oddly shaped drawers forming an arch over a patterned fringe cut in the mahogany.

"I liked that dresser," I told Elizabeth when she informed me of the latest sale. She smoked a cigarette impassively. "I liked those weird drawers at the bottom, and the bowed legs."

"Cabriole legs. It was a highboy." She didn't look up. Her Silk Cut bobbed dangerously in her lips. "It'll take some work, but I'm sure Haversham will get ten thousand quid once he's done. The dentil cornice is quite fine, and I don't think I've ever seen slipper feet on a piece like that."

"A highboy," I repeated dumbly.

"Yes, a highboy," she said absently as she left me alone.

Highboy. I mouthed the word as I ate Weetabix for breakfast. The buzzer jolted me from my depression like an electric shock. I glanced at the oven clock—just past ten thirty. I went to Hans.

"Oh, David, I hope I didn't disturb you."

"You didn't, Hans. What's up?"

"I haven't seen your Maggie around lately."

"Studying. She studies a lot these days."

"Good for her. My taxes are sending her to university, you know."

"Hans, really, I think you're a drain on the government, not a supplier."

"Well, yes, David, at present, but you have to look at the totality of the Bromwell existence, not just its closing chapter."

Dear Bet,

Or should I say Mrs. Goncalves? Mrs. Joao Goncalves, better still. How on earth do you pronounce his name?

Well, little sister, you do have a way of breaking news. I have always said it is best not to stray too far from home. Activity tends to cause trouble, whether you're looking for it or not. I for one am avoiding both at all cost, activity and trouble.

Despite my inefforts, I suppose I have some minor news for you. Nothing so dramatic as your own. Don't worry. Her name is Segolaine Chouinard, and she appears to be sharing my bed. In one of those rare forays beyond the alleys of my corner of the Rive Gauche, I found myself at a nightclub where Miss Chouinard was, let's say, dancing. Wasn't wearing very much, to tell you the truth.

We talked. She danced. I shuffled. I suppose I've taken her in, saved her from the occasional forays she was making into the oldest profession on the planet. I know, hardly a doctor trying to save Africa and Empire, one African at a time. But she is soft. She dances well, and she acts like she likes me.

Simon's father has procured us a nice flat here, all odd angles, loose floorboards and draughty windows. It is tucked away enough to avoid those dreadfully dull student protesters and striking workers. Really, sometimes I think Paris perused the oddities of the '60s and acquired only the most earnest of offerings, Segolaine excepted. Simon is doing his level best to extract as many creature comforts as he can from the old man. We eat well. I'm growing fond of cooking. If I ever see you again, I'll filet and truss a duck for you and broil it in my orange sauce. Remind me some day to tell you the exotica I've learned about, especially the various, seemingly inedible parts of the pig, and I am not speaking of le pied de cochon, mind you.

Julian's gone and gotten himself a real job, at a bank, of all things. I fear he is not long for our little club. His ambitions are considerably higher. But he'll crawl back to my cooking from time to time, mark my words. He says hello and to tell you the obvious: You've gone round the twist.

I've discovered my new favorite book, "Darkness At Noon," by this little Hungarian Jew, Arthur Koestler. Not that a life of boredom in a Parisian flat is exactly like condemnation to a cell in a Stalinist prison, but I relate. The loss of ideals, the onset of ennui, guilt, suffering, torture. Quite a good read. It's about a bloke named Rubashov, a revolutionary Soviet leader who's fallen out of favor and condemned to a show trial and death.

"We brought you truth, and in our mouth it sounded a lie. We brought you freedom, and it looks in our hands like a whip. We brought you the living life, and where our voice is heard the trees wither and there is a rustling of dry leaves. We brought you the promise of the future, but our tongue stammered and barked..."

Beats Shakespeare.

Seriously, Bet, whatever comes of this marriage of yours, and this foray into the Dark Continent, war, empire, Heart of Darkness and all that sort of thing, be proud of yourself. Think how successful your escape from Houndsheath has been and so fast. One leap, and you have cleared the gravitational field and found adventure on an epic scale. Here I was so smug that I had managed to cross the Channel.

For what it's worth, I'm behind you, though that's not worth much at all. Don't believe a word they tell you, the imperialists or the revolutionaries, however swarthy their skin may be. Stay in touch. This is fun.

Much love,
Hans

CHAPTER NINE

The Portuguese devotion to attics was a gift to the wildlife of West Africa, an inland artificial reef. Despite all experiences that told them otherwise, the colonial architects kept building them, on military bases, in medical outposts, schools, and agriculture stations. Within weeks, the bats would move in to their comfortable new caves. The large lizards would follow, their loud *tou-ka* calls waking the sleepers at all hours. The rats and swallows found nesting grounds. The attics of Portuguese Africa were teeming with life.

João had been in Bissau only two months when the orders came to rotate out into one of the Portuguese medical outposts in the interior. Elizabeth did not need to go, he was told, but if she chose to, it would be perfectly safe. She might even enjoy it. He was to take up residence in the town of Contuboel, near the Senegalese border, on the rough road north from Bafatá. The kilometers that separated the agricultural station where he would live from Bafatá were crawling with guerrillas, but the town of Contuboel itself was safe, a few shops and a dense cluster of Fulani family compounds. They were Muslim. To say they were sympathetic to the Portuguese might be going a bit far, but it was close enough. They were implacably hostile to the Christian PAIGC, João was told. An enemy of an enemy is almost a friend.

João walked slowly back toward the officers' quarters, wondering whether he wanted Elizabeth with him. She would be a worry to him, another life to fret over as he considered his own safety. But she was proving to be a useful diversion to him, a talker when all was quiet at night, save the crickets and lizards. She chased away the sounds of screams and moans, the images of amputations, glazed stares, and gaping wounds from which protruded small intestines mingled with mine shrapnel. Though often, he wanted solitude, to think over the day's carnage and ponder his future. She was making some friends, especially with the African woman, Angélica, who was a fabulous Portuguese teacher. And his wife's eyes still lit up like a golden retriever's when he returned to base. It brought him some shame truthfully, mainly because he didn't feel the same elation. In fact, there were moments when she was beginning to annoy him. Time away might be good, he thought.

When he caught sight of her, sitting under a shade tree with Angélica, his doubts dissipated. The assignment was clearly making him more nervous than he had allowed himself to accept. Of course he wanted her company. Besides, there was that flyer at the base, Colonel Brito, the air force man the wives all giggled over. He didn't want Brito to decide his next conquest would have a posh English accent and creamy skin.

"It could be a good change of scenery, a look at real Africa," he told her after explaining the orders.

"I'll go, if Angélica can come too."

"I'll make that happen."

Elizabeth turned to Angélica and smiled broadly. Angélica's gaze in return, deep brown eyes over sunken cheeks, was not nearly as enthusiastic. Already, Angélica felt light-years from the life she had grown accustomed to in New Bedford, and quite a distance even from Praia, the capital of Cabo Verde, dusty and dry but lubricated with dollars from abroad. The capital of Guiné was backwater enough. Now she was headed for the backwater of this backwater country. To Angélica, there was nothing exotic in that. But Elizabeth needed a friend, and her friend would pay her. So she would go.

Two days later, they set off in an armored convoy out of Bissau. Soldiers, dressed in freshly pressed fatigues and bush caps with bills in the front and back, piled into massive West German–built troop carriers with wheels the size of the men they carried. Unimogs, Elizabeth remembered João had called them. The three guests of honor traveled in a jeep flanked by the armored behemoths. Within a few kilometers, the pavement was gone. Children at dirt or mud junctions fanned charcoal fires and offered blackened corn on the cob or peanuts stirred in palm oil and garlic. At Jugudul, the village where a road headed north to Mansôa and Farim and, ultimately, to the Senegalese Casamance, the soldiers tensed visibly and clenched their Heckler & Koch G3A3s, thankful the West German arms market kept their nation supplied. There should have been a checkpoint there, some sign of military authority. But there wasn't. This was rebel-held land. There was no real defense against an ambush. But none came and the men relaxed.

Within two hours, the convoy had entered Bafatá and coasted down the hill to the Moorish market and the weathered Portuguese administrative buildings. Lines of tailors, each clad in a white robe and skullcap, worked foot-powered sewing machines, while colorfully wrapped women and girls carried produce to market stacked in Chinese-made plastic tubs, piled high on their heads. Bicycles plied the dirt streets, veering toward the ditches to make room for the Portuguese war machines. Men glared as they passed. Children abandoned broken swing sets and seesaws, dashed from what passed as a city park and shouted, "Tuga, Tuga," running as fast as they could to catch the Unimogs, laughing at the clouds of dust that enveloped them.

"There it is again, 'Tuga,'" Elizabeth exclaimed. "Wherever I go, 'Tuga.' What does it mean?"

"Portuguese, Tuguese, Tuga," Angélica answered patiently. Sometimes Elizabeth amazed her. "Really, just white person. Portuguese, white people, they are the same thing here. The Guineans know of no other white people."

"I suppose my British passport is no defense then?"

Angélica just smiled.

As the road veered north along the Rio Geba, the land grew lusher. Women worked fields with small, handheld hoes, babies slung on their backs. Men clustered under cottonwood trees, drinking palm wine and playing mancala on boards cut from palm trunks, rounded pebbles filling hemispherical hollows. Elizabeth would watch the laughter cease as the convoy rumbled into their games. They'd stop, mid-move, to stare as the soldiers passed. A wide wooden bridge, laid crosswise with irregular, thick planks, boards running its length to ease the passage of trucks, marked the approach to Contuboel. The river was languid, thick with lilies and reeds but inviting in the heat. "Schisto creek," João said, slightly patronizing. "Don't even think about stepping into it."

It was lovely, thought Elizabeth with relief. Coconut and oil palms dotted the landscape, along with massive cottonwoods, banyans, and the occasional baobab. It was remarkably unpopulated. A man walked toward the small cluster of rough-hewn brick buildings with an emaciated cow not much bigger than a Great Dane, his son pushing a rusty bicycle. Children walked hand in hand, some with distended bellies, filled with parasites or protruding with kwashiorkor from the lack of protein. But others looked pretty good. Adorable, really. Around each of their necks hung a leather juju, a good-luck charm carefully crafted by the local mullah or shaman, no difference. The houses were wide and cylindrical, topped by rounded, thatched roofs that built to a central peak. The walls were low, constructed of mud brick. Thick, rough tree trunks held up the lips of the roofs, providing outdoor shade.

Just before reaching the few cement buildings, the trucks veered left and roared up a steep hill to a gate manned by a languid old man. He moved slowly to lift the barrier by hand, the troop carriers and jeep idling loudly. They pulled into a flat clearing of low-slung, whitewashed buildings, a miniature of the base in Bissau. Only when the engines stopped did Elizabeth realize what a din they had created over all those miles. For a few moments, there was silence.

Aleixo Menges bypassed the troop carriers that preceded their jeep and walked straight to João and Elizabeth's vehicle.

"We have been waiting for you," he said with a broad smile, jutting out a hand through the front passenger-side window to João and introducing himself as the director of the agricultural station. Like so many other colonial administrators, he was young, maybe twenty-seven or twenty-eight. Then again, so was João. Menges sported a little goatee, a worldly affectation for an agronomist in the middle of nowhere, and little round glasses to boot. But his greeting was generous and his welcome sincere. "Word is out that a real doctor is coming to our meager clinic. The lines began to form yesterday."

João looked at him wearily, then leaned into the door to open it, as if it were the equivalent of one of those new-model, early-seventies, two-door American sedans, not the flimsy canvas-topped door of a Portuguese jeep. Menges took notice.

"But you are tired," he said. "Let me show you and your lovely wife to your quarters. Such a treat to have a young couple here."

"Elizabeth Gonçalves," she said in passable Portuguese, offering her hand. "My husband can be a bit careless with introductions."

Menges met Elizabeth's eyes, lingered a little too long, then blushed, taking her hand. Elizabeth smiled in wonder. She still could not see herself as attractive, despite João, and when she felt anything like a spark, she was quick to dismiss it as her own overactive imagination.

"This is my friend and Portuguese teacher, Angélica," she said.

Menges gave Angélica a beneficent smile, the kind colonial administrators used to please themselves with their own tolerance.

"Cabo-Verdiana," he noted with self-satisfaction. He did not take her hand.

The quarters sat at the top of the hill, just where the military convoy had leveled off and swung left onto the clearing. A few other buildings rested on a terrace below, then palm trees, then Contuboel, not far below. The rise was not dramatic enough to mitigate the heat. Once again, João and Elizabeth would be in their own unadorned white room at the end of the hall, but this hall was much shorter, just two other rooms and a fairly spacious bathroom with cold running water. No one would want hot. A porch faced into the compound, and just off the porch, an old man in a dusty dishdasha and skullcap lay in a hammock beneath two coconut palms.

He sprung up more spryly than Elizabeth would have thought possible and grabbed a thick walking stick, smoothed with use, beaming and bobbing his head obsequiously.

"Bom dia, bom dia, bom dia," he said, shaking Elizabeth's hand first, then João's, ignoring Angélica's.

"This is Guedado," Menges said. "He is your night watchman and guard."

Guedado's head bobbed again, his smile widening still further as he raised his stick and swung it through the air at some imaginary miscreant. This was the most suspect security force Elizabeth had ever laid eyes on, but she found that amusing. They were in a gated compound, in a safe part of Guiné. It was nice that the Portuguese were so generous with colonial employment.

"There's been a bit of a tragedy in town," Menges said casually. "Just beyond the gate, by one of the experimental garden plots, a group of children stumbled into a black mamba nest yesterday. Two-and-a-half-step snakes, they call them here. You take two-and-a-half steps before you die. Beasts. Six children died in seconds."

"How awful," Elizabeth gasped.

"Such is life in a country where life expectancy is around forty. There are many dangers, more lethal than the PAIGC or even the Portuguese Air Force. But it's still a shock. The funeral is tomorrow."

The convoy had parked in front of the mess hall. Around back, where livestock was slaughtered for supper, repulsively giant vultures hopped about looking for scraps. The halfhearted waves and *shoo-shoo*s from the staff were comical next to the great, bald birds, which hopped back a step, as if to pay their respects to the gesture, then hopped forward to resume their scavenging. The building on the terrace below João's quarters was the clinic, staffed by a pair of Portuguese nurses, and now, a doctor, at least for a few months. As Menges had said, a line of villagers was already awaiting João's appearance. Below and through a trail were the vegetable beds and experimental millet fields. The director spoke volubly about efforts to grow vegetable strains that did not mold and rot during the wet season or could tolerate the parching sun of the dry season, the millet seeds being bred for protein, not just pure starch. "And we're working on some insecticides and herbicides," he added.

Dinner that night was foul, some kind of starchy noodles cooked until they were waterlogged, then drenched with reddish-orange palm oil. A chicken had been rotated over an open fire to a jerky-like texture, then sliced with a meat cleaver without regard to parts or cuts. Bone and bone fragments prevented a good bite. But Elizabeth was new, so she smiled and ate, reaching into her mouth to pull out the parts that stuck in her teeth.

There was a quiet to her new home that she felt she could truly love. Only eight were on hand to eat that evening around long picnic tables. The three Guineans who joined them in the corner laughed uproariously at everything and nothing. The nation seemed at peace, and so did Elizabeth. She leaned over to João.

"I like it here."

João woke up the next morning to the sound of his wife's screams. She burst into the room completely naked, dripping wet, panting and cringing and grabbing a sheet off the bed to cover herself. João held her by the shoulders and guided her to sit on the side of the bed, which sagged under the weight of the two of them. She gingerly lay on her back, catching her breath.

"What? What? Did somebody hurt you? Did something bite you?"

The urgency in his voice revealed a genuine concern, an anguish that pleased Elizabeth to no end. She leaned over and put her head against his chest, her body convulsing slightly as he rocked her, his arms pulling her close. Water dripped uncomfortably down his naked chest. His stomach dropped as adrenaline surged through his blood.

Then he realized she was laughing. He pulled away to let her look up at him. Streaks of tears crossed her face, her eyes were watery and earnest, but her mouth was turned up mischievously.

"I'm sorry, I'm sorry, I really am." She waved her hand in front of her mouth as she giggled like a child.

"What in God's name happened?"

Elizabeth paused to choke back the giggle, looking down and finding an empty spot on the worn linoleum to compose herself.

"Well, you were sleeping so peacefully, so I got up to take a shower. The water was so cool. I was really enjoying it," she began. "Then a giant cockroach scurried in with me, right into the swirl of water at my feet. It was huge! I jumped back from it and hit my head on the shower wall. That scared one of those giant lizards. I hadn't seen it on the windowsill—you know, the *tou-kas*? It ran into a hole in the ceiling. Then there was this almighty clatter. A mouse fell onto the floor. Then about ten bats swooped down from the attic through the same tiny little hole. One of them was in my hair, I swear."

They were both laughing now, loosely, happily, unselfconsciously, deep belly laughs. Elizabeth let out a few little snorts, which only made them laugh harder.

"Leave it to the Brit," João sighed, poking his wife in the ribs, "on West African safari."

"'The kingdom of perpetual night,'" Elizabeth sighed.

"*Richard the Third.*"

Elizabeth turned on her side and propped her head up in her hand.

"You do amaze me," she said.

"Then it's working."

They lay back in bed, the sheet dropping from around her chest, and held each other to absorb some of the other's glee. João's hand traced the muscles that framed his wife's spine, down to the little dimples at the base of her fine backside, up the curve of her rear. She rolled over and offered herself to him, and they made love tenderly.

They dressed and walked outside their quarters to see if there was some breakfast at the mess hall. Guedado was gesticulating wildly from beside his hammock, beckoning them over.

"I have protected you. I have protected you. I have protected you." He grinned in delight, speaking in rapid-fire Portuguese patois as he brandished his stick in a mock threat and motioned toward the ground.

At his feet was a rat the size of a small dog, beaten to death.

The leadership of the agricultural outpost, including João, Elizabeth, and Angélica, all attended the funeral in Contuboel later that morning. They walked down the dusty grade, past the desultory checkpoint and into town, where Fula in long white robes had gathered in a great outpouring of grief from villages throughout the area. The Portuguese crew, even Angélica, looked blindingly white amid these Africans as dark as ebony, their skin smooth but for the ritual scars on some of their faces. The crowd was gracious, jovial even, with the newcomers, and Elizabeth smiled and felt fortunate to be there.

They surged forward, toward a particularly large compound where six small bodies lay wrapped in white linen under the eaves of a house. Ululations filled the air as mothers and mourners wailed over the lost children. But another spectacle had caught Elizabeth's eye. On the periphery of the gathering, two men, sheathed from head to toe in ragged orange strips of cloth, bark, and tree fiber, their faces masked in carved wood, menaced the crowd. Accompanied by a small group of young men with drums, the men in orange clanged machetes together and lunged. The villagers shrank from their approaches, feigning fear, but did not run. The two men circled the crowd, pouncing, ducking back, lunging again, brandishing their long knives, then drifting to the next cluster in a ritualized assault that touched no one. The thumping of the drums added a soundtrack that heightened the drama.

"They are spirit people, protecting the village in such bad times," Menges said quietly, leaning in to Elizabeth's ear when he caught her fascination. She swore he grazed it softly with his lips.

As the men approached her part of the crowd, Elizabeth felt a wave of panic, not knowing what was happening or how to respond.

"What do I do?" she asked Menges.

"Watch the others. Do as they do."

Nobody laughed or even smiled as the orange men leaped and leered and showed the fierceness of the protecting spirits. The townspeople played along in deadpan seriousness. It was an elaborate, ritualized performance, more than a game but somehow less than a religious rite. Elizabeth tried to follow suit, to cringe in serious silence, but she could not suppress a giggle, a noise that provoked stern looks from the Guineans around her, and in turn from her husband. Those looks wiped the smile from her face quickly. She could not keep her eyes off the spectacle. One of the orange men broke away from the group and ducked into a mud-walled house, disappearing into the blackness of the unlit home.

"Look. That orange man has gone into his house," Elizabeth told Angélica in an unsubtle stage whisper, using her best, careful Portuguese and pointing after him. "He must be hungry or need to use the loo."

Menges turned quickly toward her, grabbed her upper arm, and tore her away from her friend with surprising vehemence. In English, he hissed in Elizabeth's face, "What did I tell you? Do as the others do. Show some respect. We are guests here."

He dropped her arm, as if she were a child misbehaving in church, and turned away angrily. João glared at his wife with a meanness she had rarely seen. Not disappointment, but shame.

Elizabeth was stunned and wounded, unsure of her offense. She stayed quiet for the rest of the morning. For once, she knew she understood nothing that she was seeing, that the plainest action— a blessing, a tearful moan, an offering—was quite beyond her realm of comprehension. The simple joy of discovery that she had felt as she joined the throng of Africans was gone now, replaced by timidity and confusion and shame like she had never felt before.

"Do not challenge custom here," Angélica whispered in her ear as the crowd dispersed and they headed back to the outpost. "Who is to say what those men or spirits are? There are powerful beliefs out here. Remember what Senhor Menges said: Dangers are everywhere."

In the weeks that followed, Elizabeth became attuned to the drumming in the town below and villages beyond. On some days, in the heat of the afternoon, a cluster of women, wrapped in their best, most garish prints, would surge up the hill onto the flat high ground of the agricultural station, ululating wildly, beating drums, with spirit men dancing around them. Then they'd retreat back to Contuboel just as quickly. They appeared to seek nothing with these forays but visibility. They smiled, chanted, and disappeared.

Elizabeth remained baffled, but her trepidations subsided. She took walks into Contuboel with Angélica. She learned that beyond the simple, one-road, no-intersection town was a maze of trails leading through lush grasslands, fields, and forests. She could spend hours wandering these well-worn routes, smiling at villagers, men and women, watching the girls in the field hoeing with their baby sisters slung onto their backs, or the young men who scrambled up towering palms to pluck coconuts or check the palm-wine fermentation. She felt no threats at all. Secrets were all around her—the roundup of prepubescent twelve- and thirteen-year-old boys who were marched into the bush for weeks on end to undergo ritual circumcisions and unspoken rites of passage into manhood, the whispers about clitorectomies undergone with no such fanfare, the deaths, the births. She understood none of it, and no one offered to explain. Menges did bring a shaman up to make Elizabeth a leather juju to protect her against ill winds. The old man scribbled something on a torn piece of notebook paper, placed it in his palm, uttered an incantation, blew into his closed fist, then encased her blessing in a delicately fashioned leather pouch. She took to it immediately, wrapping the leather cord around her neck for what she vowed would be forever.

One morning, Elizabeth and Angélica sat on crude wooden chairs beneath a banyan tree going over a Portuguese lesson. Elizabeth saw Angélica as a true friend, maybe the closest she had ever had. She could confide in her, express her doubts, her worries about João, and Angélica always listened. There had been Vicki, but she was a cousin. A certain obligation came with that. Angélica could have refused to accompany her to the interior, Elizabeth thought. She had made a choice, for her.

Angélica felt differently. She liked Elizabeth, was flattered by her attention, her genuine affection, but what did this woman know of her? What did she know of a life on the verge of nothing? If anything, Angélica saw herself as a teacher, one who was fond of her pupil, to be sure, but distance had to be respected.

Guedado came slinking up behind them, eyes darting to the honeysuckle bush behind Elizabeth's chair. "Sssst, sssst," he whispered, but vehemently, his eyes wide, his hands gesticulating wildly but in small, emphatic motions. Angélica understood first, rising slowly, her eyes locked on the honeysuckle as she backed away, leaving her friend alone but beckoning to her in compact, conservative gestures. Elizabeth sat dumbly for a few more seconds, then lifted herself just past a crouch and moved toward Guedado, her eyes searching his.

"What?" she said in a strained whisper.

"*Morte negro*," he muttered, pointing to the bush. Elizabeth turned to follow the direction of his finger. There, curled around a twig, was a snake not much thicker than two of Elizabeth's fingers, olive green on the back, shifting to a yellow-green belly. Its eyes seemed to smile.

"It's cute." Elizabeth smiled. "It's harmless. C'mon."

Angélica grabbed her upper arm. "That is a black mamba, 'black death.' Didn't you hear Guedado?" she asked, as the watchman scurried off to alert Menges and to get his club.

Menges came around quickly but showed no more alarm than Elizabeth had.

"Shoo," he said with a laugh, grabbing a long stick and poking at the snake. The serpent calmly slid from its perch into the grass and silently glided away, its full length, nearly six narrow feet, stretching gracefully before the group. Guedado returned with his staff, but it was too late. He was furious. His rants in Fula grew louder and louder, incomprehensible to the other three.

That night, Luis, a staff member known mainly to Elizabeth as the guy who fetched the station's French bread on dashes into Senegal, slid next to the group at dinner as they wrestled with canned sardines over palm oil–drenched rice. He leaned forward.

"Senhor Director," he said in a low voice, addressing Menges. "The staff wishes to inform you of its unhappiness at the events of this morning."

Menges looked back at him quizzically. "What? The snake?"

"Senhor Director, when a Guinean is lucky enough to be that close to a black mamba and not dead, he kills it."

There were other surprises too, less mysterious for Elizabeth perhaps, but far more momentous. She had stopped getting her period, for one. She was not ready to tell the only doctor around, her husband—not yet. But she knew she was pregnant. She was deeply happy, happier still to keep it a secret, even from Angélica.

João, too, was happy much of the time. The adrenaline rush of trauma care was gone, replaced by the deeply more satisfying job of attending to the gratefully ill. In the little clinic, the unadorned waiting room was always full. Simple benches outside held the overflow. There were plenty of patients who came with hideous, untreated cancers, degenerative diseases that João had no equipment to diagnose, let alone treat, heart diseases that were death sentences so far from a proper hospital. But so many more came with ailments easily remedied with penicillin, eased with aspirin, or cured by simple rehydration salts. Their gratitude overwhelmed him. It seemed that everyone left his clinic content that this young Tuga had worked wonders, or at least had tried.

Elizabeth began spending more time at the clinic. She spoke in her rudimentary Portuguese about boiling water to women who did not understand even good Portuguese. She tried to dispense iodine tablets for plastic gas cans of water brought to the fields. The women didn't like the taste or the brownish water, cleansed of its bacteria. Elizabeth would laugh.

"But you are alright drinking water that tastes of petrol?" Angélica tried to translate to Kriolu, which she herself was only just starting to pick up.

"Oh, you get used to that," the women replied.

She had much better luck with the children. Many suffered from debilitating diarrhea, but the impact of rehydration salts, UNICEF-issued, with the bright blue UN logo stamped on the bag, was immediate and undeniable. The nausea and lethargy of dehydration would give way in an instant. The joys of childhood would return in a day. Mothers would beam.

João watched her, sometimes overcome with affection. She made him laugh, with her abrupt, nervous gestures, her clumsiness, her genuine need to please these people. Better still, she completed the picture. In the days before their flight to Bissau, this scene had played in his fantasies, with only small, insignificant variations, the doctor and the doctor's wife, easing suffering in war-torn Africa. He loved her, he thought.

"Old Spínola warned us you'd take to this," João said, laughing. "The coot knows a few things."

"'An honorable murderer, if you will,'" Elizabeth replied with a smile.

*   *   *

It was not yet daybreak when the thumps began, or more like thuds. The sound first entered a dream, a dull knock on Elizabeth's bedroom door back in Houndsheath, Mother coming to call: *thud*, pause, *thud*, pause, *thud*, *thud*. The thwacks on the tin grate just below the roof line, the thumps on the stucco wall, the rustle of grass outside her window, the noises went on and on, not very loud but steady, arrhythmic, and inscrutable.

She listened for what must have been an hour, choosing not to awaken João. Then, as the sun rose in earnest, the sounds faded. All was silent but a delicate rustling of grass. She evaded João's searching hands, jumped out of bed, threw on an unflattering African shift, newly tailored in Contuboel, and went out.

"*Noite estranha*," Guedado was saying, as he poked his walking stick at something in the grass. Strange night.

At his feet was a dying bat, feebly lifting a wing and letting it drop. Elizabeth's gaze focused on the grass around the building. Black splotches compressed the blades, some moving, most not. Hundreds of bats had not made it home to the daytime safety of the attic. The little corpses were all over the compound, in the thousands.

Guineans were practical people. They saw omens in such events, but they also saw the malice of the Portuguese overlords. The bats kill the bugs. The bugs kill the people. The bats are good—and now dead.

"Guedado wants you to talk to Senhor Menges," Angélica told João. "He wants to know what happened."

João disappeared into the little administration building as the two women dressed properly for breakfast.

The doctor looked troubled as he sat down with a plate of Senegalese French bread and Portuguese jam. Angélica and Elizabeth had gnawed through their baguettes already and were nursing cups of Nescafé as they awaited word of the bat holocaust. They looked expectantly at João, who remained silent as he gathered his thoughts.

"The station has been working on a defoliant, fifty-four percent arsenic. The army wants it for the elephant grass along the roads that hides the guerrillas. They sprayed it last night. They wanted to see whether dew would make it more potent or less potent. I guess they got their answer."

"I don't understand," Elizabeth said. "It's a defoliant, for plants, right? Kill the plants, not the animals?"

"It looks like it affected the insects as well. The bats ate the insects. By the time they returned home, the arsenic had taken its course."

"Have they tried to figure out how this stuff affects people?" Angélica asked. Her drawn face looked more severe than usual.

"That, apparently, was not part of the assignment," João responded.

Children were given a few cans of sardines as payment for the grim task of putting the bat carcasses into woven-plastic rice sacks. The arsenic-laced corpses were mixed with the great compost piles of the agriculture station. Whether those corpses would contaminate the soil...well, that would be another experiment.

After several weeks, another Portuguese military convoy rumbled through Contuboel and up the hill to the agriculture station. This time, the armed jeeps flanked a Unimog painted white with a large red cross. Renato Marsola Araujo bounded out smiling broadly as João moved to greet him.

"You didn't think I would let you have all the fun, did you?" he asked, putting an arm around João's shoulder. "Come to think of it, you didn't think I would let you have any fun, I'm sure."

"I don't like the sound of that," João replied, his smile fading.

Araujo shrugged. "Let's go meet this Menges. Then we'll talk."

As the doctors walked amiably toward the administration building, Araujo talked of trauma patients in Bissau, life on the base, the crazy ideas of António de Spínola.

"He's going soft, you know. He speaks of equality for the *ultramar*, something real, you know? Not Caetano's bullshit. We may be winning the battles, he says, but we're losing the war."

João shrugged.

"It's not just here," Araujo continued. "I tell you, João, it's getting ugly in the *ultramar*. The PIDE are flooding into Angola. The South Africans are bombing Mozambique with French Mirage jets. We're using herbicides on cassava fields. It's out of control, like Vietnam, I swear to you. The wars are metastasizing. The world hates us."

"Is that what you came here to tell me, current events?" João asked as they arrived at Menges's office. Araujo knocked gently and waited for the director to open the door. When he did, the two men hugged.

"Good to see you, Renato," Menges said heartily. "Our first doctor, João. He loved this place. Then he abandoned us. Ambition got the best of him. You really should take a walk down to Contuboel, Renato."

"Perhaps I will, Aleixo. Maybe I can answer this question myself. Tell me, Senhor Director, how safe is it out there? The PAIGC has camps all through the Casamance now. They own the routes from Dungal and Cuntima into Farim and almost down to Mansôa. A few more kilometers east, and I'm afraid they're heading your way."

"Doctor Araujo, what's gotten into you these few months in Bissau? You talk like a military man, not like a medical one."

"The professions are merging, my friend. I want our friend Doctor Gonçalves here to hit the road in the next few days. Winning the hearts and minds in little old Contuboel isn't going to win this war. The Tugas can't show fear."

"And you are asking what, General Spínola?" Menges said, his eyes now leery.

"If you would look out your window, you would see a freshly painted mobile medical unit. I don't imagine Cabral's men pay much attention to that big red cross. They're communists, you know, not much into crosses. The roads north to Cambaju and Sare Janque, into Senegal, are they safe?"

"How else would we get French bread for breakfast every morning?" Menges laughed.

*   *   *

The assignment shouldn't have been a surprise to João. He was in the army of a nation at war, ostensibly with itself. Spínola's counterinsurgency tactics were to become legendary, studied in war colleges, written up in textbooks as infallible, tried and refined in low-intensity conflicts the world over. His strategy: Don't seek out the guerrillas for a fight. They are too elusive. Protect the local populace from their would-be liberators, and make them love you.

With Cabral and the PAIGC pushing in from their bases in Senegal and Guinea, it was time for João to join Spínola's war for hearts and minds. Not even Fulani territory could be taken for granted; the area north and east of Contuboel soon would be contested ground, a blank spot on the PAIGC's territorial map, surrounded on three sides, east, west, and north, by rebel-held territory. Dr. Gonçalves wasn't to fight for it. He was to minister to it. He was to roll back Cabral's gains without firing a shot, though he might administer some injections.

The mobile medical unit sounded more impressive than it was: two cots and a dispensary of drugs and first aid. But as he had seen from the clinic in Contuboel, a very little goes a long way. Along with him, the unit would be staffed by an army medic and protected by two jeeps, one in front, one behind, manned by four soldiers each, lightly armed with G3A3s. Anything more would make João's professions of beneficence suspect. They weren't expecting trouble.

Elizabeth would stay behind with Angélica, the *tou-kas*, the mambas, and a far more quiet attic, scrubbed of its bats.

"I'll be back in a week or two, Bet," Gonçalves told his wife. "There is nothing to worry about. If you want, work in the clinic. You can do practically what I could. The nurses will be there, and Angélica can help with language. It'll help the time go quickly."

He held her tightly for a long time, determined not to be the first to break the clench. She looked into his eyes.

"That's what my brother calls me, Bet." She smiled.

"You need to tell me more about him when I get back."

They sat together on the foam-mattress bed in their Spartan room. He reached out his hand to touch her cheek, and she held it to her face, leaning into it, feeling the warmth. Her eyes closed. A tear rolled onto his hand. The fluid was warm, then grew cold, and he looked at it before wiping it on his leg.

"Really, Elizabeth, what are you afraid of? Nothing is going to happen to me. Nothing certainly is going to happen to you."

She nodded her head miserably. She knew this was an emotional time for her—for reasons João would not, could not, be considering. She wanted to tell him they were going to have a child together, but she wanted the moment to be right, to be romantic, to be resonant with meaning. In Contuboel, such a moment had never arisen.

He stood up and changed into fatigues as she lingered, her eyes unfocused and gazing at the floor. He turned one more time, met her eyes, and forced a smile. But he left agitated; *I'm the one going out there*, he thought. *What the fuck is she crying about?*

The little convoy rolled out just before noon, João in the passenger seat of the Unimog, a soldier driving, the medic in the canvas-covered back. The other soldiers piled haphazardly into the jeeps in front and behind, rifles—safeties on—in their laps.

They rumbled through Contuboel, then slowed to a crawl as the road north deteriorated to a barely passable track, crisscrossed by streams and deep furrows. They had gone ten kilometers in a little less than an hour when they approached the first sizeable village, Cancosita. Villagers fled as they approached. João motioned to the driver to stop and kill the engine. For a moment, they sat in silence. Then João opened the truck's rickety door and stepped onto the muddy road, walking deliberately to the back of the medical truck and slowly opening the zippered canvas flap.

The children were the first to appear, peeking from behind the openings in the mud walls that surrounded the family compounds. A boy who looked eight but was probably eleven walked slowly toward João as the physician slipped on a white lab coat to cover his fatigues. The lab coat held no significance for the boy. The fatigues meant plenty. Barefoot, shirtless, in short pants of an indeterminate color, a castoff maybe of an American, years before, brought by the boatload to West Africa by missionaries, then cycled through the rag markets in Bafatá or Farim. The boy held out a hand, open-palmed. "*Dàdiva?*" he asked tentatively. "*Cadeau?*"—in case João was an errant Frenchman who had wandered south from the Senegalese border just a few kilometers up the road.

"*Médico,*" João responded, hands tapping his own chest. "*Pais?*" he asked, gesturing for his parents.

The boy giggled, then bolted away. Other children poured out of compounds. "*Dàdiva, cadeau,*" they chanted for about five minutes, *gift, gift, gift,* before the mothers began venturing out and hushing their offspring.

Cancosita was well beyond the maw of the Portuguese. The farmers didn't cultivate groundnuts for sale, didn't pay taxes, didn't work someone else's land. They were relatively healthy, although a few kwashiorkor bellies spoke to the protein deficiencies. But this was West Africa. Guinea worms, botfly infections, diarrhea, malaria—there was plenty for João and the medic to attend to. The women patiently waited their turn.

As shadows lengthened and evening approached, the first man of Cancosita approached the throng now gathered around the medical truck. Middle-aged and dignified in a long white robe, he asked in passable Portuguese for the officer in charge.

"I suppose that would be me," João answered. "But I don't think of myself as an officer. Doctor João Gonçalves," he said, holding out a hand.

"Baboucar Sabally," he said with a slight smile, nodding but not extending his hand. "We would like you and your men, doctor, to stay the night. You are our guests."

"It would be our pleasure," he responded.

This was how it was supposed to be, dispensing medicine to

grateful natives, partaking of African hospitality. This was winning, thought Gonçalves, catching the triumphalism in his own thoughts but giving in to it anyway. He led his team as they walked behind Sabally and in turn were trailed by a swarm of children. A huge, steaming pot of stew was already boiling over a wood fire inside their host's compound, bubbling in a vast, wok-like iron skillet, pounded by hand. The smell of chilis and chicken, manioc and rice mingled with the usual wood smoke, charcoal, and shit. João was used to filtering out the bad from the good. Frankly, the meal spreading before him beat most served up at the agriculture station.

Each of João's men was given a gourd, halved and hollowed into a well-worn bowl. As was custom, the men went first, ladling rice, manioc, and stew in large quantities, taking the best pieces of chicken. The women went next, then the children. João cringed at the logic. Children were prone to die. Men were bigger and stronger and needed the nourishment to hunt, climb the palms, and tend to the fermenting wine or grab the coconuts. Of course, children would be less prone to die, and men would be smaller and need less food, if the feeding priorities were reversed. But to the Fula, adults had proven their fortitude by the mere fact of surviving. The next generation would have to follow suit.

"That Tuga woman at the funeral a few weeks back, your wife?" Sabally asked.

"Yes," said João.

"Your only one, right? Your custom."

"Yes, just the one." João chuckled.

"She challenged the spirits, I heard. She called them orange men."

"Yes, well, she didn't understand," João said, flustered.

They sat in silence for a while as they finished their meals, fingers sticky with palm oil and starch, their bellies groaning with guilt and satiation.

"My men will sleep in their tents," João said preemptively. Sabally was already motioning for the children to clear out their huts for the newcomers, but João insisted. He and the medic would stay in the compound. The eight soldiers would remain with the vehicles, to stand guard and to stay out of the way.

The night sky was aflame with stars. A sliver of moon could not compete. A few lamps came out, glass jars with a small string wick, shedding hardly enough light to see their feet. The guests shuffled forward, trying to find their way to the hut and the woven straw mat that was to be their bed for the night. The noises of Contuboel—battery-powered transistor radios, drumming, inebriated chatter—were all gone. It was dark and hushed and warm, and at just past eight o'clock, João rolled over, an army-issued wool blanket pulled over his head to ward off the whine of the mosquitoes, and fell asleep.

The roosters weren't the only things stirring at dawn. Mangy dogs snuffled around for scraps. A few women were quietly talking to each other, blowing on the coals from the previous night's cook fires. João was intent on paying his way without being an ugly guest. So he sprang to his feet, pulled on fatigues over his olive-drab shorts, and dashed out of the compound to the jeeps. The watchmen were all asleep as he hoisted a bag of rice from the truck, then a small bag of dried fish and a half-dozen hard-boiled eggs.

"Breakfast," he said with a generous smile as Sabally emerged from his hut to feed the chickens and stoke the charcoal embers of the cooking fire. One of his wives took the provisions with a smirk and set about making the meal.

He had hated this breakfast at first: white rice, stir-fried with pungent, salty dried fish, maybe an egg, usually some okra or mushy tomatoes. Now he found it wonderfully satisfying. He vowed he would eat it for the rest of his life, though he wasn't sure the ingredients in Lisbon would create the right consistency, a mix of soft vegetable mush and crunchy, chewy rice. It was especially good on day two or three of the rice, scraped from the bottom of a spoiled iron pot.

The soldiers were not savoring their meal. They had been in this village long enough, too long really, having left enough time to get word of their location all the way back to Cabral in his redoubt in Conakry on the Atlantic coast. They shifted uncomfortably on the ground, eyes motioning to the medic. It was time to go. João rose, and they rose too quickly for the Fulas' sense of propriety. They wished their hosts good health and loaded into the jeeps and truck, heading northeast, toward Sare Bácar and the Senegalese frontier.

João was feeling good about himself as he and his men climbed back into the truck. He was a reluctant soldier, but he had always hoped the army would toughen him up, help him discover the leader beneath all of that education. The military is a group activity, sure, but he had always pictured himself alone, a stalwart physician standing against the mayhem of war. Then Elizabeth had come along, and in a fit of weakness, he had married, and all that independence had receded under the weight of her need. But here he was standing on his own, a soldier, an officer, he thought.

Lost in those thoughts, João didn't notice when the first bullet pinged off the door of the cab, nor did the driver, who nearly slammed the truck into the back of the lead jeep, which had pulled to a halt when the second struck. As the soldiers dove out of the jeeps, a fusillade of automatic weapon fire poured out of the elephant grass. It was the perfect ambush spot, an intersection with an impassable dirt road that cradled the cluster of houses of Bambato. To call Bambato a village was being too generous. The guerrillas had come down from Cobeto, much farther east than any maps would put any PAIGC soldiers. The lines of demarcation were evidently more fluid than Spínola liked to admit.

João fell out of the cab onto the muddy track. The noise was overwhelming and unworldly after the silences of the evening. One of the soldiers in the rear jeep dragged the radio behind the bumper and tried to reach headquarters in Bissau. The others scrambled behind the vehicles for cover. But it was over before they could get through half a clip. Maybe thirty guerrillas tumbled through the curtain of grass, AK-47s blazing. The firing was indiscriminate. One magazine would be spent, and another would be quickly pushed into place, fire resuming. They showed no need to conserve ammunition. They were obviously well supplied. Bodies were mangled, eviscerated, limbs severed by the volume of lead pumped into a shoulder or thigh. The Portuguese patrol was overrun before João could figure out how to take the safety off his sidearm. The fighters waded through the silence, breaking it with gunshots to the heads of even the most obviously dead soldier. Skull fragments and brain tissue thudded into the West African mud. Blood poured into the ruts of the road. Only the medic groaned, a bullet in the meat of his shoulder, his Red Cross insignia preserving his life.

João sat in the mud, mouth open and silent, surrounded by guerrillas who were chuckling quietly at him. His handgun had fallen into a puddle, unused.

Baboucar Sabally appeared from around the front of the truck, imperious as he was the night before. He said nothing, just met his recent guest with a neutral stare, eye to eye.

The talking was left to another man, in well-worn camouflage fatigues and a floppy sun hat, who came up from behind Sabally. He was taller than the others, lean, with sinewy biceps exposed by torn fatigues. He had aquiline features, not West African, and was so black he almost looked blue to João. His head was shaved.

"Doctor Gonçalves." He smiled. "We were led to believe you would be coming for a visit."

He unslung his AK and placed it casually against the wheel, within easy reach of João. He ducked into a squat, at the doctor's level, close but not threateningly close. His Portuguese was perfect and accentless.

"Have you seen *Doctor Zhivago*, Doctor Gonçalves?"

"Seen it, read it. Of course," João replied.

"Read it. Ah, very good. I wish I had time for Russian novels of such length. I've been a bit busy lately.

"Remember Strelnikov, the shooter? He was nothing much as

Pasha, Lara's cuckolded fiancé, but as a revolutionary, well, then he was something."

"Feared," João said.

"Zhivago was kidnapped, or, I'd rather say, drafted. You'd know something of that, wouldn't you? I know how Caetano is sweeping up all the doctors who won't run. The Russian was drafted into the service of the revolution, you might remember. A doctor is always of great use, a medic too." He gestured with his head to the wounded man behind him. "We are not as romantic as those Russians, Doctor Gonçalves, no soaring soundtrack or love interests here. But then again, West Africa is not so cold either. It has its advantages."

The guerrilla leader stood slowly and extended his hand to João. Gonçalves stared for a second or two and then took it and allowed this man to help him to his feet.

"Welcome to the revolution, Doctor Gonçalves."

The guerrilla's weapon still leaned against the great wheel of the Unimog, undisturbed. As Gonçalves stood, the fighters loaded the wounded medic onto a stretcher. The motley force receded back into the bush, leaving the stew of corpses for the vultures.

Dear Hans,

You can be dreadfully droll when you want to. It's been some weeks since I received your letter, I must admit. So I write these words with some trepidation: How is Segolaine? What a splendid name, no doubt gorgeous, and probably cast aside already. Alas, what will I ever do with you? "But men are men; the best sometimes forget."

West Africa is so beastly hot, I can scarcely breathe. The movement of this pen is about all I can and should muster. On the other hand, I've probably never been so thin—Twiggy incarnate. They'll be selling package tours to Portuguese Guine at tony West End travel agencies, a sanatorium for the overweight, the only place you can shed a stone in a week without moving a muscle. For an extra few quid, they'll throw in amoebic dysentery to speed the process, two stone in a week with a lasting souvenir—a wrecked intestine—that the customs agents dare not challenge.

I have some time on my hands right now. You'd never believe where I'm living, some strange colonial agricultural station above a tiny, impoverished town called Contuboel. A funny story about that: the Portuguese built the Contubelians their first decent latrines a few months before our arrival here, part of a hearts-and-minds campaign we are fully part of. Quite elaborate, really, the latrines are these closed shacks with deep holes, and a cement chimney of sorts to vent the stench, covered with wire screening. The idea is that the flies that do get into the hole and sully themselves on the contents at the bottom then fly to the light up the chimney. But they can't escape because of the screen. Follow me?

Anyway, the Tugas—that's what the Africans call the Portuguese—told the natives the design would help stop the spread of fecal-borne diseases. This took some doing, apparently. It's difficult to explain how bacteria or viruses can spread from bum to mouth when your audience doesn't really understand the concept of microscopic organisms. Oh yes, they know that flies land on their shit, and they know that flies land on their food. But convincing them that yes, those are the same flies, and that they have little bits of shit on their feet, well, that wasn't so easy. In the end, the Portuguese were satisfied that their message got through. But lo and behold, the villagers don't use the latrines. They save them for the passing white people. When we asked them why, they said the white people have diseased shit. Funny, that, such misunderstandings abound. Remind me to tell you about my escape from the African menagerie that paid me a visit in the shower the other day.

Joao was sent here on assignment. I must confess it was nice to escape from the capital city and the chattering wives on base. I've brought my dear friend and Portuguese teacher, Angélica, with me. She's lovely, Hansy, speaks perfect American English with a Bastan accent, a mocha-skinned Brahman. The good Doctor Goncalves is off on a mission of mercy. He, an armed medic, and a squadron of adorable Portuguese soldiers went off yesterday in this monstrous truck to administer medicinal assistance to the natives that need winning over. You know, it just might work.

Hans, I am feeling good about my decisions now. Life is sometimes bewildering here, but it is exotic. Joao and I have loads of laughs, and I still melt at his touch. I miss him right now, miss gazing into his eyes, so brown they are almost black, miss leaning against his skinny little body. You will get to meet him soon enough. Meantime, say hello to Mum and Dad for me, and Segolaine, if the dear is still about. And write soon.

Your loving sister,
Elizabeth

CHAPTER TEN

"Mum, don't you think you're staying up a little late with David? You have exams coming."

Cristina had come in around twelve thirty, early for her. She wore patterned black tights and sleek high heels, not like Maggie's flats, frankly not like any of the shoes on the feet of the girls I knew. They elongated her legs, which stretched down from a short black skirt. A white peasant shirt hung loosely over her shoulders, but a thin, patent-leather belt cinched it around her thin waist. She pulled off a black beret and sent me a smile that sent blood coursing in a rush through my body.

"You're talking to me about late nights, young lady?" Elizabeth responded playfully.

"I'm young, Mum. I don't need the beauty sleep."

She smiled and batted her eyelashes comically.

"Hey, Cristina, I haven't seen Kelvin around lately," I ventured.

"Oh, he vanished from the scene a while ago," her mother jumped in. "They don't last long."

"It wasn't my fault," Cristina said defensively. "He went back to the States, something to do with basketball, more money there, and some club called the Pistols or the Pistons or something."

"There'll be others," Elizabeth sighed. Her daughter gave her a sweet smile.

"What are you two talking about anyway?"

"Oh, you know, the old war stories."

I was usually a little tongue-tied around Cristina, unless I had scripted out some sort of greeting, and this intrusion was a surprise. So I was maybe a bit proud of my question about her basketball-playing boyfriend and, I must admit, privately tickled by her answer.

"Which old war story now?" she continued.

Elizabeth waved a hand and dropped from her stool, starting toward the sink. Long ago I had figured out that she did not like to talk about Cristina's father around her.

"C'mon, Mum. I don't mind."

"I was talking about your father's capture, in Africa."

"Your old premonitions about death and all?"

"Something like that."

There was a beat of silence.

"David, tell us about your sister."

Elizabeth turned her body abruptly to look at her daughter. She had an odd look of dread on her face, not reproachful but scared, as if some terrible taboo had been broken, as if something frightful had been released. I didn't quite get it—even now, after so long in the UK, British reserve was sometimes inscrutable to me—but I wanted it gone.

"It's OK, Elizabeth. Americans like to talk about such things. We like to talk."

That was true, I guess, broadly speaking, but it wasn't true about me and especially not about Rebecca. I didn't like to talk about her at all, not even with Maggie. It filled me with guilt, about the way I was when I was a kid, about my teenage years spent more or less apart from my parents, and most of all about my distance from them now. I was angry and resentful, but I talked to wipe the panic off Elizabeth's face.

*   *   *

Rebecca Heller, as far as I could remember, was the most responsible child that ever walked the planet. She had curly hair, something she must have gotten from our grandmother. The rest of the family's was straight. And hers was a lighter brown than everyone else's too. She loved telling me and my brother, Noah, what to do, but not in a bossy, lordly way. She was instructive, and we generally listened.

"If you stack the single Lincoln Logs like this, along the two edges of the walls, you can put the window in like this, see?"

"Don't try to put the needle onto the record with your hands. You'll scratch it no matter how careful you are. Use this little arm to lower the needle. See? On the edge of the turntable? It goes down nice and gently, and Dad hates it when you scratch his records."

"With Pong, the little ball gets going faster and faster, so you have to anticipate it. You can't just wait, then move your paddle. That's the trick. As soon as it comes off my paddle, judge the angle and move to it."

"*Three's Company* really isn't appropriate for a nine-year-old, David. You don't get all these jokes, but someday you will and you'll realize I'm right."

I remember her tone during those little lectures—concerned, earnest, but not domineering. She would have made a great teacher.

She was studious, a voracious reader with only a few friends, and they were almost as smart as she was. As the neighborhood boys arranged ourselves in warlike configurations for a pine-cone fight or ducked out to Big Bend Road to throw dirt clots at cars, Rebecca and her friends played with Breyer horses or sat together and read books. She progressed from Nancy Drew to *All Creatures Great and Small* to *Watership Down* to *The Lord of the Rings* to *To Kill a Mockingbird* by fourth grade. As puberty stalked, she became obsessed with the southerners she wanted to claim for her own: Carson McCullers, Flannery O'Connor, Walker Percy, and finally, Faulkner. Her vision had begun to blur and headaches had come on as she read *The Sound and the Fury*.

"That's to be expected," my father had quipped when she pointed this out. "Try something easier, like *Absalom*."

Rebecca was the kind of child parents loved. She relished conversation with adults. When my parents threw parties for their book club or their mixed doubles team, Rebecca enthusiastically offered to take the guests' coats to the neat pile she made on the guest bed upstairs, or bring around plates of smoked salmon and cream cheese on cocktail bread. When she was a little older, she taught herself to mix drinks off the labels on the bottles crammed tight in my parents' bar. There was a dwarf in the book club, an odd, scruffy midget who would pick up and eat the Hickory Farms cheese ball as if it were an apple. Mom always knew he'd come and ruin her cheese ball, the smoked cheddar kind encrusted in walnuts. She bought one anyway and laid it out like an offering to the dwarf. Only Rebecca knew how to talk to him. My brother and I used to spy on them as they chatted, fascinated and a little repulsed.

At her Bat Mitzvah, Rebecca read an essay on the Equal Rights Amendment and recited her Torah portion flawlessly.

"Only you, adults of Georgia, can ensure passage of this vital addition to our nation's Constitution. Only you will have yourselves to blame for failure."

The adults nodded earnestly, lauded her civic-minded liberalism, then ignored her imprecations and voted Republican.

There had been a little glitch on the prayer she led as the Torah ark was closed. The rabbi, she said, had pointed to the wrong spot on the prayer book, and to her regret, she hesitated, looked up at his bearded face, and said, out loud, "Wait a minute, where?" The microphone had picked it up. She was mortified. None of the kids at her party had gotten drunk. The dance floor was crammed with adults.

She had grown gangly by thirteen, a little bucktoothed, with a mouthful of braces to fix that. Truth be told, she was not the most beautiful girl in middle school, but if she minded, she surely didn't confide in us. She religiously applied the prescribed wax to her braces, washed her face with Clearasil, and mixed and matched her V-necked sweaters with her broadcloth button-downs, covering what little breasts she had in cotton and knit wool. In her worst moods, she called us pests and forbade us to come into her room. But those didn't come often, if I recall right. She helped me with math, even when my parents didn't ask her to.

"We call it 'math' in the United States, not 'maths.'"

"But it's short for 'mathematics,'" Cristina protested, "so 'maths.'"

"Americans aren't quite so literal," I assured her. "'Math' is just shorter. Anyway, Rebecca would tell me, 'David, don't worry. I don't like math either.' That made me feel a lot better."

The headaches came suddenly, then blackouts if she stood too quickly. My father, once he gave up on his Faulknerian diagnosis, figured at worst it was mono, but Rebecca was not a complainer, so her complaints held grave weight. I woke one night to her wailing. It was piteous and searching and begging for mercy. I crawled out of bed, terrified, to peek into her room, hoping to glean some of the comfort my mother was trying to dispense. She was lying with my sister in her single bed, holding her tight, stroking her flyaway hair and shushing her in a soft, soft voice as Rebecca's body convulsed in sobs. I fell back to sleep in the hallway, to the sound of my mother whispering, "Try not to think about the pain, shh, try, try, try."

The next day, my father took her to one of his oldest friends, who happened to be a neurologist. The man, who had gone to medical school with my dad, didn't want to believe what he saw. He stared at the dilated veins in the back of my sister's eyes. He tested and retested her reflexes, agonized over the X-rays. Before MRIs were commonplace, he gave Rebecca one. He stared at the results, trying to find alternate explanations. Then he did what he had to do. He told his best friend that his eldest child, his only daughter, would likely die of brain cancer, soon.

I was not party to much of her treatment. I know she had surgery because half her head was shaved, showing me the sutures binding the purple wound. I know she was pumped with a medication that swelled her head so much she was barely recognizable. Her eyes sunk in the folds of puffy flesh and peered out from deep, cushioned caverns. Her mouth was a tiny, useless tear between the obscene orbs that her cheeks had become. Her lips were two adjoining lines of raw, weeping sores. Her jawline was buried in rubbery jowls that folded downward like a cartoonish frown. The sight of her frightened me terribly. My parents never told us she was dying.

Rebecca loved art. She tried her hand at it, took drawing and tempera painting classes at a friend of a friend's house after school, painted animals on canvas in thick, gloppy oil. She wasn't very good at it, and she knew it, and she took that with good humor too, because she was good at plenty of other things. If her literature was precocious, her taste in the visual arts was pure thirteen-year-old girl—Renoir, Van Gogh, and Monet, lots of Monet—to go along with her music, Olivia Newton-John, "Afternoon Delight," and "Seasons in the Sun."

"We had joy, we had fun, we had seasons in the sun, but the stars we could reach were just starfish on the beach."

We played the music in her hospital room on a portable record player—"Good-bye my friend, it's hard to die"—and plastered her room with posters of the water lilies of Giverny, boating parties, and starry nights. She could no longer read, so my mother read to her— not the ending of *The Sound and the Fury* but *The Runaway Bunny*.

"'If you become a rock on the mountain high above me,' said his mother, 'I will be a mountain climber, and I will climb to where you are.'"

We no longer knew whether Rebecca could hear or understand, but my mother kept reading. She was sure she could.

"'If you become a crocus in a hidden garden,' said his mother, 'I will be a gardener. And I will find you.'"

She was reading the moment my sister slipped from this world— and took with her my mother and father, who could not bear to stay behind.

"'If you become a little boy and run into a house,' said the mother bunny, 'I will become your mother and catch you in my arms and hug you.'"

My older brother, just twelve, took down all the posters of all those Impressionists who have made me sick ever since. They are in my closet, at home in Georgia, and my parents are asking me to come back. They think I want them. They say they will be there when I return, all of them.

"'If you become a bird and fly away from me,' said his mother, 'I will be a tree that you come home to.'"

Elizabeth stood in silence, leaning against the kitchen counter and staring at the floor. I wiped my eyes, and sniffed, but the tears kept coming. Cristina's hands gently reached for mine and held them. She was crying too. Finally, she leaned over and kissed my cheek, her lips lingering on a tear track.

CHAPTER ELEVEN

The world doesn't change with the death of a child. Children die every day. The world changes with the changing minds of Great Men. António de Spínola's mind had changed, and he began writing by candle-light the book that would change his nation forever. Electric power in Bissau had become intermittent, much to his shame. Saboteurs, guerrilla rockets, and the occasional lucky mortar round were taking their toll on the capital of Guiné. Caetano's junta in Lisbon, and the decrepit president of the republic, Admiral Américo Thomaz, knew nothing of PAIGC shelling, or the Neto trail, named after the intellectual revolutionary hoping to lead a new nation, that burrowed deep into Angola from guerrilla training camps in Zambia, or rebel sabotage on the rails linking Beira in Mozambique to Rhodesia.

The old cavalry officer sighed through his pen—the age of heroics was coming to an end. He strained his eyes in the dim light as he authored *Portugal e o Futuro*, "Portugal and the Future." He recalled the carnage of Leningrad, the triumph of Franco, his own rise through the ranks of the Portuguese armed forces, and then looked around at the dimly lit corners of his study, where mold grew on the ceiling and slime rose from the baseboards.

"We are exhausting ourselves in a war that cannot be won. We are defending the wrong foundations of the nation," he wrote. "We cannot admit that many Portuguese lose their lives today with the only effect that still more will die tomorrow. In this war, we are fighting for ideals that neither are moral nor serve the people."

The Portuguese expeditionary force in Guiné now totaled one soldier for every fifteen civilians. The future of Portugal lay in Europe, not in empire, he wrote, yet how could our little, isolated country of eight million souls join our continental brethren when half our national expenditures go to support the armed forces and their wars? Offer our African brethren true equality. Let them decide their future, as true citizens of Portugal or as autonomous states nominally under our flag. And let our boys return home.

The helicopters rumbled into earshot as Elizabeth Gonçalves was finishing her second Nescafé with Angélica and Luis, the bread man. She had let herself sleep in a bit that morning. She had been married five months and was nearing only her twenty-first birthday. But already it was strange sleeping alone, with the stirrings of a new life inside her, even stranger waking up alone in West Africa.

Luis had given her a big smile that morning. Responsible for the frequent forays by jeep into Senegal for baguettes from the town of Kolda, or the much bigger city of Ziguinchor if he was feeling profligate with the station's money, Luis had taken a fancy to Elizabeth and had pressed her for a few English lessons. Unsteady in João's presence, now he was jovial.

"Penis butter, ees good." He laughed, holding up a giant tin of peanut butter the Portuguese had carted in from Bissau. A loud peel of laughter rose from the only other English speaker in the room, Angélica. Elizabeth looked at her, and they laughed together. Luis had no idea why, but he joined in.

The thumping of the rotors drew Elizabeth from her seat. The armada came into view, flying low on the horizon from the west. There were four Alouette IIIs, the kind of choppers Raquel Brito had told Elizabeth her husband coveted for his *Páraquedistas Caçadores*—"Hunter Paratroops"—and two American Hueys marked with large red crosses on white fields. As they roared by the agricultural station, Elizabeth could see the gunners clearly in their open doors, their weapons and eyes trained on the ground.

The radioman in João's patrol had not had time to make contact with Bissau, but the distress signal was alarm enough. They had radioed in their position the night before and could not have gotten far on the roads of northern Guiné that early in the morning. The helicopters found what they were looking for quickly. Weapons, provisions, medical supplies, and medicines were all taken. But the jeeps and the medical truck were left behind, intact. The PAIGC moved by stealth, not by car. The vultures fled as the helicopters landed, and what was left of the soldiers was transported back to Bissau. There was no sign of the doctor or the medic.

Elizabeth knew the air patrol had something to do with her husband, and it set her fantasies spinning into dangerous territory. She sat down in the shade of the palaver hut, a wall-less, thatched-roof structure where the staff came to talk over assignments and catch the occasional Guinean breeze. *João could be dead*, she thought. If her husband was killed in action, surely the Portuguese military would see her safely back to Britain. It was a rash and guilt-inducing thought, and she scorned herself immediately for it, but it had come quickly, this fantasy of widowhood. This was war after all, she indulged. She could be back at her parents' estate within days. Daddy would arrange for a good Tory abortion in London and a convalescence at Houndsheath. She would look for a way to London and a use for her strange education. This little adventure would be like a dream; it would linger in her mind, fading over time, but would have no real impact on the course of her life. How strange a chapter of her life: Such momentous happenings could end up having so little import, she thought, clinically, soberly.

It was not until the next day that she learned the details of her husband's disappearance and presumed capture. Aleixo Menges asked if he might have a word with her. Her Portuguese was good enough to leave Angélica behind. If Menges ran into trouble, he could muster his own limited English.

"It has to do with the helicopters from yesterday, doesn't it?" Elizabeth started in.

"Yes, Elizabeth. There was an ambush. They tried to call for help, but the helicopters were too late. When they arrived, João was not there. There were a lot of bodies, a lot of death. All of the soldiers, but João was not there."

"Could he have escaped, run away? Could he have somehow been left behind?"

"Maybe, we'll have to see. He had spent the previous night with villagers nearby. Perhaps they protected him. But this was a big force that attacked, very efficient. By the looks of the mess, it didn't take long. A surprise assault in Fula country. The medic, Augusto, wasn't found either. I believe he and João were probably captured. All of the medical supplies were taken from the truck. They would want the doctors as well."

Elizabeth remembered books and movies where war widows fainted or wailed or beat the chest of the uniformed messenger at the door bearing the bad news. She wondered why she was not overwhelmed, but she was not. It was an embarrassing thought. She stared down at the dirty floor beneath Menges's flimsy folding chair, noticing the scuffs on the floor around the legs, which scraped the ground with bare, rough metal. They sat in silence for a long while, Menges waiting for a response, some sign that would tell him to comfort her or to leave her alone. Nothing came.

So he spoke again. "Elizabeth, I am sorry, but you and Angélica must leave here. You will be better off in Bissau waiting for word of João. There is nothing for you here."

"But I must wait for him. If he escaped, he's nearby. I should be here if he finds his way back, or if he's found." She strained to enunciate the words, not just because she was translating from English to Portuguese but because she did not believe them. João was gone. This place seemed suddenly absurd. She didn't want to be here, with the mambas and the dead bats and the big, empty bed. She wanted to be home, in England.

"Elizabeth, if João is found, he won't come back here. He'll go to Bissau as well. I'm not even sure I can stay much longer. What happened to that patrol is not supposed to happen here. It's no longer safe."

Menges reached over to Elizabeth, draping his left arm clumsily around her back, his hand squeezing a shoulder, his head leaning toward hers, their knees touching. It was not for her benefit. He was seeking her comfort. "I always thought this day would come," he said softly. She leaned a little forward to put her forehead gently against his. Her hand, which had lain inert in her lap, moved to his thigh. His free hand moved to hers. Their hearts raced. It had been a very long time since he had touched a woman. She felt for the first time the sinful thrill of adulterous possibility. But they went no further.

José Mendes de Farinha was only seventeen when he went underground in Luanda, hunted by the secret police as a boy radical. He had been Spínola's ideal, an *assimilado*, educated in the best Catholic schools in Angola to aspire to be a true citizen of Lusitania. But he was swept up in the liberation movements all around him, egged on by the Jesuit priests who ran the schools and the mestiços chafing at the falsehood of their alleged equality. Comrade Henda, they called him at the meetings held in dark basements or back rooms of the lovely seaside city in the midst of a furious revival fueled by newfound oil to the north. On the run, he found his way to Kinshasa, where Mobutu was an inconsistent patron of the Angolan revolution, then to Cabral in Conakry.

Now he and his men were punching through Fula country, absolving liberated villages of their debts to the colonialists and freeing their farmers from the hated cash crops the Portuguese demanded. The PAIGC would extract their tributes eventually, but first they would take just a chicken or two. They would try to traipse lightly.

This ambush had been good for that. They had rice and provisions now. The medicine they would keep for the base, along with the services of this whining doctor. It was no secret why Spínola was bringing doctors to Guiné; hearts-and-minds campaigns could go two ways. But this skinny conscript couldn't even pick up a weapon. His boots hadn't even been broken in. He was limping from the blisters. What kind of training did the Portuguese even offer? At this rate, it would take them a week to get back to the base outside Kolda.

"You speak perfect Portuguese, not Kriolu," João said, wincing at the pain in his boots but trying to tone it down, mindful of his obvious physical inferiority.

"Good Catholic education," Farinha said.

"In Bissau?"

"Luanda. There is no education in Bissau."

"Angola? You're a very long way from home."

Farinha was silent as they walked on through the narrow track skirting the forest. He was trying to decide whether to engage this man or treat him like a prisoner. The wounded friend was already a horrible burden. Two men had to carry him. Other men were carrying their packs and weapons. He should have just shot him.

"What is your rank, Doctor Gonçalves, so I can address you as a military man?"

"Major. But don't. I'm a doctor. Do you want my serial number?"

"Do you want mine?" Farinha asked.

"I'd like your name."

"José Mendes de Farinha, but you'll hear everyone call me Henda. Don't ask why."

"Nom de guerre?"

"You speak French too?" Farinha grumbled.

João shuffled on. He was finding it difficult to navigate the ruts in the trail. His boots were killing him. The short walk from his quarters to the clinic and back had not softened them at all. No one had given him any tips on the matter, any training really at all. He was on the first forced march of his life, and the only other Portuguese military man was on a stretcher, barely conscious and probably heading into shock.

"Where are we going?"

"Now you're looking for sensitive information, Doctor Gonçalves. But it will be no news to your Spínola to learn we are heading into Senegal."

João's head was swimming. He was exhausted and scared, still processing all that had transpired.

"Do you mind if I ask how you won over that Fula man, Sabally? I should not have been surprised, I guess, but I was. His welcome seemed so genuine last night."

"It was genuine. Muslims regard hospitality as a religious duty. Trust me, it was nothing personal."

"But what does he care about the PAIGC or the Portuguese? We've hardly touched his life. That village hasn't changed for centuries. When he catches a glimpse of the Portuguese, it's a patrol passing by or someone like me, dispensing medicine. What do you have to offer?"

Farinha shrugged his shoulders with exaggerated insouciance. He wanted his message to get through without turning around.

"Do you really want to have this conversation?"

"Yes," João responded. "Yes, I do. I've been in this country for four months. I've had one semi-meaningful exchange with a Guinean, wounded in battle and in my hospital. Otherwise, the natives take my medicine and my advice in silence and shuffle away."

"I'm not a Guinean."

"You'll have to do."

"Doctor Gonçalves, are you from Lisbon?"

"Yes, I am."

"I've been there, you know. Boring. When you look around you, at the cafés of Paris, the clubs in London, even at the political turmoil and excitement or tragedy in West and East Germany, do you feel like your benighted little corner of Europe has been left out? Do you feel like you're looking into the window of a party that you weren't invited to?"

He paused. The question was not meant to be rhetorical, but João didn't answer.

"You are the joke of Europe, the last empire with nothing to show for it. London swings. Lisbon, what, languishes? You won't put up with that forever. At some point, the young people will want some decent live music."

He chuckled at that. Even in the worst of times, Africa bursts with musical joy. A nation devoid of such rapture was to be pitied.

"I don't see why insulting my country has much to do with our conversation."

"No? Doctor Gonçalves, this is one thing we have in common. We are the jokes of Africa. We're like the dog that gets kicked by the runty kid who's bullied by his father. Humiliation trickles downhill.

"Kwame Nkrumah declared Ghana independent of Britain fourteen years ago. Fourteen years," Farinha continued, his voice starting to rise. He had intended to keep his cool, to preserve his energy. But he was always amazed how clueless the Portuguese were. "Ghana has already had time to see its first African leader rise, fail, and be deposed by a coup d'état. Your governor, Spínola, meets secretly with Léopold Senghor, who has been president of independent Senegal for more than a decade. It's true. I'd love to be a fly on the wall for those meetings. Senghor has ruled for more than a decade, and we're still suffering under the colonial control of a two-bit nation that peaked four hundred years ago."

" 'Suffer' is a strong word. Do you believe it?"

"Doctor Gonçalves, you are not a very good listener, are you? Independence for a country like Guiné, even Angola, may not mean wealth or development. I'm not a fool. I can see the fighting that will follow. It might not even mean freedom. The Russians, the Cubans, the Chinese, they're all licking their chops. But we have our pride. We are surrounded on all sides by independent nations. Senghor and Sékou Touré in Guinea may not have done much for their people, but they are proud men. Kaunda in Zambia, Kenyatta, Nyerere in Tanzania too. That pride does not recognize the borders drawn up in the back rooms of London and Paris and Lisbon. They tell us to rise up, and our failure to do so only makes us feel worse.

Your presence is a daily humiliation, whether you give us medicine or the heel of your boot. We will win our independence to relieve ourselves of embarrassment. It's as simple as that.

"In the meantime," he concluded, "I'd suggest you save your strength. You'll have some patients to attend to soon."

"Ah, Senhora Gonçalves." António de Spínola rose ostentatiously from the table. He was in his finery: white gloves, monocle, even the jodhpurs of the cavalryman he was. Elizabeth was joining him in a darkened dining room off the main officers' mess on base. She still had not seen the governor's palace. She wore the same flowered dress she had worn when João and she dined with the governor on their first night in the country. But Spínola seemed like a different man, weary and miserable despite the costume.

"Senhor Governor, my husband..."

Spínola raised his gloved hand to silence her.

"I know of João's capture. I have no doubt that he is safe, Elizabeth. He is with one of Cabral's most capable lieutenants, a man named Farinha, all the way from Angola. They have probably made it back to Senegal by now."

Elizabeth was incredulous.

"If you know this, why don't you do something?" she demanded.

"Elizabeth, intelligence is one thing; action is quite another. We learn much from our spies in the countryside, but not always because they want to help us. More often than not, they are taunting us. They are letting us know how helpless we are. I don't have João's exact location. That, I'm sure, is by design. The base they will be heading for is in the Senegalese Casamance, south of the Gambia, outside the town of Kolda. My friend President Senghor will make sure João is protected, but he will make sure the base is protected as well."

"General Spínola, what am I to do?" Elizabeth pleaded. Her brave face was already crumbling at what she saw as the general's indifference. "This is my husband you're talking about. He doesn't even know I am pregnant."

It just slipped out. No one knew she was pregnant but her, and now the governor and commanding general of Guiné. She reddened with embarrassment.

She was there not exactly on a mission, more like a quest for absolution, for self-forgiveness. Her convoy had rumbled onto the main base in Bissau three days before; the scene that had greeted her on her arrival in the country had repeated itself tediously: the Guinean women ironing out the botflies, the aimless milling of young Portuguese men, the heat and dust. It was annoying somehow in its changelessness. On cue, Paula Pelegrin, Ana Aveiro, and Raquel Brito showed at her door within minutes to express their concern over João's disappearance and offer up what gossip they had. Of course, she was the best gossip of all. A doctor had been captured. What on earth had he been doing? How did he get himself into this predicament? The women pressed her for details, her limited Portuguese frustrating their demands.

"I'm sure you are doing everything you can to get your husband back," Paula said with feigned admiration.

"Yes, of course," Elizabeth said with a serious look.

In fact, she had not done a thing to secure her husband's freedom or even ascertain his whereabouts. She thought of those potboiler stories in the newspapers of mothers who moved heaven and earth to find their missing children; the Christian wives of arrested Berlin Jews, holding public vigils and protests to confront the Nazis and free their husbands; Antigone, defying King Creon to bury her brother Polynices; Henry at Agincourt; "fight till the last gasp."

She was no hero, but she could make an effort. She would seek an audience with the governor. No sooner had she put out the word than a dinner invitation had arrived from the governor's mansion for the next evening.

"Congratulations are in order." He smiled, raising a glass of red wine. "This is wonderful news. I am sure your parents will be thrilled."

"And my husband? Will he be thrilled? Can your friend Mr. Senghor get word to him?"

"Elizabeth, is it really so bad that these freedom fighters have the service of a good doctor for a few months? Guiné is lost, my dear. João is safely behind the lines now. The food is better in Senegal anyway, but he will be in Bissau soon enough, watching his comrades hail Amílcar Cabral's ascension to the governor's palace. I assume it will be called the presidential palace or some such thing. They can have it. As empire recedes, your husband will wash up unharmed on the beach."

Spínola paused to take a deep drag from a cigarette, stub it out, and light another. A veil of smoke obscured his lined face for a moment, then cleared. Elizabeth sat silently and watched, feeling hopeless and alone.

"Ah, senhora, I can see the impatience on your face. I'll have a word with Senghor, see if he can have your husband released. But it's not really in my hands, as you can see," he continued, his palms and shoulders raised in exaggerated helplessness. "Elizabeth, I'll let you in on something. I'll be gone from here soon. I have been recalled to Lisbon. Someone is not happy with the state of things in Bissau."

The general looked at his hands, sheathed in white calfskin, then into Elizabeth's eyes. This was not how it was supposed to end for him. He had failed. But there was no one to pity him. "My advice, if you want it: I would suggest you await word from your husband from wherever you call home in the United Kingdom."

During the general's monologue, a tuxedoed waiter had entered silently and laid a plate of prawns in tomato sauce in front of Elizabeth, with a glass of red wine. Only the overcooked macaroni divulged the meal's African origins. Elizabeth now sat in silence. She was not about to make small talk about West African geopolitics with the most decorated military officer in the Portuguese *ultramar*. She couldn't, even if she had wanted to. After four months in Africa, she was still an uneducated, inexperienced child of wealth and neglect.

Spínola stood and smiled down on her beneficently. "Senhora

Gonçalves, if you will excuse me, I have duties to attend to. I know it's rude of me, but please, enjoy your meal. I will make sure that Renato Araujo looks after you, should you decide to stay. He can make arrangements for your return to Britain as well. Is your friend, the Cabo-Verdiana, still with you?"

"Angélica." Elizabeth nodded without meeting his eyes.

As he opened the door, he turned back for a moment. "I'm writing a book. I'll make sure you get a copy."

Elizabeth ate alone, absorbing the silence. The prawns were delicious.

It was three months before João worked up the courage to speak to Farinha about his captivity. The commander wasn't an easy man to track down. He led forays into Guiné, consulted with superiors at a larger base outside Ziguinchor, and occasionally made the long, circuitous trip to Conakry when Cabral summoned his leadership. At times, he played host to a Cuban or Algerian goodwill delegation bringing supplies and best wishes. He was the model of the disciplined guerrilla commander, not yet thirty, not even Guinean. João liked to think they had something in common.

If João had expected the guerrillas to be living in squalor, he was disappointed. The base outside Kolda was tidy and well provisioned, under the protection of the Senegalese government, stocked by the Cubans and armed by the Soviets and Czechoslovakians. As promised, he was treated that first day to a warm baguette, but that proved to be nothing special. It was a staple of the base, served at breakfast, lunch, and dinner. His most difficult patient was the medic, Augusto, who was recuperating slowly. The other combat wounds João saw were mostly superficial. More dire combat casualties were left on the battlefield to be treated by Araujo and his medical corps in Bissau.

"Very useful, that hospital." Farinha had chuckled when he explained where the real trauma patients were heading.

"But they don't let the guerrillas return to the battlefield," João protested. "If they recover, they're taken away to Angola or Mozambique."

Farinha laughed.

"Some, yes, but we've had plenty of escapes from the hospital. Besides, our comrades could use them in Angola and Mozambique."

João kept himself occupied with an odd variety of respiratory problems—hacking coughs, shortness of breath—and strange skin ailments, all from the increasing use of defoliants. João thought of the bats. They would be someone else's problem when these strange maladies turned into cancer down the line. There wasn't much he could do. It was of no real medical consequence that he had gone to see the commander.

"José," the doctor started. His voice quavered—not too much, he hoped. He didn't fear what the commander might do to him for his impertinence. He feared what he was doing to himself, the humiliation of the supplicant.

Farinha looked up from a metal desk, surprised by the familiarity. It was the kind of desk you would see in a schoolroom, functional and ugly, beneath Farinha's dignity, João thought. Farinha didn't seem to care.

"I have not spoken of my personal situation. I hope you don't mind if I plead my case now. I have a young wife."

"In Africa?" Farinha asked.

"At the agriculture station in Contuboel," João said. "At least, that's where I left her. I couldn't say where she is now. I dragged her into this. I married her and brought her to Guiné. She's British. She has nothing to do with any of this."

The fingers of Farinha's hands laced together. He swung his body to the side and crossed his long legs, smiling.

"Are you petitioning for your release, Doctor Gonçalves, or would you like us to capture your wife for you?"

João stood in sheepish silence, looking from his feet to the man behind the desk, then back to his feet.

"Do you think your personal life is of any interest to me? You are

rendering valuable service. We dragged your friend from the battlefield on a stretcher instead of putting a bullet in his head. He still
hasn't done a thing to repay the favor."

Farinha gave him a withering stare. "You are not going anywhere."

João's head bowed.

"Can I get a word to her then, through the Red Cross? I am a
prisoner of war. I have rights." The words may have been defiant,
but they were spoken almost apologetically. João felt like the pampered bourgeois doctor's son that he was. He had nothing to plead
but his young wife, not heroism, not service, not threat. In captivity,
his thoughts of Elizabeth had swung wildly from carnal to affection-
ate, to distrustful, to contemptuous. One moment he was imagining
his head lying on her chest, her fingers gently combing through his
hair, or her head moving deliberately back and forth as he watched
and moaned. The next instant, his thoughts flashed to the same
scenes but it was a different man her hands or mouth would be caressing. Menges, perhaps, with his little glasses folded neatly on the
bedside table, or maybe Luis, the bread man. Come to think of it,
she did spend inordinate amounts of time with him. João would lie
in his bunk, seething. She would not have waited for him. Of course
not. She was likely already gone from the continent altogether.

Farinha had no wife. He was, thought João, a better man for
that. Presumably he had a mother or some semblance of a family in
Luanda, but that was a million miles away. He was unencumbered
by any of these thoughts, the tender, lustful, or sinister.

"You probably don't realize how many of your countrymen we
hold captive in Conakry. The Portuguese send spies, commandos,
sometimes warplanes to see if they can free them. It hasn't worked
yet. But we have their attention down there. Here, we don't need
attention. For all I know, you are presumed dead. We have heard
nothing from your army or your governor about you. And we have
channels, through Dakar and Senghor."

He fell quiet, seemingly tired out by the conversation. His eyes
drifted to a few papers scattered on the desk.

"Get out," Farinha said quietly, waving a hand as if he was shooing a fly. "Don't you have something more important to attend to?"

João shuffled out, with nothing to show for his efforts but mortification. The medic, Augusto, was no more sympathetic. Unlike João, he was a real soldier. He wanted João to be free, but free on Portuguese terms. It was his duty to escape, he told João. Augusto was not well enough, not yet. But João was being used to aid the enemy. If he did not have the fortitude to withhold his services, he could at least try to get out of there. João listened as Augusto chastised him, thinking it was all nonsense. He promised he would try if the chance presented itself.

"Make it present itself," Augusto growled.

The explosions knocked João from his bed, concussive, pounding blasts that felt like they were shaking his brain. There were orders being barked, screams of fear and of pain, the twisting of metal. A fighter's body stood upright and bleeding, impaled on a crossbeam that had torn from the Quonset hut's frame. His head was half blown off. João lay on the ground, covering himself as best he could but looking at the body. He was fascinated by it, by the head wound, which looked like a cross section from medical school, only wrought with a meat-ax. He wondered if he would be better off outside.

"What the fuck are you doing?"

He heard the shout through the smoke. Portuguese, not Kriolu. Augusto was cursing him again.

"Get the fuck out of here, Gonçalves. This is your chance. Go."

It took a moment for João to understand the medic was serious. It was chaos in the predawn gloom. The guerrillas who had not found shelter were dead or wounded. The planes had dropped their bombs in one run but were returning to strafe.

"I'll die if I go out there," João shouted back.

"What makes you think you won't die in here?"

A long moment passed. The whiz of bullets, clatter of AK-47s, *pop pop* of handguns, screams of pain, shouts of orders and anger, all of it resolved into a background roar. The dashing Colonel Almeida Brito and his Esquadrão 121 had attacked the base with merciless efficiency, a last gasp from Bissau like an aerial Battle of the Bulge— inflict as much damage as possible before inevitable defeat. João imagined himself elsewhere, in the bed of his boyhood, at his clinic in the Algarve, cradled in Elizabeth's thighs.

"Go!" Augusto bellowed.

So João ran. He ran out of guilt and shame, disappointment and loneliness, a sense of responsibility, a fear of abandonment. He didn't even know if she'd be there. She could have abandoned him months ago, rejoined her parents in England. In his four-odd months of captivity, that's what he had figured, that this marriage of his had long since dissolved.

The grounds of the base were glowing from fires that burned dully. There was not much to ignite but some grass and a few primitive wooden structures. The Quonset huts erected by the Cubans looked like an industrialist's rendition of *Guernica*, a mass of twisted metal. João had plenty of light to escape, but he was fairly certain he could remain unseen in the chaos.

After only a few hundred yards, he was clear of the base. There were no gates, no perimeter fences. He probably could have managed this escape months ago. Once clear of the battlefield noise, he stopped and sat beneath a banyan tree to catch his breath. He had no idea where he was or where to go. Guiné was only a few miles to the south, he was sure. But his white skin would be more of a liability in the Portuguese war zone than it would in Senegal. He might be taken for a Frenchman here, maybe even a tourist who had wandered a little far afield from the beaches at Cap Skirring. He would at least not be a threat. He had penicillin and aspirin in his pockets, as always. He could trade it for food perhaps, find his way to the capital of the Casamance, Ziguinchor, and from there, get word to Bissau.

He was far too close to the ruined base for comfort, so he started walking away from it, hoping for the best. Within minutes, he stumbled into a group of market women who eyed him warily but said nothing. He fell into line behind them, on a road better than any he had seen in Guiné beyond the capital. On their heads, they balanced tubs of vegetables bound for a market that had to be large. Kolda, João reasoned.

As it turned out, the market at Kolda was close, maybe another kilometer. It was open and bustling. Portuguese aircraft had bombed the countryside just hours before, but the Senegalese appeared to pay no mind. That might as well have been happening in a different country, on a different continent. João ducked into a bakery to trade some medicine for bread. It was a small, one-roomed cement building with a colorful, hand-painted sign outside showing a brightly festooned woman holding a bouquet of baguettes. They looked like an arrangement of phalluses splayed out before her smiling face. João's French was good. Most of Lisbon's educated spoke French. He figured he could hold his own inside the store. Only his now-faded and beaten fatigues made him nervous.

But before he began to barter, something caught his eye. A man was speaking rapid-fire Fulani, buying dozens of loaves of bread. João stared in disbelief. Even from behind, he recognized him, something about the way he seemed to be laughing as he talked, his shoulders pulsing up and down joyfully. He was shelling out money with great disregard. It was obviously not his.

"Luis?" João asked tentatively.

The man spun around, then broke into a blinding smile. João had a full, bushy beard now. He had tried to keep his hair combed, but it hung down to his shoulders. Luis recognized him immediately. He took the few steps that separated them in the tiny shop and threw his arms around him. The bread man of Contuboel—there must be a God.

CHAPTER TWELVE

It was past one a.m., and the windshield wipers swatted feebly at the mist that was enveloping me in panic. I was in the dreary southern outskirts of London, driving Hans's oversized blue "ambulance" van. The road signs loomed up in the fog like pop-up targets on a shooting range. Hans's wheelchair was locked in over my left shoulder. They didn't design this thing to have him ride shotgun. I could sense his anxiety growing, even if I couldn't see him.

"I've got this, Hans. Really, go to sleep."

"I can't sleep in my bed. How do you think I'm going to sleep with your driving?"

His words sounded slurred and breathy, like a whisper. They matched the soft rain that enshrouded the streetlights. It was spitting, as the British said. Like Eskimos with all their words for snow, the British had lots of words for rain: spitting, pissing, soft. *Odd*, I thought of his tone; Hans had been breathy before, but he usually grumbled with gusto. Still, I couldn't argue with the sentiment.

March was proving to be no better than February, when the damp of England seeps through the lousy insulation and soaks you to the bone. Only in May can you finally warm up. For Hans, though, winter was lifting; March was within smelling distance of summer and Tuscany—what he lived for.

James and Wills had scored two tickets to *La Traviata* at the

Royal Opera House. James took ill, and Wills decided to give the tickets to Hans. Without a third, the poor man had no choice but to spend the evening with me solo, throw those pearls before the swine. I liked to think of myself as a sophisticate—literature, symphony, art, films—but opera was beyond me. I found it dreadfully boring.

Elizabeth, nervous about the excursion, had seen to it that we had given ourselves plenty of time. I began hoisting Hans out of his bed at four o'clock, rolling him onto one shoulder, pushing the canvas under his body, rolling over the other shoulder, harnessing him in, hooking up the winch, and lifting him from the bed.

"Watch out, David, watch the catheter," he shouted as I lunged to stop the winch. I had forgotten to unhook the urine bag, a potentially lethal mistake, or at least a messy one. Even with no nerves, he could sense the tug on his cock. Don't ask me how.

"Sorry, sorry, sorry," I said, flustered at making such a basic mistake after so long.

"David, really, are you up to this?" Elizabeth asked. She had been leaning against the doorway, watching the process. Now she was standing bolt upright.

"Yes, yes, I'm sorry. I'm, I'm looking forward to it."

"You're a really bad liar."

In truth, my mind wasn't on my work. I was worried about my parents and their increasingly insistent letters begging me home, feeling conflicting obligations toward them, Maggie, and the Bromwells. It was spring now. I had made it through the Brighton winter, which was an accomplishment. Maybe it was time to go.

I bundled Hans into his coyote-fur straitjacket, carefully tucked the coyote throw on his lap, gave his thinning, dull hair another comb-over, and began wheeling him backward from the room, through the front door and onto the stoop. Elizabeth offered a steadying hand but not much strength as I tilted her brother back down the ramp that covered half the front steps. It was one of the more unfortunate design flaws of the house, but houses were not built for quadriplegics in the nineteenth century. It brought the two of them into closer contact than I had seen for some time. They didn't exchange a word.

We were on our way far too early, just past four thirty, going against the traffic, north into London. Even driving at the dawdling speed Hans demanded, I made it to the opera house in less than two hours. A colony of homeless men, women, and children greeted us at the car park. Thatcherism was at its most dangerous stage of breaking the welfare state, tough love with no economic growth to absorb the casualties. The Iron Lady was staying the course, regardless. Her voters were perfectly happy with the state of affairs, their taxes dropping, dirt-cheap shares of formerly state-run enterprises like British Airways falling into their laps. Amid the human detritus of the age, Hans seemed only mildly more pathetic than the rest of humanity.

I drove past their vacant stares. No one stuck out a cup or asked for money in any way. As I unlatched the wheelchair, lowered the ramp, and backed Hans down, no one jeered at his furs. They just watched me wheel the corpse to the elevators, perfectly civil.

"C'mon Hans, I'll buy you a beer," I said as the doors opened on the broad, brightly lit foyer of the opera house. "Are you hungry?"

"Not for anything here." Hans sniffed.

There weren't many people milling around this early, but there was beer to be had. I ordered Hans a half pint of bitter. I took the full deal. This was a mistake. If I was to help Hans sip his beer, I had to put mine down. With no place to sit and no tables in the hall, that meant putting a full pint on the closely cropped carpet.

"American," I imagined all the Londoners thinking to themselves as I picked my beer off the floor for a sip.

I made small talk with Hans for what seemed like an eternity. "How long have you been going to the opera?" "Tell me something about *La Traviata*." "Not a bad drive in." "Do you like Verdi? I've always liked *The Four Seasons*."

"That's Vivaldi," he said wearily. "David, are we on a date? Why all these questions? You're exhausting me."

"Sorry," I mumbled, as an elegantly dressed woman entered the picture.

I assumed Hans knew her. He looked up and smiled, seemingly in recognition as she gave him an effusive "Well heellllooo."

"Hello to you," Hans said cheerfully. He sounded like someone wracking his brain for the name of someone he clearly once knew but couldn't place.

She wore a long, sequined black dress, accordion pleats swishing at her ankles, with a little patent-leather bag whose gold chain draped across her shoulder. Her face was pleasant enough, if wrinkled and fiftyish.

"Going to the opera?" she asked-stated.

"Obviously," Hans said.

This is where I expected Hans to ask, "Oh, where is so-and-so?" or, "Your husband couldn't make it?"—some hint of recognizing her personal status. Instead, he stared up at her blankly.

"So what happened to you?" she blurted out, running her eyes over his body and then shooting him an expectant, quizzical gaze, as if she was saying, "Now this ought to be good."

I snapped out of my disinterested observation. This woman, I realized, was a total stranger.

"Broke my neck, my dear, snapped it right at the base of my skull. How do you like that?"

"Really," she replied enthusiastically. "How did it happen, darling?"

Hans glanced at me beseechingly. I had never seen such a look of need from him, not levitating dangerously in his winch, not even when the hippie was hell-bent on stripping him of his coyote skins.

"Hans, I think I see Wills over there, at the end of the foyer," I said, quickly swinging him around and sending my beer spilling onto the woman's strappy feet.

She danced away from the cold fizz, cursing the Yank as Hans was saying, "Ah yes, I think I see him as well." We made our getaway cleanly, leaving our guest angrily shaking a foot as she made her way back to the bar for a handful of cocktail napkins.

"My God, that was ghastly," Hans said with relief.

He looked up at me. He didn't quite have the dexterity to swivel his head around enough to meet my eyes, but he tried. I was touched.

"I don't see how you put up with stuff like that, Hans."

"David, I put up with a lot worse than that. In the house, two pretty young things wipe my arse every morning and insert a tube into my pecker. And I know their names. That's humiliation."

I smiled.

"Tell me about Cristina."

"Why? Are we on a date?"

He smiled.

"No, David. How is she? She's becoming a woman. I'm not blind. What kind of woman will she be?"

"An exceedingly attractive one, I should think." I thought that would do the trick, but Hans looked at me expectantly.

"I don't know, Hans. She's very self-assured. She has a thousand times the confidence I had when I was her age. I can't imagine anything really holding her back if she puts her mind to something."

Then I paused. "Except maybe Elizabeth, you know?"

"How do you mean?"

"I don't think Cristina would abandon her mother. They're such a team."

Hans sat silently for a time.

"That's good, I hope. Maybe it's not. David, the furniture won't hold out forever. Nor will I. I want you to help Cristina, use some of that American ambition you've got. I know it's still there, under that layer of English dust. I want you to help put her mind to something."

"How?"

"I don't know. I'm sure you do, though. With her studies, with her—how would you say it—with her direction. Take an interest in her, and not the interest I know you've taken. A different interest. Will you do that?"

"Yes, Hans. I'll do that."

He looked at me skeptically. And it was true that the thought of taking Cristina seriously scared me as much as asking her on a date would. I feared her rejection.

"I don't ask for much, David," he said with a sly, tired smile.

There were no wheelchair slots in the opera house, no ramps down the gently graded stairs or any other manner of assistance. I propped Hans up on the back wheels and made the trip as gentle as I could to our row, five back from the orchestra pit. I unhooked his urine bag, tucked it under the coyote throw on his lap, and then lifted Hans up, imploring an usher to lend a hand moving the rubber penis mat to his seat six in from the aisle. Hans sunk down uncomfortably in the folding chair. I tugged him unartfully into the best sitting position I could manage and settled in for a very long evening. I could smell the piss.

Midway through the second act I stopped fighting it and allowed my eyes to drift shut. I have no idea how long I slept. When I reopened my eyes, Hans's body had keeled dangerously over. He slumped down in his chair, his upper body leaning into me, his head lolling sickly to the right as the music soared on stage. Adrenaline rushed through me in a panic as I lunged to push him back up. I had failed him, shamed him, amplified his helplessness in an auditorium full of people he would want to impress.

His eyes met mine. There was no anger there at all, only rapture. Violetta—desolate, inconsolable, in love—was trying to renounce Alfredo. "*Amami, Alfredo.*" It meant nothing to me—and everything to Hans.

As I felt my way south toward Brighton, I had the sensation of blindness. The street signs and roundabouts seemed to crash upon me through the misty rain. I was incapable of anticipating the next obstacle. In between those moments of panic, the image of Hans's inert body lolling in its seat kept flashing before me. I felt sympathy, but mainly I felt incompetent. There wasn't much required of me in this job, but I sucked at it anyway.

"David, I'm not feeling too well." Hans's voice rose like a whisper in the fog. The A23 had finally cleared Gatwick. Pease Pottage signaled the break I was waiting for, as the suburbs gave way to open road.

"I'm not feeling too well myself, Hans." I smiled over my left shoulder and caught just a glimpse of him, strapped into his chair at the waist and chest. His head bowed slightly forward. His face looked puffy, pale in the glow of the streetlights. Even from my vantage point, I could see purplish, veined lines across his swollen cheeks. His lower lip was protruding, with a bit of spittle on his chin. He looked terrible, even for Hans.

"Yes, quite right," he said quietly, his words slurred with fatigue. I heard nothing more from him that night, not even as I wheeled him out of the ambulance or hoisted him into bed. Elizabeth had appeared in the hallway in a long, flannel nightgown, too tired to be of much help but satisfied to see us, home and alive.

" 'Night, David," she yawned and walked off as I tucked Hans in beneath the piles of covers.

The next morning, Hans could barely lift his head from the pillow.

"Long night," Elizabeth said with feigned cheer as I mashed up some Weetabix to offer Hans in tiny spoonfuls. His lip protruded as sickly as I remembered. The paleness of his skin had not been a trick of the streetlamps. He ate nothing. I was more relieved than usual when the nurses arrived.

"Hans needs to go to hospital right away," one of them said before the morning ablutions were complete. She was not chipper at all.

"What's wrong with him?" I asked.

"Dunno exactly. Kidneys, I 'spect."

It would have been more difficult to load Hans into the ambulance than push him up the steep, two-block climb to the Royal

Sussex County Hospital, so I hoofed it. "You go on," Elizabeth had implored me. "I've got a class. I'll try to catch up in a bit."

The Spartan, Victorian, redbrick façade gave way to a dreary, fluorescent-lit admitting room, where Hans was greeted like a regular, if not an old friend.

"Good morning, Mr. Bromwell," the round, porcine lady behind the counter said with a slight trace of cockney. It was one of the rare times when someone behind a desk had greeted him and not me, the attendant. Hans was in no shape to be effusive. He just grunted.

I walked behind as peroxide-haired men, their piercings removed for work, rolled Hans to a room with a window overlooking Imperial Lane. For so long, I had looked up at this hospital, which menacingly stood watch over us. Now I was seeing the other vantage point. It was lovely. The wait was long, but not as long as the scolds in the States would have you believe was endemic to socialized medicine. As it turned out, diagnosis was instant. The doctor took one look at Hans and turned to me.

"Will you call Elizabeth?"

"It could take a while. She was heading off to the poly."

He sighed.

"Hans's kidneys are going, and I need to talk to his sister."

"OK."

He showed me to a pay phone and gave me ten pence when I had to admit I had nothing in my pockets. There was no answer. I tried again in five minutes, then again in another five. Finally, she picked up.

"Elizabeth," I said, "I'm sorry to bother you, but the doctor needs you here."

They greeted each other like old friends as she walked into Hans's light-filled room.

"Doctor Worthy, I'm delighted it's you," Elizabeth said with a relieved little swoon.

"Elizabeth, it's been a while." He planted a kiss on her cheek that she clearly relished. She was blushing when he told her, "I'd be sur-prised if he had much more than a quarter of a kidney left."

He led her away with a gentle tug at the elbow, not so far that they were out of earshot but far enough to confer on Elizabeth a re-sponsibility that would be hers alone.

"We can keep him here for a few days, flush his system, get rid of the salt and potassium. I've got some phosphorus-lowering med-ication. Some iron supplements may goose up the red blood-cell counts. He'll feel better, a bit more chipper. Or..."

He hesitated just for a moment. "We could do nothing." He gave her a knowing look. She looked at Hans, then at me, her face mo-mentarily stricken. Then she looked at the floor, composing her thoughts.

"What about a transplant?" I blurted.

"Hans, what do you think of our young American friend?" Eliza-beth called to her brother. "I believe he's offering you a kidney."

Hans said nothing, just looked tired.

"Blimey, David, you are a little thick sometimes," Elizabeth con-tinued. "Did you draft those letters to the Voluntary Euthanasia Society in duplicate? You might want to take another read."

Kidney failure was a common conclusion to quadriplegia, and a fairly painless one at that. She turned serious and looked up at Wor-thy's expectant face.

"Do what you can, Peter. Make him feel better." She walked over to Hans, took up a lifeless hand, and stared into his weary eyes. They stayed that way awhile, he in silence, his expression inscrutable.

She leaned toward him on some signal I had not or could not de-tect, and put her ear near his lips.

"'Kill thy physician,'" he whispered.

"'And the fee bestow upon the foul disease,'" she said, completing the quote and giving him a sad, sweet smile. She kissed him on the forehead and signaled for me to leave with her.

*　　*　　*

"'The true beginning of our end,'" Elizabeth said with a smile as she handed me a glass of red wine that evening. The sky was darkening as we walked home. Elizabeth had raided Hans's stash of Barolo and asked if I would be going to Maggie's while Hans was "in hospital," as the Brits put it.

"Maybe," I had said with a shrug. "Not tonight."

"Splendid," she said, cocking her head, smiling just a touch and giving me a look of genuine affection. I saw for a moment how attractive she could be. "Then let's have something Hans would hate."

That would mean a run to the chippy down on the Marine Parade. She knew I loved it, especially the chips deep-fried in the same oil used for the cod. I couldn't explain the appeal, but French fries with a slightly fishy taste, salted with vinegar, were enormously pleasing. Expensive Italian red didn't go at all, but I wasn't complaining. Neither was Cristina, who had joined us, a rare occasion and another pleasure for me. I thought of my promise to Hans.

"David, if I didn't love you like a brother, who knows where we might go?" she sighed that night in the kitchen, her voluptuous lower lip rising in a teasing pout. Her black hair, combed to a shine, swung pleasingly before her eyes. She had the most perfect mouth.

"Story of my life," I grumbled. "Elizabeth, does she always act this way?"

"Only since puberty," Elizabeth replied, flashing a look of mock disapproval at her daughter.

"Oh, c'mon, you two. I'm only joking. Sorry to tease, David. Really, I can be a right cow." Instead of meeting my eyes, she looked down at the counter. I smiled. Her eyes, dark, almost black, lifted and locked on mine.

It was a silly exchange, but it felt good, normal. OK, better than normal. I felt something stirring, beyond the lust I had felt the first time I laid eyes on Cristina. I didn't try to suppress it under the guilt of unfaithfulness to Maggie or the self-loathing I had carried for months, knowing I could never win her. I had to admit to myself I wanted Cristina in some new way. Maybe it was folly, but I harbored ambition, and I didn't care how wrong it was on so many fronts.

That night, we spoke of Hans's demise for the first time, as if it were imminent and inevitable. I hadn't given it much thought, but Elizabeth's studies, her preparation for the world of work, made sense now.

"You've been amazingly patient, waiting him out, David," Elizabeth said, searching out the last crumb of a chip from the greasy tip of the paper cone her meal had come in.

I looked at her with a shocked expression.

"Don't get me wrong. Pathetic as this might sound, he's the man in my life. I certainly can't count the boys this one brings round," she said, nodding to Cristina.

"Mother!" came the obligatory huff of protest.

"Or the volunteers, no offense. Hans saved my life, David, and Cristina's. He rescued us. He treats me like dirt at times, but I can hardly complain about this little world we've made here. Better than the alternative. Anyway, that chapter's about to end, isn't it? A blink of an eye, really."

And it was a blink of an eye. I had assumed the life that I beheld that first day in October had been fixed like that for years, and would be for years after. Not so. I was stumbling into a denouement. Charlotte Bromwell had died of breast cancer in 1981, just seven years before my arrival. She had seen her son ignore the wishes of his physical therapists, doctors, and nurses and sink into the worst kind of quadriplegia. She had seen her daughter return from Africa with a new appreciation of what she had left behind at Houndsheath, even if no apologies were on offer. She had seen her beautiful, olive-skinned granddaughter. But she hadn't seen the cancer. The Bromwells were conscientious objectors to the National Health Service, but by then, they were too cash-poor for private practitioners. So Charlotte simply didn't go to doctors. By the time it was caught, it was virulent and everywhere. A mastectomy, then another, chemo, round after round, all for naught. Charlotte didn't stand a chance.

Gordon Bromwell soldiered on for a while after that. He still had his politics. He had been much older than his wife. He had never considered that he might outlive her. It was easy enough at first. The servants did the cooking and cleaning. In London, cheering Thatcher on was a singular joy, especially from the backbenches of the House of Commons. In the end, however, the tragedies that had beset his family were too much for even him. It was bad enough when his foppish, gallant son had been reduced to a grumbling skull attached to a lifeless body. With Charlotte's death, he was left with "Oh, Gordon, we are so sorry for your troubles;" "Oh, Gordon, really, anything we can do, just let us know;" "Oh, Gordon, you are a brave, brave man." Like his son, Gordon Bromwell was not one for heroics.

He came to enjoy the screaming students of the Animal Liberation Front more than his fellow members of Parliament, with their sickly sighs and expressions of support. The ALF came round pretty much every weekend to scream and stomp and spray garlic on the fox trails. At least he knew where they stood. It was the treacle at Whitehall that drove him to retirement, and to the rifle in the guest room, which he trained on the foxes and rabbits, and one day in 1985, on himself. It had been tricky, no doubt, placing the business end of a rifle in his mouth and firing it with the big toe of his right foot. But Gordon Bromwell used the tools at his disposal.

A suicide, even late in life, nullifies a life insurance policy. Estate planning, such as it was in Britain, was no match for despair. Innumerate and orphaned, with a quadriplegic brother to care for, Elizabeth turned the fate of the North Downs estate over to a lawyer in Basingstoke she barely knew.

"'Liquidate,' he said. 'Render unto Caesar.'"

Elizabeth poured the last of the bottle.

"The National Trust was only too happy to take such a lovely estate off our hands. They're turning it into some kind of conference center, business training or some such. Americans like that sort of thing, even if it is a bit drafty.

"The collapse of the Bromwell fortune was swift. For a time— maybe just two months, it seemed like longer—Hans and I stayed at the house, just the two of us, and Cristina of course. She was getting to be a handful. One by one, the servants left. You know, it's not like the old days, where the home of service is the only home they know. They have family scattered here and there now. They have places to go. And when we stopped paying them . . . well, loyalty will only get you so far.

"That was when I first met dear Haversham. I had gone alone into the village, to a little antique store my mother used to humor. I only wanted someone to come back with me to Houndsheath to look at a few things. We needed cash. The one person I could not afford to lose was Hans's nurse, and she needed paying. There was this doddering old lady at the shop. She was tall, I remember, like she would fall over with the next breeze. She had very long fingers. She told me a London furniture man would relish a look round the old house. She had some idea of my parents' taste. She had been indulging them for years. Next day, the little Jew—oh dear, David, I'm sorry, I've done it again—Haversham pulled up in that little lorry. First thing he took away was the dining room table. Louis the Fourteenth, I remember. It was an almost-black mahogany, deep, deep red, inlaid with light burled walnut in the corners. The patterns were these intricate damask swirls, two heavy legs on each side splaying out into these dramatic, four-footed buttresses. It brought me what I thought was a fortune. Twenty thousand quid. I'd love to know what he sold it for. It cost me nothing in my mind. I always ate in the breakfast nook. And without that big heavy table, the dining room became this grand play space for Cristina. Got her off the banisters for a while."

"I remember that," Cristina spoke up. "You piled up pillows and blocked off the entrance with chairs, so I could flop about on my own. I was getting pretty old by then, Mother. It wasn't like I was a baby in a crèche."

"I know. We had so much on our minds then. It was hard to find you a playmate. I tried."

"There was that boy from the village, William."

"Yes, I remember him. His father had been a gardener at Houndsheath. Of course, we had to let him go, but on good terms. His son quite fancied you."

Cristina smiled. "Don't be ridiculous."

I imagined Cristina as a child, beautiful and utterly unselfconscious, lustrous dark hair a little unkempt, gangly arms, skinny legs, running wild—an only child in such an odd environment. Where was her father? How had she been wrenched from the Africa that had given her life? How had she gotten here, to No. 4 Imperial Lane, from there, a dying estate from a dying era? It broke my heart in some little, sweet way. I recognized the tenderness, allowed myself a glance at Cristina's beautiful face, then turned from it.

"But even that twenty thousand wasn't going to pay the tax collector. I could've sold every stick of furnishing on the estate and not come close. Funny, my father the loyal Tory found no fault in anything Thatcher did, but in the end she did nothing for him. We pretty much lost it all, except the furniture that we could stuff into this flat."

"I'm, I'm sorry," I stammered.

"'When sorrows come, they come not single spies, but in battalions.'" She lit a cigarette, drained a vodka shot, then stood to do the dishes.

"I wasn't in when he did it. I had taken Cristina into Basingstoke to do some shopping, take care of a few things. Hans was, of course. He heard the shot, he reckons, but gunfire from that room was constant. It wasn't till a servant knocked Dad up for dinner that the body was found."

I winced.

"By then, you know, it felt like just me and Hans anyway, brother and sister against the world. I was protective, but truth be told, we were drifting apart. The bitterness over our entwined and ruined fates was just beginning to creep in. My father was an odd presence, like a hovering angel even when he was alive. He kept watch over me, kept me safe, always knew what I was up to. He had people, you know, seemingly all over the world, spies who knew how to get things done. He directed them, like a puppeteer, but always from afar. It doesn't feel a lot different now, except he doesn't appear to be as effective."

"Do you mind me asking," I said gingerly, "why didn't Hans do the physical therapy? It just seems like a self-preservation instinct would have kicked in."

"Ah, those cunts—pardon my language—the nurses and physical therapists, especially at Stoke Mandeville, fawning all over poor Hans. Expect they wanted into his pants, if you ask me. Probably why they wanted to talk to him about sex. They would have given anything to teach him the way, climb right on top of his gurney and sit on his face."

"Mother!" Cristina snapped. She wasn't teasing. She was angry.

I looked at her, stunned. I had seen pictures of Hans before the accident, a dashing young man in Paris in a little flat, cooking or posing with some tarted-up girlfriend or his friends Julian and Simon, who have aged only slightly better than Hans. But he was a quadriplegic at Stoke Mandeville, with a lot of other cripples. All of the stories, from Hans himself even, pointed to his own willful self-neglect, a decision that life was not worth living in his state. Surely he wasn't being exploited by the staff hired to care for him.

"You're joking, aren't you?" I mustered.

"Oh no, my dear David, you can hardly imagine the attraction: eligible bachelor from a posh background, father an MP with a title, and still so needy. The short life expectancy only heightened the attraction. I had to take him away from the harridans myself, get him back to Houndsheath. I could take care of him as well as they could. Of course, Mother accused me of sabotaging his recovery."

"These are flights of fancy, Mum, and you know it," Cristina said, getting up to leave. "You don't have to justify those days. Nobody faults you for what happened to Uncle Hans. Don't try to find fault in anyone else."

Cristina gave me an appraising look, as if she wanted to know where I would carry this conversation, whose side I was on. My response was supposed to be reassuring. I was with her. She left the two of us alone in the kitchen, the usual state of things. But as she left, she allowed her bare arm to graze mine lightly, and she glanced back at me for one final estimation, her chin dropping slightly so she would look at me through thick eyelashes. I felt my cheeks burn.

With her daughter gone, Elizabeth opened the cupboard and reached for the vodka. She took a shot and settled herself.

"Cristina's right. I apologize," she said through a shy smile.

"Don't apologize to me. You might want to have a word with her."

"Those were the worst days of our lives, you see. My mother's death was so sudden. My father had had enough time to say good-bye to us, in any case. By the time he pulled the trigger, he saw what was happening to us, to his family. He probably felt like a third wheel, or a fourth. Cristina never paid much mind to him. A bit stuffy for a twelve-year-old girl.

"Anyway, we hemorrhaged money. Funeral expenses—we had to have a big show. It was in all the papers, none too flattering of course. There were lawyers' fees, taxes..."

She paused for a while and smoked in silence. I didn't want to interrupt, but I wanted to hear the rest.

"Funny, that was when James and Wills really came throgh for us, became friends, I s'pose. They had bought some first-edition Thackerays or some sort that I had sold to Haversham. Paid a bloody fortune for them. The next time Haversham popped round to their shop, they laid it on thick. They're good at that, sort of coaxed it out of him where the pieces were coming from. They decided to drive down to Houndsheath themselves to try to cut out the middleman.

They were supposedly book people, but they bought some objets, I remember, an ivory carving of Wellington, a bronze escutcheon my father used to swear dated back to the Roman invasion, some oil paintings—I never understood who on earth would buy a painting of one of my relatives to adorn their living room. But mainly they were taken by us, by Hans. Don't ask me why. S'pose they didn't have children of their own. They've been around ever since.

"Anyway, we ended up here to be close to the hospital, as I'm sure you've figured."

"Why didn't you go back to Stoke Mandeville, or whatever it was called?"

"Didn't trust 'em. Anyway, Hans fancied the idea of being by the sea. I told him you could hear the waves from the house I had found. It wasn't really a lie. When the breeze is right, you can. He just never opens the window. We tried to hang on to a full-time nurse, but it didn't take long to realize that wouldn't last. You're only the third volunteer. That's why we're not sick of ya." She gave me a wink.

"Really, only three? I heard about the one that fancied Wills."

"Oh, you heard about him? Didn't last long. A bridge, really, between the nurse we let go and Italy. Something not quite right about him.

"And the last one. God, Hans can go on about him. Rode a motorcycle, always getting into trouble.

"Hans did live vicariously through Paul," Elizabeth said after taking a deep drag. "He got through the winter. That was alright. I wasn't taking so many classes then and could pick up the slack."

"Wait. So I made it the longest?"

"But I need you the most, David. You're the one to see us through to the other side, you know. The last, I'm sure. You should be honored. 'When beggars die there are no comets seen.'" She stabbed out the cigarette and reached for the pack. "I just hope he's well enough for the trip to Tuscany this summer. He'd so love to die there."

I wandered into Hans's room that night to read. It was a violation, really. Of privacy, to be sure, but mainly of etiquette, of the tightly drawn world Hans had created for himself. But then again, I always thought I was just some hired help, passing through on eighteen quid a week, doing what was expected of me. Now I discovered I was only the third in a very short line, and the only one to feel the coming of spring at No. 4 Imperial Lane. I was due some license. I went to the top drawer of the dresser, or maybe it was a highboy or a lowboy or whatever, to pull out the next letter in the pile, when the phone rang.

"David, it's for you," Elizabeth called out.

I shoved the paper letter into my pocket and hustled into the kitchen, a little embarrassed.

"The hospital," she said, rolling her eyes as she handed over the phone.

"Hello?"

A woman's voice on the other end of the line said she was calling for Hans Bromwell.

"Is this David, the volunteer?"

"Yes?"

"Sorry to be calling so late, love. Hans here said he'd like some reading material. Frankly," she continued conspiratorially in an exaggerated stage whisper, "I think he's looking for a little company."

Dearest Bet,

I apologize for being so tardy with this letter, the suffering of the slothful. The less you do in life, the less you are inclined to do. Writing a letter can be so daunting, especially to one whose life is so bloody interesting. To clear up matters immediately, I have not thrown aside Segolaine, as you so rudely intimated. She is bleeding me dry with her incessant need for affection, but I have not withheld even once—well, maybe once or twice, but I was too pissed to pop.

I trust that I can no longer scandalize a woman, now married, who has seen it all. Just lie back and think of Lisbon. Isn't that what that old bat Victoria said?

I am under dreadful pressure from Sir Gordon Bromwell to get on with my life. I can't imagine what he means by that, but I am humouring him by at least looking for a job. I believe I told you Julian had gotten a job at a Parisian bank. It sounds dreadful, but it is a regal structure with wonderful art deco and art nouveau touches inside, lots of young lasses to chat up. They run in and out all day doing errands for their bosses. They like nothing more than to be waylaid by a dashing young man who might give them an excuse to stay a minute or two longer away from the office. If I don't be careful, I might just have to accept Julian's offer for a post there. Ah, but then Segolaine might get sore. She does have a jealous streak, remarkable for one of such questionable virtue. Maybe I'll try graduate work, get a D-Phil in something or other.

I and the Bromwell stash of cash have been able to keep my Segolaine off the streets for some time, though she still dances in some rather seedy locales. She says it's her art form. I suppose one could call it that. Her customers do get excited by it, though I'm not sure the trousers are supposed to be the body part aroused by art.

But listen to me, sounding the prude. This is the sexual revolution, the 1970s, and in Paris, magnifique! As Rubashov would say, "The masses have become deaf and dumb again, the great silent x of history, indifferent as the sea carrying the ships." The opiate has changed, however, to libertine delirium. Better to be a Parisian intoxicated on free love than a Russian, lost on the tide of history, no?

Simon wishes you well. He's potentially balking at Tuscany this summer, says Julian is too tiresome even to suffer through wine and pate with under the Italian sun. I really must talk him out of that. If he backs out, I will have no choice but to foist Segolaine on Julian's family. I'll need the company. That should spice up matters, wouldn't it?

Write soon, dear, and while you're at it, get the hell out of Africa. I trust you've gotten the gist of the place.

Your peevish brother,
Hans

CHAPTER THIRTEEN

The news of João's escape crackled across the radio in the officers' club from the agriculture station in Contuboel. From there, it swept through the Portuguese wives auxiliary of Bissau—real news, not just gossip. Lovely Raquel Brito burst from the low-slung building into the bright African sunlight, giddy with the good fortune of being the one to bring Elizabeth the word. Her cotton dress, softened by repeated washing by hand with the harsh lye soap of West Africa, clung to the front of her thighs while billowing behind her. She found Elizabeth in the PX, sniffing a wrinkled tomato.

Elizabeth had gone on aimlessly after João's capture and Spínola's departure, having called off her crusade. Spínola's halfhearted appeals to Senghor apparently went unheeded, if they happened at all. Elizabeth busied herself cashing João's paychecks, cooking for Angélica, keeping up with her Portuguese lessons, and trying the language out listlessly on the chittering wives. She had tried to will herself to be useful at the hospital, but she felt like an imposter. There had been a young soldier, recuperating from a bullet to the spine, just below the neck. He was paralyzed from the chest down, with only marginally functioning arms that feathered by his sides as he tried to sit straight in a wheelchair. He had lit up the first time he saw Elizabeth. She beamed back at him. She was lonely. But she could not relieve him of his anguish. They talked about the past.

There was no future to discuss. After a week of effort, she never went back.

She was showing clearly by now; not much was expected of expectant Portuguese wives. At night, she set deadlines for word of her husband's return. If she heard nothing in a week, she'd go home. The week passed, and she'd give him another week, then another. Soon, two months had passed, then three, then four. By summer's end, she'd be back in Hampshire, she swore.

"Elizabeth, Elizabeth, *seu marido*, your husband, he's alive," Raquel blurted out, bouncing on the balls of her feet, her whole face radiating joy. She wanted to throw her arms around the Englishwoman, but Elizabeth just looked at her blankly for a moment.

"What?"

"Your husband, they found him. Maybe he found them. I don't know."

"What?" Elizabeth repeated, but this time her face showed comprehension. A smile was breaking out, a smile of disbelief, but joy as well. "What?" she asked breathily. "How?"

Raquel wiggled her head in a silent laugh. A cute little squeal involuntarily escaped her chest. Then she threw herself forward, wrapped her arms around Elizabeth's neck, and squeezed her ebulliently. "I don't know. I don't know. My husband said something about a bread man."

For João, it had been shamefully easy. He had crept to the same jeep that he had seen so many times roaring in and out of the agriculture station's feeble gate. The euphoria of finding Luis had faded a bit. He was petrified he would be caught by Farinha's men and hauled back to the guerrilla camp to face what his countrymen had done. Head bent, shoulders hunched, he climbed into the back and tried to pull the loose canvas covering over himself. Luis laughed.

"Doctor, what is the problem? Do you think they care about you that much, or even want you back?" He laughed again. "You must think very highly of yourself."

João knew Luis had a point. A commander who had just sustained heavy casualties after a brutal surprise attack could use a doctor, but he would have far bigger things to deal with at the moment than hunting down an escaped prisoner. The camp was a wreck. There were bodies to dispose of, salvage operations to mount, and then there was the matter of appealing to the Senegalese government, which was supposed to stop such cross-border counterattacks. João knew all this. He just couldn't make himself believe it. He tried to lie as flat as he could, as his traveling companion climbed behind the wheel, let a huge bag of baguettes slide off his shoulder and onto the passenger seat, and started the engine.

"Suit yourself, man," Luis shouted over his shoulder.

João motioned frantically from under the canvas for Luis to turn back around and stop talking to him. Was he determined to let the world know a man was hiding in the back of his jeep? *For God's sake*, he thought. Luis couldn't see the gesticulating. He just chuckled as the jeep got into gear and stuttered into motion.

The ride back into Guiné was completely uneventful. After forty minutes, the decent Senegalese road had given way to the barely passable Guinean furrow. João had had enough of being slammed around in the unpadded, steel storage space. He was more likely to die of head trauma than meet up with guerrillas again. As Luis maneuvered through the ruts and potholes at a crawl, João uncovered himself and climbed into the front.

"Watch the bread, man," Luis shouted, reaching over to make sure Gonçalves didn't kick it out of the vehicle. "That's what I was sent to fetch, baguettes, man, not you."

Luis didn't talk like this when Elizabeth was around, João thought to himself, cranky as he struggled to wedge the bread back behind his seat.

"Hey, grab me one of those baguettes," Luis demanded, elbowing João playfully. Suddenly João was starving. They split a loaf, still a little warm, as they tossed from side to side. It was already starting to taste of Guinean dust and clay, a taste João knew well from his meals at the agricultural station.

When the jeep passed through Contuboel, the children ran out to ask for bread. Seeing João in the passenger seat proved far more interesting. They dashed ahead.

By the time Luis swung the jeep up the slope and through the gate, word had reached Menges. He stood there, in the dusty flat landing outside the complex of buildings, smiling like an imbecile.

"Dammit, João, you lucky bastard," he said as the doctor walked up to him, beaming. The two men embraced.

The helicopter ride back to base took a half hour at most. By the time the chopper touched down, Colonel Brito had taken full credit for the doctor's liberation. His only regret, he said with a shrug, was that he could not bring helicopter commandos to rescue João, but he said he had rightly calculated that escape would be easy enough, once Esquadrão 121 had done its job. Elizabeth lost track of Brito's boasts. She had more pressing concerns. How exactly was she to greet this man? What was expected of her? A passionate kiss? A look of ecstatic joy or admiration or wonder? Was she to slap him for his abandonment, or take him by the hand and lead him away for sex, right then and there? At twenty-one years of age, she still didn't really know what she was supposed to do around men, much less her husband, who had disappeared without a trace for a good chunk of their marriage.

João had not taken the time to shave or cut his hair before leaving Contuboel, though he had showered in the same stall where his wife once confronted a cockroach, a lizard, and a dozen bats. He stepped off the Alouette III, its round, glassed front giving the crowd an early glimpse of their hirsute Robinson Crusoe. He was immediately mobbed. Men and women, in uniforms and dresses, rushed to slap his back, mock his beard, and welcome him home. Elizabeth stood on the outside, gingerly waiting for the crowd to clear.

João, tall and lean, searched for her and caught her eye. The crowd parted. He approached her hesitantly, looking at her rounded belly for a good long time, and then pulled her to his chest.

"I didn't think you would stay."

They were not the words Elizabeth had expected or had wanted. "I missed you," "I'm sorry," or a simple "I love you" would have done nicely, maybe something about the joy of learning she carried his child. He didn't think she would stay? Was that a hope or a lament? Was he worried or wishing? Well, what did she know? He had just been through a trauma she could hardly imagine, violent deaths, captivity, threats, she was sure, beatings maybe, and escape. What right did she have to expect anything from him? He was holding her. She was smelling her husband, her face buried in his familiar, bony shoulder. Everything would be alright.

João Gonçalves's head was spinning. She was plainer than he remembered, her face doughy, her eyes a little vacant, her body swollen. She was wearing one of those ample, formless African shifts the women tailors of Contuboel made, stiff and unattractive, festooned with color to make up for their lack of style. Formless, but stretched tight over her belly. His wife was pregnant, what, four, five, six months? This woman was going to bear him a child, and soon. What was it his father had said? You will have ugly children? Maybe he did deserve better. He was still young at twenty-eight, a physician, trim, fit, and now a combat veteran if not a hero, an escaped prisoner of war. Why wasn't one of these pretty little things his? Raquel Brito, Paula Pelegrin, Ana Aveiro? Look at the way they smiled at him. Admiration, pity, desire. How did his life take this turn? He felt sick. He held on to his wife like a drunk holding on to a telephone pole.

"Gonçalves," a voice boomed, "there'll be time enough for that. We need you now."

Colonel Eduardo Medeiros, the new base commander, clapped a big hand on João's shoulder. Relieved beyond words, Gonçalves pulled back, locked eyes with Elizabeth for a moment, then walked off with the starched uniforms that led him to base headquarters. It would take hours to be debriefed. They needed it all: the number of fighters who had attacked, the weapons, the look of their clothes, the condition of their boots, the hours and days marched to their camp, the route taken, as best he could remember, the layout of the camp, the sources of supplies, the command, any names he could remember at all. Were there Soviets, Cubans, or Chinese? Did they eat well or were they desperate? Did they drill or train? What services had he rendered? How was he treated? What of his fellow captive, the medic? They had no word of him since the air raid.

João was eager to share, and he spoke in a great verbal fusillade until he was spent. It was liberating. He felt no remorse for the guerrilla fighters he had lived with and cared for. Many of them were dead already. The survivors would be targeted again with the information he was imparting. Nor did he relish aiding the Portuguese army. He had no belief in the cause, whatever it was, empire, rescue, punishment. He just wanted to talk, to tell his story, and, if truth be told, to avoid his pregnant wife.

Darkness had fallen by the time Medeiros poured an ample brandy and pushed the snifter across the heavy, shellacked wooden table. Then the colonel walked through a door and returned momentarily, with a straight-edged razor and a white-glazed metal basin.

"You're a good man, Major Gonçalves. You've served your nation well. Now"—he smiled, handing him the razor—"go find that wife of yours. She'll be ready for you, if you know what I mean."

João shaved, collecting the remnants of his beard and throwing them in the trash, worried that he would clog the sink in the headquarters bathroom. He looked in the mirror and liked what he saw. Then he stepped into the sticky, hot night, surprised by the streetlamps that illuminated the dusty parade ground. By Lisbon standards, the stars were a light show. But they were washed out compared to the heavenly firmament he had taken in for the past four months, outside a town called Kolda, on a guerrilla base darkened each night for fear of an air force that for so long had failed to show, and then had shown as brutally as they had feared.

He breathed deep, then stepped toward the officers' quarters, where his wife was waiting.

Elizabeth was cooking dinner over the small communal stove. The two weak burners took their time, but João's debriefing had provided plenty of that. *Caldo verde*, with potatoes, collard greens, and smoked pork sausage from the PX, simmered on one side. *Carne de porco à alentejana*, without the clams and with salt pork substituting for fresh, cooked on the other. For once, Angélica was not around to enjoy it. The smell of Portuguese cuisine pulled João to the kitchen. Elizabeth beamed with pride, and João could not suppress a grin. Some of the heaviness melted away.

"A lot to tell, I'd imagine," she said awkwardly.

"Yes, a lot. I'm sorry that took so long," he said, reaching into the simmering soup with a wooden spoon. Even in the heat of the West African night, the taste was exquisite.

"I won't ask you to repeat it all, not just yet," Elizabeth said shyly, staring at the simmering pots. It was the most awkward moment of their relationship, more awkward than their first meeting in the clinic, their first beer together at the seaside bar, their first lovemaking. She was his wife, she was pregnant with his child, and she didn't know what to say to him. Her mind flashed back to the pond in Hampshire where she chatted effortlessly with her dog as a little girl. She felt so far from home.

João was immersed in his senses as he stole another taste from the pot.

"Hmmm, a man could expect no more," he marveled.

"'Small cheer and great welcome makes a merry feast.'" Elizabeth smiled up at her husband. She blushed like a girlfriend serving her first meal to a promising suitor.

João stood behind his wife as she stirred, dropped his chin on her shoulder, and wrapped both hands around her belly. She sighed and leaned into him.

"Why didn't you tell me?" he asked.

"I was going to, really. Then you were gone."

"How long has it been?"

"Five months, I expect, maybe five and a half."

She spun around to kiss, but he was not done.

"Have you seen a doctor, an obstetrician? Is there one in this bloody country?" he asked.

She silently shook her head, looking shamefacedly at the ground. She felt like she was speaking to her disapproving father, his questions shouting, "How could you have done this to yourself?"

"João." She looked up into his eyes. "Before, before you . . . disappeared, we made love almost every night. We have done nothing to keep this from happening. How could you be so surprised?"

Her words accused, but her voice pleaded for mercy.

"I know," he said, pulling her to him and lifting his head to nestle hers under his chin. "I know."

They still hadn't kissed when she served him dinner quietly.

They sweated over Elizabeth's piri piri peppers and saffron creations as João told his stories of captivity. He did not dwell on the violent beginning and end. They were fleeting, ugly moments, not his real experience. He didn't let himself think of them. Instead, he spoke admiringly of Henda, the young guerrilla commander, of Augusto, the medic he had nursed back to health, then abandoned, of the respiratory ailments he could not help and the guinea worms that were delaying the PAIGC's ultimate victory. Young fighters by the dozen were laid up for weeks on end, doing nothing but wrapping the head of a protruding worm around a stick and slowly, painfully, pulling it out, millimeter by millimeter. And he told her of that moment, lost and with no real idea what to do next, when he ran into Luis buying bread for the agriculture station.

"You're kidding," Elizabeth said, laughing uproariously. "Truth is stranger than fiction. You know, Raquel Brito said something about a bread man when I asked how you had escaped. She had no idea what that had meant."

"I was petrified, even after I had found Luis," João said, laughing as well. "I was sure I would be captured again. I crept to his jeep like a thief. You know what he said? 'You sure have a big opinion of yourself.'"

"He fancies you, you know."

"Who?"

"Luis, the bread man, he wants you."

"Don't be daft."

"No, he does." Darkness swept down on João like a shroud. "He does. I'm sure he rescued me to get into your pants."

A moment passed.

"'Black men are pearls in beauteous ladies' eyes,'" he said coldly, meeting her gaze.

"'O, beware, my lord, of jealousy; it is the green-ey'd monster, which doth mock the meat it feeds on.'" She tried to break the spell. "João, have you taken leave of your senses?"

There was a pause, a moment when João could choose to escalate or not.

"Yes," he said, shaking his head in short, violent spasms. "Yes, I'm sorry."

He made love to his pregnant wife that night, roughly, possessively, heedlessly. He buried his hands in her thick nest of hair and held on to her head. It had been a very long time, she thought. She held her tongue as he propped himself over her on outstretched arms and tucked-in knees, trying to avoid her belly as he thrust inside her, avoiding a look into her eyes even as he averted his gaze from her body. Elizabeth was overwhelmed with shame. She was ugly, she too had thought, round in the front, plump from behind, breasts turning pendulous, disgusting. But she needed his love, his reassurance. She had prayed a man would like what she was becoming; certainly a man who loved her would. And yet, she could not allow self-pity. *Who knows what this poor man has been through?* she thought, over and over, as her hands reached around his head and her fingers soothed his long hair. She looked up into his face, but his eyes were turned elsewhere. And soon, he was asleep.

Then, in the early hours of morning, one o'clock, maybe two, João set himself on her.

"João, the baby," she whispered, slowly waking to what was happening.

He was half-asleep. Maybe it started as a dream, but he too was waking now, fiercely. He was tearing at her nightgown, pushing it over her swollen belly, pulling her legs apart, heaving himself onto her.

"João, João, slow down. João, please. Please, stop," she whispered, urgently.

He didn't respond. He just pushed, pushed hard. It burned and tore.

"Wait, wait," she cried, not willing to reject him but not ready for this, not ready to accept him. "You're hurting me," she said, crying now, tears pouring down her face. Her body heaved, not with excitement but with sobs. He was in now. Her hands dropped into the small of his back and felt the violent, insistent rise and fall of his hips, each thrust burning and tearing. "Please stop, please, please stop," she cried.

He collapsed, his head buried in her pillow. He too was crying. Neither spoke for a long time.

Then finally, "I'm sorry, Elizabeth, I'm sorry. I'm sorry. I'm sorry. Can you forgive me? I'm sorry."

"Shhh," she said. "Shhh." She stroked his head, smoothed his hair from the crown of his skull to his thin, muscled neck. "It's alright. It's alright."

She lay on her back, wide awake, hurting, bleeding, and petrified. He slept.

"It's not rape if you're married to him." Angélica shrugged as she fried up an egg for Elizabeth over a single gas burner in the low-ceilinged kitchen of the dormitory the Portuguese army put her up in. She slept in a room with four other Africans in the employ of the *metrópole*—cooks and washerwomen. Her light skin and New England accent may have helped her get a roof over her head, but it did not get her much more than that.

"Angélica," Elizabeth responded with a huff. "I thought…"

"Did he hit you? Did he kick you?" she asked, pausing just long enough to register her friend's silence.

For so long, Angélica had indulged what she viewed as Elizabeth's spoiled streak, the weakness of one who had never struggled, even in her neglect. She was a student after all, a task to be accomplished, and Angélica had grown fond of her pupil. But for one used to misuse by men, this was too much.

"You know, you're like the white women I used to see sometimes in the nicer restaurants in New Bedford, in America, always complaining about their men not coming home on time, not buying them flowers and such. You've got funny ideas about men. I half thought João was never coming back, not 'cause he was dead or something but because he found something better."

"Angélica, just shut up," Elizabeth wailed.

"I'm sorry, girl, but—"

"I thought you were my friend. You're being mean. It's hurtful."

"I am your friend. I'm trying to save you from yourself."

Angélica was voicing just what João had been thinking that morning. He rose stiffly, muttered another apology to Elizabeth half under his breath, showered, shaved, and left before his wife had gotten out of bed. She was awake, listening to every sound he made, shuffling through drawers for pressed fatigues, blowing his nose in the shower, urinating in the flush toilet. She kept her eyes closed, not fooling him but avoiding conversation, not that he wanted any.

João kept his justifications to himself. He had taken what belonged to him. He had been through a lot. She was lucky to have him. Unlike Elizabeth, who at least had Angélica, unsympathetic as she was, he had no one to share his experiences with, no one he could unburden himself onto honestly. He thought of his father. Maybe for once in their lives, they would have something to talk about—women, desire, anger. But he was not there. Had he known Angélica's response, he may well have tried to confide in her. Instead, he grabbed a ride to the hospital from an army private and tried to get back to work.

"Doctor Gonçalves, please, come in," the voice of Renato Marsola Araujo boomed through the open doorway of his office.

He stood to clap his left hand hard on João's shoulder as his right arm reached for a handshake. "My friend, you look remarkably well for a prisoner of war." He laughed. "You must tell me about your little adventure."

"Must I?" João asked ruefully.

"Very well, João, when you are ready. They fed you well, I see." Renato patted his hands on his own belly and laughed again. "Good French bread on that side of the border."

João turned to go, but Renato pulled him back.

"João, I know a lot has happened in these last six months or so, out there. A lot has happened here as well. Please, sit down.

"Maria," he shouted.

A raven-haired nurse attentively appeared. "Maria, please get Doctor Gonçalves some coffee." She nodded to João and ducked away.

"Spínola's gone, Elizabeth tells me," João said.

"Spínola's war is gone too." Renato sat down heavily in the chair behind his desk. He propped his feet up, laced his fingers together, and looked at João quizzically. "Look out there," he said, motioning to the emergency ward. "You won't be seeing many Africans flown in here anymore. No more guerrillas and no more civilians. They're on their own now. There's fewer of everything really. Brito's in charge. This is an air war. Not many small-arms wounds to mend when the infantry stays in barracks. We get the odd wounded soldier from a lucky mortar strike, but even those seem to be diminishing."

"Then we're winning?"

"We're pounding the shit out of them, if that's what you mean. Bombs, napalm, defoliant. Everything's fair game, to the gates of Conakry."

"We've bombed Guinea?"

Renato shrugged. "Oh yes. Senegal too, but you would know more about that than I."

João was silent.

"We're at a stalemate, though," Renato sighed. "We've pushed back the guerrilla lines. Militarily, we have them on their heels, but Cabral isn't going anywhere. He was in New York again, delivered Caetano an ultimatum at the UN: Guiné would be declared independent by the end of 1972, the beginning of 1973 at the latest. We've lost the world. They hate us."

He sipped his coffee and fell silent, his eyes drifting to an unadorned corner of the office where a bloom of mold was taking hold.

"We'll lose soon enough, when we're broke."

João waited for Renato's final pronouncement. This was leading somewhere, he thought. Maybe he would be going home soon.

Renato smiled.

"There's no place for us here anymore, João," he said. "You'll be moved soon, I expect to Angola, unless the Cabora Bassa project takes off, then maybe Mozambique."

"Not Lisbon?" João asked expectantly.

Renato laughed. "Maybe Nova Lisboa, in the Angolan highlands. You don't get time off for good behavior or heroics, João. Caetano's not giving up southern Africa. You'll like it in Angola. The cities are real, the architecture, the food, walks on the waterfront. Luanda is full of Portuguese cabdrivers and chambermaids, bartenders and cooks, all the fools who got swept up in Caetano's promises of land and help. They'd never picked up a plow in their lives but figured, 'Hey, how hard could it be if an African can do it?' They failed in the highlands just as they failed in Lisbon. Now they're back doing the menial jobs they left, only they're doing them under the African sun.

"Nova Lisboa's nice, I hear," Renato continued. "It's cool and green. It could get hot, though, in the military sense. If it falls, it'll be a shock. A big, beautiful city, movie theaters, pink ministries, yellow palaces, cars, motorcycles. There's a big car race there; famous, I guess.

"When this place falls, no one will care. If Nova Lisboa goes, they'll care. They'll care from Washington to Moscow. They'll care from Johannesburg to Lisbon. It won't be so easy for Caetano to keep that quiet."

Elizabeth and João circled each other for days like two giant planets, permanently in each other's orbit but unable to touch. They were pulled apart by centrifugal force but bound by gravity, at equilibrium in their shared helplessness. He would make attempts, mumbled apologies, an outreached hand, a guilty glance. But each pass whooshed by her, and they were back into the circular dance of a couple unsure of the next step.

For Elizabeth, Angélica had become worse than worthless, an unsympathetic scold.

"Look around you," she'd say. "Look beyond these gates. You think you have it so bad?"

João whiled away time at the half-empty hospital, tending to guinea worm and dysentery, directing hot compresses onto botfly boils and doses of Flagyl to giardia sufferers. At night, he'd often eat at the officers' mess without his wife, who seemed to grow heavier and more distant every afternoon when he wasn't watching. Elizabeth tried to cook and eat for herself and the baby. At night, with nowhere else to go, they'd come together in silence, dress in pajamas that were too hot for West Africa, and climb into bed, each clinging to the outer edge of the foam rubber.

Ultimately, it was boredom that brought détente. Elizabeth liked her husband still. She was carrying his child. She wanted it to work.

João had no one else to talk to.

"Let me take you out tonight, Elizabeth, in the city."

"The city?" She chuckled. "Bissau?"

"There's a restaurant, believe it or not. It serves passable Portuguese food. It'll give us a chance."

"I can't pitch a fit there?" she said with a quiet, slight smile.

"No," he answered, and released a laugh more like a long-awaited exhale. "No, there will be no fits. At least that's the plan."

"You'll be humiliated by me. I look awful, a fat cow."

He looked at her for a good long time. The silence hurt.

"No," he said finally, "I'll be proud."

The restaurant was a white concrete slab perched atop a narrower concrete block, with a staircase leading up to the dining hall. It looked like a giant's large white table, somebody's idea of space-age architecture. It might have worked as a modernist conceit elsewhere with good building codes. Los Angeles, say. In Bissau, it looked like it would topple over. There was an attempt at a picture window opening up on the Rua Da Boe, but large support slabs traversed the panes, as if the architect had taken a look at the unsupported exterior wall and thought better of it at the last minute. Portuguese men—officers, businessmen, traders—dined with thin Guinean women with gloppy mascara, wearing taut African fabrics clinging to their finely shaped buttocks, prostitutes mainly but well-mannered after so many years of colonial trade.

João ordered a dish of *bacalhau* and an *espada* of grilled fish to share. There was no music, just the low murmur of Portuguese and the practically whispered Kriolu of the Guinean waitstaff.

"How did you know about this place?" Elizabeth asked, straining to keep her suspicions from her voice.

João shrugged. "Renato, the other doctors." He understood the accusation in the question but held back.

Elizabeth looked at him straight. "Do you come here with these women?" she asked, a flick of her head taking in the entire population of female diners, their long, braided hair extensions piled flamboyantly atop their heads, bright red, shiny lipstick accenting provocative, rich mouths.

"Elizabeth," he sighed. "No, I don't have the courage for such things."

It was not an encouraging answer, just a pathetic one. Her next question was a thought—*Would you if you did?*—but she kept that one to herself, afraid of the answer, which was obvious. It would be humiliating to them both.

João spoke now of captivity, of missing her and worrying. He allowed himself to tell her of his guilt, his failings of courage as a soldier, the scorn of Augusto, his fellow captive and the only real man to have survived that first attack, his belief that he had abandoned her. She talked of the baby, of names—if it was a boy, maybe António, after Spínola, she laughed; if it was a girl, something English but not too, something passable in Portugal as well, like Isabel or Cristina—of leaving Africa as a family, getting her figure back, such as it was. She talked of the things first-time pregnant mothers talk about—her fatigue, troubles sleeping, the first trimester, hiding nausea at first, then giving in to it when he was gone. And she talked of things most women of her background don't think about.

"João, do you think I can really have this baby here?" she asked plaintively. "I have no obstetrician. The hospital is a wreck. I'm scared."

"You won't be having the baby here," João said softly.

"What?" Elizabeth leaned forward, smiling at first. For a fleeting moment, she thought they would be going home, wherever that would be—Lisbon or London, Hampshire or the Algarve, anywhere far to the north of Guiné. But João's eyes were downcast, as if he was not sure whether this news would be welcomed or cursed.

"We'll be leaving here. Soon. That's what Renato says. I'll probably be sent to Angola."

The next unknown washed over Elizabeth's face, cleansed it of expression. She stared blankly.

"This is good news, Elizabeth. Luanda, the capital, is a beautiful city, a real city with good hospitals, far from war. The highlands are cool and lush. We can get an apartment, have a real life. After Guiné, Angola will seem like the UK."

He smiled reassuringly.

"Why am I only learning this now?" Elizabeth asked.

"I just got the news from Renato myself. I'm still awaiting my orders."

"We're never leaving this bloody continent, are we?"

João reached across the table and took Elizabeth's hands in his. It was the first time they had touched in a week.

It would be more than a month before the orders came to leave. Elizabeth was into her seventh month. She was huge, hot, and tired. Brito called João into the officers' mess. Renato Marsola Araujo was waiting. The air force officer poured a healthy helping of *vinho tinto* into a mason jar and pushed it to the doctor, then poured another for Araujo and another for himself.

"To your next adventure," Brito bellowed, self-satisfied. It was just past nine in the morning.

They would stay in Luanda until the baby came, maybe a few weeks after that. Then it would be out of his hands. General Costa Gomes, commander in chief of Portuguese forces in Angola, would be handing out orders.

"Quite a survivor, General Gomes," Brito said. "I don't trust him a bit. They call him the Cork because he's always floating out of trouble." Brito's hands waved along an invisible ocean, his voice rising in mockery. "He lost his post in Lisbon—what was it, under-secretary of state for the army, I think—back in sixty-one after his name surfaced as a plotter against Doctor Salazar. But damn if he didn't get back into it. A brigadier general three short years later."

Brito glanced at his own rank, festooned on his chest, then shrugged. "You won't see much of him. Angola is not Guiné. It's a big country—excuse me, a big province of our beloved country," he said, his voice dripping with sarcasm. "I envy you, though, Major

Gonçalves. I'll be the one to lower the flag here and fly it out myself, tucked between my legs."

"Before you head off to bed, David, I want you to tell me something," Elizabeth was saying.

I looked up from my cup. I was tired. Hans was still in the hospital, and much as I loved these listening sessions, I could have used a rest that night.

"When you go to hospital to see Hans, what are you doing?"

"We read letters."

"Letters?"

"From your days in Africa. He has a pile of them in the chest by his bed. You didn't know that?"

"Well, I suppose I must have."

She took a moment to light a cigarette.

"Well, then, how are they?"

I thought for a moment.

"Corroborative, mostly."

"Will you show me one?"

I must have rolled my eyes. I wanted to go to sleep.

"Oh, c'mon, David, just the one. Then I'll leave you and Hans to your little game. I wrote the bloody things."

"He wrote half of them."

"Well, then show me one that I wrote, for fuck's sake, David."

I couldn't argue with that.

Dearest Hans,

I pick up this pen with terrible trepidation, so much to tell, so much of it horrible, a tale "whose lightest word would harrow up thy soul, freeze thy young blood."

Harrowing things have happened since I last wrote. Joao was captured by the guerrillas while in his mobile clinic. He just disappeared from me. I came back to the capital, Bissau, and was close to abandoning him, to returning to Houndsheath. But I couldn't be so cruel. You see, I am carrying his child. A shock, I know, you are soon to be an uncle, and a frightful uncle you will be, teaching my son or daughter all your vices and sloth. That will be a happy day. I do so miss you.

Without Joao, the loneliness and uncertainty were unbearable. My friend Angélica was some comfort. I awaited word, tried to somehow press his case with the governor of this colony, and then suddenly, he was free. The prison or guerrilla base or whatever you want to call it was attacked by the Portuguese, and he just squirted free. But Hans, he is a changed man. It is as if whatever happened to him these past months, whatever he saw, whatever they did to him, whatever he did, has sucked the gentleman from his marrow. I realize he had been without a woman for a long time, but what he did to me our first night back together was unforgivable. I don't know if I can look at him the same way again. I had so longed for his touch, his embrace, and his caress. Now, the thought of such things makes me shudder with revulsion. He took me, Hans. He took what he wanted and spit me out, like an animal, the savage bull.

But it is still more complicated. The war in Guine is all but lost. We are to depart, to Angola. Have you heard of it? Joao tells me I will like it, that the capital of Luanda is a real city, with cafes and restaurants and theatres. My baby will be delivered in a modern hospital. I am so tired of it here, the stench, the rot, the hopelessness. But what of this lovely land I am promised if I can no longer trust the man I am to share it with? I fear for my child, Hans. I fear for myself sometimes, though I know I am being a silly cow. It is not as if Joao has beaten me. I know—he has been through a lot, and I must give him time.

I am glad to hear you are still with Segolaine. You really must send me a photo. She sounds breathtaking. Watch out for those lasses at the bank, Hans, lest they lead you into temptation. Your Segolaine does not sound like a woman to be trifled with. I would ask you to pray for me or some such, but alas, neither of us was raised with such convenient outlets. So instead, I will say be happy for me. I am to bring a life into this world, such as it is. I will write from Angola.

Yours truly,
Elizabeth

CHAPTER FOURTEEN

"Guiné?" Francisco da Costa Gomes murmured. "You have seen a little war with big heroes: Senhor Cabral, with his speeches to the UN; our own brilliant, sad General Spínola. I hear he's writing a book about it all. Well, I hope you look back at that valiant little conflict with some fondness, Doctor. Here, you will find a big war with no heroes at all, only villains. I'm afraid I count myself among them."

João sat in an uncomfortable plain wooden chair, watching the general across a vast desk of mahogany, carved from the forests of the Congo. He had to decipher Gomes's introspective tone without the benefit of reading his eyes; the general wore dark glasses, even though the room's thick wooden shutters were drawn tight against the southern sun. Costa Gomes's boxy head was made more prominent by his receding hairline. The wiry, graying hair of his long sideburns framed prominent ears. He had a strangely thick lower lip that accentuated drooping eyes and a melancholy face. His bushy brows rose skyward. João understood why a military man like Brito wouldn't trust him. He seemed saddened by his position.

The original sin in Angola was Lisbon's, no doubt, the commander conceded. In Baixa do Cassange, in 1961, forced laborers, fed up with sowing cotton for their Portuguese, German, and British overlords, burned their identification cards and roughed up a few white traders. Crowds of Africans had gathered along the streets of Nambuangongo, the main market town of the province, to laugh and cheer the protesters. Musicians beat drums and strummed Portuguese guitars. Revolution, or at least change, was in the air, but it was a festive sort.

To the west, a more serious rebellion was under way. Some two hundred fifty fighters for the MPLA, the Popular Movement for the Liberation of Angola—soft intellectuals, mestiços, with no fighting experience among them—had the temerity to attack the main prison in Luanda. To that point, the MPLA, under the command of a Lisbon-trained medical student named Agostinho Neto, existed only in smoky cafés, basement plotting sessions, and revolutionary-sounding posters plastered on Luanda's walls in the dead of night. Now the professors and their students had guns. Seven policemen were killed. No prisoners were freed. The assailants were slaughtered with dispatch.

For their troubles, hell was unleashed, armed with napalm and revolvers. Seven thousand Angolans were incinerated in the villages of Baixa do Cassange. Portuguese settlers mobbed Luanda's slums—the *musseques*. To the north, in the fledgling nation of Zaire, Holden Roberto was ready for the next round of bloodletting. An ambitious mestiço with a rural army all his own, Roberto was not about to take orders from the city slickers of the MPLA, who were neither of his tribe, Bakongo, nor of his temperament. His UPA fighters, Union of the Peoples of Angola, maybe four or five thousand strong, armed with machetes and old shotguns, poured southward from the border, killing anybody or anything in their way. Women and children were strapped onto tree trunks and sent lengthwise through sawmills.

"The do-gooders at the UN say fifty thousand Africans died in that first year of war," Costa Gomes was saying a decade later, taking a deep drag from his African-rolled cigarette. "I don't doubt the number, but I can't corroborate it. We didn't count.

"I do know another number: two thousand. That's the number of

Portuguese who died, and let me tell you, that is not good for business when your business is settlement.

"We made a deal with the devil then. The South Africans have been loyal allies ever since. Their air force patrols the border, even bombed Tanzania for us. That shut Nyerere up. Don't get me wrong. We are doing our part. Last year, we secured twelve additional battalions—airborne, paratroopers, Marines, you name it, nearly twenty-thousand additional troops. Caetano's not about to give Angola up. But our propeller planes are no match for South African jets. We need those bastards."

João didn't understand his role, why he was here. The silences, he thought, were for effect, not engagement. So he waited.

"How long do such deals last before you are dragged to hell to pay your dues?" the general continued. "God does not like deals with the devil. Tell me, Doctor Gonçalves, when does the reckoning come?"

"Is that a rhetorical question?" João asked.

"Only if you don't have an answer, Major."

João owed this meeting with the commander of forces in Angola to his wife. There weren't any stuffed teddy bears or pink balloons to greet her and their new daughter postpartum, but there was one unruly tropical bouquet.

"Congratulations on your new arrival and may your recovery be a quick one," it read in English, with perfect penmanship. "Your father sends his best and would like you to write sometime. Sincerely, General Francisco da Costa Gomes."

The note sent a strange shiver through Elizabeth.

"'I can call spirits from the vasty deep,'" she murmured in wonderment to her husband, smiling over the paper.

She had felt so isolated for so long, so removed from home, it was as if she had found some kind of message in a bottle, a wayward, lucky break. She was too exhausted to contemplate its meaning or origin. But the general followed up two days later with a formal introductory letter, which arrived while she was still in the hospital.

"I hope that my last note did not cause undue surprise," it read. "Allow me to introduce myself. I am Francisco da Costa Gomes, commander of forces in Angola and an acquaintance of your father, Sir Gordon Bromwell, Member of Parliament. I met your father many years ago, when I was on NATO headquarters staff, in Norfolk, in your East Anglia. I realize that is quite a ways from your home in the south, but your father, in the House of Lords then, was and likely still is quite the military aficionado, as you no doubt know. And, I would add somewhat sheepishly, he was an admirer of our leader, Doctor Salazar, and our Iberian neighbor, Generalissimo Francisco Franco. This is an arena he and I did not see eye to eye on, but I try to avoid talking politics.

"Regardless, he received word that you might be heading in my direction, and he has asked me to keep an eye out for his daughter. His kindnesses were many as a gracious host in England. I am obliged to ensure your safety, which I am in a position to do. As I noted before, Sir Gordon would like a letter from you every now and again. As a father myself, I am full of sympathy.

"Truly yours,

"General Costa Gomes"

For an entire childhood and adolescence, Elizabeth had virtually no relationship with her father. That he had tracked her down, even through an intermediary, filled her with wonder and gratitude. Was this love? she thought. What would that feel like? She had never felt the warmth of affection; no kind words, no shared laughter, no compliments on her face or piano playing or singing voice, not even recriminations that reminded her that anything was expected of her. She wracked her memory, trying to conjure an instance when her father had told her he loved her, and it didn't come. He surely knew he was a grandfather. Perhaps he was looking after her after all.

She looked down at her baby daughter, Cristina, olive-skinned, already with lustrous black hair, latched on to her nipple. How could a creature so beautiful, so delicate, so tender emerge from troubles as deep as hers? Could this tiny baby be a solution, any solution? She delicately held that soft, dark skin with one pale, English hand, cradled that black crown with the other, and the very notions of troubles to be reckoned with, issues to be solved, they disappeared. And tears flowed.

For João, the entire first four months in Angola had been an escape. He and Elizabeth had flown out of Bissau on a troop transport full of soldiers, reinforcements for the Angolan war, a charitable person might say, evacuees from a defeat more likely. The men were crestfallen. Like him, they had hoped the loss of Bissau would mean an end to their tours of Africa. Instead, they were merely relocated. It was a strange-looking plane, with a bulbous passenger section nestled between narrow twin fuselages that rattled loudly behind the propellers. The arrival had been nothing like the shock of those first impressions of Bissau. Luanda was hot, but cooled by the wide expanse of seaside. The city teemed with life, thousands of Portuguese civilians mixed with hundreds of thousands of southern Africans in bars and restaurants along the bay, graceful colonial buildings, weathered by Africa but not ruined by it.

The army put them up in the Hotel Le Presidente, the oldest in a city founded in 1575 by the Portuguese explorer Paulo Dias de Novais. Slaves made Luanda prosper; palm and peanut oil, ivory, cotton, coffee, and cocoa made it legitimate. Now oil was making it rich. Luanda was oblivious to war and the draining coffers of the national bank in Lisbon. The oil discovery in Cabinda was fortuitously timed. The Six-Day War and its aftermath had plunged the West into a frantic search for its lifeblood anywhere but the Middle East. Luanda was a forest of construction cranes in the middle of a war of liberation, but the fighting was so far away that the residents chose not to believe in its existence.

No one seemed much to notice the doctor and his wife. Their room in the hotel overlooked the bay, in the heart of the city. João took long walks on the seafront, sipped freshly picked and roasted coffee in the cafés on the ocean, checked in on his wife—

huge and miserable—and then headed into the city again. At night, there were endless diversions. The thrum of Latinized African music mixed with the flouncy miniskirts of the era. It was a sensual cauldron.

Elizabeth ached. She had wept as she said good-bye to Angélica, her only real friend in Africa. "'May violets spring! I tell thee, churlish priest, a minist'ring angel shall my sister be,'" she whispered in her ear as they held each other. Angélica smiled and patted her on the shoulder. "There you go again with that."

Their relationship had been strained to say the least, but the thaw between João and Elizabeth had defrosted the women's friendship as well. Angélica came to understand Elizabeth's hurt at João's hands not as the self-indulgence of a pampered child but as a glimpse at her friend's vulnerability, so far from home, so dependent on this man. Elizabeth forgave Angélica as the Cabo-Verdiana's scorn softened and her ribbing turned good-natured again.

Angélica came by her newfound empathy honestly, for her own sense of vulnerability had overwhelmed her. The loss of her white patron meant everything. She would be reduced to a charwoman at best, or thrown off the base to try to find her way in Bissau or find a way back to Cabo Verde. For Elizabeth, solitude meant finding her way back to her husband, if she could. And it meant starting over, in a new African country, even farther from home, with a baby due in weeks. Parting had been agony.

Like João, she was cheered by her new, temporary home. But an ocean view could keep her occupied only so long. The endless cycle of hotel meals, fitful naps when she could not find a position to rest around her great abdomen, fifteen-minute walks, and lonely convalescence wore her down quickly. She badly wanted the baby to come, to free her from the grotesque body that she believed was sending her husband into the streets, and to break up the monotony. Those last weeks of pregnancy were God's way of making childbirth an acceptable alternative, she thought.

Though he was not an attentive husband, João was a conscientious doctor. He treated Elizabeth like his most important patient, making frequent rounds, ensuring proper nutrition and hydration, preparing for the best care available. As promised, the hospital in Luanda was a far cry from Bissau's. It had obstetricians, well-trained nurses, a real maternity ward. And João apparently had been forgotten by the Portuguese army, which had brought him to Angola, installed him in this fine hotel, and seemingly lost interest in him. It was a temporary lapse, no doubt, but he had no intention of raising his hand, not with his first child on the way. Professional courtesy for the wife and firstborn child of the new doctor ensured fawning service for Elizabeth. She found she was spending far more time than necessary making the final arrangements for her approaching due date. She had nothing else to do. Easily available, chatty Portuguese cabdrivers and an obliging hotel doorman made trips to and from her obstetrician's office a painless diversion. João sometimes came along to check on the state of medicine in the Province of Angola.

"How does the heartbeat sound today?" he'd demand of the day's nurse.

"Strong and steady, Doctor Gonçalves."

"Have you considered an X-ray, just to be sure?"

"I don't think that will be necessary, Doctor Gonçalves. Do you insist?"

"Let's check the fetal heart rate tomorrow. I'll make my decision then."

Elizabeth would watch her husband through these interrogations, aghast. She was aware there was a time when his knowledge and forcefulness would have filled her with admiration, even desire. Now he just seemed a bully.

The actual birth was something less dramatic than Elizabeth had at once feared and hoped for. The initial contractions hurt; even young Elizabeth knew that was coming. But when they were frequent enough, she was put to sleep. If Europe was beginning to cotton to natural childbirth, or at least cognizant partum and an epidural, colonial Portugal remained fond of general anesthesia, which kept the mother nice and quiet. Elizabeth awoke, groggy, sore, with a nasty tear that no one had warned her about, a husband napping beside her, and a beautiful baby girl in the arms of the nurse standing over her.

The nerves of motherhood would wait, the worries over her marriage, her larger displacement in the world. At that moment, she belonged.

"Cristina," she murmured, her arms reaching out to her daughter, almost weightless in her delicacy. She nuzzled the infant's face to hers, bathed it in tears, then, guided by the hands of a flaxen-haired nurse with olive skin, brought her to her breast. For the first time, she felt the welcome pain as her baby latched on, then the letdown and the moment of maternal understanding. In that instant, she loved that child like she had never loved anything before. João stood to put a hand on her sweat-drenched hair, another on the baby. She didn't notice.

At almost twenty-two, Elizabeth was not experienced enough to worry about whether she could handle the sleepless rigors of infancy, nor was she mature enough to cope with a difficult child. Cristina, as it turned out, was a delight. The first two weeks, she was almost silent. Even after she truly awoke to life beyond the womb, she took it all in with quiet, wide-eyed wonder. Physically, she was her father's girl, with a long, delicate face, high cheekbones, black hair, dark, dark brown eyes set along an aquiline nose. She was the kind of baby that won gasps from passing mothers, not squeals of playful laughter.

Both parents delighted as Elizabeth shed pounds by the stone, fat coursing from her belly into her milk and through plump breasts to the voracious, growing baby they adored. Elizabeth was convinced João's youthful appetite for sex had disappeared without complaint as she closed down to his desires. At first, she felt guilty. Not much later, she figured her husband had overcome the fears he confided at the restaurant in Bissau. The pickings were far more tempting here, and he still had long, unexplained absences in the Luandan night. She surprised herself with her acceptance of it. In this moment, she had all that she wanted.

When he was there, he was all she could hope for in a father. He loved his daughter joyfully. The family, now looking and feeling complete, strolled along the bay with a pram purchased at an upscale department store. They sat in the cafés together, João gallantly shielding his breast-feeding wife and baby from view and then showing them off to the housewives and swing-shift bar girls taking in the southern African sun. The girls discreetly acted as if they were meeting the young doctor for the first time, hiding the knowing blush on their cheeks or suppressing the giggles of a carnal recall.

Once out of the hospital, Elizabeth took it upon herself to make contact with her protector. She found the address he had left for her and nervously drafted a letter to the general, telling him all was well and thanking him profusely for relaying her father's message. She promised to write to Hampshire, and she did. In fact, she decided to reconnect. She dashed off letters to Hans, to Cousin Victoria, to her parents, even to her childhood tutor. She was happy and proud. She had something to express beyond fear or regret or confusion.

With the healthy birth of Dr. João Gonçalves's child came the inevitable end of the Portuguese army's indifference to his sloth. A note greeted him one afternoon at the hotel front desk after a particularly long lunch in the sun, typed on medical corps letterhead.

Major Gonçalves, your presence is requested at Medical Aid Service headquarters, 23 November 1971, 0800 hours. Colonel Hugo Calheiros, commander, Angolan Medical Corps.

"Have a seat, Major Gonçalves. I am Colonel Calheiros," he said, sitting heavily in the functional chair behind his nondescript desk. "I gather you're having a pleasant time in Luanda."

João couldn't tell if that was a question or an accusation. He leaned to the latter and blushed. Calheiros's smile was even and sustained; João saw it as lascivious.

"Well, sir, it has been eventful. I had my first child."

"Yes, we know, congratulations, and please, no 'sirs.' We're both doctors. I've done my duty addressing you as 'Major.' Can I call you João?" Calheiros asked.

"Of course," João said, smiling with relief.

"We know a great deal about you. This is the military, after all. Your experience in Guiné makes you highly valuable to us. You know the real Africa, not this," he said, gesturing vaguely to Luanda's city center below. "You know how it smells. You've seen tropical diseases, parasites, you've treated combat wounds and trauma, and"—he paused for effect—"you've seen combat."

Calheiros smiled in a patronizing way; strange, João thought, in the context of the conversation.

"I have to admit I've grown a little soft since I've gotten here."

"We've noticed. We have been watching, João. Don't think the secret police operate only in the *metrópole*. We need you now, João. Your orders have come in. You've seen things most doctors in theater haven't. Don't be deceived by Luanda, or even Nova Lisboa, where we're going to send you. There's a real war going on. We're winning it, and unlike in Guiné, we have a reason to fight. For a lot of us, this is home, the only home we've ever known. I was born in Lobito, to the south of here. I can't imagine leaving this continent. But it's a hard fight."

"I've heard bad things about Nova Lisboa," João said.

Calheiros laughed.

"You'll love it, or at least your wife will. Trust me on that."

João had a week before the family was due to report to their new home. Elizabeth decided it was time to meet the general.

"Dear General Costa Gomes," she wrote in English, hoping that was not too presumptuous. "My husband and I will be leaving in seven days' time for Nova Lisboa and his new post. I would very much like to make your acquaintance in person before our departure. If it is not too much trouble, would you mind sharing a cup of tea with me? Sincerely, Elizabeth Bromwell Gonçalves."

It was the first time she had referred to herself that way. She liked the sound of it. Rather than wait for the post, she bundled Cristina up, had the doorman hail a cab, then rode to the imposing fortress above Luanda Bay, Fortaleza de São Miguel. That was, in fact, not where the offices of the top leadership was. Those offices were on the grounds but beyond the forbidding walls, in a far lovelier, orange-hued colonial building with gracious windows and plantation shutters, a veranda on the inland side, a garden framing the ocean view on the other. Her request to have a letter hand-delivered to the general was greeted with more amusement than suspicion. She did not wait for a reply before heading back down the hill.

The general sent word to the front desk that afternoon that he would be at the Café Ultramar, near her hotel, in the morning at eight and would be pleased to meet. João offered grudging admiration for her initiative. He, too, saw the merits of the meeting and promised to watch the baby.

She had never seen General Costa Gomes, but he was easy to pick out by the quantity of brass on his chest. She stood out too, washed-out and awkward amid all of that Latin insouciance. As she approached, he stood regally and offered to kiss her hand. The general lacked the battle-hardened bravado of Spínola, no monocle or white gloves, no flash behind the tinted glasses. His strengths were political, outward modesty masking a knack for ingratiation and an ability to find the seams for advancement. He had grown up in the impoverished north of Portugal, Trás-os-Montes, "behind the mountains." Like many other poor boys, he never conquered the sense that he did not belong and did not deserve his success. In a singularly reticent autocracy, that only assured his continuing ascent.

"It is a pleasure to make your acquaintance, senhora. You remind me much of your father," he lied graciously. "Please sit. I'd order you tea with milk, but that is one thing I would not recommend in southern Africa."

"Thank you, General, I have long given up on the milk."

"Very wise. That explains your good health."

A waitress had already approached, and she let Costa Gomes order tea for her, Earl Grey, from the shipping port of Goa, no longer under Portuguese control but alive in the imperial memory.

"I only have the vaguest understanding of how you came to Luanda, senhora. I know of your husband. Military doctors are much prized in these wars of ours. I don't doubt the wisdom of General Spínola's campaign for hearts and minds, only his timing. We're already down to the dregs of conscription, the dullards who could not find a way to escape. Our young doctors are scattered to the winds—Britain, France, the United States. You'll have to tell me why Doctor Gonçalves showed up, especially with his King's College degree."

"I expect it was something dreadfully old-fashioned," Elizabeth said. "Duty, or some such."

"I expect it was something more primal than that, his father for instance." Costa Gomes laughed softly, sipping his second espresso. "It is amazing what men of a certain background will do not to disappoint their fathers. It is even more amazing the valiant lengths their women go to see the best in them."

"I suppose so," Elizabeth said.

"I gather I should not put you into that category?"

"Which?"

"The bit about striving to please your father." His tone sounded a touch reproachful.

"No, daughters are different. They have mothers. There are only two kinds, the ones who cannot leave and the ones who cannot stay."

"Ah, and I can see which one you fancy yourself to be."

Elizabeth looked down at the table sheepishly. Family duties were different in Britain than in Portugal. Costa Gomes might have gathered that during his time at NATO Command, Norfolk, but that didn't mean he accepted their equivalence. Elizabeth felt the flush of guilt on her face.

"Senhora, I don't mean to pry. We have all seen love sweep up the young. It is a swift river at your age. Your current happened to be an especially strong one."

He smiled at his cleverness. She did not meet his insistent gaze.

"When I was your age, I was swept to Macao by a more blunt force, the Portuguese military. I've told your father I'd look after you…"

"That's why I'm here," Elizabeth blurted out, so rudely she gasped. "I, I, I'm sorry. That was quite forward."

"Senhora, you're speaking to a man who talked his way out of the gallows and into a command in southern Africa. They called it sedition, you know. I didn't like the fascists all that much, but when it came to it, when I had to grovel, I convinced them I did. I do not stand on ceremony or pride."

"Then you won't mind if I ask a…a favor?"

Costa Gomes tried on a beneficent little smile.

"Ask away, my dear. Just as long as you know I don't have to agree."

"João, my husband, has already been through a lot, in Guiné. It's not me I'm worried about. It's him."

"How so?"

"Well, captivity hardened him. I'm just starting to see the contours of the gentleman I married begin to re-form. I'd hate to lose that again."

"Elizabeth, this is war. Doctor Gonçalves's experience in Guiné is very valuable to his country at the moment. That hardness may not be so great in a husband, but it is in a fighter. I will keep you and your daughter safe. But your husband, he belongs to the Portuguese army."

Two days before leaving Luanda, João was summoned to Costa Gomes's office for a briefing.

"Doctor Gonçalves, I don't know what to make of you. Your generation has all but forsaken the cause. The intellectuals, the doctors, they no longer bother to burn their draft notices. They board a train to Paris or Rome without even opening the envelope. I have no doubt you could be in London right now, on salary with the National Health Service, holding a pensioner by the balls and telling him to cough."

To João, the conversation was going from bad to worse. He could defend his decision and speak of his love for the motherland or some such crap Costa Gomes wouldn't believe, or he could stay quiet and let the general have his truth, that João Gonçalves showed up because doing what he was told—by his government, by his father, by the woman in his bed—was almost always the easiest thing to do. He stayed quiet.

"Your wife loves you very much," the general continued. "She asked that I protect you."

"I did not ask for that," João said hotly. They were the first meaningful words to pass through his lips, and they came out angrily. He had encouraged Elizabeth to reach out to the general. He figured it was best to have such a man on their side. But not for protection. Elizabeth may have been well meaning, but she had humiliated him, and General Costa Gomes was rubbing it in.

"Sir, I apologize, but I want you to know I gave my wife no message to deliver you about my status. I am grateful for your kind offers to watch out for my family. But I have every intention of serving as a military physician. I've seen combat..."

Silence fell as Costa Gomes appraised the doctor. He seemed pleased he had a soldier sitting with him, angry but contained, the mooring of his wife loose and distant.

"Good, Major. I told Senhora Gonçalves as much. Nova Lisboa has three bull's-eyes painted on it. That has more to do with our three enemies and their hatred of each other than anything we've done, but we can't be caught in the crossfire. They've already got a name for it, Huambo, as it was called when it was just a cluster of thatched mud houses and an open-air market. God help us if the three of them reach the city together."

* * *

Husband, wife, and child reported to the airstrip at seven in the morning, their belongings packed in three overstuffed duffel bags that João and the cabby managed while Elizabeth pushed the pram. They were escorted to a Do-27, a turboprop that looked like a private plane a sportsman might own for quick fishing trips. Angola was full of them, German castoffs. The Portuguese would have liked something a little more substantial, but the Americans were souring on Caetano's colonial policies. NATO assistance was drying up.

At just over five hundred kilometers away, Nova Lisboa was not a hop, a skip, or a jump from Luanda. It was a long-enough flight for anticipation to build. Elizabeth envisioned a war zone, or at least a city besieged, enveloped in fear, beset by shortages and dreading the end—something like Bissau but with more white people. The small plane rose above the coastal plain, flew over impenetrable forests, and then skimmed over the lush green grasslands of the highlands. They touched down on the tarmac and stepped into the first temperate air Elizabeth had felt in over a year. An army driver took the family by jeep into a city neither had expected. The wide, graceful Avenida Cinco de Outubro led them past kilometers of modern, nondescript, but tidy apartment blocks. They traversed the Jardim Américo Tomás, drove past a vast outdoor theater, empty in daylight but capable of seating a thousand or so. A towering Florentine fountain graced an expansive central park with winding paths through subtropical flowers. Clutches of young mothers held the hands of their children or pushed strollers through the Parque Infantil. The art deco Cinema Ruacaná and Club Nova York awaited the night's revelers. It was all immaculate. What were missing were the Africans. A few Angolan women waited at bus stops or tended sidewalk fruit stands, but Nova Lisboa was a white city, a colonial construct, beautiful but doomed, built on sand. Elizabeth suffered a few moments of liberal guilt, but then she turned to João and smiled. He smiled back.

The jeep approached the gates of a large military compound not far from the center of town. *A Zona Central do Comando Militar*, a large sign proclaimed, "Central Military Zone Command Center." Two Portuguese soldiers lifted the barrier and waved them through. This was not a city in panic. The barracks and buildings of the base were arranged in tidy rows of uniform white structures, all but indistinguishable from one another. The driver pulled up to one of the last and helped João carry the duffel bags into a little anteroom. The base commander stepped out of his office, and with a pleasant smile, extended a hand to the new doctor.

"You have friends in high places," he said as he ushered husband, wife, and baby into his military-issue office, drab but sun-drenched. "General Costa Gomes offers his regards and has asked us to set you up in an apartment off base."

Elizabeth looked quizzically at her husband.

"That seems entirely unnecessary," João said, "really."

The commander shrugged. "It's an order." There was something troubling about his expression, incongruous with the surroundings. His face was clean shaven, his hair fashionably long, not military issue. The crow's-feet around his eyes and worry lines between his brows were more deeply etched than his age should have wrought. He seemed somehow disloyal.

"Is that safe," João asked, "for Elizabeth and the baby?"

Elizabeth gave the major a concerned look as she rocked back and forth and gently bounced her baby. The commander didn't give her a glance.

"My friend, an apartment on the avenida is far safer than here. On base, you are a military target. On the Avenida Cinco, you're just another Tuga, a settler family with a new Angolan child. I suppose in the largest sense, no one is as safe as we'd like to believe. But there is safety in herds. That's why the wildebeest run in them."

He walked back around his desk and sat heavily in his chair, sighing and reaching for some paperwork.

"You will be part of the great white herd of Nova Lisboa."

CHAPTER FIFTEEN

I had stumbled out of bed to go to the toilet when I ran into Elizabeth staring intently at a pair of dusty bookcases in her upstairs parlor. I stood in the hallway in my boxer shorts, surprised by the sight of her and struggling to cover a useless morning hard-on. The sun was out. It must have been getting late, but there were no windows in my room, tucked against the wall that adjoined the house next door. With Hans in hospital, there wasn't much reason to wake up.

"My father absolutely forbade me to sell them." She said it vaguely, her mind clearly on the furniture.

"The books?" I asked. I was embarrassed to be standing there in my underwear, my recalcitrant erection mocking my situation, but Elizabeth didn't so much as give me a glance.

"The bookcases."

They were clearly old, soiled by fingers that rubbed over the intricate brass grilles, which were browned with tarnish. Those grilles would have been startling if polished, even I could tell. The sides had these delicate fronds—leaves, I guess—that no one would bother to carve these days. I had never really noticed the bookcases but had looked at the books quite a lot—rows of uniform, graying sets of Thackeray, Coleridge, Pepys, Samuel Johnson, the kinds of British authors you read about without actually reading. *Who the hell was Pepys?* I thought to myself as I looked at the spine of the great volumes. They looked ancient. I wouldn't dare touch them for fear that the pages would crack like dried leaves. To me, the books more than the cases spoke of the ancientness of the Bromwell line. I was more drawn to the Africana in the room: brightly dyed fabrics stretched over cheap wooden frames, a carving of a threatening-looking little man in a loincloth holding knives in each hand, a colorful etched gourd with a long, slender handle I once warned Maggie I'd use on her one night.

"He was beginning to go round the twist, really. He hadn't said much when I started selling it all off. Sometimes he'd get angry at the racket the transactions made. But when they came for these bookcases, he came alive. He practically barricaded himself in the library."

"They must be worth a lot."

"A bloody fortune, I'd imagine. They're kingwood; sixteenth century, my father insisted. I can't be sure." She approached them and reached out to touch the carved edges. "Fronds of ormolu. It's a bit hard to see them, but a quick once-over and they'd be as good as new. Haversham's on his way. I've promised him something good."

We both stared at the bookcases for a while in silence. I was tempted to put an arm over Elizabeth's shoulder. But I was standing in boxers and a T-shirt, my breath, I feared, stale from a long sleep. I was suddenly aware of my Americanness, uncouth in the eyes of Hans, for sure, unsure of Elizabeth's opinion of me.

"Go back to bed, David," she said, turning to me for the first time. Her face was sad, maternal. "I've got a bit of a stomachache. I think I drank a bit much last night."

I nodded, not knowing whether it was OK to say, "Yeah, Elizabeth, I think you drink a bit much every night." Instead, I asked, "Sorry, can I use the loo first?"

"After you, kind sir."

I slunk off to the bathroom and back into my room.

With all those letters clattering around my brain, one on a shredded aerogram was pressing down on me in particular. It had come from my mother.

Dearest David,

We haven't heard from you in a long, long time. I hope you are well. Please write. We miss you. I know your father and I haven't always been there for you—since Rebecca's passing. We've never really talked about it, and I'm sorry for that, really. I don't have to tell you your parents did not take your sister's death well. Some day, I pray, you will have children of your own, and you will better understand the anguish we have suffered—we continue to suffer. But that is not why I'm writing, dear. I'm not making excuses.

In your absence, I've had a lot of time to think about you and your teenage years. I realize now I hardly noticed you turning into a man. Those years are all a blur. I can barely recall a thing. We didn't give you a bar mitzvah. We didn't give one to your brother either. Rebecca was still too raw, but still, I'm sorry for that. I have this memory of driving to Providence to drop your brother off at college. Somehow we met you there, but I don't remember why you weren't in the car with us. We didn't take you to college at all. You flew off on your own.

I can't complain that you are off on your own now. We gave you little choice in the matter. I want you to know I see all this now. I didn't see it then, but I have wanted to understand why you didn't come back after your year abroad. I blame myself.

David, we are learning to see our sons, I swear. Last week, your father and I cleared out Rebecca's bedroom. We're turning it into a guestroom. It was hard. We did it together. I cried, but then in the morning, I looked at the empty walls and the stripped bed, I opened the dresser drawers to see them bare, and moved the garbage bags full of her clothes to the curb for Goodwill. I felt better and thought of you. It's spring now. You have to start thinking of your future, and I hope that your future is here, not there. My heart is thawing. There is room for you now, and I want you to know I love you and am waiting for you.

Please come home soon.

All my love and kisses,
Mom

I had been in Washington when my parents took my brother to Brown his freshman year of college. Noah was a skinny kid then, with gray eyes and light brown hair that seemed to come from some other gene pool. I joked about the mailman, something he didn't find amusing in the slightest. He had a way of making his presence known to my absent parents. He was smart, polite, a striver in the ways parents liked. I had my own mild ambitions, but they were a little off key. I had started an Atlanta chapter of the Children's Campaign for Nuclear Disarmament, a ridiculous little venture that mostly resulted in well-meaning parents scolding me in Piedmont Park for asking their gullible children to sign petitions they could not possibly understand. A group of us had converged on the nation's capital to deliver those petitions. I was sixteen. I took a Greyhound with a friend, met a few young senators and congressmen, fell in love with another sixteen-year-old activist named Kirsten, then boarded another bus for Providence. My father had given me the money for bus fare and food. With the arrival of my mother's letter, I realized they didn't even remember giving me permission or sending me off.

My propensity for falling in love—or at least infatuation—came from my mother, Ruth. At barely five feet, she was an overly sensitive woman, buffeted by the world's storms and carried along on its currents. She married my father when she was nineteen and at Barnard. My ability to navigate those currents on my own came from my sister. I have this vivid memory of her. I had been reading comics, when I decided to become the Hulk. I took great big oil crayons and colored myself green, covering as much of my body as I could till the greasy utensils broke into bits too small even for my little fingers. My brother laughed and laughed and I loved his laughter. My mother was off at work (she was a social worker with a master's in sociology by then). My father was at the hospital—a cardiologist.

I ran into my sister's room, squealing with joy. Rebecca looked at me with pursed disappointment.

"David, Dad is going to kill you."

"No one can kill me. I'm the Hulk."

"You're an idiot. You touch one thing and you're dead."

It was a little late. Green smears had followed me up from the basement, lurking on walls, banisters, doorknobs, and doorjambs. Rebecca stripped me bare and scrubbed. She scrubbed silently and intently until not a trace of green was left. Then she retraced my steps back to the basement, scrubbing away the evidence. When she finished, she looked at me, sighed, and went back to her book.

I pulled myself awake an hour later amid the clatter of furniture moving. I caught only the back of one of Haversham's men walking awkwardly down the stairs. I checked the parlor. The bookcases were still there. The Empire-era end tables were gone, though, along with the jade chinoiserie lamps that had rested on them, with their depressing yellowed-silk shades.

I felt wonderfully rested by the time Hans was discharged from the hospital. It had been only five days, but those were days filled with sloth. There hadn't been much they could do beyond some IV drips and infusions of A-positive to flush the blood and restore iron levels. I visited him each day of his stay. Elizabeth made the trek once. He mainly slept. Cristina had dropped by as he was nearing his discharge, to see if she could interest him in a Belgian truffle she had picked up in The Lanes. I told her that perhaps she could dress a little more conservatively, and she managed a pair of jeans and a cropped cotton sweater nicely.

"I do like that you notice what I wear, David," she told me. "So many men couldn't care less. Maybe we could go shopping sometime."

The thought thrilled me, but I felt a twinge of sadness. She was so delicate, so lovely, and so far from possible.

"Anytime, Cristina," I sighed. "Just say the word."

It was not that Cristina and I had no relationship. By this time, I considered her a friend. I wanted more, but I would not dare to seek it. I had worked up the courage to ask her if she needed any help with her studies, intent on making good on my promise to Hans.

"Why David, do you fancy me that much?" she had said with a slight, suspicious smile.

My cheeks burned, but I held my ground. "No, Cristina, it's not like that. Really, I want to be of some help. With Hans away, I might as well work for my eighteen quid a week."

She regarded me quizzically. We were where we always were when we spoke, in the kitchen, and she offered a test. "Alright, David, where should we go?" she asked suspiciously.

I shrugged. I understood the test. If I suggested my room or hers, her suspicions would be confirmed.

"How 'bout the upstairs parlor? Your mother made some extra room with Haversham's last visit. There are still a few lamps up there."

"Alright then," she responded with a smile.

After that first study session, Cristina and I began spending quite a bit of time together. High-stakes testing wasn't part of my educational experience. I didn't appreciate the pressure of A levels—she was taking three: History, English Literature, and Biology. But I knew history, even British history, I had a passing knowledge of literature, and I was eager to help.

"Do you really have the royal line of succession memorized?" she had asked during one of my first tutorials.

"From Ethelred the Unready to Elizabeth the Second," I bragged.

"Alright then, who was before Elizabeth?"

"You mean Bloody Mary?"

"No, the current Elizabeth, you sod."

"George the Sixth, the one with the stammer, assumed the throne after Edward the Eighth abdicated to be with one of ours, Mrs. Simpson."

"Very good, David."

She let her hand fall gently on mine, then pulled it away—but slowly—when my searching eyes met hers.

As it turned out, Cristina could be serious when she wanted to be, and as the first generation of Bromwells to attend state school, she had much to prove—if only to herself. Her grandparents were dead. Her Eton-educated uncle had no pull to hoist her back to the class that was for so long the domain of the clan. Her mother, who hadn't gone to school as a child at all, was impressed with her daughter's mere willingness to get up every morning and leave the house. That act alone, the discipline of normalcy, made Cristina the rock of the Bromwell household. If her mother was in a particularly lazy or bad mood, or nearly comatose after a solo bender, it was Cristina that made sure her education stayed on track—a before-dawn wake-up, bus fare into town, assignments organized and done. And with my opening offer, I became increasingly roped in as part of Cristina's act. I still found her enticing, even over early English history. A sly smile and a twinkling eye through her dark, dark locks, and I'd do anything—even long quiz sessions on Labour politics between the wars. But that desire, I figured, was my problem, not hers. I would not burden her with my longing.

"The Irish Potato Famine came in what years?"

"The Great Famine, David. Only Americans call it the Potato Famine."

"Really?"

"Really. Eighteen forty-five to eighteen fifty-two, death toll about a million."

"Cause?"

"The subdivision of land, overdependence on the Lumper potato, and of course the Corn Laws."

Literature was my favorite subject for these sessions, even if history was my strong suit.

"'The world is too much with us; late and soon, / Getting and spending, we lay waste our powers,'" I read from a well-worn textbook, its spine long broken.

"Wordsworth," Cristina chimed back, "written I think very early nineteenth century, no?"

"Bingo."

"Bingo?" she asked mockingly, her eyes twinkling.

We were sitting on the floor, backs to the wall of a room in a house steadily emptying of its possessions. Her mother, no doubt, was drinking in the kitchen. Her uncle lay still and silent beneath his wool blankets. And Cristina had again laid her soft, long fingers on my forearm. My heart thudded, so loudly I thought surely she could hear it, as I flipped through pages, trying not to scare her away.

"Tell me about this one:

> Listen! you hear the grating roar
> Of pebbles which the waves draw back, and fling,
> Begin, and cease, and then again begin,
> With tremulous cadence slow, and bring
> The eternal note of sadness in."

"I love that poem," she said quietly, her hand still there, burning my skin, "'Dover Beach.' Any schoolgirl who grows up on the South Downs knows it."

"What do you hear in that section?" I asked.

"The sea, of course, you twit. I hear it every night if I listen carefully.

> Ah, love, let us be true
> To one another! for the world, which seems
> To lie before us like a land of dreams,
> So various, so beautiful, so new."

I rejoined.

"Swept with confused alarms of struggle and flight,
Where ignorant armies clash by night."

It was late. I put my hand on hers and squeezed softly. She lifted it and enveloped my hand in both of hers, and I brought the precious package to my lips. Our eyes met. I moved my head toward hers, eyes open, riveted by the soft beauty of her lovely face. Then she smiled and turned her head to offer a cheekbone sheathed in perfection. My lips found not what they were looking for but lingered on what they found. She gave one more reassuring clasp, dropped my hand, and stood.

"Best we get to sleep, love."

"Cristina, wait. I . . ."

"Our next session, David. Biology. Promise."

Then she was gone.

On Hans's last morning in hospital, I climbed the two blocks on my own to fetch him. Elizabeth was in typing class.

"Well, David, my welcome wagon, I trust all is well on the home front," Hans said, strapped tightly back into his wheelchair, snug in his coyote fur, a greasy brown paper bag in his lap with his tooth-brush, comb, and some dirty clothes. It was odd seeing him so expertly put together, none of it my doing. I had come to believe I was the only one who could do it properly.

"Hans, you're looking a lot better. I won't get too carried away, but really, I mean it," I said. And he did look better. The puffiness in his face, the lolling eyes and drooping lip were gone. He looked attentive. But he was still tired. I wondered if that would ever change.

"Have you shagged that niece of mine yet?" he asked, in a way that would sound serious to anyone who didn't know better. I had been circling around to the back of the wheelchair to relieve the orderly. A nurse giggled, not knowing how else to act.

"Cheeky bastard," she said to him.

"No, Hans. On my best behavior, not that it'd matter if I wasn't," I muttered, jerking the wheelchair a little roughly and heading toward the large double doors.

Getting myself and Hans back into a rhythm proved surprisingly difficult. Hans was eating nothing now. Elizabeth made a small plate of food for him at meals, knowing he would take a bite or two of each offering and then turn his head away. I no longer ate the leftovers by his side. With so little food on the plate to begin with, swallowing the few forkfuls after Hans would be too mortifying, even for me. Hans was dispirited. I would put the music on for him, more often than not. With so little nourishment, operating the stereo was too heavy a lift on bad days. He could manage turning the pages of a book, though mainly he just stared at the words. I'd set up his reading desk, strap on the rubber-tipped stick, and prop up a very worn copy of a book called *Darkness at Noon* by someone named Arthur Koestler.

As he read, his urine bag would cloud over with the strain on the bit of kidney still functioning. I offered one afternoon to take him down to the Imperial Arms, or just for a push along the boardwalk. The weather was finally clearing. It was still cool, but clear. A long look at the ocean would do him good, I assured Hans. He sighed, and I dropped it.

"I could compose a note to the Voluntary Euthanasia Society, expressing on your behalf your sincere ingratitude as you face the loss of kidney function. We could have some fun with it." I smiled at him, overeager to add some gallows cheer to the changed atmosphere.

"Yes, David, why don't you do that, this afternoon, while I'm napping," Hans said wearily.

James and Wills had screeched down from London one afternoon in their aging but potent Jaguar. I was happy to see them, to break up the sad monotony. I'm not sure Hans was. They sashayed through the front hall, unannounced, and into Hans's room, bearing a bottle of Barolo and a tin of foie gras, not the homegrown variety of the pre-accident crowd but they knew what he liked. They couldn't help but notice Hans's down state, and they acted accordingly.

"Oh, darling," Wills said to Hans, leaning over him with flamboyant intimacy. "You've looked better, but haven't we all?"

I had seen Hans play along with such displays a dozen times. This time, he sighed.

"Hans, really, we heard about the kidneys and all. I'd say what a pity if I hadn't heard your grousing about the state of your life—you know, the state of actually living—for so long. Now's your chance. Do not go quietly into that good night and all that twaddle. Rage, rage, rage."

He shook his fist at him dramatically, his face scrunched into mock passion.

"I'd love to rage, Wills, really, but there's not a lot of petrol in the tank. David," he said, turning his head to me, "maybe you could rage for me."

I smiled and made a cursory fist at the sky, well, the ceiling.

"Bravo," said James, "having a young man at your side to express your death rattle for you. I couldn't imagine a better way to go. And he's not that bad-looking."

He checked me out from head to toe with exaggerated lecherousness. "I'm thinking of getting myself one of these Community Service Volunteers, you know. I'll say life is too much of a strain at my age. Do they let you look at their pictures before you choose?"

"He's not a rent boy, you know," Hans said, trying to engage.

"I asked for a volunteer, didn't I? I have no intention of paying him."

Wills sensed the joie-de-vivre gambit was getting them nowhere. "Really, Hans, why so glum?"

There was a long, deliberate rolling of the eyes at that one, then, "If only I had actually accomplished something, you know? Trite, I'm sure, but these are the things one contemplates at the end."

"Oh, pshaw," Wills scoffed with a wave of a hand. "Darling, you've accomplished a lot. Elizabeth, come help here. Elizabeth?" he called out into the hall, but there was no answer. She was at the poly. "There you go, you accomplished Elizabeth. You made coyote-fur straitjackets fashionable in certain circles."

"Young David here was nearly beaten up for that fashion."

"I said *some* circles, love. Really, Hans, nobody accomplishes anything. Maria Callas had a few really good records that will be forgotten by the next generation with their bloody compact discs." He said "compact discs" with an exaggerated drawl, as if they were a disease. "Even old Maggie Thatcher, once she's sold off British Rail, British Air, British Telecom, British tea, Lord knows what else, to the Americans I expect, who'll remember her beyond the *Spitting Image* puppets? You can't get caught up in all that achievement stuff. It's all far too American."

"You know," Hans said, "if I could just take a really good shit before I die, maybe I'd go happy."

"I think we can help with that," James said semi-seriously.

They stayed maybe an hour, talking that way, cheering the old bugger up, then gunned the Jag off Imperial Lane on an excursion to Lewes, where the old ladies serve high tea with all the crusts cut off.

"I need to leave."

I said it flat out. I was sitting on Maggie's bed, thumbing through a *Melody Maker*, an article on That Petrol Emotion. A friend in the States—well, a girl I had been in love with who hadn't loved me back—had given me a tape of them before I left. It hadn't taken, but of course context is everything. Now I was reading about John O'Neill and his old band, the Derry Hitmakers, and the near miss "Big Decision" had with the Top 40—charted at 42!—as if it meant something, really meant something. Maggie was lying on her stomach beside me, her head propped up on a hand, reading a thick sociology textbook.

"Alright. Late, isn't it? I can give you cab fare," she offered absently.

"No, Maggie, I need to leave Britain, to get on with my life. I've gotta get a fucking job this summer, you know."

She looked up. Our eyes met, and she let hers linger as she took off her glasses. But she was miffed, and I wondered what line I had crossed this time.

"David, whadya want me to say? 'Don't go'? 'Stay with me'?"

"I dunno. That might be a start. Or how 'bout, 'I'll come with you'?"

Her eyes drifted downward to the well-worn white sheets—bedclothes, the Brits call them.

"You don't mean that, David."

"Mean what?"

"You don't want me to come home with you."

"What the hell, Maggie? I thought those were the plans all along, at least for the summer."

"Plans change."

A little edge had crept into her voice. She was working up to something.

We lay in silence for a long time, the Cocteau Twins carrying on unintelligibly on her vertical turntable.

She sat up finally.

"David, I have something to tell you."

Now I looked up.

"We can't go on kidding ourselves. I think it's best that we, well, maybe, David, I'm sorry, I think it's not working anymore. I'm sorry, David."

"What? What about your fucking courgettes and cucumbers? Was that just bullshit?"

"David, I'm sorry. I really am. I know you stayed for me. It's my turn to follow you. But I can't. We're just different people now. I'll love you forever, David. I will."

" 'I'll love you forever' is the thing you say when you've stopped loving someone."

She sat looking at me, her mind whirring almost visibly, trying to decide whether to deliver the next blow.

"There might be someone else."

Now it was my turn to sit bolt upright.

"Might? Might? What the fuck does that mean, 'might'? Who?"

"Well, we haven't slept together. I'm just, you know, interested. He fancies me. He's, he's bloody English, David."

"Who is it, Maggie?"

"You don't know him."

"Who? You owe me that."

"His name is Grod."

"No it fucking isn't Grod. What's his fucking name?"

"Grod. David, I'm doing you a favor."

She threw off the bedclothes, reached over to put on a bathrobe ("dressing gown," she'd say), and headed toward the door. I lay there, utterly incredulous—and thought of Cristina.

Maggie turned back. Tears were streaming down her face; she clearly wanted to show me that—and to see if I was reciprocating. I looked into her eyes, sadly, but for all the wrong reasons.

"Big Steve was right," she said. "There is something about you."

I walked all the way home from Buxton Road, down past the train station, through the darkened Lanes and their shuttered, precious shops, past the Pavilion, flowers just beginning to appear, coaxed out by professional gardeners, a few tourists still lingering on the grounds, and along the Grand Parade to Kemptown. I ran through the long history of my love affair with Maggie as my body hurtled downhill toward the sea, flowing with gravity. "Grod," I kept repeating in my head, "Grod. Who the hell was Grod? One last trick for Maggie Fucking Highsmith to play on me. Probably didn't fucking exist."

I knew my anger was just some show I was putting on for myself, some momentary bit of self-pity. As the terrain flattened at sea level, I felt my back straighten and my spirits lift. By the time I climbed up the stoop at No. 4 Imperial Lane, I was feeling alright, really. It was three a.m. I was alone—for the first time in a long, long time. I slept well, till long after Hans's nurses had left. I don't know why, but he let me sleep.

A week later, I came in late to empty Hans's urine bag one last time before retiring for the night. I drew his curtains and pulled the thick woolen covers over his head. The stereo was silent. His rubber-tipped stick was still strapped to his hand, but he was not reading the book open in front of him. He was staring out at some invisible point in the room, propped up on his pillows. He was staring, I suppose, at the end.

"Leave me uncovered for a while longer," he said, in a barely audible exhale.

"Of course," I said.

I came around the far side of his bed and sat down, compelled to stay. I reached over his emaciated chest and unstrapped his pointer, then lifted the book and reading pallet from his bed and brought them to the end of the room.

"David," he murmured softly, "do something with your life—no, do more than one thing, more than one thing."

"I will," I answered, almost in a whisper. Sound seemed out of place in the gathering darkness and near silence. Hans's vacant eyes were bereft. The sadness was overwhelming. I had not seen that in him.

"David, I'm not one to impart any wisdom. Lord knows, I have none to give. I did one thing of importance in my life. One. I like to think I saved a life, probably two."

He paused to catch his breath. His head rolled slightly toward me.

"Whose?" I ventured.

"Tell me about Cristina."

"I did what you asked me to, Hans. I offered my help."

"Did she take it?"

"Yes, she did, much to my relief. I've been helping her prepare for her exams."

"Wonderful."

"She wants to go into fashion design or something like that, but she knows first she has to go to university. She's going to read history, I'm pretty sure, maybe English literature. She's good at both, I mean really good. But she's been reading up on how to get into the fashion industry. She's serious about it. And smart. I'm impressed."

"What did I tell you about American ambition?"

"I don't think I gave her that."

His head turned to face me, and our eyes met without quickly averting. I wondered if it was the first time that had happened. He held that gaze, his mouth turning up in the slightest of smiles.

"I was a pretty young thing too. All the benders at university wanted to claim me as one of their own. I enjoyed the attention. I think I invited it, to be honest." He stopped to swallow.

"My loss of beauty may have been a little more dramatic than most, but it was nothing special when you think about it. Happens to us all. I look at Cristina"—he paused for several seconds—"and I imagine what she'll look like in fifty years.

"Beauty is not meant to last, but it's also not meant to be wasted. It's a trap, a lure, maybe a means to a greater end if you're lucky, or skilled. I did nothing with mine. There was a girl for a while, Segolaine. You know her from our little reading sessions, I'd imagine, David. I loved her name. I loved her too. But I didn't know then how much that matters. She was my last chance, as it turned out, but I didn't know that at the time. You're not meant to regret what you couldn't have foreseen, but…"

He caught his breath.

"I had thrown my life away even before all this, before my beauty was taken from me. I was born with more chances to find meaning than almost anyone. And here I am, unable to see beyond my bed skirt."

He motioned me to draw near.

"If I lose Cristina, if she amounts to nothing, it'll be for nothing. She's the one—she's the life I need to have saved."

We sat in silence for a long time. He turned his face back to the ceiling, the light from the streetlamp peeking through the curtain and illuminating one side of his face.

"I'll protect her, Hans."

Then tears flowed. They rose from nowhere, or maybe some long-dry well that was disrupted by a tectonic shift deep within the heart. I was startled, out of control. I moved to wipe my face with a sleeve, but I kept crying. Drops flowed in tracks down my cheeks, dripped off the end of my nose, fell from my eyes as I leaned forward to compose myself.

"David, are you going to be alright there?"

I laughed and sat in silence for a while.

"Yes, Hans, sorry." I sniffled.

"Should I read you a letter from the stack?" I asked in a hush.

"Take one for yourself, David. I know you enjoy them."

I stood and gestured with his blankets, a slight lift of the edge of his voluminous wool pile. He nodded, almost imperceptibly. I covered his head, drew the curtains more tightly, turned out the light, and left him alone.

Dear Bet,

Don't say I never take the initiative. I contacted Sir Gordon who miraculously had your address at some hotel in a place called Luanda, very posh I'm sure. I was quite distressed at your last letter. I believe the word you were looking for is "rape." You said he took you. I take things all the time and barely ever elicit any anguish. You seem to be suffering quite a lot of that. You could have hardly known this man you call your husband before he became that. You say he is a changed man. I ask, "Changed from what?" The lover of those opening days and weeks of a romance is a miraculous thing. Every word he utters is magnificent poetry, every gesture both gallant and gentlemanly or, if coarse, in an utterly attractive way. You shake the drug from your system and pray that what you behold as you nurse your hangover is an acceptable facsimile of the lover you thought you had. There, I sound like Mother.

Still, I trust things have settled down. Far be it from me to pretend to understand the torment of war suffered silently by your young doctor. Men are resilient creatures. Dr. Joao, by now, has surely resumed life as himself. It is up to you to decide whether that is the man to share your life with. For most of us, that decision comes before you kneel before the altar, but Elizabeth Bromwell has always followed a slightly different path. Please keep me informed about all this, darling. I may have to saddle up and ride to the rescue, or at least inform Papa.

As for me, well, I have done everything you have told me not to, and it has cost me dearly. Segolaine has flown the coop. For someone who has shared her bed with innumerable clients for money, she was awfully touchy to learn that I was having a few birds on the side.

Yes, I took that confounded job at the bank. I am a loan officer, putting my political and historical education at the University of Edinburgh to good use listening to the sobbing appeals of aspiring homeowners, the petit bourgeoisie of Paris and its suburbs. I really am soft. I've approved all but one loan, and that poor fellow was dead broke, determined to open the ten-thousandth cooking school in this saturated city. To drown my guilt, I sautéed sheep's kidneys in cream and butter for one of the lovely young clerks who was consoling me for the loss of my girlfriend. You must try them some time, the kidneys, not the clerks.

I do not mean to be so flip, but I can't help myself. I miss Segolaine a lot. She stuck by me ever so long. I don't know what she saw in me, but I fear no one else will ever see either.

You must tell me about this new land of yours. I did look it up on a map. It's large and far south. Just thinking about it makes me sweat. And by the time you read this, no doubt, you will be a mother—and I an uncle, fancy that. Tell me what brand of genitalia the little dear has, and I'll send a proper present. I am serious about this Joao character of yours. You must keep me abreast.

Your loving and worried brother,
Hans

CHAPTER SIXTEEN

A half-dozen Alouette helicopters swept over Serpa Pinto like bulbous-eyed giant mosquitoes in a menacing swarm. The grasslands passed below, seemingly unpopulated. But that was deceptive. Neto's MPLA, those once-soft intellectuals from Luanda, had brought down four Alouettes in 1973. João Gonçalves watched the landscape of Eastern Angola sweep beneath his boots, a London-educated physician trained in trauma care through three years of war, readying for combat as an ordinary medic.

"Your turn, Major, go," a lieutenant yelled inaudibly. Gonçalves fell from the chopper, hit the marshy grasses, and rolled as he was trained. He grabbed the pack that had been thrown down beside him, unslung his weapon, and took off after the other soldiers for the relative safety of a small copse on the edge of the elephant grass.

The enemy could be canny, reluctant to engage. They knew time was on their side. That past September, not four months before, liberated Guiné declared independence. Amílcar Cabral had been assassinated in January '73, gunned down by at least thirty of his comrades, dark-skinned, real Guineans tired of the platitudes and orders of the Cabo-Verdiano half blood and his intellectual elite. What the Portuguese took as a sign of chaos, the Africans knew to be the final chapter of purification playing out before Guiné was swept into history. Moses would not be crossing to the Promised Land, but that didn't mean the Israelites wouldn't be taking Bissau.

In April of '73, Almeida Brito and his Fiat G.91 were blasted from the sky. Lovely Raquel returned to Lisbon a black-veiled war widow.

João's response to slow-motion defeat was to fight harder. His wife and child had formed a nuclear bond so tight he felt like a rogue electron buzzing in frantic orbit, the nurturing core just out of reach. He was living the sum of a man's domestic fears, exactly what his father had warned him of, an outsider looking in. Female kindness toward men, sex, charm, warmth, all these things are merely means to her end, his father used to tell him in slightly inebriated tones: marriage, stability, family, children. Once that end is attained, affection slows to a trickle, if it doesn't shut off altogether. The trick, the elder Dr. Gonçalves advised the younger, is to bathe in a woman's kindness and love, then, just as she senses she has attained her goal, just as her affections begin to shift elsewhere, find another. Experience only the best in women. Maintain your illusion of the fairer sex as always warm, always generous, always giving of herself, her body, radiant in her love for you.

Well, João was a soldier now. He'd go drinking with his comrades, whoring on occasion. He would have pangs of guilt. The excitement of transgression would draw him to the brothels around the base where the choices of skin tone, body type, and demeanor were laid out like a carnal buffet: black as coal, mocha mestiço, Algarve bronze, and Lisbon porcelain, soft and round, taut and lanky, demure, raunchy. He would make his selection and take her off in a rush, his heart pounding, but the fever of lust would break, and his conscience would return, flowing into his heart as the blood ebbed from his groin. He thought at these moments of his mother, her weeping fights with a father who in the end wasn't so different from him.

He had to admit that at times—too many times—he took his shame, grief, guilt, and anger out on his wife. He tried not to leave marks, and he strained not to disturb Cristina. But he was the dupe here, the victim, the cuckold, lured into marriage by a woman of once-volcanic desires, eager to please, charming, loving, grateful. That woman was gone. If he lost his temper, well, who really was to blame? He would slam the door of their flat, take a long walk down the Avenida Cinco de Outubro, maybe take in a movie at the Ruacaná, and seethe at his lot. Then, with the pyrotechnic brew of emotions burned off like a flare, he would climb the stairs to their apartment, apologize and mean it. He didn't want to lose this family of his. He wanted to have his wife's body to warm him in the morning. He loved waking up to his beautiful daughter, hearing her squeals of delight, feeling her hands around his neck, cold, soft, and moist all at once. Cristina was the last love they shared.

Such concerns were blissfully forgotten as he looped north and east with a dozen men toward the Zambian border. They forded a waist-deep river, wide enough to soak them through, hands held high to keep their rifles dry, and left the open grasses for a sparsely treed woodland. Lieutenant Fernando Alonzo took the lead.

Then he exploded. He seemed to vanish, although in truth he was very much still there, just spread with blinding velocity in great chunks. The patrol was under heavy fire. The men scattered. Some slithered on their bellies. Others dashed for the trees. João crouched down, then lunged for the cover of a pecan tree.

"Medic! Medic!" A piercing cry went up over the gunfire. João scanned the chaotic battle scene but could see nothing. He crept toward the screams and practically fell upon the private, writhing in a patch of grass that formed a trampled ring around him, like a giant bird's nest. Gunfire had blasted his foot off. Scraps of flesh hung livid red from bone exposed halfway up his calf. Gonçalves grabbed a preloaded syringe of morphine and stuck it in the·man's shoulder, then twisted a tourniquet below the knee to stanch the blood gushing from his leg. Sporadic fire still rang out, but the battle was subsiding.

"It's going to be alright, just a minor wound. Where are you from, Private? You just got a ticket home. I'll let your mother know you're coming. You sure know how to break up a good patrol."

Someone unfolded a crude canvas stretcher, bloodstained and browned, and four men converged around the fallen soldier. They set off, back in the direction they had come from, Lieutenant Alonzo left in pieces for the hyenas.

Elizabeth was making compromises too great for a woman her age, but then again, her windfall had been a sudden one. She hadn't worked to become a doctor's wife, like many other women had. It just happened. She had a beautiful, olive-skinned daughter, a spacious flat in a city with lovely weather, and perks like a PX and officers' club. She could not question the bill when it came due, steep as it was. The whores and drink, the lashing vituperation, the raised hand and occasional blows would be followed by apologies, caresses, and idyllic absences. She accepted the trade.

Elizabeth fell into the leisurely life of an army wife, making friends not only with Portuguese women but with South Africans and Rhodesians. The white wives of southern Africa were painfully friendly, determined to prove the stereotypes of vicious racism wrong, but proving it only to the white people. They invited strangers to tea, praised their decision to visit or live in the glorious highlands of Africa, and fawned over their babies.

Elizabeth was not one to stand on principle. She was young, without politics, and almost without guile. She was holding Cristina by the fingers, watching her toddle unsteadily around the grand fountain in the Jardim Américo Tomás, when she met Greta Vanderbroek.

"Oh, she's beautiful," the woman said in Portuguese, with an accent Elizabeth knew to be Afrikaner. "How old is she?"

"She's just turned two," Elizabeth replied, her Portuguese now effortless. She was used to the attention but was taken by this woman—big boned, tall and blonde, with braids swept back around a prominent head. She wore a conservative, western-style floral print dress that fell below the knees and could do only so much to hide her voluminous breasts and broad hips. She was clearly not Portuguese.

"I have two of my own," she continued, "in school right now. It's so peaceful walking in the park alone."

Elizabeth wondered then why she would break that solo revelry by talking to a stranger. But she kept quiet and pretended to be intently focused on her daughter. The other woman hovered.

"*Meu nome é Greta*," she said, jabbing a hand out to be shaken.

Elizabeth looked at her closely and, without taking her hand, said in English, "You're not from around here, are you?"

The smile on Greta Vanderbroek's face spread like a burst dam, her large mouth swallowing the lower half of her head.

"No, I'm from Johannesburg," she said, as if Elizabeth was the silliest woman in Angola. "South Africa."

"I'm English," Elizabeth said simply.

For perhaps an hour, the women talked, telling their stories: how they had come to be in the highlands of Angola, both dragged by husbands involved in a war that should not have been their own. Like so many other times, Elizabeth realized how little she knew about the world she lived in. Greta Vanderbroek's husband had a bland-enough-sounding job; he worked for the South African board of armaments. What it meant was he armed combatants across the board.

"It's survival really, us versus the communists," she said earnestly. "Samuel and I met at university. Stellenbosch. Have you been there? Lovely, really lovely. Ah, but I suppose my husband had a higher calling. Too bad the Portuguese are such frightful allies to have to count on. They're weak, but what choice do we have? We can't let Mozambique and Angola fall. Rhodesia would be next, then Botswana, and South-West Africa."

Greta and Elizabeth became fast friends, grateful for the ease of speaking English and the absence of their husbands. Elizabeth took great satisfaction in being with a body of such stature, a mighty

Brunhilde among weaker women. She did not confide much, nothing about her marital troubles or her uncertain future with the man she married so hastily. In fact, she took it upon herself to cultivate a friend to the family. She wanted João to become friends with Greta's husband, Samuel, and to prepare the older Vanderbroek children to one day be Cristina's guardians and babysitters. A domestic cocoon, why not?

It wasn't easy. The men both traveled or were otherwise indisposed. But they got together often enough. Elizabeth was fine with entertaining in their flat, with its two bedrooms and open, combined dining and living rooms. It wasn't Houndsheath, but it was modishly contemporary, and how much could be expected of a twenty-four-year-old army wife? The Vanderbroeks, on the other hand, had a house near the park, small by the standards of Elizabeth's youth but generous in Nova Lisboa, charming and comfortable, with Cape Dutch furniture dragged up from South Africa. The women would chatter in the kitchen or fuss over the children. Samuel, much older than João, beefy—thick really, not fat—with thinning blond hair and leathery dark skin, deeply furrowed, would take João to the veranda, break out cigars rolled with Angolan tobacco, and inquire about the war. João smoked his offerings and drank his scotch but was parsimonious with his war stories.

"It's an unpleasant business, no doubt," Samuel would say, waving a meaty hand over his head to disperse the smoke and swat a mosquito. "South African pilots have taken to using defoliants on the cassava in the so-called liberated zones. The people may not have anything to eat—brutal work, no? But we can't give them a haven. If they have to traverse those long corridors from Zambia and Zaire, our planes and gunships can pick them off. If they find shelter in the villages closer to Nova Lisboa, it becomes entirely too messy—burning thatch, inquests at the UN, pressure from NATO. No, my boy, we must remain vigilant."

Such talk had seemed ridiculous to João before his transfer to Nova Lisboa; now he understood, even if he didn't quite sympathize. Cape Town, Johannesburg, and Salisbury in Rhodesia must be just the same, white cities built by white people who no longer thought of themselves as colonists or even settlers. They thought of themselves as at home, and they would defend their cities as such.

"They're patient, you know. They're waiting us out," João said through a cloud of smoke. "They're closer than you think. The other day, I was inserting an IV in a soldier who had taken a bullet in the gut. We were maybe one hundred fifty kilometers southeast of here. That can be a nasty wound, infects fast. I looked up after connecting the drip and met the eyes of one of the guerrillas. Don't ask me who he was fighting for. He was behind some brush, just watching me. He could have killed me easily, but he just watched—yellow, jaundiced eyes, a look of pure contempt."

"Maybe he was out of bullets, eh?" Samuel said in his singsong South African English.

"Maybe." João shrugged. "Maybe he just wanted to watch us take another dying Portuguese boy away."

"Nah, you're too pessimistic, my friend," Samuel said gregariously, leaning forward in his wicker chair to give João a slap on the shoulder. "We've got them tied up. We're not going anywhere. Just as long as the old men in Lisbon can carry on."

On February 22, 1974, one of those old men, António Sebastião Ribeiro de Spínola, nailed his "Portuguese Myths" to the door of Lisbon's Belém Palace. The effect may not have been as consequential as Martin Luther's defiance at Castle Church in Wittenberg, but the reverberations shuddered from the western shore of the European continent to the southeastern edge of Africa.

Myth One: Portugal's wars in Africa were defending the West and Western civilization itself.

Myth Two: Lusitanian history had somehow bound all overseas governance to the command of Lisbon.

Myth Three: The provinces of the *ultramar* could at once be a part of Portugal and be populated with second- or even third-class citizens.

Myth Four: The essence of the Portuguese nation was the civilizing of the wider world.

"The populations are still favorable to us but they will cease to be so when they feel themselves held back from fulfillment of their legitimate aspirations for a better life and full participation at all levels," Spínola wrote. With sentences like that, the old general's masterwork, *Portugal e o Futuro*, could well have put the *metrópole* to sleep, but not even its author had guessed how dry the kindling in Iberia was. Portugal needed only a spark, and Spínola's turgid but caustic lament was it. The streets had the joyful feel of freedom seeping in.

Admiral Américo Tomas, the seventy-nine-year-old president of the republic, responded to Spínola's challenge just as the near dead come to full lucidity before they succumb to the smothering pillow. The armed forces were put on high alert. Spínola was cashiered. Infuriated, loyal young officers tried to respond. On March 16, Lieutenant Colonel Almeida Bruno, who once stood sheepishly by in Bafatá as the new commanding general of Guiné rallied his bedraggled men, mustered that moment in his agitated mind.

In jeeps and half-tracks, Bruno's Fifth Cavalry Regiment drove from its barracks at Caldas da Rainha south toward Lisbon, convinced an uprising would follow. To their horror, the nation may have been stirring but it was not ready. Military command in Lisbon sent a far greater force to confront the rebels. Bruno was the first in chains. Hundreds followed. The prison fort of Peniche was filled. The officers who could not fit were exiled to the Azores. The first battle of the revolution ended in a rout.

Far away, in Nova Lisboa, the soldiers of empire knew only that something odd and important was happening. For three weeks, they had been confined to barracks. The helicopters were idled on the tarmac. The fear of battle was replaced by a fear for their future.

Only the angry screech of South African jets continued. They were under someone else's command, fruitlessly trying to hold at bay the guerrilla armies rushing toward Nova Lisboa in the sudden absence of Portuguese patrols. A new world was closing in.

On March 28, a month after Spínola's publication date, the troops gathered around a black-and-white television set in one of the barracks to watch the prime minister deliver what their officers said was a critical address. João watched as well that night, in the living room of his flat, while Elizabeth rocked Cristina to sleep in the nursery.

"Foreign elements within the armed forces launched a mutiny from Caldas, determined to see Portugal lose its overseas provinces," Caetano began, dabbing sweat from a broad forehead that swept up and back toward a receding hairline. His heavy horn-rimmed glasses seemed to weigh him down as he stared at the papers clutched in clumsy hands. "They have been repelled, their leaders dealt with severely."

Caetano tried to rally a nation and an empire behind a cause of such antiquity that its mere mention made mockery of it. "It is Portugal who made Angola," he continued, his intended inspiration delivered in a drone. "It is Portugal who created Mozambique. We fight in defense of the Portuguese of all races and of all colors."

The screen flickered, went blank, and flashed back up to an American comedy dubbed in Portuguese, *Sanford and Son*, about an old black man, his hip, mustachioed son, and a junkyard.

João shook. Angola, he knew, was remaking itself, and the home that he once knew, that he long ago left and had refused to return to, was slipping away. He walked quietly to the nursery to make sure mother and daughter were asleep, as expected, then hustled into the night, not to the base—there would be no answers there—but to Samuel Vanderbroek.

"Your Caetano is a fool," the South African said, seething quietly. "We have been watching this for a year, more than a year. The Armed Forces Movement has not been subtle."

He poured João a scotch in a cut-crystal tumbler, no ice, no water, and walked toward him with the offering. "I'd half believe you
were a part of it, João, if I was not watching your face right now.
They are Spínola's men, under his spell. You know him well, no?"

"Not well," João said defensively.

Samuel cut him off. "Well enough. But never mind. Our intelligence was apparently not good enough for your government.
Foreign elements indeed. You know, for fascists, you Portuguese are
pretty pathetic."

"Is it over, this rebellion?"

"Ha! Not by a long shot. Tell me, João, have you been to Évora,
back home?"

"Of course, our Roman city. Every schoolchild goes to see the ruins."

"Yes, an appropriate place to plot empire's end, I should think—
conspiracy amid the rubble. There were a series of officers' picnics
there—wives, families, wine, bread and cheese—lovely affairs near
various barracks in the countryside. Last September was the last of
them, quite an outing. Officers from all over the country, perhaps all
over the empire. They talked and plotted all night. We knew. How
the fuck didn't Caetano?"

He downed his drink and poured another.

"The Armed Forces Movement Coordinating Committee," he
said with exaggerated grandiosity. "They call it the MFA. Why is
that?"

"Armed Forces Movement, in Portuguese, would be the *Movimento das Forças Armadas*, MFA."

"I can never keep these things straight. I'll grant you, the rebels,
they were smart. They spread. I'm quite sure there's a cell in Nova
Lisboa. There's a major, the commander of your base here. Know
him?"

João shrugged. "He got us our apartment."

Samuel led his friend onto the veranda, but they didn't sit.
Samuel paced, sipping scotch and looking at the stars. João stood
and waited.

"No," Samuel said, gently placing his tumbler on a glass-topped mahogany table. "It's not over. The real leader of the group has gone completely unnoticed, a public relations man of all things, Major Otelo Saraiva de Carvalho." He chuckled, muttering under his breath, "You Portuguese with your names."

"Otelo?" João repeated in mild astonishment. "I knew him, in Guiné. Spínola's hearts-and-minds man."

"Spínola's man." Vanderbroek nodded in recognition. He sighed—a long, slow exhale. "That figures."

Military commanders in Lisbon, eager to show they were still in charge, delivered stern orders for offensives to be mounted out of all five military districts in Angola: Cuanza Norte, Cabinda, Cuando Cubango, Lunde, and Bie. Guerrilla forces that had taken advantage of the lull were to be pushed back, and hard. The offensive was suicide. Spare parts for the helicopters and fixed-wing fighters were running low. The army's African conscripts were abandoning their posts in the night, joining guerrilla patrols now in hailing distance of the Portuguese bases. Junior officers, looking over their shoulders for Caetano's secret police and worried that insufficient zeal would land them in the brig, dutifully ordered their men back into the Alouettes. Three days after Caetano's address, a helicopter was blasted from the sky. It was overloaded with troops, and nine men died. After that, no one wanted to be the last to die in a dying war.

João's hunger for combat evaporated. The base was seething with tension, divided between rebel sympathizers and regime loyalists, everyone convinced their comrades were either PIDE or communists. A muffle had descended over the base. João imagined plotting in dark corners, secret cells, doors being kicked open in the night, unknown brigs filling with soldiers.

After nearly a decade of combat, after so much blood had trickled onto African soil, the action had shifted to the cobbled streets of old, stagnant Portugal. There was nothing left for João but to stay home.

*   *   *

The decisive blow to Earth's last African empire would be delivered by a man in a monocle, unarmed, in a black Peugeot.

On April 24, 1974, just before midnight, Rádio Clube Português, a pop music station consumed at the time with John Denver's "Sunshine on My Shoulders," Terry Jacks's "Seasons in the Sun," and, if the urge hit, ABBA's "Waterloo," broadcast an odd mistake to the youth of Lisbon. "It is five minutes to eleven," an unfamiliar voice said, followed by a syrupy Portuguese song, out of place among the foreign soft rock: "*E Depois do Adeus.*"

The listeners of Rádio Clube Português likely would not have turned the dial to the Lisbon Catholic Church station, Rádio Renascença. If they had, they would have noticed a second airwave oddity: church radio broadcasting the Portuguese pop song "*Grândola, Vila Morena*" at half past midnight.

But Portuguese men in uniform knew to change channels and listen. Otelo Carvalho had engineered a mutiny signal to be broadcast right over the public airwaves. Twelve vehicles and one hundred fifty cavalrymen, under the command of Captain Salgueiro de Maia, rolled out of the garrison at Santarém, a cavalry school sixty kilometers from the capital, as the last notes of "*Grândola*" sounded. In Lisbon, the Fifth Infantry Regiment and the Seventh Cavalry were waiting. The First Engineers Regiment, in the suburb of Pontinha, had already been prepared as the headquarters of the rebel government.

By three a.m., as the city slept, Captain Maia's troops were taking their positions in Black Horse Square. Lisbon's commercial and military airports were seized without a shot. The studios of Portuguese television and radio, as well as the central post office, were all taken silently by rebel forces. Air traffic was halted in and out of Oporto airport in the north and Faro on the Algarve.

At 4:20 in the morning, an anonymous voice crackled across Rádio Clube Português, apologizing for the break in music, appealing for calm, and imploring the people of Lisbon to remain in their homes. The secret police, the voice said, were to "abstain from any confrontation."

The message was repeated at 4:45. Then at 6:45, a spokesman from an organization no average citizen of Portugal had heard of, Movimento das Forças Armadas, declared that military units had encircled the capital.

The sun rose over a Lisbon liberated after forty-eight years of fascist dictatorship. Joyful crowds descended on the Largo do Carmo, the headquarters of the Republican National Guard, shouting by name the members of the government they wanted handed over to the mob. As noon approached, Otelo Saraiva de Carvalho—his hair grayer than it was in Guiné, the softness of his neck replaced by lean sinew—led a small group of officers through quiet residential streets to the modest home of General António de Spínola. Phone calls were made, talks ensued. And at 5:40 p.m., April 25, General Spínola drove in his black Peugeot through a throng of cheering Lisboners to the Largo do Carmo.

Twenty minutes later, a loudspeaker announced Caetano had handed over his powers. António de Spínola was now the head of the Portuguese government. The Carnation Revolution had come and gone.

"Your story is coming to an end, isn't it?" I asked Elizabeth.

She smiled.

"'Like as the waves make towards the pebbl'd shore, so do our minutes hasten to their end.' Am I boring you, David?"

"Not at all," I objected, and I meant it. I was more puzzled than anything. Obviously my biggest questions had yet to be answered: Where was João now? How did she and Cristina escape Africa? Most of all, what happened to Hans? But the wars in Africa would surely be ending now. My own days in Brighton were numbered. The centrifugal force of home was growing stronger as the warmth of spring was taking hold. But then there was the gravitational pull that was Cristina.

Elizabeth seemed to read my mind.

"Hate to break it to you but we've got a ways to go."

My study sessions with Cristina had slowed with the crush of more pressing work as her final secondary-school year was drawing to a close. I imagined she was pulling away, that she had come to her senses. I was disappointed, but I understood. She would be starting college soon. Her uncle was moving on, and with him, her mother—somewhere, who knew where? I would be leaving as well.

I climbed the stairs past midnight, and there she was, standing in the doorway of the parlor. She wore loose flannel pajamas and fuzzy slippers, not exactly seductive, yet she was. Her hair cascaded over the floppy collar. Her face, so delicate, so lovely, was trained on mine. Her breasts, unconfined beneath pink striped flannel, made me ache.

"Do you still have time for my history, David?"

I looked at her in surprise.

"You know, just wondering. With all of Mother's stories and that Portuguese silliness, I thought you were done with our lessons."

"I thought we were moving on to biology?" I rejoined with a sly smile I hoped passed for seductive.

"We have other things to master first, don't we?"

Tired but buzzing, I sat down on the floor again with Cristina to hash over the significance of the Magna Carta, whether a document empowering dukes and barons had any real lessons for a democracy centuries away. My heart wasn't in it. I was waiting for a sign from Cristina, some invitation, and it wasn't coming.

"What's wrong, David? Do you need to go to sleep?" she asked.

I felt a surge of exasperation, fueled by fatigue but also genuine confusion.

"Cristina, what's going on here? I thought...I...I thought something was happening between us. I don't know. I, I think I need help here."

Cristina looked down at her hands and was silent for a moment. The quiet enveloped us.

"David, are you always so forward?" she finally asked, shyly. "I need to study. I thought you were helping me."

I tried to take her hand but she pulled it away.

Then it just slipped out. I blurted. "Cristina, I think I'm in love with you."

She looked startled, as if I had slapped her. Tears welled up in her eyes, and she looked out through a window into the darkness. I stared at her in silence, waiting. When she finally turned her head to me, her face, creased with tears, was hardened slightly.

"This seems like a load of bollocks frankly, David. You're trying to sneak off a last thrill with me. I don't think that sounds like love."

Her eyes dropped to my lap, and mine followed, as the elation over my confession, the unburdening of a rock I had carried around, seemed to flatten me now. I was drained and hurt.

"Don't be mean, Cristina." I paused. "I'm sorry; what should I have said? I have very strong feelings for you. I do, OK? You don't want me to say I'm in love. Fine, we'll call it something else, call it X. I'm X for you."

She started laughing.

"OK."

Another long pause, then her face softened a little.

"Whatever X is, I swear, Cristina, it's real. Please believe me. Please. I need you to believe me."

"I'm sorry, David. I was cruel. I didn't know what to say. Give me some time to think about it, OK?"

I nodded.

A delicate finger touched under my chin and lifted my head. Our eyes met. She was smiling.

"OK, Mr. X?"

Dearest Hans,

What was it you wrote, about the masses floating on an indifferent sea of history? I understand that all too well. My little family, Cristina, Joao and I, feel like castaways in a violent ocean. I do not know what you hear in your insular world of the events rocking Lisbon and, by extension, my corner of the world. I fear my life is about to change dramatically, perhaps for the best but perhaps for the far, far worst.

My physician of a husband has become a soldier boy, playing at combat even when he does not have to. War has become his escape from us, it would seem. "O! wither'd is the garland of the war, The soldier's pole is fall'n; young boys and girls are level now with men." He reports for duty as often as he can, as if he has a death wish, a trained doctor masquerading as a combat medic. When he is at home, he is a bully boy, carousing, whoring, and on occasion, hitting me. It is as if the passionate young man I fell in love with was captured by guerrillas and replaced with a tormenter, determined to drive another white interloper from Africa by slow torture.

It is not all so bad. Our latest city, Nova Lisboa, New Lisbon, is wonderful—temperate, lush, charming even. I have a dear friend here, Greta Vanderbroek, a South African Boer. Lord knows what persecutions her family has rained down on the blacks of her country, but we don't talk politics. I'm sure you would approve of my studied indifference. Her husband appears to be some sort of secret agent or gun runner, no doubt up to nefarious acts. But they live in a lovely, tropical bungalow, and I need the reprieve. Samuel serves the finest scotch. And their children are old enough to relieve me of childcare every once in a while.

Not that I am looking for much relief. Truly, I love motherhood, and our daughter, Cristina, is growing into a raven-haired angel, sweet and brave and loving, "prodigious birth of love it is to me." Even you would swoon.

I fear, though, we will soon be swept away from all this. The coup in Lisbon has brought to power my old friends, the tired generals of Guine and Angola, exhausted of war, determined to let empire go the way of our own Pax Britannica. I am no die-hard imperialist, but what is to become of us when the armies of Lisbon's enemies have the run of this place? I only hope Joao has the sense to know when all is lost. Then, we shall say, "Now go we in content, to liberty and not to banishment." Ah, just to write such lovely words makes me wonder if I am clinging on long past the death knell.

Watch the newspapers for me, Hans. I fear I will not be able to keep you abreast of such tumultuous changes.

Yours,
Elizabeth

CHAPTER SEVENTEEN

News of the Carnation Revolution had shocked Angola, not only the ordinary citizens and soldiers but the men who would shape or destroy its future.

On the day of the coup, Agostinho Neto was in Canada, courting support from the American Gulf Oil Company. A protection racket really, Gulf would provide money and guns to the MPLA, and Neto would provide the muscle to protect the company's operations from the rival guerrilla gangs, especially in the hot zone of Cabinda, where the oil was. He flew back quickly to open quiet peace talks with Lisbon. Holden Roberto issued a statement saying his forces would fight on until complete independence was won. Secretly, he too reached out to the Armed Forces Movement. Jonas Savimbi, South Africa's stooge, declared a ceasefire even as his ragtag army, UNITA, closed in on Nova Lisboa.

The combatants met in an Algarve beach resort in Alvor for what Spínola was determined would be a final political solution, one way or the other. They set November 11, 1975, as Angolan Independence Day. As the Portuguese washed their hands of Angola, an MPLA negotiator was asked what the Alvor accord meant. "It means we need to get more guns."

As their world crumbled, Elizabeth and João were finding some of their happiest times in Africa. Like a camera lens, the aperture was closing, darkness was falling, but as the focus sharpened, the Gonçalves family became only more rooted to the last patch of Angolan ground available. And that patch was seeded by an odd little man named Dr. Fernando Real e Rui Vaz Osório.

Whether out of willful oblivion or hopeful defiance, Dr. Osório had arrived in Nova Lisboa just after the New Year, 1975, as Lisbon was cutting the cord. He was dispatched to set up the Institute of Biomedical Sciences. In isolation, it seemed logical enough. The city was already home to the Institute of Veterinary Sciences and the Institute of Agronomy. Five hundred first-year medical students from Luanda were adrift, cut off from a capital city in chaos. They needed a university to complete their training. Nova Lisboa, so long considered the most vulnerable target, was now viewed as a refuge.

For João, Osório's arrival was a welcome diversion—from the military, which had become pure tedium in the interregnum; from home, where the cycle of fighting and contrition was wearing him down; and from his own sense of alienation and his growing understanding that his stay here would be ending soon. He petitioned the base commander to discharge him honorably from the military.

"João," the commander said, smiling, "this isn't a job you simply tender your resignation from and walk away."

"Sir, I have served for more than four years. Have I dishonored the Portuguese army?"

"No, Major, but you reenlisted, and that reenlistment was not month-to-month."

"But…"

The colonel held up his hand for silence from behind his military-grade desk. His hands entwined behind his back, he made a few grandiloquent paces in the small office.

"Major Gonçalves, rules are rules. I will let you join the faculty at this strange new institute; Lord knows how long it will last. But you will remain a reservist. This war could well be over for the likes of you and me. Or it could explode in our faces tomorrow. We live in odd and unpredictable times."

He extended a hand, and the men shook formally.

"Oh, and João," the colonel called out, as João was walking out of the Quonset hut, "keep the apartment, but I wouldn't get too comfortable."

The courses João taught brought him steady, challenging tasks, late nights grading papers and drafting lesson plans, and a regularity he hadn't felt since leaving the clinic on the Algarve. He drifted away from the soldiers' orbit. Elizabeth and he warmed to each other. They were even learning to make love in silence as their young daughter slept. She'd meet him on occasion at school with Cristina, her arm swinging a picnic basket, and the three would walk to the park for a lunch of bread, mangos or jack fruit, and expensive imported cheese. He dipped his face on occasion into her neck, under her arms, between her legs, no longer intoxicated by her smell but sufficiently aroused to forget things. War may have been closing in, but in their new domesticity, João and Elizabeth convinced themselves it was receding.

Evidence to the contrary mounted. In the early hours of July 11, 1975, in the slums of Luanda, the body of a white cabdriver was found strangled to death. On July 22, five hundred or so white thugs marched to the governor's palace, jeering at, kicking, and beating blacks on the way. When a black policeman was pounded nearly to death, the *Ultras* were beset by black Angolan defenders. The riot that followed left more than fifty dead and hundreds wounded.

The flight from Angola began then, slowly at first, but it built up steam inexorably. Luanda, then Nova Lisboa became cities of crates and boxes. Entire factories were emptied and loaded onto ships for Lisbon and São Paulo. In the growing vacuum, the rival guerrilla armies stepped up their slaughter. Rotting corpses poisoned the water supply in Malanje, the opposing fighters throwing the dead into the wells. Artillery fire thundered into the outskirts of Luanda. Refugees packed the central city. The capital's Craveiro Lopes Airport was overwhelmed with whites clamoring for flights to Lisbon. On the beaches of Luanda Bay, Lobito, and Benguela,

Africans awaited steamers and container ships, hoping for safe harbor in ports to the north.

The last governor of Angola flew to Portugal in mid-August for consultations about the final handover of power with a Lusitanian government that no longer cared. "Perhaps they can just mail the flag to Lisbon," he grumbled as he looked over his shoulder at what remained of Luanda.

João Gonçalves did not seem to care. The highlands that nestled their home in Nova Lisboa were far away. Life was good. Lulled by her husband's confidence and good temper, Elizabeth did nothing.

It was early when Samuel Vanderbroek knocked on the apartment door. September had just arrived. It was still cool in the Southern Hemisphere, but temperatures were beginning to creep up. João was getting his notes ready and stuffing a satchel for school. It had been months since the two families had seen each other. João and Elizabeth read the newspapers with some trepidation but did not let even the sight of refugees from the highlands intrude too much on the rhythms of a life they were finally enjoying. Domesticity was a welcome change—the quotidian of sandwich making and laundry hanging and cigarette butts tossed absentmindedly in gutters and the faint smell of garbage that needed attending to.

It was simple joy after so much strife. Neither was ready to disturb it, even though when they reached for each other, there was a thin sheath of indifference between them. Here they were, waiting some sort of end.

"Samuel, what a surprise," João said, as he opened the flat door, startled by the burly blond man in the hallway. Samuel's hair was longer than usual, his face hastily and roughly shaven, with little patches of untended stubble.

"I am sorry for this visit. I'm sure the time is inconvenient."

"No, no. Come on in."

Cristina had dashed toward the door to check out the commotion but had recoiled behind Elizabeth.

"Good morning, Elizabeth," Samuel said with a feeble smile, bowing his head slightly.

"Samuel, it is so good to see you," she said, hands on her daughter's shoulders. "How is Greta? It's been a while."

"I sent her home with the boys last week." He sighed heavily. "All that trouble in Luanda. The word from the highlands is not good either."

There was an awkward silence as the three adults stared at one another, João feeling challenged and ashamed that he had not thought of the safety of his family, Elizabeth suddenly wondering, not for the first time but now acutely, if her trust was simply foolishness.

"How is that university of yours holding up, João?"

"Surprisingly well, thank you. I was just heading off—"

"João, might I have a word with you, in private?" Samuel interrupted in a sotto voce, compounding the discomfort but seeing no choice. He nodded to Elizabeth as he led her husband off to their bedroom, with no regard for privacy, as if what they owned was his.

He shut the door gently but gave it an extra push to make sure it was sealed, then walked to the far end of the small bedroom. African carvings adorned teak bedside tables and Elizabeth's dresser. A swatch of brightly dyed cloth, pulled tight over a wooden frame, took up maybe a third of the far wall. Samuel pretended to be captivated by it as João gingerly crossed toward him.

"João"—he spun around—"I need your help, your medical help."

"I, I, I haven't been practicing much lately. What is it?"

"I need absolute assurance that you will maintain discretion on this. You will stay silent, even to Elizabeth."

"If it is a medical matter, I have no choice. I would never divulge the medical condition of a patient without permission."

"Patients," Samuel interjected forcefully.

"Patients, yes," João returned, quietly but quizzically.

"This is all ending, João, at least for you, for Portugal. Angola will descend into chaos and communism. We cannot allow that to happen."

"We?" João said, puzzled. "You and me?"

"No, no, no," the older man said with an irritated smirk. "We South Africa, Rhodesia, what is left of civilized Africa. And we won't."

"Samuel, but it seems you've failed already. The bombings, the defoliants. Hardly civilized, and they've done nothing."

"That was just an opening act, my friend. We don't control when the finale begins. We must take our cues from our Cuban friends, who will be arriving soon. The Soviet subs are already patrolling the seas. We're not sure what they are up to, but we know they're there. When they show themselves, the real battle begins."

João began to think his friend had gone insane, that paranoia had finally gotten the best of him. He glanced at his watch, thinking about the first class of the day.

"Samuel, is this all, because I really have to go?"

"No, João, it is not all. When those cues come, we must be ready. We're just offstage, but we're not ready. Yellow fever. I know the Portuguese medical corps has dealt with it before, discreetly. We need a little of that expertise and a lot of that discretion right now."

Samuel was right. The Portuguese medical corps had quietly tended to outbreaks of yellow fever throughout Angola. In some cases, hundreds had died in hospitals and on bases, mostly Africans but some Portuguese as well. The scourges had been kept quiet, the bodies buried, as heroes if white, in unmarked graves if black. There was no need to cause panic or stoke still more questions in Lisbon. But the doctors had become more adept at containing the outbreaks. It was a point of pride, and Samuel Vanderbroek was encouraging it.

"We need you."

"What about my family, my daughter? It's a bit of a dodgy time to be flitting out on a secret mission."

"Don't worry," Vanderbroek growled. "We'll take care of them."

The Alouette took off heading south, a lone chopper with no escorts. João wondered aloud how safe this was. He had no desire to tempt death on one final mission, certainly not for the South Africans. Samuel assured him there would be no combat involved.

"We're flying over UNITA territory," he shouted into the brand-new headset, his voice ringing clearly in João's ears. "Savimbi's friendlies, as the Americans like to say."

"Where are the Americans in all this?"

"Mainly on the sidelines, but they'll come round."

The helicopter swept low over grasslands that grew more arid as they flew south. Every now and then, they'd fly directly over clusters of armed guerrillas, who merely raised one hand over their eyes to shield them from the sun and the other in a friendly wave. They were boys, mostly, in ragged short pants ripped from long trousers, and T-shirts discarded by American or British families. João had told Elizabeth next to nothing, only that he had a mission he had to accept, that he'd be back soon. She had pleaded with him, scolded him, accused him of abandonment. His own misgivings caught the retaliatory accusations in his throat. Just once, he thought, he would like his wife to support him, to say, "João, I know you have to do what you have to do. You're a doctor, go." Just once.

He said that to his wife, not angrily, sadly really, shaking his head. "Just once, Elizabeth."

"Just once what?"

He turned without saying another word and bolted from the flat.

The pilot touched down in Evale to refuel. UNITA occupied the iron-mining outpost, but it was a fair-haired, muscular white man who brought the fuel in huge jerry cans. Samuel and he talked into each other's ears at the top of their lungs, with serious expressions. To João, only a few feet away, their words were inaudible over the helicopter's roar. A few scrubby trees dotted the arid, dusty landscape. Angolans wandered around huts of stick walls and thatched roofs, seemingly befuddled by the strange happenings around them. Topless Himba tribeswomen in bright cotton skirts and elaborate grass-and-stick jewelry encircling their bellies and necks looked sullenly at João.

They stayed just long enough to top off, then took off south once more.

Maybe forty minutes later, Samuel gestured down to what looked like nothing, an arid track beneath them.

"South-West Africa." He smiled. "It's not much, but it's ours." Within minutes, they were in sight of Oshakati, a surprisingly bustling border town of ramshackle shops, tin structures like Quonset huts, jeeps, and dust. The chopper banked hard to the right, toward the Atlantic. In minutes, João caught sight of their destination.

A blond officer dashed toward their chopper as it came to land. He was holding a large floppy hat onto his head and squinting against the swirling sand that blasted his face.

"This is the doctor I was telling you about, Colonel Kuntz, Major João Gonçalves," Samuel shouted at the top of his lungs as they jogged away from the Alouette, crouching in fear of the rotors, which were too high to pose a danger but seemed dangerous enough.

"Good to meet you," the South African said in English, British-inflected, not Afrikaans. "You speak English, I trust?"

"My wife is from Hampshire," João shouted back.

"Good show," the officer said in a feigned posh accent.

They climbed into a jeep and headed straight for the hospital unit.

"You'll be needing this, I presume," the officer said to João, pulling out a surgical mask as they approached the door to the large, tin structure, its primitive windows open to the desert breeze.

"I'd rather have something to cover my arms," João replied, looking at his dark forearms, exposed by his short-sleeved fatigues covered in dust. "Do you have a lab coat?"

The man looked at him quizzically. "Well, I'm sure we can manage one. Come in."

By Portuguese standards, the field hospital wasn't half bad. Neat rows of beds, trim, well-coiffed nurses, the occasional IV pole, and lots of sick men. João stopped in his tracks.

"This is the yellow fever ward?"

The officer looked over the scene with a puzzled, embarrassed expression, before admitting that yes, this was epidemic central.

"Looks like it's in pretty good shape to me, clean at least," the officer said.

"If you can't close these windows, I want mosquito netting around each bed, tucked in tight. The vector is the mosquito, not the cough or the diarrhea or the blood. It's the mosquito."

João said this incredulously. How such a mighty army did not have this knowledge was simply bizarre.

"We don't have yellow fever in South Africa," the officer protested. "We're a temperate climate."

"It's your damned war," João snapped. "You ought to know where you're fighting it."

For nearly two weeks, João took charge of the ward, supervising mosquito control efforts, the spreading of netting, and the isolation of the most ill soldiers. Internal hemorrhaging can be severe and ugly; bleeding out in a crowded ward is no way to boost morale. João barked at nurses who gave their moaning patients aspirin to kill the pain.

"Have you no sense? Don't you know what acetylsalicylic acid does to internal bleeding?" he'd bark, thrusting a jar of paracetamol in their faces. He showed them how to measure the lost water content in the bedpans of puke and shit, how to rehydrate the right amount, which of the soldiers needed precious IV fluids, and which should be made to drink, protests or not.

It was Samuel who ended it. He stood by the door of the yellow fever ward, watching in amazement as João made rounds, oblivious to greater meaning, or even to his wife and child.

"João," he finally said when the doctor had drifted within earshot. "The news from Nova Lisboa is not good."

João looked at his friend as if he had just woken him.

"News? What news?"

"Major Gonçalves, it's time to go home."

* * *

"It's alright, Cristina. It's going to be alright. Just hold on to Mummy's hand, love. Hold on tight."

Elizabeth tried to sound reassuring, to mask her panic and guilt. Out of weakness and indecision, she had made a terrible mistake. She had waited. Now her husband was gone, she knew not where, and her four-year-old daughter was suffering the consequences.

Cristina, her cascade of ebony hair a tangled mess, whimpered softly. She held a soiled teddy bear in one hand, her mother's sweaty hand in the other, as they picked their way through the human detritus littering the smooth, polished floors of Nova Lisboa's modern train station, two more heartbreaks in a profusion of many, mostly women and children fleeing the Angolan highlands.

The smells of shit and piss were overwhelming, the station's toilets overwhelmed. The African street vendors joyfully sold jugs of water, fruit, gum, and cigarettes outside at outrageous prices, in Angolan escudos that would soon be worthless. But the inventive merchants could do nothing about the plumbing or the trains. The refugees had to make do in the darker corners of a building with too few dark corners; as for the trains, all the tickets were long gone.

"Mummy, I don't like it here. It smells," Cristina pleaded in a strained but hushed voice. Her little nose, already aquiline and delicate, scrunched in self-defense. Her eyes squinted to filter out the sights she could not understand.

"I know, love, I know. I know."

Elizabeth pushed forward toward mobbed ticket windows to try to find any space on a train for Benguela, on the coast. Luanda, where a flotilla of ships awaited, wasn't on the rail line, which was built not to transport humans from population center to population center but to empty Angola's interior of its resources and get them to the industrial port of Lobito Bay for the world beyond Africa's shores. The occasional shout of protest greeted an errant footstep, but mainly the refugees watched in sad silence as another white woman set off to plead her case, child in tow.

For five days, Elizabeth had been trying to get out of Nova

Lisboa, out of Angola, out of Africa. The air bridge set up in early September 1975, first by the Portuguese, then joined by Britain, France, the United States, and even the Soviet Union, was winding down. Nearly a quarter-million Portuguese had fled, as the province they thought was their home disintegrated into anarchy. But in Nova Lisboa, the settlers kept coming, in long, ragged caravans from coffee, cotton, and sisal plantations, market towns, and iron and diamond mining outposts days away.

The army was no longer offering protection. "We spent fourteen years fighting and dying for you lot," the soldiers would say, "so you could live in your villas, oversee your laborers, and sell your crops and metals. That's over. We don't bleed for settlers anymore."

Now the settlers were bleeding, from bandit ambushes, accidents on the rutted African roads, and crossfire between rival guerrilla forces preparing for independence and the bloodbath that would surely follow. The convoys—heavily weighted toward women, their men still fighting—would limp into Nova Lisboa, overloaded with belongings that would soon be abandoned in the streets, left to the Angolans fending for themselves in a newly independent nation, stripped bare save for such hand-me-downs.

Elizabeth could have left on one of the early airplanes. General Costa Gomes, still in touch with her father, personally sent an emissary from the Nova Lisboa base to escort her to the airport. But her husband was on "one last mission," he had said. And so she waited for him. She waited against all logic for the man who had brought her to the highlands of southern Africa, only to sour on her. Deep down, she still had faith that the João Gonçalves of the billowing white shirt and ocean breeze would return. So Elizabeth waited.

She used the lull of early morning, when the guerrillas were sleeping off their gin-soaked hangovers, to sneak out of her flat for food, braving gang rape for her daughter's sustenance. She had plenty of money. But the stores were empty, only the motley assortment of errant fruit, gum, and cigarettes the vendors were pedaling at the train station. She had to walk to the African market two kilometers away. She'd tell her four-year-old to stay inside and be quiet, kissing her gently and waving a doll or stuffed bear in her face to elicit one last giggle that would stave off guilt for a few paces. It was the best she could do. The building was practically empty. She knew no one who could take care of Cristina in her absence. She dared not take her with her. The African markets were laden with fruits, vegetables, and starchy cassava. But the rice, imported from other parts of Africa or beyond, was gone. Bread was a memory. Elizabeth had stopped wondering how she was going to get out and had given herself to fate. Somehow something would happen, she kept telling herself. Every time she returned to her apartment to find her daughter alive, she thanked a God she had rarely thought to thank before.

One day, desperate for adult conversation, she ventured to Fernando Osório's apartment for a visit, Cristina tagging along. The professor, beyond middle-aged but still vital and proper, surely must be going as stir-crazy as she was, she thought. The stairwell of his building had been eerily quiet as they climbed the two flights to his flat. She knocked gingerly.

"Fernando?" she called. "Fernando?"

Foolishly, she opened the unlocked door to the abattoir. He had tried to run, obviously. His body was backed against a wall near the door to his bedroom, slumped in a deep puddle of congealed and stinking blood. His eyes were glassy but terrified. His throat was slashed so deep his head had nearly been severed. The apartment was ransacked, drunken fighters no doubt motivated more by greed than hate.

She gasped—cried out really—and turned away, to shield Cristina from the sight and flee. She could never be sure her daughter had not seen the carnage. She never asked. And when they hurriedly returned to their own flat, she hunkered down and would not leave.

The next day, she hailed a gypsy cab to the airport. The mass of refugees sleeping on the floors and the tarmac were quick testament to her mistake. On that first foray, she found an army colonel she recognized, and anxiously produced a British passport. As Britons so often do, she assumed the embossed lion and unicorn—*Dieu et mon droit*, "God and My Right"—was her ticket out, her right.

"I'm sorry, Madam. First priority is to citizens of Portugal. Please contact your embassy," he said blandly.

"My embassy? That's in Luanda."

"I am sorry, but I cannot help you right now," the harried officer said, turning to the rest of the throng clamoring for his attention.

She heard that line over and over, before each night limping home with an exhausted little girl and her teddy bear. She would unlock the door in hope of finding João inside. But all that would greet her were the rapidly depleting shelves in the cupboard of a flat she had once loved.

João jiggled the key in the balking lock of his apartment door. Outside, dusk was settling on the city, but in a hallway he never much noticed, darkness had fallen. The low ceilings felt dingy, the unadorned walls depressing. A hush of abandonment hung on the building. He stepped into a barely lit flat, tentatively asking, "Hello?"

Everything seemed to be in order—a little untidy but, given the tumult outside, not bad. Drunken UNITA rebels, Savimbi's child soldiers, were making forays from their bases outside of town down the wide avenues of Nova Lisboa, firing their guns in the air and catcalling anything in a skirt. The odd artillery shell or mortar randomly whizzed into a government building or thudded into a park. There didn't seem to be any purpose to the explosions, just the revelry of heavily armed juvenile delinquents.

"Hello?" João said again, this time a little louder.

The door cracked open in the bedroom, then opened wider.

"João?" a small, English voice asked.

"It's me," he said, those two syllables catching in his throat.

Elizabeth and Cristina crept out of the bedroom, into the semi-gloom of the apartment. Gonçalves had expected if not a hero's welcome then a rush of gratitude. He had returned, safely. Instead,

Elizabeth stared blankly at him, deciding whether to scream in rage or collapse with relief.

Her voice emerged in a whisper, out of practice and tentative. "Do you have any idea what we have been through?" she asked, anger tinged with grief, the words choked by the urge to sob. "You left your family to die, João." She paused. The silence hit violently. She waited another beat, composed herself. "I waited for you, and waited. We lost our last chance to get out."

She wanted to scream. Her husband not only gave her reason to rage, he offered her the protection to raise her voice beyond the whispers that she and Cristina had been using for days. But she couldn't. Her eyes locked on his instead, wordlessly accusing. A defensive anger rose in João's throat. He had been saving lives, practicing medicine, doing what he was trained to do and doing it damned well. This woman, supposed to be his wife, would never understand him, would never appreciate how good he could be.

"Daddy?" A meek, miserable sound broke the tension. Cristina slid from behind her mother, careful not to let her head break contact with Elizabeth's thigh. Her hair was greasy. Water pressure was gone. Bathing was a ritual that had been sacrificed to war. Her once-chubby cheeks were noticeably hollowed, such a rapid change that mirrored the sudden collapse of the city around them. Her hungry, vacant eyes looked up at her father, whom she adored. João saw in her something haunting and desolate. His heart sunk. He crouched down and held out his arms. She walked slowly toward him and lowered her head onto his chest. Her arms hung limply by her side. He wrapped his around her in silence. Then, after a long while, he looked up at Elizabeth. "We've got to go. Now."

They frantically packed the same three duffel bags they had come with. Elizabeth stuffed a few carvings she loved, a colorful etched gourd, and the weaving from the wall, ripped from its wooden frame, into her bag. She tossed out the flowered dress she was married in to make room. João looked at it on the floor for a moment, then zipped the bag.

"What the hell took you so long, man?" Samuel demanded as they dashed by him in the building's atrium. He had been waiting there the whole time, not wanting to intrude on the reunion but refusing to stay in the car on the street, his white face glowing in the light of the one streetlamp still working on the block. The helicopter that had ferried him and João back to Nova Lisboa was gone, heading south again to the border. His escape and the escape of this family were his responsibility now. João saw something in Samuel's face he had not seen before: fear.

They would sleep at his place that night—he had bought some armed protection—and leave at first light for the station. A train would be leaving for Benguela.

"It's no use," Elizabeth said. "You can't get on. They come in to Nova Lisboa packed already. There are mobs already waiting to take whatever crack of space they can find."

"Don't worry, love." Samuel forced a smiled. "We've got this worked out."

The next morning, a driver took the four of them to a small house alongside the main station, just up the track. Samuel told João and Elizabeth to wait inside with Cristina, and slipped back out. A few minutes later, he returned, furtively waving for them to hurry out the side door. A train sprawled out beyond the main platform, and beyond the last car, another car was being pushed down the track by maybe thirty UNITA soldiers, guns slung casually by their sides. They yelled at each other, alternatively angry and laughing as they latched the single car to the main train. They then circled it in an armed phalanx. Within minutes, the people inside the station noticed the commotion. Seconds later, a throng heaved toward the car. The soldiers brandished their weapons and, with the stocks, knocked back the odd train-station denizen still brave enough to beg them to open the door.

Amid the desperation, Samuel was still able to grin at Elizabeth.

"Your carriage, Madam," he drawled, as he held out a hand to help her up.

"What? How?" she said in disbelief.

"You don't think Gordon Bromwell would let his daughter rot in Huambo?"

For weeks, Elizabeth's father had been expecting some kind of confirmation that his daughter had escaped from Africa, a letter of thanks with a Lisbon postmark, maybe a phone call, or at least a communiqué from his friend Costa Gomes. His daughter's ingratitude he had come to expect. It was his fault, really. Beneficence was something the Bromwells bestowed; it was not bestowed on them. His family did give thanks, of course, for its latest conquest, but not really to God, more to a vague metaphysical course of events. "We thank you for the success Gordon has found in lowering the top marginal tax rate," or some sort. They did not thank other people, certainly not each other. But this was a matter of some seriousness. And he heard nothing.

Phone calls were made, messages sent, and word reached Pretoria's man in Nova Lisboa, Samuel Vanderbroek, who, incidentally, was scrambling for his own escape route even as he was delivering an experienced doctor to the ailing forces amassed on the South-West African border.

"It's a colonial government railcar," Vanderbroek said to Elizabeth, looking around with satisfaction at his sumptuous if somewhat dusty surroundings. "They've kept it hidden in its own garage for years. Rarely used, as you can see. Once it was clear you hadn't gotten out on the airlift, your father began inquiring about rail links or roads. Damnedest thing, I get a call from Pretoria. 'You've got to find an Englishwoman named Elizabeth Bromwell.' I just laughed. 'I'm with her husband.'"

And he did laugh, a long belly laugh, as he settled onto a plush, deep purple velvet bench.

"I got in touch with some of the Portuguese administrators who had made their escape already in the airlift. This popped up—cost Mr. Bromwell a pretty penny, I'm sure."

Fifty or more stranded souls could have piled into the extra car. Elizabeth thought of those vacant stares and the beseeching looks that she had shared with the other refugees who had crammed into the train station. She felt ill. But as the train built up steam, leaving Nova Lisboa behind forever, she settled in and enjoyed the first-class remove. She was leaving Africa, she thought with some relief but more than a little sadness. This is where she learned to be married, to accept, where she had borne a child, the jewel of her life, where she had made her first home and a life truly free of Mother and Father, or so she had thought. Already, it was gaining the glow of retrospect, warmer still because she—like all the whites fleeing the highlands— knew full well it would never be the same.

"I can't believe I'm paying these punks," Samuel murmured to himself.

Cristina at first sat silently on the velvet, huddled closely against her father, who wrapped an arm around her in a tight, quiet hug. She fiddled with his fingers, scrunched and unscrunched his army cap—the bush variety, with sun visors on front and back, and glanced up at his face occasionally for reassurance. He would kiss the crown of her head; she'd smile to herself, then look back down at her busy little hands. As the train gained speed in its long, slow descent from the Bié plateau to Angola's coastal plain, on its way to Lobito Bay, her four-year-old self burst forward. Soon, she was running to the front of the car, then the back, to one side then the other, giggling and showing off as the locomotive coasted from Nova Lisboa's 5,581 feet of altitude, past the high slopes of the Lepi range, past sisal, coffee, and fruit-tree plantations at Alto Catumbela, already going to seed, over the dramatic Lengue Gorge, then down to sea level, along the salt pans, sugar plantations, lime kilns, and stone quarries outside Benguela. A few desultory workers could still be seen going through the motions of labor. But mainly, the fields and quarries were still, abandoned for the safety of the village or the encampments on the beach, where the Angolans had fled as independence approached.

And now a British aristocrat and her Portuguese husband were making the journey created for copper, on the caboose end of a train filled this time with human cargo. Cristina flitted happily around the cabin, leaving João free to fall into silent self-doubt. He was being rescued by his wife. Just days ago, he was directing triage operations at a vast military encampment, dictating to the fair-haired South Africans. Now he felt again like a man incapable of controlling his destiny, regardless of his efforts, education, or competence.

And there was something else. He never was an outward advocate of empire, throughout the long years in Africa. But as he and his countrymen made their ignoble escapes, he could not help but feel the sting of humiliation. He was being hustled out of a Portuguese province, the richest of the empire, with the help of the British and South Africans.

When Elizabeth and he were in Guiné, before Cristina, before the fights, before defeat, Luis the bread man and a cluster of Guinean staff told the couple a joke. There was a bird in Guiné, the jambatutu, which flew in spurts of fifty feet, making its way languidly through the steamy fields of West Africa without grace but without care either. It was the national symbol of the nascent state that would become Guiné-Bissau. "Jambatutu woke up one morning feeling particularly lazy," Luis had begun. "His mother said, 'Hey, Jambatutu, get up. Go fetch some firewood for breakfast.' 'No, Ma, I'm not feeling so well.' He stayed on his mat and watched his sisters and brothers go to work. 'Hey, Jambatutu, go and sweep the house.' 'No, Ma, I'm not feeling so well this morning.' 'Hey, Jambatutu, come here and stir the pot. I've got to go feed the baby.' 'No, Ma, I think I really am sick.'

"Well," Luis said, his joy building, "this went on for a while. Jambatutu wouldn't wash, wouldn't help build the fire, wouldn't pound the rice, until finally, his mother said, 'Jambatutu, breakfast's ready.' 'Alright,' Jambatutu said, all excited, and he hopped out of bed, grabbed his bowl, and dug in."

At that, Luis and the Guineans broke out into uncontrollable laughter—knee-slapping, tear-inducing, snorting laughter. Elizabeth stared blankly, but perhaps, João had thought, she hadn't understood the language. He had, every word of it, and at the time, he could not fathom why this story was funny. He heard the joke a few more times, each telling eliciting the same rip-roaring hilarity. He thought about the story often, until the joke became the emblem of his wider bafflement at the world around him. He could explain the Portuguese interest in Africa, the rivalries between Neto and Roberto and Savimbi, tribalism, a class structure imposed by his forefathers, but then he thought of Jambatutu and realized he understood nothing.

Until now. He smiled to himself as he watched the highlands recede. A little chuckle slipped through his nose, a puff of recognition; he was Jambatutu. Like the bird, he was taking another short hop that would take him gracelessly, aimlessly elsewhere, hoping for a handout. He had failed to take flight.

"'The blood-dimmed tide is loosed, and everywhere the ceremony of innocence is drowned; the best lack all conviction, while the worst are full of passionate intensity.'"

João murmured the words softly, but not to himself. He wanted Elizabeth to hear.

"I don't know that one," she said in a hush. "Something violent. *Troilus and Cressida?*"

His eyes met hers. They were filled with a sadness she had never seen in him, distant, pained.

"It's Yeats. What would your bard know of the end of days?"

Elizabeth watched her husband intently. She felt his sadness, not at its depths but she felt it nonetheless. Her nation's empire was long gone; that João was feeling such a loss would never have occurred to her. But she understood his sense of failure, an emotion she had felt often. She reached for his hand. For a moment, she felt it all rush back. Then he turned away to watch the scenery float by.

CHAPTER EIGHTEEN

As I waited for Cristina, I decided to indulge Hans in his dissolute fantasies of my country, and catch up on a little of the history I might soon be returning to. I took him to see *Mississippi Burning* at the Duke of York's, where we watched Gene Hackman confront the homicidal Klansmen Hans later told me he imagined lurking in every corner of my crack-besotted country.

Hans was weakening. He lived in something of a twilight, never quite fully alert, never truly able to sleep—but stubbornly alive. I watched him out of the corner of my eye, his eyes seemingly glazed as he stared at the screen. In a flood of sympathy and premature nostalgia, I rested a warm, young hand on his skeletal claw. He gave me a slight smile, of gratitude, maybe even affection, but he couldn't muster a full glance. I realized I was watching his face intently, trying to divine a response. I turned back to the screen.

I was going through my own private torment. My brother, Noah, was planning a quick tour of Europe before his second year of law school. My parents were offering up a little money if I wanted to join him, then return home to Georgia. That would mean foreclosing on Cristina and abandoning Elizabeth nearly a month before Hans was due to ship out for Italy, not enough time to find a new volunteer but plenty to wreck her studies and leave her to care for Hans alone. In my impoverished state, I hadn't crossed the English

Channel since last summer, and Noah was pressuring me—not for his sake, but for my parents. Phone calls were tricky, but at a time prearranged by aerogram, he had called me at the Bromwells' late one night. I picked up the phone in the upstairs study. I was trying to stay out of earshot of Hans, but I was regrettably very much in range of Cristina.

"C'mon, David, your little sabbatical is over," he said. "Time to smell the fucking coffee."

"What the hell do you know about my life, Noah? Don't you think I have obligations here?"

"Well, your little girlfriend dumped you, didn't she?"

"Charming, man. You have a really enticing way of getting me to join you on the Continent."

"The Continent? Is that how you talk over there now?"

"Europe, OK? I was just trying to, you know, delineate one side of the Channel from the other."

"Oh yeah, the Channel," he snorted. "David, look, this isn't about me. Mom and Dad have gone through a lot since, you know, Rebecca and all. They're ready. It's...different here now."

I paused.

"Did they tell you to tell me that?"

"What's it matter? I'm telling you, asshole. C'mon, David, we'll have a little fun. You can show me some of your new favorite spots, I'll drag you to some places you haven't been to, we'll get a little high, you can get me laid, maybe. That'll be a challenge for you. Then we can head home together, see the 'rents. A blessing on your head, mazel tov, mazel tov."

(The highlight of my brother's teenage years was his star turn in *Fiddler on the Roof* senior year of high school—cast as Tevye because he was big enough and looked Jewish. He wasn't a bad singer, it turned out. My parents showed up for closing night but forgot to bring a camera.)

"Let me think about it, Noah. You haven't even asked about my quadriplegic, have you? He's not gonna just pop up and say, 'Hey, don't worry about me. You just run along.' I've got, you know, re-sponsibilities, jerk."

The truth was, I wanted one last space cake in Amsterdam, an-other walk along the Seine, some European adventure. My brother had plans to go a few places I hadn't been, touristy spots my snob-bish pretentions or my wallet hadn't allowed: Carcassonne, Nice and Cannes, Monaco, Cinque Terre. I reasoned that I had at least as much of an obligation to him as to Hans and Elizabeth. (I didn't feel it, though.)

It was a cool, pleasant evening when I pushed Hans out of the movie theater. Misty, cold March had relinquished Brighton to April. Days were warming, with tulips and irises in bloom around the Royal Pavilion, the ersatz Mughal pleasure dome built by the future King George IV for his assignations with the scandalously Catholic Maria Fitzherbert. The Victoria Gardens were an explosion of color. The Old Steine bustled with tourists. I had parked the am-bulance some blocks away from the theater to feel the spring air, maybe wake Hans up a bit or at least offer a little cheer.

"What do you say we go to a pub, Hans?" I asked. I was oddly buoyant considering I had just sat through a movie about the mur-der of young civil rights activists at the hands of vicious racists. But it had been nearly two years since I had touched American soil. The film seemed like an anthropological study, depressing in the same way a documentary on the dying Yonomami would be, or the Rape of Nanjing.

"Why not?" Hans replied, more an exhale than an expression. "Nothing for me, though. You drink away."

The late-night lorries rumbled past on their way to the farmers market as I pushed Hans down the Viaduct Road. With each clat-tering truck, I wondered whether Hans still wanted to die, still fantasized about a timely push from me into the traffic. Really, though, as death approached he seemed to cling to life. There were no more dictations to the Voluntary Euthanasia Society, though a letter had recently arrived from them.

"We have good news, dear members," it read. "We have secured a quota from the British government allowing some terminally ill patients passage to the Netherlands for consultations with physicians licensed to administer lethal doses of morphine. We are accepting applications, which must include two physicians' testimonials defining the nature of your condition, the pain entailed and the hopelessness of your situation, along with your own signature, certified by a notary public and a psychiatrist attesting to your sound mental functions."

I laughed as I read it aloud, expecting Hans to muster a chuckle. He didn't. I tucked it away with the other junk mail and hustled out of the room.

"Did you recognize any of your kin in the film, David?" Hans asked in the pub as I returned from the bar with a pint of bitter and a small glass of water.

"I particularly identified with the burly Jewish Klansman," I said. "I think I saw my father under one of the hoods, but one can never be sure with those things."

"I was thinking more of the murder victims, David, the earnest one with the curly black hair—your kind, I should think."

I laughed. I was still quick to think the worst of Hans's intentions when it came to me, but he was coming around. In truth, he'd come around some time ago. I pushed Hans beside a booth, not worried we were taking up too much space on a quiet weeknight. I sat down heavily on the worn, lumpy velvet pillow covering the wooden bench and gave Hans a tender smile.

"What's that look?" he asked suspiciously. "Are you up to something?"

"Hans, there is something I have to tell you. I'm thinking of leaving. In early May. My older brother's going to be in Europe. I've got one last chance to travel around before having to go back to the States. And..."

My chatter trailed off. We sat in silence for a moment.

"I know Elizabeth's counting on me until you go to Italy."

Again, silence. I thought Hans had tuned out; maybe he was going into one of his dormancies. Then he breathed deep.

"What about Maggie?"

"Maggie?"

"Yes, Maggie."

"Hans, we split up ages ago. Well, she dumped me for some guy named Grod."

"You made that up, didn't you?" he said with a slight, breathy chuckle.

"Well, that's what she told me anyway."

He was quiet for a while, letting that one sink in—had he really not noticed the bunnies had been stilled upstairs? I was saddened by his disappointment.

"I understand you were a communist last year, a pretty pathetic one," he spoke up.

"You've been talking to Elizabeth, haven't you?"

"My sister doesn't much like to talk to me, but she seems to like to talk to you, and about you. I should congratulate you, David. You've done more to bring us together than anyone, maybe ever."

"Cheers," I said ruefully, holding up my glass to Hans's sardonic smile. But Hans wasn't being sardonic, I could see. It wasn't hard to tell when the man was serious. It was almost comical. A smile seemed to be such an effort that when he let it go, his whole face drooped in a sudden swoon. It was as if gravity took hold with a violent yank.

"Can you stick with anything, David?" Hans gave a short, raspy exhale, paused a moment, then breathed deeply, as deeply as he could. The conversation was taking a lot out of him. His lungs had little capacity left. He had to satiate every remaining alveolus. There was a long break. Then he continued.

"I had a girl once. Segolaine."

"I know, Hans. You loved her name."

"Yes." His eyes were yellow and watery, and he looked at me straight. I shuffled, and then offered him some water. He took a sip.

"She loved me, David. She was a whore, but she loved me. Someday you'll find a woman who loves you, and you'll learn that's something. That's really something."

Cristina and I had a date the next night, at least that's what I told myself it was. She had used the word, but to her, I was sure, it was just another study session. First, she promised, a drink at the Imperial Arms.

We walked together down Imperial Lane in the almost-warm spring night. Once No. 4 was out of sight, she reached for my hand.

"It's like a date, David," she said brightly.

"*Like* a date?" I asked.

"*Just* like a date."

She grasped my hand with both of hers, tucked it against her short skirt, and leaned her head playfully on my shoulder. A seductive thumb caressed my skin.

We sat in a quiet corner of the nearly empty pub, Cristina sipping a half pint of lager while I nursed a full one of bitter. We talked easily about the future, about Elizabeth's job search, about my final year of university, her coming first. She had been provisionally accepted to the University of East Anglia outside of Norwich, pending the results of her A Levels, which she'd take in June and hear back about in August.

"I'd love you to visit East Anglia. It's nothing like Sussex. The boys all wear khakis and polo shirts and talk about punting and the Fens," she told me.

"Sounds horrible."

She laughed a delicate, breathy laugh, and I reached for her hand under the table, clasped her fingers, and leaned in to her ear. "I'll visit you anytime you like. Just say the word." She pressed our hands against her thigh, cocked her head into my breath, and let her long hair envelop my lips.

" 'Ello, Cristina, fancy meetin' you 'ere," a loud voice interrupted. A lad in a black shirt, opened well down his chest, Doc Martens, and black skinny jeans stood over us. Peroxided hair, long on top and parted in the middle, was feathered along pocked and hollow cheeks.

"Hello, Leander, how are you?" Cristina answered flatly.

" 'Oo's your friend? You're thick as thieves."

"Sorry, this is David. David, this is Leander, a bloke from school." He knelt close to her other ear.

"Not your usual type, Cristina. He doesn't really have a chance, right?"

"A chance for what?" she answered caustically.

A naked toe touched my bare ankle and climbed up my calf, caressing rhythmically, up and down my leg. A surge of heat and blood rushed to my groin, and I squeezed Cristina's hand hard.

"Let's get out of here," I said.

"I'll come with you two," Leander said. "Night's young. Where to?"

"No you won't," Cristina barked.

I watched the numbers count down along Imperial Lane, praying for liftoff, but as we neared No. 4, Cristina dropped my hand and a space grew between us.

"Do you think I was rude to that bloke back there?"

"Leander?" I mocked. "No, not at all. Cristina, you're always gonna break hearts. You've gotta accept that."

"What are you saying, that Leander fancies me or something?"

"Cristina." I smiled, and she smiled back.

She turned the key in the door, then led me up the stairs, back into the parlor, grabbing her literature textbook as we went in. My heart sunk. This time, though, she went to the remaining sofa, which sat bereft, without end tables or a coffee table to adorn it. She sat hard against one end. I took my place at a respectable distance. Then I looked at her. There was something in those eyes, surrender, acceptance, desire maybe. Her mouth was open just slightly, and I could hear her breathing. She locked a gaze on me, and I lunged—without a thought, without a plan. We were together in an instant.

My left hand grasped her hip, then slid up the gentle curve of her waist, my right wrapped around her head, fingers rising through her hair at the nape of her neck. I pulled her to me, and our lips met, her hand pressing my head to hers.

This woman, this beauty I had desired and dreamed of and wanted for so many, many months, just there. It was so easy. My hand reached to feel her narrow frame, to caress the supple rise of her breast, to graze a nipple through silky fabric, to pull her toward me from the small of her back. She slid down slightly, and I reached a hand between her knees, then up her skirt, along her impossibly soft, surprisingly delicate inner thighs, slowly, deliberately stopping a fraction of an inch below the apex to feel the heat rising, to tantalize. Her hips trembled. Her legs parted ever so slightly farther. Her breath grew at once shallow and insistent as we kissed, tongues gently touching. I ached for more.

Where I expected relief or wonderment I felt instead gratitude. I was grateful, to Cristina, to Elizabeth, to Hans, to a world and a God that had delivered this moment to me, against all expectations for what would happen, what I deserved.

"Cristina, Cristina, Cristina," I whispered, over and over, wanting to hear her name in my voice, wanting her to hear my reverential thanks. "You're so beautiful."

"David," I heard back. "David, wait," she said more insistently, sitting up.

"What is it?"

"Uncle Hans."

I looked at my watch.

"Oh, shit. Cristina, wait for me."

"This will sound peculiar to you, but I used to love scratching my back, just like a great, filthy bear."

I was shuffling around Hans's room. I was trying to be consciously diligent as my head hummed with excitement. Cristina was upstairs, but we both knew such duties could not be shirked. His back and thighs had been checked for bedsores, his urine bag emptied, his catheter given a gentle tug to see that all was set. I sat down on the barstool by his pillow to hear his quiet voice.

"I had this rough-hewn four-poster bed in Paris. Sounds posh, but it wasn't. The finishing had been rubbed off the posts, which were plain and sharp-edged. Every night, I would lean my bare back against a post and scratch. 'Ahhh.' It drove Segolaine mad. 'You look like an animal, Hans. Come to bed. I'll scratch your back.' 'No, darling, I prefer it my way.'" He chuckled. "I miss that, a lot."

"Would you like me to scratch your nose or something?"

He gave me a long, sad look of pity, one that told me I hadn't grasped the point of his story at all. "Don't let this go to your head, David, but I've grown to like this time of day. I used to hate it, all the fussing around the bed, for what? So I could lie in bed some more."

He paused.

"Now we have a little ritual, don't we?"

I reached gingerly under the blankets and fished out a hand to hold. It was an awkward, self-conscious gesture. His skin was so thin I could feel the sinew of useless tendons binding the bones. Hans lifted his head to see the spectacle.

"You know I can't feel that, David, not a thing. You might as well be fondling my urine bag."

I let out a frustrated breath.

"I'm trying here, Hans."

"I can feel my face," he said that night.

The whispered voice broke into my thoughts. I leaned over and, with the back of my fingers, tentatively stroked Hans's cheek. He let his head sink back into the pillow and smiled.

"I'm glad I have something to offer, Hans. Really, thank you."

"Thank you," he repeated, as if trying out the words for himself. "People used to always be thanking us, for this charity ball or that bit of magnanimity or perhaps just the Bromwell presence. Funny how we British can be with our aristocracy. My father never really stretched to serve, mind you, but he had his moments, sometimes even when he wasn't campaigning for reelection. Just showing up at some village dinner was considered an unbelievably noble gesture on the part of my parents."

He sighed, but he often sighed. I had a difficult time discerning an exhale from an expression of feeling.

"I haven't been thanked in a long while."

I slicked back a greasy wisp of hair threatening to fall in front of an eye.

"Do you think Elizabeth will make it, you know, when I'm gone? Is she still studying?"

"Yes, Hans, I think she'll make it."

"I don't have life insurance, you know, and it's not as if when I'm gone Haversham will give her a fortune for my hospital bed and tin cabinets."

I laughed. "I hardly think she's counting on that, Hans. I think she really wants to work, you know, be normal, like everyone else."

"So she's looking forward to..."

"No, that's not what I meant."

"Yes, yes, I know. And Cristina?"

I blushed and smiled shyly.

"What is it?" he asked.

"Can you imagine Cristina not making it, Hans?"

"No, no, I suppose not. There was a time, but not anymore.... Thank you, David."

I covered his head, turned the knob to make sure his door closed silently, then ascended the stairs to make love to Cristina Gonçalves.

Dearest Elizabeth,

Now you have me worried. I do love our little communications, but I fear we should be widening our circle. There comes a time when all children of privilege must use their privilege, claim their birthright. I'd imagine a lady of the realm, beaten by her ne'er-do-well of a husband and swirling in the cauldron of African revolution, has found her moment.

It sounds as if by the time you receive this letter, you may not even be at the address of this Nova Lisboa place of yours, lovely as it may be. But if by chance this correspondence should find you, please write back as soon as possible to advise. I do not wish to betray your trust, dear sister, but I am sure our Member of Parliament of a father could effect a rescue of some sort. It pays to be a militarist Tory in times of strife. That's why our benighted countrymen called on that drunk Churchill after all.

Father, apparently, is gaining some stature in Whitehall with the insistent clamouring of this wench named Margaret Thatcher, conservative revival and all that sort of thing. I believe he is finally allowing himself some enjoyment in politics. Until now, he's just been the humbug on the backbench, yammering on about fox-hunting and inheritance taxation. I like to get his goat with my debauched-son act, but I suppose it's nearing time for me to return to England and assume my dull position in society, to the manor born are we.

Is it terribly presumptuous for me to ask whether I should be taking you along, dragging you along even? You have a husband of sorts, and a lovely child, but remember, Elizabeth, you have a place here as well, a comfortable nook carved out of English society by generations of Bromwells. It can be a claustrophobic little notch, no doubt, but it's a safe one. I'm quite sure it can accommodate all three of you if that is what you wish.

I for one am feeling the tug. Sloth has been kind in a meaningless sort of way, but I can't stay in Paris forever. My first mistake was taking the initiative and finding work at a bank. If that isn't enough to propel me across the Channel for more edifying assignments, I don't know what will. But before I drag myself from my flat on the Rive Gauche, I could take a little jaunt into the Heart of Darkness to fetch my baby sister, if that's what's been called. Mistah Kurtz, I presume, is not yet dead.

Please, please, let me know your wishes on this front soonest.

Your loving and anxious brother,
Hans

CHAPTER NINETEEN

On November 10, 1975, Commodore Leonel Cardoso, the last Portuguese high commissioner in Africa, lowered the flag flying over the palace in Luanda and boarded a skiff for a troop ship bobbing in the bay. Four hundred ninety-two years after the king's caravels dropped anchor at the outpost to be christened São Paulo de Loanda, the remnants of empire set sail for Lisbon, retracing the route Diogo Cão had blazed—in reverse.

Elizabeth Bromwell followed the collapse of Angola the way most everyone did, if they chose to: She read it deep inside the newspaper. She was adjusting fitfully to a new life in Johannesburg, biding her time, waiting to leave Africa—soon, she figured, though she didn't know how.

Her escape train had pulled into Benguela in the early morning darkness, just weeks before Independence Day. Electricity was already running scarce, but the lights of the station were kept off anyway to avoid mortars. The screech of the wheels awoke the passengers in the sumptuous last car. Samuel hushed his companions.

"Stay quiet, and don't light anything. Best not to attract attention. We're staying on until Lobito," he said in a whisper. "Not much further."

Maybe half the train disembarked in Benguela, hoping for rail transit south, into South-West Africa, or a plane ticket out. The rest remained on board for Lobito and the faint hope of a freighter.

Elizabeth and João had not asked Samuel what awaited them at the end of the line. Their guide seemed confident enough. He had produced a magic carpet out of the highlands. They could trust him not to improvise the last, most crucial leg.

An hour and a half later, they reached the great natural seaport of Lobito in the early dawn. On the wide beachhead just beyond the station, a tide of African refugees huddled around driftwood campfires, cooking rats or cats or dogs or whatever could be found. Children heaved jerry cans, still smelling of gasoline but filled with water from a single faucet outside the Benguela Railway office. A ragged line, maybe fifty meters long, of disheveled women and children waited their turn at the tap. In the deepwater harbor, just meters from shore, was a flotilla of freighters. Some were there to get the refugees out. Most were there for one last looting; whole factories and warehouses waited on the docks in massive wooden crates and on pallets.

Samuel Vanderbroek pushed two of the child soldiers out the door in front, weapons at the ready, then led Elizabeth, João, and Cristina out, followed by the other two boys with guns. They were steps from the offices that housed the railway and port authorities, which appeared to be empty, barred and barricaded. The refugees kept their distance, watching the party with a mix of anger and envy as they crept around the back of the building. Samuel pounded on the door in a rhythmic knock. No one came. He did it again. Still no one. He gave his companions a "don't worry, everything's under control" kind of look, then pounded on the door again, this time with such ferocity the wood splintered around the lock. Finally, a faint voice came through, muffled and unintelligible to anyone but Samuel. He shouted something back in Portuguese, and the door opened just enough for the crew to pile in. A little African man, light of skin and bespectacled, bowed obsequiously as they passed, even to Cristina, but not to the soldiers. Samuel barged past.

"What took you so long, man?" he barked.

Samuel knew where he was going. The others had to hustle to keep up as he burst into the radio room.

There sat two large white men, in uniform, sipping tea from military-issue tin cups. Dutch blood had given the South African army an imposing stature.

"Samuel, nice of you to join us," one man said in his clipped accent, a rueful smile crossing his face.

"Good morning, Captain Van Heerden, Lieutenant Roos."

"You're a bit late, Vanderbroek, almost a week," Roos said.

Samuel shrugged. "I had a little problem to attend to over the border"—he gestured to João—"with this man. Doctor Major Gonçalves, I'd like you to meet the forward guard of the South African army, Zulu Company."

"We're coming." Van Heerden chuckled. "South Africa's going to send those dirty Cubans back to their little island in the sea, yah?"

João stood in silent wonder, suffering yet another revelation that he had absolutely no idea what was happening in the land he had lived in for the past four years. The South African army was here, in Angola? Pulling the strings, controlling the sluice gates of colonial history? Fighting Cuba? He felt like an idiot.

"Doctor Major, the pleasure is all ours," Van Heerden said, with a big, mocking guffaw that Roos joined in with obvious glee. "Your departure means we get to do things our way now."

Samuel stood patiently, allowing the mirth from their little joke to ease off in its own time, in on it but not amused.

"I'm not so sure those dirty Cubans are going to be so obliging," he grumbled, as he pushed his way past Roos to the South African receiver to radio a ship in the harbor, receive some instructions in Afrikaans, then herd his team back out the same way they came.

"Give my best to your commander when he arrives," Samuel called out to the South Africans as he reached the door.

"Shouldn't be long," Roos and Van Heerden shouted in unison.

The little Angolan man smiled, bowed and muttered, and let them out the back again before slamming the door and latching it violently behind them.

The launch was already at the dock when they arrived, oversized for the task and bristling with large guns held by menacing white men. Not far from shore, a freighter awaited, actually a military materiel transport. With no government of any kind left in Lobito, the South Africans simply floated into the harbor and began off-loading weapons, officers, and supplies for an army on its way. Its load dumped on the docks, the ship rode high in the water, the officer cabins available for Elizabeth, João, Cristina, and Samuel. But even the biggest cabin was a spare affair, whitewashed neatly but with only two narrow bunks, one of which Elizabeth and Cristina would share.

The Angolans hoping for escape did not dare approach Samuel and his band. Instead, they parted like the Red Sea to allow two white men, a frazzled white woman, and a raven-haired child to reach the dockside. Samuel had already slipped payment to the four young soldiers. Now he was cutting them loose. In Portuguese, he assured them their comrades would be there soon, within days. In a panic, the boys' voices rose. They gesticulated wildly, pleading for passage. One of the men from the launch stepped into the fray, holding aloft his FN MAG, an imposing heavy machine gun of South African vintage. The boys backed off and watched silently as their travel companions stepped into the skiff and headed into the harbor.

"You'll stay with us in Johannesburg, won't you? At least until you decide what to do with your lives. You know, João, there is always room for a good doctor in South Africa." Greta Vanderbroek was beaming with happiness. It all seemed like a great adventure and joyous good fun for Greta. Her friend Elizabeth, looking a little tired but all in all not too worse for the wear, was standing before her on a dock in Cape Town. The Vanderbroek children would be caring for little Cristina again. Samuel, back by her side and in her bed, would be sipping brandies with the dashing young Dr. Gonçalves. And all of this far, far from war and strife. Angola be damned. Deliverance was complete, thank you very much, and her husband had been the shepherd. She was proud.

The shepherd, of course, had only been taking orders. Four days before, Elizabeth climbed into a tiny cabin aboard a South African freighter, relieved and exhausted, to find a telegram resting on the pillow of her bed.

"Elizabeth, dear, it is time to come home. Your father."

For four nights, Elizabeth and João had fought sotto voce, trying to win the night without waking their worn-out child. The game was over, Elizabeth said that first night at sea. It was time to go home, to Lisbon if not to London. They could book a flight from Johannesburg as soon as they landed. There may even be direct flights from Cape Town to London. As Elizabeth pressed her case, João dug in deeper. There was still a future for them in Africa, possibly even in Nova Lisboa, if they had the patience to wait it out, see how things settled. This was where they were almost happy. He could see it on the horizon.

"I've seen the whole damned South African army on the border. This could be over in a month or two, a friendly government installed, the university back up and running."

"João, what has happened to you? You have a family too. They're waiting for you. They miss you. Where is this obsession with Africa coming from?"

"Obsession? Obsession? You saw all that we had. A life we had made on our own, without your bloody father meddling, without my father and the church and expectations. You just want to throw it away because Daddy called you home? Pathetic."

Exchanges like that made Elizabeth wish João had not spent so much time in London, perfecting the English verbal uppercut. He must have known some vicious women there, she thought.

"That's over now, over, and you know it. Nova Lisboa doesn't even exist anymore. What do you want, a wife and child in Huambo, begging mangoes in the market? You've heard Samuel. There will be no end to war."

"Samuel, Samuel. Maybe you're fucking the man. He's so damned wise."

"You're one to talk about fucking."

He shot her a look of boiling rage. He raised a hand as if to strike, then turned away. The quarters were too close for violence, his sleeping daughter practically underfoot.

They made their way to Cape Town, not a thing settled between them about the life to come.

The freighter, unencumbered by cargo on a calm sea, slipped quickly past the Blaauwberg Coast. It was early still when the ship eased into Table Bay, but the sun was already bright. They cruised past a forest of loading cranes on the outer reaches of Duncan Dock. Rusted trawlers jostled with modest cargo vessels and military ships.

The city of Cape Town shone under a blue sky, hard pressed against Table Mountain, with only a few short tendrils tentatively reaching up its sheer rock walls. To the west and south, Lion's Head and Signal Hill reared up above the buildings and homes to watch over the cloistered city. The rocks, massifs, and mountains were a grand amphitheater for the city below. Robben Island, a low, almost formless gray hump on the horizon, concealed its prison and its human contents, the leaders of the African National Congress seemingly sealed away in perpetuity. Nelson Mandela himself would be waking now. Perhaps he had already turned to the day's task, breaking more rocks.

All of that was unknown to Elizabeth and Cristina, who stood on the deck and watched the future approach. As the Victoria and Albert Waterfront came into view, so did its wondrous sights: gray-stuccoed Cape Dutch customs houses with their elaborate white trim and flat-fronted rooflines cut into marvelous dips, curves, and peaks, a French-balconied office building, red wharves piled on top of each other and bustling with black, brown, and white traffic. Successive waves of colonialists, empire builders, and interlopers had built the Cape: the Dutch, who populated it with slaves from Malaysia and Java and built their trading realm; the French Huguenots, who fled Catholic persecution only to slaughter the Khoi tribesmen and elephants impeding the establishment of incomparably lovely towns like

Franschhoek, with their lush gardens, statues of Marie Antoinette, and estate wineries grand enough to challenge the Loire for bragging rights; and finally and most thoroughly, the British, who made up for their lack of charm with blinding ambition and the organization to make it work. A Victorian gingerbread clock tower greeted Elizabeth, João, and Cristina at the end of the dock. At its base stood Greta Vanderbroek, smiling broadly.

João took satisfaction in Greta's greeting, a vindication of sorts. Life would be good and possible here, until he was ready to declare it otherwise. That may be in six years or six weeks. He didn't know. In truth, he didn't really know why he was insisting on staying. He understood the visceral desire to resist Elizabeth's entreaties, to dictate the terms. But he could have overcome that if he saw a reason to return home. He couldn't find one. He also could not allow himself to be another combat veteran adrift, addicted to the adrenaline high of mortal danger or haunted by what he had seen and done. In his psychiatry rotations, he remembered seeing grainy, jerky old films from World War I of trembling wrecks suffering from shell shock, proto-psychiatrists chasing them around English gardens with cattle prods. It had actually been funny, Chaplinesque. The med students could imagine the sound of an old, tinkling piano belting out a rag as the soldiers waddled around in the antiquated herky-jerky films, leaping forward with each painful but ineffectual shock, their doctor-cum-tormenters waddling behind with their odd weaponry.

Cristina stepped off the gangplank and gawked silently. African-born, she had never seen such wonders. Greta stooped to her level and pointed to the enormous rock perched atop a mountain behind them.

"It's called Lion's Head," she said, making claws with her hands that swiped at the child playfully. "Roar! He protects us all."

Then she stood and held Cristina's hand, leading the family off the dock and onto the waterfront. She smiled at her husband, who signaled he would catch up to them after he finished a little business. Porters would carry the Gonçalveses' scanty cargo after a respectable time had lapsed to get them clear of the unrespectable pile.

"Are you tired? Do you want a hotel?" Greta asked, as they walked past the Queen Victoria. The sky was a rich blue, the sun friendly, warming the air to the perfect temperature of a British day in June. Elizabeth gazed at the pink faces sipping tea with their breakfasts inside a sunlit lobby. She could not imagine anything more civilized.

"You know what I'd really love, Greta? I'd really love some good English food."

Greta smiled down at Cristina.

"Does that sound good to you too, love?"

Cristina, her mouth closed tight but a smile wide across her face, nodded happily, pigtails bobbing by her side.

They spent three days in the warm, dry bliss of apartheid Cape Town. In the townships of Langa, Guguletu, and Khayelitsha, far from view, young men idled away another day of unemployment drinking or sealing their shacks with pillaged corrugated scrap, while women hustled for domestic work or sold their bodies for a few rand. The Group Areas Act of 1966 was building steam. The authorities had taken to the pencil test to sort the blacks from the Malays, Indians, and mixed-race coloreds and decide where to put the carefully separated races. If the pencil stayed in the hair, the test subjects were black, destined for the worst of the shantytowns. If it fell, they would still be leaving their homes, many of which had been in their families for centuries, but their shacks would be slightly larger. If the pencil dangled inconclusively, the Afrikaners would have to resort to complicated charts measuring lip size and nose breadth to make a determination.

Elizabeth and Greta strolled through the Company's Garden and De Waal Park unencumbered by such things. The flowers—mesembryanthemums, proteas, leucadendrons, and restios—were anarchic, the royal palms burst like fireworks, the baobabs and magnolias were a British pensioner's dream, a Victorian garden in the tropics. Cristina chased long-beaked guinea fowl and red-winged starlings. Only once did Elizabeth take note of the throb of bulldozers on a hillside above the harbor.

"They're clearing District Six still. It's been taking ages really, Lord knows why, but they're in the last stages," Greta said with relief.

"District Six?" Elizabeth responded.

"There." Greta pointed to a barren area, largely scraped of its homes and the sixty-six thousand people that once lived there. "That had been a colored area, a real mess and in such a nice area. Look at that view. Now Cape Town will be able to make something of it.

"Oh, don't worry, Elizabeth," she continued, responding to the anxious look on the young Englishwoman's face. "They're being relocated to Cape Flats. It's better for them there. Lots of room. And the ones with jobs will have their Dumb Passes to get into the city. It'll make things so much more orderly, you know?"

Like their Portuguese colonial brethren, white South Africans were gracious hosts to the white outsiders who washed up on these shores. A friend of Samuel's lent João his car so he could take Elizabeth up the coast road to Camps Bay. They drank South African pinotage wine, ate springbok and ostrich carpaccio, and walked hand in hand along Glen Beach, watching the white surfer boys in the cove. Under the Twelve Apostles, ancient, eroded pinnacles standing guard on the bottom of the unfrozen world, Elizabeth and João tried to mend their marriage.

"I know I've been a horrible shrew. It's been hard, but I'll try not to be so, so... I don't know, domineering," Elizabeth said, swallowing her pride as they stood on the white sand and watched fruitlessly for whales.

João looked out to sea. Elizabeth tucked a hand in the crook of his arm.

"Domineering," João repeated absently. "Yes, that would be good. Try, Elizabeth."

He gave her a quick glance and a wan smile. She searched his face for more, for some reciprocity. But he turned it back to the sea.

"It's beautiful here, no?" he said quietly, patting her hand. "I told you it would be alright."

*　　*　　*

After three days in Cape Town, Greta and Samuel took their visitors to Johannesburg, or rather to their tidy suburban house in Sunninghill, north of the city and an easy drive for Samuel to the Board of Armaments in Pretoria. The rolling hills, green in the South African spring, and gracious live oaks reminded Elizabeth of pictures she had seen of California. The Vanderbroeks' guarded and gated community was nothing special, a bureaucrat's haven far from the lifestyle afforded the expatriate in a place like Angola. But if Greta missed her gracious, subtropical home in Nova Lisboa, she didn't let on. Elizabeth enjoyed Greta's company well enough, though their talks in the back garden somehow lacked the romance of strolls through Nova Lisboa's parks.

The Vanderbroeks had a piano, a cheap upright with a tinny sound, like the dance-hall pianos in American westerns. It beckoned to Elizabeth. She would eye it as she walked by, and in her mind she went over fingerings from her childhood, tempos, dynamics. She tried to blot out the phantom sound of her mother's yelling, the dynamic that had driven her from the instrument years ago. It would be a comfort, or at least a distraction, to sit down and play, to ease into the music that she really did love. One day, she did. She sat down on the plain wooden stool to run through an aria dragged from her memory.

"Chopin?" a voice asked softly. Greta's hand rested lightly on Elizabeth's shoulder.

"Purcell," Elizabeth responded without looking up.

"I didn't know you played."

"I don't, not really."

But she kept playing, simple pieces like Bach from his *Notebook for Anna Magdalena*.

"But you do. That's lovely," Greta encouraged.

"This? This is just something I learned when I was eight. It's nothing."

She played on. She felt herself swept up in something. A hand lifted from the keys to wipe away a tear, and her friend sat down carefully beside her.

"Are you alright, Elizabeth?"

"Yes, yes, I'm sorry," she said, hiding her face in her hands. Greta put a great, heavy arm around Elizabeth's narrow shoulder and pulled her closer.

"I never wanted to play piano again, you see. It reminded me too much of home, a home I hated desperately." Elizabeth spoke in an almost whisper. She wanted to be heard, but not to hear herself. "Now home is all I want, and it is so very far away."

"Home is never so very far away, dear. You'll see."

Samuel introduced João around at Sunninghill Hospital, one of the better hospitals in Johannesburg, he assured him, and Gonçalves quickly took a job as an emergency room physician. He was all the more desired because he was willing to care for the blacks and coloreds from the townships in the clinics dotting the less desirable areas of the city. They moved into an apartment complex close to the hospital, and once Elizabeth found a preschool for Cristina, she was alone and miserable. She'd spend her mornings grocery shopping, preparing for meals, looking forward to picking up her daughter at lunchtime, and plotting against her husband. At night, they'd fight.

She knew her grievances were hackneyed and tiresome, the bored housewife locked away while her husband pursues life and career. But that did not diminish the sting. She had lived the ultimate cloistered childhood, had found the wherewithal to escape, and was now back in purdah. Christmas was approaching. Christmas dinner would be at the Vanderbroeks, thankfully, but Elizabeth set off one morning to prepare a festive flat—a little surprise that might soften João, who so often came home in a foul mood. She had never grown used to Christmas in the summer, but in the suburbs of Johannesburg, the stores were well-stocked with the trappings of winter holiday, the vestiges of Dutch and English pasts. She bought fake pine garlands and wreaths. She splurged on a hand-painted wooden nutcracker from West Germany and picked up some Christmas lights, though she skipped the tree.

She and Cristina spent a joyous afternoon festooning the flat, baking cutout cookies, and destroying a candy recipe Elizabeth could not quite remember. When they heard João's heavy footsteps on the stairs, they lined up smiling, Cristina leaning happily against her mother's legs, Elizabeth's hands lightly holding her daughter's shoulders. There was no shout of surprise as the door opened, just two beatific, satisfied smiles.

João looked into his wife's eyes, gazed casually around the apartment, tossed his keys on the counter, and kissed his daughter's forehead. Then he walked into the bedroom to change.

Elizabeth whipped together a dinner of chicken and the shapeless noodles that seemed to exist only in Africa. João sat down and sighed as he tucked his napkin onto his lap and looked at his dinner.

"The flat looks very festive," he murmured without affect. "Thank you." He granted his wife a perfunctory smile, picked up a fork, and ate in silence. Elizabeth fussed over Cristina to keep herself busy. She was building to a boil.

No doubt, she did not wait long enough after tucking Cristina in. She could not fool herself that her daughter was asleep. She could also not coexist with João in that apartment without confronting him.

"Thank you, João, you have a delightful way of ringing in the holidays," she said dryly, as she closed the door to Cristina's little nursery room.

"You're welcome."

"That's it?"

"That's it," he said. His blood pressure was rising, but he was not going to take the bait, not tonight.

"No, that's not it. That's not it." Elizabeth's voice was climbing decibels fast. "You go off on your merry way. I try to make this God-awful flat a little cheery and—"

"Elizabeth, you can have your little holiday. That is fine with me. But don't expect me to be a part of it. You did not ask if I wanted this. I don't. Enjoy it for yourself."

He turned to some mail sitting unopened on the counter and pretended to be interested in the task of sorting the chaff from the bills. Elizabeth was raging by now.

"You bring me here against my will. You leave me, day in and day out, then at nights, when you're doing God knows what. You can have the decency to play along once in a while."

"Oh, here we go again. Elizabeth the neglected, Elizabeth the forsaken. Let me guess, I'm as bad as your parents."

"Worse," she screamed at the provocation. "Worse. At least they were generous enough to provide a little entertainment for my cell, a cousin, a brother—and a nice cell it was. You've locked me in solitary confinement with nothing, while you're off having the time of your life, doing exactly what you want to do, in and out of that hospital."

João's eyes narrowed to slits. He walked toward his wife now on silent footfalls, an index finger in the air in front of his face. They were furiously pushing each other's buttons, and she had tripped the wire.

"The time of my life? I trudge out every morning to work, to provide for you and Cristina, to earn my keep and yours. I work my ass off, and I get nothing, nothing from you, no appreciation, no admiration, no, no, no sex. You know, this may not be the lifestyle you grew up in, but it's a damned sight better than you were going to earn on your Shakespearean party tricks."

"Try me. I think my—"

"I am a doctor, for God's sake. What more do you want from me? Isn't that what every fucking woman wants?"

"Wants? Wants? How about a little affection every once in a while? How about love? If you won't give it, let me go home, where I can find it."

"Love is supposed to go both ways, dear, both ways, and you're a dry well. And what is this? Now you come from a loving home? That's rich. Let me guess: You were fucking the servants."

His hot breath was now in her face.

"You bastard," she shouted, recoiling. "You damned, stubborn bastard. We'll never leave here because you can't admit you failed at whatever brought you here in the first place."

João's right hand went up to strike, but Elizabeth lunged first, a feeble slap that ended with her wrist squeezed tight in her husband's right fist. His left slapped her face. She turned fast, hit her head against the wall, and wrenched her arm loose. João slapped her again and again. Her arms were cradling her head, the corner of the living room shielding her side. Enraged, he hit her hard in the gut, then again in the ribs. The slaps were gone. These were fists.

"Get out of my face," she sobbed in fear and pain and contempt. "Get out of my face, do you hear me?" Then she did something she had vowed never to do in one of their fights. She fled to Cristina's room.

He hesitated, then pursued.

"Out of your face? Out of your face?" he hissed, his leering visage next to hers. "How's this? Is this out of your face enough?" Even in the gloom of the nursery, Elizabeth could see his purple-red rage. She turned away, her hands hiding her face from his blows and her eyes from his fury. He hit her hard in the side, and this time, she crumpled in a heap. One last kick, and then, aggrieved and impotent, he flew out of the nursery, stormed down the three short flights of stairs to the GM Ranger waiting in the street.

"Mummy," a shaky little voice called from under the covers. "Mummy, why is Daddy hitting you?"

Elizabeth did not get up to comfort her daughter. She sat on the floor, rocking and sobbing and steeling herself to finally do something.

There would be other fights, similar, in the weeks that followed. She kept her protests down to a whimper to try not to awaken Cristina. He tried not to leave a mark. She'd retreat into her daughter's nursery, a sanctuary João recognized after that first violation. He would screech into the night, maybe to a bar in Johannesburg or to Alexandra, the closest township, where he might find a cheap whore or, he often hoped, a quick death, a knife to the throat for the wallet he carried conspicuously—suicide by slum. It never happened. The townships weren't as deadly as they were made out to be.

Elizabeth's letters to Hans were growing more rambling and desperate, but his last one contained an offer: *"I could take a little jaunt into the Heart of Darkness to fetch my baby sister."* She thought on that for weeks. Finally, she fired a flare, not in Hans's direction but where it would matter.

Dear Father,

I know I have not been much of a daughter to you these past few years. But you have been my guardian angel. I wanted you to know I have known that. When I have needed reassurance most, I have gotten it, a sign from General Costa Gomes, an escape route offered up once, forsaken, then offered again. I owe you so much, and I have not even shared your first granddaughter with her gran.

Oh, Dad, you should see Cristina. She is a beautiful raven-haired darling. I only wish I could offer her more, more love, more stability, more peace. Things are not well with Joao, I must confess. "Oft expectation fails, and most oft there where most it promises; and oft it hits where hope is coldest, and despair most fits." He is a good man, I swear. He has found medical work at the hospital here. He cares for blacks, whites, anyone who needs it. And he has gone through much more than I could ever know in his country's wars. He was on a mission during the air evacuation of Nova Lisboa and Luanda, one last tour of duty, you might say. That is why I did not get on that plane. And perhaps that is why he cannot bring himself to return to Europe now. The government sent him to combat, and then disappeared with him in the jungle still.

He does take it out on me too often. I fear I bring it upon myself, with my silly complaints and whining. He says nothing is ever enough for me, and perhaps he is right. I'm a silly cow, as Mum used to say. But I must confide, Father, that we have terrible rows.

He is careful not to leave too many marks. But I am marked none-theless. I am ashamed, and I so fear for Cristina. She pretends to be asleep, and maybe she is. But is this a way for a four-year-old to see her parents? I don't know what to do, Father. I have but one friend here, and since we moved into this flat, she is far away. I hate to trouble you, but I thought perhaps you could help. Maybe a family vacation in southern Africa, you know Cape Town is lovely, and I'm sure our friends Greta and Samuel would show you the parks and wildlife.

Of course, a little jaunt to South Africa might not look good these days for a man in your position. But it was just a thought. Write soon, Father, and give my love to Mum. And thank you again, for all you have done for me and my family. You are truly a lifesaver.

All my love,
Elizabeth

She wept as she wrote her return address in bold, black ink and sealed the envelope.

The phone rang at eight in the morning, the harsh double jolt of a Parisian telephone. Gordon Bromwell figured it was late enough to catch his son in a sleep light enough to roust him, but early enough to ensure he was home, if he had come home the night before at all. He let it ring and counted. On the eighteenth ring, Hans Bromwell picked up.

"This had better be good," he said into the receiver to no one in particular.

"Hans, this is your father."

"Yes?"

"Your father, Hans. Get up now."

"Oh, Father," Hans said, a groggy smile crossing his face. He was naked in a wide bed, its sheets falling off his trim body in a heap.

The wet cold of a Parisian January was kept at bay by monstrous radiators cranking out heat at full blast. "Father, I am a bit old for you to be issuing orders like that, and from across the Channel no less. But I digress. To what do I owe the pleasure?"

His words slurred in an affected play, both more tired and drunk than he actually was. He enjoyed antagonizing his father like this.

"How's Parliament treating you anyway, old boy? I suppose that little Labour victory last year set you back a bit."

"Hans, I'm not calling to chitchat, entertaining as you are. I have something I need you to do. It's about your sister."

Hans knew better than his father about her precarious domestic situation. But he was torn about the question of intervention. Action was not like him. *We're all adults*, he'd reasoned to himself. *If she could run away from home to latch on to this chap and fly off to Africa, she bloody well could fix this sticky wicket when she's ready to.*

His father's concern penetrated, however.

"Hans, I'm not asking much," he said. "Just go down to Johannesburg and check on her, see if she's alright. If she needs an escape, she'll take it—you just need to open the door. I'd go myself, but you know how it is—Labour Government, apartheid, and all that nonsense. It wouldn't look good at all. Besides, I don't get the feeling this João fellow much appreciates my efforts."

Hans muttered some halfhearted excuses about having to quit his job, take care of a few things. Then he relented. He'd meet Gordon in London and fly from there.

"Son," his father finally said, "thank you. I'll see you in a week's time. You know where my office is."

For Hans, the trip was at least a diversion. He reasoned maybe it was a useful break. He'd see the sights, meet Elizabeth's God-awful husband, bring some Cadbury sweets to the niece he'd never met, then maybe come home to study. Perhaps a post with the new government would be an entertaining little irritant for his father. Paris was over anyway, he thought with some relief on the deck of the ferry steaming from Calais to Dover.

*   *   *

"You knew about this?" His father was incredulous. His voice, usually exasperated, was angry. "When did you learn about the abuse?"

"Well, Father, 'abuse' may be a bit harsh. They fight. You don't fight with Mum?"

"We don't speak of marks left or not left. We don't hit," Gordon said defensively, pacing his dingy little office in the majestic Parliament building.

"Father, Elizabeth's a big girl now. She's not a little mouse, cowering in the corner."

"Hans, you know nothing of such matters, nothing. Frankly, Hans, you know nothing of matters of the heart at all."

Hans let out a sardonic laugh at that one.

"And you do, with that bleeding heart of yours?"

They stared at each other in silence for a moment. Gordon walked around to his desk, slid open a drawer, and produced a British Airways ticket.

"You'll leave tomorrow. Your sister is expecting you."

Jan Smuts Airport was not much to look at, but sadly, it was nicer than Heathrow. As Hans gathered his luggage, he began to wonder what most Britons abroad were wondering at the time. *Why bloody go back?*

"Are you Hans Bromwell?"

Hans turned to face the lanky, dark-eyed stranger smiling at him, his hair tousled, a hand extended.

"That would be me, yes."

"João Gonçalves, your brother-in-law."

They shook hands warmly, Hans feeling a rush of relief. He had made his connection for one. For another, this soft-spoken man could not be a threat. He had read the situation correctly. His father was wrong. João made a quick grab at Hans's suitcase and set off for the Ranger.

"I've been looking forward to meeting you for years," he said as he walked, his soft accent softened further for the charming. "I feel like I know you already."

"And me you," Hans answered awkwardly. They both winced, but almost imperceptibly. "How is Elizabeth?" Hans asked. "And Cristina? I'm so looking forward to meeting my niece."

"You won't be disappointed. She's a beautiful child. She'll sweep you off your feet, as the Americans say."

"I must tell you." Hans chuckled. "I don't know what the Americans say."

"I wanted to bring her to the airport to meet you. Your sister said no."

"Pity, I would have liked that."

"I figured, but you know Elizabeth. When she gets something into her head, she won't let go. Somehow the journey wasn't safe suddenly." He shrugged, heaving the suitcase into the ample trunk. "Ah well, you'll see her soon enough." He slammed the trunk shut with a smile, wiped his hands on his jeans, and walked to the passenger side to unlock Hans's door.

The Ranger wasn't terribly impressive: a Chevy engine and an Opel design in a dull brown mustard color, the shine burned off by the African sun. But the springbok badge on the hood signified it as South Africa's own. It smelled of fast food and the old clothes of the many previous owners. João had gotten it cheap, on hospital credit. He had higher ambitions—a Mercedes soon, to go with his MD. That ambition alone revealed something he had yet to admit to himself, much less his wife. He was staying in South Africa. Success beckoned. The country was beautiful. The people welcomed him, at least the white people did. Why not accept the hospitality on offer? Hans climbed into the spacious bench of a front seat. João's foot hit the accelerator before his brother-in-law's door was fully closed. He turned on the radio. Rodriguez's "Sugar Man" wafted over the clanking of the engine.

Hans stretched out, arm casually draped over the back of the seat. American design had left ample leg room for an insouciant slouch.

Besides, Hans did not want to seem uptight or nervous. These two could have a long life together.

"So tell me about life in South Africa after your adventures on the Dark Continent," he opened playfully.

"We are still on the Dark Continent, my friend."

"True," Hans said with a laugh.

"It's boring, if you must know, boring in all its peacefulness," João responded, his right arm sticking through the window, his fingertips drumming to the music, softly, on the roof of the car. The radio hummed. "Sugar Man, met a false friend, on a lonely, dusty road, lost my heart, when I found it, it had turned to dead, black coal."

He laced a finger through a crossbar on the steering wheel, driving the car with mindless panache.

"Well, all warriors must lay down their weapons." Hans smiled. "Not that I'd know much about that."

"No, you wouldn't."

The highway dashed by the sprawl of Johannesburg, then the hills of the suburbs. João kept up the banter at a nervous clip. "You know your father has a penchant for rescuing us. Elizabeth always thought he didn't care much about her. Then we find out he's been tracking her whereabouts like a hawk. He seems to have eyes everywhere."

"Oh yeah? Sounds interesting. Howja figure?"

"It hasn't been subtle. The commanding general of forces in Angola tracked your sister down in a Luanda maternity ward with a note from dear Dad. A South African secret serviceman was dispatched to help us escape from Nova Lisboa. We got another note from Sir Gordon on the South African freighter waiting for us in Lobito Bay."

The names floated uselessly over Hans's head, but he caught the sentiment.

"You don't know the half of it," Hans said, laughing.

"How's that?"

"I'm on a bit of a rescue mission myself, agent of Sir Gordon

Bromwell. He can be a bit of a fool, prone to overreaction when his daughter's involved."

He smiled broadly at João, the wind whipping through his fashionably shoulder-length hair. João shot him a suspicious glance, but not suspicious enough to shut him up.

"Seems Gordon got the idea there's trouble in paradise. I've been sent to see for myself, check for bruises and the like."

That elicited a pained pause.

"On Elizabeth?" João's voice betrayed a little strain.

"Well, I'll check you too if you'd like. My sister can be wicked, I know," Hans said, laughing at his own joke.

This time the silence was a beat longer, a tick more painful. João's face tightened, his eyes locked on the road.

"What are you on about?" João asked. "What do you think is going on between my wife and me?"

"Nothing," Hans said, belatedly catching the changing tone of the conversation. "Nothing at all. As I said, my father can be a bit paranoid. Not me, though."

"What has Elizabeth been telling you?" João demanded.

"Nothing really."

"Don't try to play innocent on me, Hans. I know your father's type. I saw this coming."

"Saw what coming?"

"You're not taking her, if that's what you're thinking. You're not taking either of them."

João's cheeks flushed red. The speedometer was creeping upward as the four-lane blacktop shrank to two.

"I assure you, I have no intention of taking anything, or anyone," Hans said. "I'm quite sure my sister can make those decisions for herself."

"Oh, can she?" João fired back.

"Can't she?" Hans was aiming for exasperation. João heard it as accusation. He shot his brother-in-law an interrogative look, the car swerving a touch toward the shoulder.

"Don't get involved in things you don't understand."

"Is that a threat?"

"What do you understand? The alleyways of the Rive Gauche? The best whorehouses in Paris? You're a wasted life at what, twenty-seven? Twenty-eight? And now you presume to intervene in mine?"

"Are you going to hit *me* now?"

It was a provocation, intentional perhaps but probably not. Hans lived in his subconscious. He would think back on that line—"Are you going to hit *me* now?"—for years. He supposed he had to see for himself.

João's right hand snapped back into the car and onto the wheel. He lunged toward the passenger with his left. It was an awkward, ineffectual gesture, not so much a punch as an odd gesticulation of warning. As his left arm moved, his right followed involuntarily. The Ranger swerved toward the shoulder, then snapped back toward the center line. Neither of them saw the lorry, ever. They only heard the blast of the horn, which startled João into overcorrecting left, then right to avoid the shoulder, then left again to avoid the oncoming traffic. The car hit the shoulder gravel at one hundred fifteen kilometers an hour. The fishtail was a whip, turning the Ranger around and tossing it like a pinwheel into the ditch stretching along the road. As it flipped, the unlocked, hastily closed door on the passenger's side sprung open and disgorged Hans. He flew like a rag doll into the wheat field, green and ripening. At the same time as Hans's side of the Ranger was aloft, the driver's side crashed down onto the earth. Metal crumpled. His door ajar, his body half-free, João Gonçalves was crushed under the cartwheeling steel.

The car came to a rest in the drainage ditch upside down, wheels still spinning.

CHAPTER TWENTY

"'For God's sake, let us sit upon the ground and tell sad stories of the death of kings.'" Elizabeth took a deep drag from her Silk Cut and smashed it into the chipped saucer she was using as an ashtray.

I had not anticipated the final chapter in her bedtime tales to be so abrupt, so violent with finality. Cristina held my hand at the kitchen table, silent, and let her mother draw their story to a close.

Elizabeth had not been pleased when we let her know that her daughter and her live-in volunteer were shagging upstairs. I remember she had pursed her lips, given me a little glare, and rolled her eyes. Then it passed.

That had been a week before. We eased back into the rhythm of Bromwell life as comfortably as could be expected. Cristina was not shy, no sneaking around. I was in her bed nightly now, still astonished at my luck but more bedeviled than ever about my looming, still-unannounced departure. Cristina knew, and she insisted I do what was right for me, whatever that was. And now, the end of the story had come, like Scheherazade's last dawn. Like her torturer king, I had fallen in love, though not with the storyteller, with her daughter. Now I had two to abandon.

"I suppose Hans did save my life. Lord knows, I shouldn't have done him the favor in return. 'A fellow of infinite jest, of most excellent fancy, he hath bore me on his back a thousand times.'"

She knocked back what was left of her vodka.

That small kitchen on the south coast of England was so far from the exotic backdrops of the Bromwells' tale. It was like leaving a movie theater after a particularly fantastic, engrossing film to find yourself in a mall. I wondered if Elizabeth felt that too, felt it every day of her life these past years—not in Lisbon or London or Hampshire, not in Angola or South Africa or tiny Guinea-Bissau, not anywhere she was meant to be. I tried to formulate something to break the silence, something that would not sound asinine.

"You know, Elizabeth, it wasn't your fault."

I guess it was no more asinine than anything else. Cristina and I were sipping tea, but my cup was growing cold on the counter. The milk was beginning to separate into sickly swirls on the surface of the liquid. It was nearly May, but still the room went cold as the warmth of the stove dissipated. I loved Elizabeth at that moment. I wanted to help her, wanted to carry her to wherever she was going, a job in a secretarial pool or behind the counter of a sandwich shop. I wanted to ask her if she'd like to show me Houndsheath, "the heap." We could leave Hans to his slumber and take the ambulance out for a drive.

My stomach dropped. A wave of nausea swept over me as I looked into the milk congealing in my cup. I could feel tears welling up. I ducked my head and sniffed them back.

"Are you alright, David?" Cristina asked. She didn't seem all that concerned, really. She thought of me as an emotional guy, and I suppose I had become one. She patted my hand.

"I'm not so sure I can be so easily absolved, David. I sent out a distress signal, all the way to Hampshire, and it destroyed my brother's life. It's a little difficult to get past that. Ah, but 'things without all remedy should be without regard. What's done is done.'"

"Is that Shakespeare? What's done is done?" Cristina asked. "It sounds so..."

"Prosaic," I chimed in. I looked up, relieved to have something to say that was acceptably banal.

"Yes, Lady Macbeth, and are you two already finishing each other's sentences? My Lord." She waved a hand caustically, lit up another cigarette, and took a deep, satisfying drag.

"It took two bloody hours for them to find him in the field." Smoke billowed from her lungs with her words. "They cut João's body out of the car and figured he had been alone, the bastards. I'm sure I was hysterical when they reached me, but I managed to ask them if my brother was alright. 'What brother?' they said."

"He was just lying in a field with a broken neck for two hours?"

"Hmmm. And a broken leg, and a broken arm, and a dislocated shoulder. I doubt he was conscious, of course. He doesn't remember much. Has this vague image of João lunging at him, a punch of some sort, and some memories of clouds in the sky above a wheat field. I had to call a cab to take me to the crash. They didn't want me there, not least because I had this one with me." She nodded to her daughter. "I often wish I hadn't gone. I'll never forget them walking out of that wheat field, carrying Hans on this board contraption, like a stretcher only hard. His head was sandwiched between these two massive foam pads. His arm was an absolute mess. The lacerations on his face were a horror show. I was sure he was dead, sure of it.

"You saw him like that, you know," she said to Cristina. "You still talk about it when you're nervous."

Cristina shrugged. "Not for ages, Mum."

"No, maybe not. You're all grown up, aren't you?" she said appraisingly. "Anyway, they thought about just amputating the broken bits once they had sussed out the damage to his spine. I screamed bloody murder, let me tell you. Think about it. It had been more than five years since I'd seen my brother, and my first sight was of this creature, absolutely wrecked, then trussed up in casts and a neck brace that looked like something out of the Tower of London, tubes pouring out of his nose. But I didn't want him waking up to a body that grotesque. Funny, when you look at him now, but I still think I made the right decision."

"And your husband was dead," I said.

"Yeah, well, there's that too." She chuckled. "'Nothing in his life became him like the leaving it.'"

"Mum!" Cristina protested.

I dumped out our tea and poured fresh cups. Elizabeth tipped back some more vodka.

"Do you miss him at all?"

"João? You know, I do. I really do. 'These violent delights have violent ends, and in their triumph die, like fire and powder, which as they kiss consume.' He would have known that, you know. *Romeo and Juliet*. He was soft for that one. He was a beautiful man. I know I didn't give him his due. He was fond of the whole Shakespeare thing, but what he really loved was medicine. He really loved it."

She wiped her eyes and looked at me squarely, her mascara clumping. Then she smiled. "Haven't had a shag in donkey's years. Pardon me, dear," she said to Cristina, shaking her head.

"All things glow in retrospect, even João Gonçalves. God, he's the crucified Christ to you. Convenient for a teenage daughter hating her mum, having a fallen saint for a father."

"I don't hate you, Mum, and you know it. You're just being a silly sod now."

"Well, you've gotten through it, I suppose. You know, I really do believe João was a good man. He just had demons I never guessed at. I loved him. I did.

"We moved in with Greta immediately. Samuel took care of getting out of the apartment lease. It took three months to get Hans stable enough to bring back to Britain. You know, I hadn't seen my family in all those years in Africa, and suddenly there they all were: Mum, Dad, and of course Hans, all come to see me under the worst of circumstances."

"A little bitter about that?" I asked.

She paused, shrugged, and agreed. "Why would they have come to see me? My plight hardly compared to Hans's."

"I don't know about that," I offered.

"You're lovely, David, really," she said, wagging a finger at me. "'Yet do I fear thy nature. It is too full of the milk of human kindness.'"

"Your standards are low."

"You got that right.

"It all made the headlines on Fleet Street: Tory Tragedy; Sir Gordon's Misfortunes; and the like. Even the Labourites overlooked the South African backdrop, the story was so awful. It could have been good for my father's career if he had gotten through it. But he couldn't. He couldn't."

"Last year, there was this Tory politician who was supposed to speak at Sussex, at the university," I said, offering up a diversion. "He was literally stoned. Not on drugs, I mean, with rocks. His driver had to beat a retreat in a hail of rocks. He never even got out of the car."

Elizabeth looked at me.

"Stupid, that, 'full of sound and fury,'" she said with real contempt. "I'm as Labour as the best of them. I even like Kinnock, the wanker. But we're all human in the end. A life, a world, an empire can collapse in an instant, even Sir Gordon Bromwell's. You know, when I want to remember my parents, I remember them in those weeks in South Africa. We were all together, all grieving, all thoroughly miserable. They never even met my bloody husband. I remember standing by Hans's hospital bed. My father came in and put his arm around me. Then he pulled me close to him, hard. He was crying, really crying. Mum walked round the other side and squeezed my hand."

She was crying now, softly. She was looking out the little kitchen window, into the tiny back garden. There was nothing much to see in the light of day. At night, it was a void, just darkness. You could pretend there was real space in that void, like you weren't staring at a patch of brown earth hemmed in by brick. I like to think she was staring at the infinite space of her imagining, the kind of space she must have had in the Houndsheath nights of her childhood, lonely but vast, gone now to the National Trust. There was possibility in that kind of loneliness, the loneliness of youth when dreams could be expected to take flight. Elizabeth's adult dreams could still take flight, I supposed, but the flight of the jambatutu, a short burst taking her somewhere else, but still in sight of here, of this patch of Brighton, cold and broken and with a quadriplegic in the living room.

Cristina stood to join her, put an arm around her waist, and laid her head on her mother's shoulder. Elizabeth turned to plant a kiss on her daughter's lustrous head. Then they looked into the night together, while I did the dishes, stacked next to the sink, encrusted and cold. Elizabeth had made skate that I picked up from the fishmongers that afternoon, coated with an amandine breading and sautéed in olive oil. The purplish, heavy meat wasn't really to my taste, truth be told, but many of her concoctions weren't. Hans had eaten two bites.

In the hallway outside the pediatric intensive care unit of Northside Hospital is an oversized train that rolls back and forth on a track, maybe fifteen feet long. It's brightly colored, with stick figures, the kind that adults draw to appear as if they were drawn by children. It's heavy, and, for a little kid, hard to push. But boys love large things on wheels that they can push, especially the kind that crash. My brother and I took turns sitting in the train while the other hurled it along the tracks to the rubber stopper and a pounding collision. We could do it for hours, and we did—lost in the action, oblivious to our surroundings, laughing at the pounding our still-small bodies could take—over and over again. No adults ever told us to stop or to shush.

Then one afternoon my father tapped my shoulder as I counted down for one more heave.

"Come say good-bye to your sister, boys."

He held our hands under the fluorescent hospital glare as we skirted the nursing station, then tiptoed into Rebecca's darkened room. The blinds were drawn, the nurses gone. My mother's face was buried in the hospital gown that shrouded my sister's newly formed breasts. Her wails were muffled, but to me they were howls, unworldly, incomprehensible, shocking. I looked up at my father. His lower lip trembled, like the first stirrings of an earthquake. I looked into my brother's face, which was as bewildered as my own.

Then I looked at Rebecca. Her face was still swollen, an ooze of red iodine and yellow pus smearing her shaven scalp. Her mouth, a ring of sores, had lost its livid red glow, but it shined with the Vaseline my mother had just applied. Her cracked lips formed a silent, screaming "O." She stared at some spot on the wall high above Van Gogh's *Starry Night*, oblivious to her mother's sobs, which rhythmically rocked her body. Her eyes were glazed with a film I had seen before somewhere, transparent but somehow enshrouding— the eyes, I realized, of the whole fish that peered from the ice at my mother's butcher. I used to poke at those eyes in fascination, my brother shouting, "Eww, David, don't do that," my mother turning to slap away my hand. Rebecca's were larger, even more distant, the dead eyes of my dead sister.

"David, say good-bye to your sister," my father coaxed.

I shook my head.

"Please?" he asked.

I turned my body away, arms crossed, eyes smashed shut.

For ten years, I refused to look back. I entered adolescence, obsessed over girls, watched in the mirror as acne sprouted, then faded, as the first hairs surfaced on my smooth face, as baby fat slowly, slowly receded, as my body changed and became a new, unanticipated trial in my life, something to beat down, indulge, try to tame. I went to high school, left home, went to college, left the country for another college, changed clothes, changed images, and all the while, I refused to see anew Rebecca's vacant stare.

Elizabeth confronted the death of her husband and her past every day, perhaps every moment of every day.

"David, go check on Uncle Hans," Cristina said gently as she touched my hand with a fingertip. "Then let's take a walk to the beach."

I went into Hans's bedroom and reflexively walked over to the bay behind his hospital headboard to draw the curtains tight, although no light was leaking through. It was dead quiet. The stool beside him beckoned. I went to sit, to absorb the stillness.

Then a muffled voice came from under the blankets. I lifted them from Hans's face.

"So you have reached the present, David?"

"What?"

"The walls are thin. The story is over. My neck is broken in a South African wheat field, and you're fucking my niece."

He was almost invisible, the room was so dark. But in that quiet, I could hear him well.

"Yes, Hans," I said, almost in a whisper, not wanting to break the silence. "I'm so sorry."

We paused.

"About which part? The niece?" he whispered.

I leaned over him and couldn't hold back a smile.

"I'm not sorry about that part at all."

I smoothed the wet, ragged strands of hair on his head.

"No, I'm just sorry that this happened to you, how it happened."

I reached to touch his face. I laid my full palm on his sunken cheek this time; my fingers pressed gently on the hollow of his temple.

"I accept your pity, David. You know, there are plenty of cripples who have handled their infirmities with far more aplomb than I. But that's just for public consumption. When they say, 'Oh, this was the best thing that ever happened to me,' or 'You know, we all have our disabilities,' don't believe them. Inside, they're raging at the injustice of it all."

The quiet enveloped us for a while longer. "Do you two tell your story to all the volunteers?" I asked.

"No, never."

He stopped to catch his breath.

"Have you told Elizabeth you're leaving?" His breathing was labored, but determined.

"Not yet. Well, I haven't decided. I mean, I was just thinking I sort of have to stay."

"Don't lie to me, David, you're bloody awful at it. Just tell her. The longer you wait, the harder it will be on her. She has a lot to prepare for without you."

"Well, there's Cristina now too."

"Yes, you really bolloxed that up, didn't you? Well, if that's to be, that's to be, David. You can't hold her back."

I nodded in silence. He couldn't see me. The gesture was for myself. I needed the encouragement. I'd come to believe that leaving now was the meanest, most selfish thing I could ever do.

"Is it alright?"

"Is what alright?"

"To leave, now."

"David, you have this absurdly quaint notion that you can pass through life without hurting anybody, without even disappointing anyone. But because you won't make the decision, you merely force others to. You don't want anyone to dislike you, so soon enough, the world will be full of people with David Heller on their guilty consciences. Is that really better?"

I shook my head, but he could not see.

"There is no clean path through. There's no way to do it right. You will have to cheat. You will have to take others down, some perhaps more worthy than you. But you will find humans are a forgiving lot, or at least a forgetful one. It's one of the better parts of our nature, forgetting."

"Who made you so wise, Hans?"

"You'd be surprised the experience you accrue lying here doing nothing."

He stopped to regain his breath. I sat silently.

"It's just as well that you leave now, David. I'm fading. My parents are gone. When I go, I want it to just be Elizabeth and Cristina here, just the three of us."

"If you're sure, then I will."

"Yes, David, I'm sure."

He paused for a moment.

"You've heard those stories about near-death experiences—running to the light and all?"

"Uh-huh."

"I think of them a lot. The stories all start with some bloke hovering against the ceiling, looking down on his body. With a body like this, you can't imagine how liberating that fantasy is."

"No, Hans." I chuckled. "I can't."

"I imagine myself floating over Brighton like some withered dirigible, looking for Wills and James and Julian and my butcher, and Elizabeth and Cristina of course. Lord, I hope they show up to the bloody funeral. You're not invited, by the way."

"You'll have quite a party. I have no doubt about that, and I wouldn't dream of coming."

"Yes, they probably will come out of the woodwork. 'He was a good cripple, kind enough to let us sit by his bedside as we gathered our absolutions.' I suppose I have served that worthy purpose."

"Hans." I had something to say to him, something about how much more he was than that, how much he would be missed. How much I loved him, really. Instead, I leaned over and gently kissed his damp forehead.

"All those years of wanting to die, you know what I really wanted? To move. It's not the light I dreamed of. It was the running to it."

"You need some sleep," I said, an unconvincing escape phrase.

"Yes, David. Before you go, under the medicine cabinet, at the end of the room, there are a couple of bottles of wine. Julian brought them round the other day, the idiot. I can't drink them, and they won't store properly here. Take them. Grab a tin or two of the foie gras while you're at it."

I turned on a small lamp and opened the cabinet. There were

three dusty bottles of red, without any labels, the creation of the family vineyard in Tuscany, and maybe twenty tins I assumed were the pâté. I took two of each, then turned off the lamp.

"Did you find them?" Hans asked in a whisper.

"Yes, Hans, thank you."

"There's one more thing. Come around."

I walked back gingerly to his bedside, juggling the wine and the tins while trying to preserve the quiet.

"In that top drawer"—he gestured with his head to the drawer below where the reading platform rested—"there's an old book I'd like you to have."

I set down my gifts and pulled out the dog-eared, yellowing copy of *Darkness at Noon*, the novel I had propped up in front of him countless times.

"It was my favorite in the years just before the accident, don't ask me why. Koestler was a little Jew, like you—braver than you, but..."

I smiled at that. Hans could be brutal.

"He questioned. He questioned and stumbled, like you're doing. 'One must tear the umbilical cord, deny the last tie which bound one to the vain conceptions of honor and the hypocritical decency of the old world.' David, you're doing the right thing. It's time for you to go."

"Thank you, Hans."

"'Thank you, thank you.' I suppose I am a Bromwell after all."

"Shall I cover you up now?"

"No, no. I think not, not tonight. I won't sleep."

"Good night, Hans."

Cristina and I headed out into the night, hand in hand, drawn to the ocean.

"I just got you," I said. "I still can't believe I can say that. How could I let you go now?"

"How do you know you're letting me go, David? Don't I have a say in the matter?"

She leaned into me and clasped my hand in both of hers, tucked against her thigh.

"Maybe there's a way to work in Norwich. God, I could be a volunteer again. Maybe there's some other cripple there, a nicer one."

She was silent a moment. She was thinking about it, I could tell.

"David," she began quietly, "you couldn't get a work permit last year. You're not getting one this year. You're not going to be a CSV for the next three years."

We had descended the concrete staircase from the Marine Parade to the beach, the ornate Victorian banisters, painted over hundreds of times, going untouched. We held each other for support, then stepped unsteadily onto Brighton's rock beach, our feet wobbling on the small round stones that passed for, what, sand? I never got it. The ocean whispered to us.

"'Begin, and cease, and then again begin, with tremulous cadence slow,'" she whispered in my ear. Her throat caught, and I thought I heard a little cry.

"We could get married," I answered.

She looked into my eyes, a sad, sweet smile on her closed mouth. She dropped one of my hands to delicately dab away the beginning of a tear. I kissed her tenderly where her finger had touched her eye.

"Go home, David," she said softly, her gaze drifting to our feet. "Go back to your life, and let me work on building mine. Write to me. Call when you can."

"I love you, Cristina."

"I know, Mr. X."

She rose on the balls of her feet and kissed me.

"Walk me home, David. Think about standing on your own. No patrons. No one to float you. I want to see you do that. Show me you can. Then maybe I can come to you."

And so I did as I was told. I escorted Cristina home, then I walked. The water lapped the stones on Brighton beach, the sound gently percussive, like a soft roll on a hi-hat, but richer than that, water seeping through a million round rocks, receding, then rising again. I wandered a ways, down to the garish pier where lovers and tourists were eating candy floss and playing pinball machines. Pac-Man, Space Invaders, Frogger, and that funny shoot-the-centipede game, video junk I played in high school, still hadn't made it to Brighton Pier. But the ring of the bells and the heavy roll of the metal pinballs fit the scene much better than amped-up laser shots and electronic racecars. Brighton was preparing for summer.

I stood on the far edge of the pier, the lights behind me, the darkness spreading expansively over the southern tip of a small island, once just the beginning, now empire's end.

Dearest Cristina,

You don't know me yet, but I am hoping we will be the best of friends. I am your Uncle Hans. Yes, it's a silly, silly name, but think of Hansel and Gretel. Do you know that story? If not, I'll tell it to you. It's a little scary, but you are a big, brave girl, and I think you will like it.

I have heard so much about you. Your Mummy and Daddy love you very much, and I hear you have long, shining, black hair and a kind smile. And you know what else? I hear you like to hold hands on long walks in the park. I knew a girl like that once. Her name was Segolaine, a beautiful name.

I would like to take you for one of those long walks. I am coming soon to see you in your new home, and maybe, if you like, I can take you for a visit to where your Mum and I come from, in England, to see your granddad and grandmum. Oh, they'll treat you like a princess in your palace, and it is a grand palace, a big house we call Houndsheath—with sweeping, carpeted staircases and banisters you can slide down forever.

And you know what's best? Dogs, lots of dogs, puppies, playful mummy dogs and sleepy old daddy dogs, horses too. When we get there, you and I will go riding. Bet you haven't tried that yet. You'll love it. Maybe you and I and your Mum will run down to the pond for a swim. It was one of our favorite places when we were your age. Your Mummy had a sad old dog named Suzy who would lay her head on your Mum's lap and listen to all her stories, maybe the way you do now.

Best of all, best, best, best of all, it will be peaceful there, no yelling and no hitting and no angry men. Oh, Cristina, you and I are going to have a grand time. I hope this letter, my very first, finds you well. We're going to be such good friends. I will be coming soon.

All my fondest, fondest love,
Uncle Hans

One last letter was tucked into Hans's copy of *Darkness at Noon*, in a carefully opened envelope marked Return to Sender. Address Unknown. The watermark was a springbok stamped roughly in red ink. I handed it to Cristina the following summer, and she read it for the first time, sunk into an overstuffed old sofa in my bright apartment in Chicago. She cried almost inaudibly.

I knelt in front of her and kissed her hands.

"I miss him," she whispered.

TIMELINE

1932—António de Oliveira Salazar, a conservative Catholic economics professor, is appointed prime minister of Portugal and bloodlessly begins one of the longest authoritarian dictatorships in modern European history.

1959—A dockworkers strike in the West African colony of Portuguese Guinea, organized by the African Party for the Independence of Guinea and Cape Verde (PAIGC), is violently suppressed by Portuguese colonial police. More than fifty die in the Pijiguiti Massacre.

1961—Uprisings in Angola, first by peasants in the north, then by urban, educated *mestiços* of the Popular Movement for the Liberation of Angola (MPLA) and the Union of Peoples of Angola (UPA) under Holden Roberto, begin the wars for independence for Portugal's African colonies.

Under the leadership of the educated, charismatic Amílcar Cabral, the Guinean PAIGC links with the MPLA of Angola and the Mozambique Liberation Front (FRELIMO) to create the Conference of Nationalist Organizations of the Portuguese Colonies in a rough alliance to end Portuguese rule in Africa.

1963—War begins in Portuguese Guinea when the PAIGC attacks a Portuguese garrison south of the capital of Bissau.

1964—Jonas Savimbi breaks from the other liberation movements in Angola to form the National Union for the Total Independence of Angola (UNITA), aiming at Angolan highlands and the region's main city, Nova Lisboa, from bases in Zambia.

1968—António Sebastião Ribeiro de Spínola, a colorful and seasoned Portuguese general, is appointed military governor of Portuguese Guinea and launches a hearts-and-minds campaign to win over the population.

That year, Salazar suffers a brain hemorrhage when he falls from a chair (some say it was a bathtub). Marcello José das Neves Alves Caetano, a Salazar loyalist, takes control of Portugal and maintains the policies of the fascist *Estado Novo*, "New State," including the wars to maintain Portuguese control in Africa.

1970—Francisco da Costa Gomes, a Portuguese military general who ten years earlier had been involved in plotting against the Lisbon government, is appointed commander of the Military Region of Angola.

1973—Spínola returns to Lisbon but refuses a post in the Caetano government as he completes his book *Portugal e o Futuro*, "Portugal and the Future," a dry treatise on the ills of the Portuguese empire that helps launch the Carnation Revolution.

1974—The Armed Forces Movement, a group of disaffected, liberal military officers, rises up to overthrow Portugal's fascist government in a nearly bloodless coup known as the Carnation Revolution. The group, led by Major Otelo Saraiva de Carvalho, a Spínola loyalist, appoints Spínola as the first leader of post-fascist Portugal. Costa Gomes becomes Spínola's second-in-command, then, later that year, president of the republic.

Portugal grants Guiné its independence.

1975—With South African forces openly battling Cuban troops and factional civil war erupting, Portugal unceremoniously quits Angola, leaving the country to years of bloodshed.

ACKNOWLEDGMENTS

For the inspiration and great good humor they offer me every day, I would like to thank Hannah and Alissa Weisman.

For wisdom, ear, and language, I am forever indebted to my greatest reader, Jennifer Steinhauer.

This novel could not have happened without Rayhané Sanders, who believed in it from the beginning, Helene Cooper, who helped me find the path, Libby Burton, who took a chance, Susan Lund, who maintained her patience, Jamie Weisman, who meticulously edited, Mark Weisman, who dragged me to Europe at the perfect time, and my earliest fans and supporters, Evan and Nancy Weisman.

I would also like to thank my eagle-eyed copy editor, Rick Ball, and the whole Twelve team.

For a better understanding of the fall of Portuguese Africa, I give credit to Neil Bruce's *Portugal: The Last Empire*, Arslan Humbaraci and Nicole Muchnik's *Portugal's African Wars*, and John P. Cann's *Counterinsurgency in Africa*.

Lastly, thank you Wolf and Joanna, wherever you are.

ABOUT THE AUTHOR

Jonathan Weisman is a Washington reporter and economic policy writer for the *New York Times*. In his twenty-five-year journalism career, he has covered the White House, Congress, national politics, and defense for the *Times*, the *Wall Street Journal*, the *Washington Post*, *USA Today*, and the *Baltimore Sun*, among other publications. His freelance work has appeared in *Spin*, *Washington Post Magazine*, *Outside*, and the *Bulletin of the Atomic Scientists*.